THE MUTANT FILES
DEADEYE

WILLIAM C.
DIETZ

THE MUTANT FILES
DEADEYE

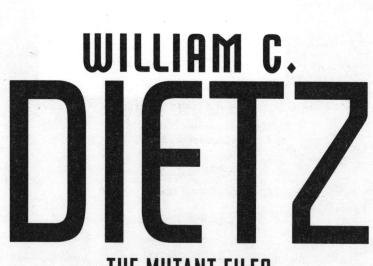

TITAN BOOKS

THE MUTANT FILES: DEADEYE
Print edition ISBN: 9781783298747
E-book edition ISBN: 9781783298754

Published by Titan Books
A division of Titan Publishing Group Ltd
144 Southwark Street, London SE1 0UP

First edition: May 2015
2 4 6 8 10 9 7 5 3 1

For my dearest Marjorie, friend, lover, and pirate

ONE

The air was deliciously cool as the sun rose, and the city of angels was flooded with pink light. The traffic light changed to green, and Police Detective Bryce Conti put his foot on the gas. He was driving an unmarked car. That was something of a misnomer, however, since the vehicle had been tagged so many times that it looked like a rolling Picasso. The radio was on, and Conti smiled as a patrol unit was sent to deal with a 288. That was the code for indecent exposure and usually meant that a drunk was wandering around a park without his pants. What a way to start a new day.

Conti's destination was a neighborhood that had been called Little Italy prior to being reborn as New Chinatown in 1938. As Conti took a right, he passed the charred remains of a burned-out house. One of thousands left empty after the plague.

Some of the homes in the area were occupied, however, and easy to identify because they were the ones that had iron bars over the windows. And in some cases there were patches of carefully kept grass out front. *God bless 'em,* Conti thought to himself, *and protect them from evil.*

Conti found the address he was looking for halfway down the block and on the right. It was the type of four-unit building often referred to as a "dingbat." A not-so-complimentary name that referred to thousands of formulaic three-story-high apartment buildings built during the middle of the twentieth century. A sign that read la buena vida was fastened to the front of the structure's dingy white facade.

Parking places were easy to find in a city where the population was half what it had once been. Conti pulled over, got out, and thumbed the remote. The lights flashed to signal that the car was locked.

Conti had been a street cop for six years and a detective for two. During that time, he had developed habits, one of which was to pause before parting company with whatever car he was using and perform a quick 360. Someone was watching. He could *feel* it. But he expected that. It paid to keep your eyes peeled in LA—and chances were that one of the neighbors was peering at him through partially opened blinds. Conti followed the path that led past the ground-floor garage back to where the stairs led up to the second floor.

Detective Lee lived in unit 201, and once Conti arrived he saw that the words fuck off had been spray painted across the front door. Conti smiled. It looked like the stories he'd heard were true. He pushed the doorbell.

Cassandra Lee was searching for someone important. An alley led to a door that opened into a dark room that . . . She awoke with a jerk and opened her eyes. Bars of dusty sunlight slanted through the blinds to etch lines on the wall. The doorbell rang again.

Lee swore, rolled out of bed, and snatched the Glock off the dresser as she left the room. She passed the bath and took up a position next to the front door. Someone knocked. "Who is it?"

The voice was muffled. "Detective Conti."

"Who do you report to?"

"Deputy Chief McGinty."

There were three locks. Lee opened one after the other. "Come in."

The door opened, and Conti entered. He was dressed in a sports coat, shirt, and jeans. She figured Conti was six feet tall, give or take an inch, with black hair and brown eyes. Rumor had it that he was a ladies' man, and Lee could see why. The bastard

8

had dimples, for God's sake . . . They appeared as he smiled. "I was starting to wonder if I had the right place."

"Sorry," Lee lied. "Make yourself to home. I'll get ready."

Conti saw the weapon and watched as Lee placed it on a side table and walked away. As far as he could tell, the oversized tee shirt was the only thing she had on. It hung down over what he imagined to be a very nice butt. Her legs were bare and slim. He liked that. *Don't do it with your partner.* That was the rule and a good one for the most part. But, depending on how things went, Conti was willing to make an exception.

He heard a door slam and the shower come on as he entered the living room. Drawn curtains made the space feel gloomy, and the brown paint made the situation worse. Interestingly enough, there wasn't any of what he thought of as "girly stuff" in sight. No colorful prints, no stuffed animals, no flowers.

Two matching bookcases occupied the right-hand wall and were filled with cop memorabilia. That included photographs. Lots of them. Most featured a man with black hair, almond-shaped eyes, and high cheekbones. Lee's father? Yes, a sergeant, judging from the chevrons on his sleeve.

In addition to the photos there was a plaque for marksmanship, a presentation nightstick, and a display case containing three medals. One of them was a Medal of Valor. The highest honor a cop could receive. Frank Lee had been a real fire-eater then . . .

"I'm ready."

Conti turned to look at her. He'd seen Lee before but usually from a distance. She stood about five-five and might weigh 125. A halo of black hair framed her face. She had big brown eyes, a perfect nose, and full lips. Her clothing consisted of a waist-length leather jacket, khaki cargo pants, and lace-up combat boots. Conti watched as the Glock went into a shoulder holster, and something shiny slipped into the small of her back. "What was that?"

She looked at him. "What was *what*?"

"The backup . . . What is it?"

"It's a Smith & Wesson model 627."

Conti made a face. "A wheel gun, huh? I carry a Kel Tec P-11. I think semiautos are the better option."

Lee's eyes narrowed. "Who cares what you think? Let's go."

And with that she walked out through the door. Conti followed, checked to make sure that it was locked, and took the stairs two at a time. She was waiting next to the car when he arrived and extended a hand. "I'll drive."

"Why?"

"Because I don't know you. Maybe you can handle a car and maybe you can't. Time will tell."

He placed the keys in her hand and watched Lee pull a 360 on the sedan, even going so far as to peer under it. Paranoia? Not really—a device placed by the Bombas Gang had been responsible for the death of 1-George-12 two weeks earlier. That meant any car that was left unattended, no matter how briefly, had to be checked.

After completing the 360, Lee slipped behind the wheel, and Conti got in beside her. Lee started the sedan, eased down the street, and took a right. More cars were out and about by then. Most of them were one-offs manufactured by various fabricantes. Form followed function in most cases, but there were some especiales as well. They were sleek affairs, low to the ground in most cases and tricked out with fanciful paint jobs.

The police officers were headed south on North Main Street by then. Lee pulled over to the curb six blocks later. Conti checked his watch. "It's 6:50. Roll call begins in ten minutes."

"You need one of Maria's breakfast burritos," Lee informed him. "Wait here, I'll be right back." Then she was gone.

All Conti could do was sit and fume as Lee entered a tiny hole-in-the-wall restaurant and soon emerged with a cardboard box. She passed it through the passenger-side window. "I stop here every morning," she explained. "I hope you like ham and scrambled eggs because that's what you got."

As Lee drove, both of them ate. And Conti, who was having his second breakfast of the morning, had to admit that the burrito was good. As was the coffee. Aztec coffee brought north through San Diego.

Both were still in the process of eating as they arrived at police headquarters. The building's facade consisted of two triangles. One was made of reflective glass and positioned at a right angle to the other. A real statement back in the day but not so pretty since the rocket attack five years earlier. The city council still hoped to restore the original look but hadn't been able to find the right kind of glass.

Lee drove down into the underground parking garage. After showing their ID, the officers were allowed to proceed through the checkpoint and down the ramp. Lee chose a parking spot in a row of vehicles similar to their own. "We're ten minutes late," Conti said, "McGinty's going to have a cow."

"Screw McGinty," Lee said darkly. "*And* the lieutenant he rode in on."

Conti sighed and followed her inside. Nobody liked Lee—nobody he'd met, anyway. So why was she still around? The answer could be summed up in a single word: results. She solved crimes, she caught perps, and she was so good with the Glock that the uniforms at the practice range called her Deadeye. Which was why he wanted to ride with her. To learn what she knew.

An elevator carried them up to the sixth floor to the Detective Bureau. After more than a half century of hard use and tight budgets, the walls were a dingy green, filing cabinets crowded once-wide hallways, and offices were crammed with tiny cubicles.

Lee could see that, *knew* that, but couldn't fully connect with it. Because the building would always be a special place for the little girl inside her. It was the place where the good guys worked, where the bad guys got caught, and justice was done.

That's why she had joined the force right out of college and remained part of it. Even if she had come to realize that some of the good guys weren't so good, some of the bad guys weren't so bad, and that "justice" was often in the eye of the beholder.

The sixth floor was home to the Chief of Detectives, her staff, and about sixty "real" detectives. "Real" being Lee's designator for people who logged more street time than chair time. All of them were housed in an open area that had been subdivided into a maze of cubicles called the bull pen.

Of the larger force, only twelve men and women were members of the elite Special Investigative Section charged with going after the city's most dangerous criminals and taking them off the street. That was the unit Lee belonged to—and the one Conti wanted to join. She led him back to the corner where half of the S.I.S. detectives were gathered around a long table. All of them were dressed in variations of street clothes and said their hellos as Lee and Conti sat down.

Deputy Chief of Detectives Ross McGinty was there along with Assistant Chief Sean Jenkins. What hair McGinty still had was military short. His eyes were the color of faded denim, his face was narrow, and his lips were thin. "Well, well," he said. "What have we here? Detective Lee and Detective Conti. A word to the wise, Conti. In spite of what Lee may have told you, members of the S.I.S. team *are* expected to show up for roll call on time."

Lee smiled sweetly. "Conti *made* me stop for breakfast burritos. That's why we're late." Nobody believed that, and, with the exception of McGinty, all of them laughed.

They spent the next half hour on HR stuff, arrangements for an interdepartmental softball game, and updates on active cases. "Thanks to Detective Howe and his team, the Bradley brothers are living in the slammer now," McGinty told them. "But our work is never done. Now there's a *new* set of assholes to deal with. They call themselves the Freak Killers, or FKs, and claim to be folk heroes out to protect norms from the plague."

He looked from face to face. "And they *are* mutant killers. They're killing mutant merchants who enter the city on short-duration visas. There have been three murders so far, which means we need to find the FKs and do it fast. Once this meeting is over, Lee and Conti will report to my office for a briefing."

Lee felt a rising sense of anger. The mutant thing was a shit detail . . . McGinty's way of punishing her for calling him "a jerk" two weeks earlier and for being her father's daughter. Frank Lee and Ross McGinty had been partners once. Back when both men were patrolmen. And, according to the stories she'd heard, they'd been friends. Then something happened. No one knew what led up to it, but there had been a fistfight. McGinty came out on the losing end of it and, according to departmental lore, had been pissed off ever since.

The meeting ended shortly thereafter, and the two detectives followed McGinty to his office. Jenkins, coffee mug in hand, brought up the rear.

In contrast to many of his peers, the walls of McGinty's office bore no pictures of him shaking hands with the mayor, accepting a commendation, or fly-fishing. And every item on his desk had a purpose. It was as if everything about the inner man was locked away. "Okay," McGinty said as he pushed a pair of manila folders across the desk. "Here's what we have on the Freak Killers. They are both an underground hate band *and* a gang. Their leader is a three-time loser named Cherko. His street name is Popeye."

Conti opened his folder. "Like the cartoon character?"

McGinty shook his head. "Nope. *This* Popeye has protruding eyes. Thus the name."

Lee was looking at a mug shot by then. Cherko had no visible eyebrows, which served to make his bulging eyes even more noticeable. In that particular photo, he was sporting a nose stud, a "fuck-you" smile, and a goatee that was supposed to hide a weak chin. "So what have we got?"

Jenkins had black hair, green eyes, and brown skin. "Popeye has a tendency to shoot witnesses," he replied. "But one of them survived. She was married to victim three. We have a hold on her."

"How 'bout family?" Conti wanted to know. "Does this piece of shit have one?"

"He had a mother as of six months ago. That's when he was released from Corcoran," McGinty answered. "But it looks like she has moved since then. Another family is living in the apartment now."

"Or Cherko moved her," Jenkins offered. "It's all in the report."

"Okay," Lee replied. "That brings us to Conti here."

McGinty frowned. "How so?"

"I don't want a partner."

"Nobody cares what you want."

"He'll get himself killed, or worse yet, get me killed."

"You're way out of line," Jenkins said ominously. "Conti has an outstanding record. That's why he's being considered for the S.I.S."

There was a long moment of silence. Lee looked from face to face and knew it was time to back off. "Okay . . . We'll find Cherko."

McGinty looked as if he might be about to say something, didn't, and nodded. "Get out of my office." They did.

Lee left the office, cut across the room, and was out in the hall by the time Conti caught up with her. He reached forward to grab an arm, and she turned on him. "Don't touch me."

Conti allowed the hand to fall away. He was angry and let it show. "What was that all about? You don't even know me!"

As Lee looked at him, Conti saw something unexpected in her eyes. Sadness? Yes, he thought so. "No," she said quietly. "I *don't* know you. And I don't want to. Because if I do, I might come to like you—and the people I like have a tendency to die. Look it up Conti . . . I've had five partners since I joined the force. Two of them are dead."

Conti shook his head. "I don't need to look it up. I did my research . . . And three of them are alive."

Lee looked away, then back again. "Okay, Romeo . . . Have it your way. Let's find Popeye."

After retrieving the car from the parking garage, Lee drove it up and out into bright sunshine. She put a pair of shades on at a traffic light, checked the rearview mirror, and drove the car onto 101. That took them east to the North Soto Street exit. From there it was a short ride to Morengo, State Street, and the hospital.

It had been the Los Angeles County General Hospital once. But that was before a terrorist who called himself Al Mumit (the taker of life), turned *Bacillus nosilla* loose on the world in 2038. The bioengineered bacteria was delivered to *Kaffar* (unbelievers) all around the world by 786 *shaheed*, or martyrs. Some were elderly couples, some were students, and some were infants. All chosen because they had spotless records, looked Western, or were clearly innocent. Like the babies.

Twenty-two of them were prevented from entering the country they had been ordered to attack for one reason or another but the rest got through. Once they became ill, the *shaheed* sought out sports events, music festivals, and transportation terminals. Any place where there were lots of people.

The results were just what Al Mumit had hoped for. *Bacillus nosilla* spread, thousands fell ill, and unknowingly communicated the disease to others. Within a matter of weeks, hundreds of thousands were infected—and they swarmed hospitals like Los Angeles General demanding a cure that didn't exist.

Sadly, people who were trying to get medical attention for the flu or some other common ailment contracted the plague while waiting in line. Some of them dropped dead and were stacked like cordwood until such time as hazmat-suited sanitation crews could come and haul the bodies away.

Lee hadn't been born yet. But her father was twenty-three at the time and a street cop. He told her about the panic, the lines that stretched for miles, and the violence that took place as people tried to crowd in. Neighboring Hazard Park had been fenced off and turned into a holding area where exhausted medical personnel worked day and night to sort people into three categories: those who were dying, those who might be infected, and those who were okay. Unfortunately, very few people fell into the third group.

Some people survived the disease but suffered terrible mutations because of it. Of that group, some were carriers, and others weren't. That made no difference however. "Norms," meaning those who were found to be free of disease, didn't want to mix with those who were infected, or to witness what *B. nosilla* did to its victims. So the mutants were forced into "recovery camps."

But it wasn't long before the recovery camps were referred to as "relocation camps," and the mutants were shipped east into states like Idaho, Nevada, and Wyoming. Meanwhile, a similar sorting process was taking place in other parts of the country. That resulted in the creation of norm-run states like Pacifica on the West Coast, Atlantica in the Northeast, and the

Commonwealth in the Midwest.

Meanwhile, mutants took charge of the Republic of Texas, which lay east of Pacifica, as well as the New Confederacy in the Deep South. Territorial disputes had been common during the early years, and wars had been fought, but a new normal had evolved. And the government of Pacifica wanted to preserve it.

The sign over the entrance to the hospital read: the california center for infectious diseases. But in all truth it was there for the purpose of treating *one* disease, and that was *Bacillus nosilla*. Before they could enter the hospital, the detectives had to pass through the screening center and put on disposable masks with the word visitor printed across them.

Most of the staff were wearing masks that had been customized to look arty, funny, or featured caricatures of themselves. Such devices were popular on the streets as well—where many wore them for extra protection. Because so-called passers, meaning mutants who looked normal enough to "pass" as norms, continued to infiltrate Pacifica, hoping to better themselves.

After showing their IDs to the security guard at the front desk, the detectives were allowed to enter the lobby beyond. The witness's name was Reba Fuentes, and she was staying in room 326, awaiting a clean bill of health and the legal clearance that would allow her to leave LA.

An elevator took the detectives to the third floor, where the doors opened onto a nurses' station. Conti showed his ID, and the detectives were sent down a hall to room 326. The door was partially ajar, and Lee knocked. A female voice said, "Come in."

After pushing the door open, Lee stepped into a small, cell-like room that had a window, a hospital bed, and hookups for various types of medical gear. A woman stood as they entered. Like most females traveling in norm-controlled territory, she was dressed in a head-to-toe burqa or "baggie." It was midnight black, and all Lee could see were two brown eyes. And even they were partially obscured by a strip of horizontal mesh. "Mrs. Fuentes?"

"Yes," Mrs. Fuentes said hesitantly. "They told me that someone would come."

The woman's voice was soft and had a tremulous quality. Lee

could understand that. Mrs. Fuentes had lost her husband, was a long way from home, and surrounded by millions of people who feared and in some cases hated her. "I'm Detective Lee— and this is Detective Conti. We're here to talk to you about your husband's murder."

There was only one chair, and the room felt crowded. "We passed a lounge on the way in," Lee said. "It was empty. Why don't we talk there?"

Mrs. Fuentes allowed the detectives to accompany her to the lounge. She could smell herself and wondered if the normales could do so as well. It was difficult to keep up with the drainage. Gary had sworn that he couldn't smell the pus, but that was a lie. "A love lie," her mother called it—and proof of his feelings for her. And now he was dead. Killed the way she would swat a fly.

Were the normales really trying to find Gary's killer? Or were they going through the motions? From what she could see, the woman was pretty . . . Like the pictures in old magazines. It was difficult to believe that such a person would avenge her Gary.

Lee ushered Mrs. Fuentes into the lounge and closed the door. There was a table and chairs to sit on. Conti placed a small device on the surface between them. "This machine will record everything we say."

Through a combination of good luck and skill, most of Pacifica's commercial infrastructure was still up and running. But according to news reports, tech-related services were spotty in the Republic of Texas, where some residents saw the plague as a message from God. Specifically, Revelation 15:1. "And I saw another sign in heaven, great and marvelous, seven angels having the seven last plagues; for in them is filled up the wrath of God."

Mrs. Fuentes nodded. "I know about such devices. That's why Gary and I came to Los Angeles. We have a shop . . . *Had* a shop . . . Where Gary would take broken machines and make them function again. But he needed parts, so we came here to buy them."

The burqa rustled as Mrs. Fuentes brought a white handkerchief up to dab at her eyes. There was something universal about the gesture and the grief associated with it. "I'm sorry," Lee said sympathetically. "I really am. But we need to hear what happened so we can find the person who killed Gary."

Conti cleared his throat. "That's right. What happened?"

Mrs. Fuentes looked down at her lap. "We crossed the border at the Blythe checkpoint. Then we rode a bus to LA and rented a room in Freak Town. Gary placed an ad on the computers that night."

"The Internet," Conti suggested.

"Yes, the Internet."

"What did the ad say?" Lee wanted to know.

"It said that Gary wanted to buy used hard drives, video cards, and old motherboards."

Conti turned to Lee. "Chances are Popeye looks for ads like that . . . He knows it's the sort of stuff a mutant would buy—and that a mutant would have to carry gold."

Lee looked at Mrs. Fuentes to see if Conti's use of the word "mutant" would bother her. The mesh in front of her eyes made it hard to tell. One thing was for sure however . . . Something smelled, and Lee thought it was Mrs. Fuentes. Almost anything could be concealed under the baggie. A shriveled limb, a misshaped torso, or an open abscess. "Yes," Mrs. Fuentes said. "The ad was a mistake. But it was our first trip, and we didn't know."

"Of course you didn't," Conti said sympathetically. "So you were there? You witnessed what happened?"

"Yes. The man you call Popeye sent a message. He said he had components to sell. Gary agreed to meet him across from a restaurant in Compton. We went there by taxi. I wanted to keep the car, but Gary said no, that would cost too much money. So we waited. A gray especiale passed us two times."

"They were checking you out," Lee observed. "Looking for a trap."

"Then the car stopped," Mrs. Fuentes said. "A man got out. He had bulging eyes and rotting teeth."

"*This* man?" Conti inquired as he pushed a picture of Cherko across the table.

"Yes."

"So he wasn't wearing a mask."

"No."

"What happened after that?"

"The man got out of the car and spoke to Gary. I was too far away to hear what was said. But it was only a minute or two before the man pulled a pistol and shot my husband in the chest. Then he spit on him and called him *un maldito mutante*."

A fucking mutant, Lee thought.

At that point, Mrs. Fuentes started to sob, and Lee circled the table to put an arm around the other woman's shoulders. The smell was worse than before. "Then what happened?" Conti asked.

"I ran. He shot me in the back. The impact threw me forward. It hurt, but I knew he would come, so I played dead."

Lee returned to her seat. "And it worked."

"Yes. He kicked me. It was hard to remain silent, but I did. Then he went back to get Gary's money belt."

The interview came to an end shortly after that. Lee signed the legal release that would allow the mutant to leave the hospital—and promised to let her know when they caught Popeye. "So," Lee said, as they left. "Tell me, Romeo . . . What, if anything, did we learn?"

"Not a damned thing. Everything she said was in the initial reports."

"That's right," Lee agreed. "You were paying attention."

"Does that mean I can drive the car?"

"Hell, no."

Conti grinned. "Just checking."

They went to lunch after that, followed by a long afternoon spent chasing leads that didn't produce anything. Around four thirty, Lee parked the car in front of her apartment. Lee got out and Conti came around to the driver's side. "One last thing," Lee said as she looked up at him. "You gave Mrs. Fuentes something just before we left. What was it?"

Conti looked embarrassed. "Fifty bucks."

"You're a sucker. You know that."

"Yeah, I know."

"Here's twenty-five," Lee said as she peeled some numoney off a small roll and handed it to him. "I'll see you in the morning." Conti wanted to say something, but Lee was walking away.

Once inside her apartment, Lee traded her street clothing for a tee shirt and shorts. Then she went out for a five-mile run. The badge and the revolver added some weight but made her feel more secure. Lee was careful to vary the routes she used, but all of them took about thirty minutes.

After returning to the apartment, she showered, microwaved the same chicken-and-veggie dinner she ate every night, and sat down to watch the news. None of it was very encouraging. *B. nosilla* was continuing to mutate while scientists searched for a cure . . . And it did so with such speed that they hadn't been able to catch up.

There were rumors that a terrible storm had devastated coastal Atlantica. Forest fires continued to rage unchecked in Washington State. And based on some iffy reporting, norms in India were battling mutants from China. It seemed like the whole world was fucked up. Lee sighed and turned the TV off.

In keeping with a long-established routine, Lee dumped the empty container into the trash and put a load of laundry in the washer. Then it was time to start her *second* job—which was to find the person or persons responsible for her father's death.

Lee made her way back to the second bedroom. What had been her *father's* bedroom before his death. She'd been living in her own place back then—and moved into his apartment a few days after the funeral. The theory was that maybe, just maybe, she'd find something in among Frank Lee's effects that would help to solve his murder. That hadn't occurred as yet, but she was determined to keep working the case until someone solved it.

There was nothing elegant about the hasp and combination padlock on the door, the primary purpose of which was to keep Mr. Henry out. He handled maintenance for the building and was an inveterate snoop. But it was more than that. The room and everything in it was private. A window into Lee's soul that she planned to keep closed.

Lee entered her father's badge number into the lock, heard the usual click, and removed the lock. The single window was blacked out, so it was dark until she flipped the track lights on. They lit walls that were covered with a mosaic of photos, diagrams, and notes. They were held in place by hundreds of multicolored pushpins. Enough pins to ruin the wall and cost her money when the time came to move out. But that would mean her father's murderer had been found—and for that she would gladly pay.

It wasn't just her father, however. No, *eight* policemen and -women had been killed over a period of fourteen years, all victims of the serial killer called the Bonebreaker. A psycho who liked to dismember his victims and mail broken bones to the police.

But *why*? The Bonebreaker had a grudge against the police department. That was obvious. But there were thousands of people who had reason to hate the LAPD. So in the absence of eyewitnesses or other evidence, the team assigned to the case was spinning its wheels. And because of her connection to a victim, Lee had been instructed to stay clear of the investigation. An order which, like so many others, she chose to ignore.

Her father's bed had been removed and replaced with a utilitarian worktable. As was her habit, Lee started on the left side of the room and began to circle around it. Her hope was that by scanning all of the latest bits and pieces, something would click. It didn't.

Acting on an impulse, she removed an old-fashioned photograph album from the shelving unit on the north wall and carried it over to the table. The technique was far from reliable, but every now and then, a random excursion into such materials served to trigger a new thought or a new line of inquiry.

Lee opened the album and began to page through it. According to the handwritten dates, it covered the period of time just prior to the plague. There were pictures of Frank Lee posing with the departmental baseball team, standing next to his cruiser, and receiving medals. But one photo stood out. She'd seen it before, of course. Hundreds of times. But the events of the day caused her to pay more attention to it.

Lee kept a magnifying glass on the worktable—and once she looked through it, her first impression was confirmed. Her father and a much younger Ross McGinty were in uniform. And there, standing between them, was a young woman.

Could it be her mother? No, her mother had very dark skin, and the girl was lighter. So, who was she? The date under the photo fell after the release of the plague and the now-famous fistfight. Had the girl been involved somehow? *Who cares?* Lee thought to herself. *That was then. This is now.* She went to bed an hour later. There were dreams, lots of them, and none were good.

TWO

The beep of Lee's alarm merged with the sound of the doorbell to pull her up out of a troubled sleep. She slapped the clock, knocked it onto the floor, and swore as it continued to bleat. The plan was to be up and dressed by the time Conti arrived, and the bastard was early!

Lee rolled out of bed, silenced the alarm, and grabbed the Glock on her way out of the room. Then she took up her usual position next to the front door. "Who is it?"

"Conti."

After dealing with the locks, Lee opened the door. She was about to chew him out when he gave her a familiar-looking box. "It's a breakfast burrito," he said. "From Maria's."

It was a plan. An evil Conti plan to arrive at roll call on time, avoid McGinty's wrath, and become chief of police. Lee wanted to say something cutting but came up empty. So she put the box on the kitchen counter and walked away.

"No need to thank me," Conti said as he took his breakfast over to the table. "That's what partners are for."

Conti's plan worked. Not only did they arrive for roll call on time—they were five minutes early. And that caught McGinty by surprise. "Well, well," the deputy chief said as he entered the room. "This is a first—1-William-3 is on time. Make a note, Sean . . . Miracles *can* happen."

Lee scowled, and Conti kept his face professionally blank.

Once the departmental bullshit was out of the way, Jenkins turned to Lee. "I have some good news for you . . . Cherko's mother applied for welfare. That triggered an alert that came straight to me. We know where she lives."

Lee felt a sudden surge of optimism. She knew that Mrs. Cherko had gone to see her son in prison. So it stood to reason that he would visit her. All they had to do was watch and wait. "Now we're talking," Lee said. "Where is she?"

"Right off the corner of Fairfax and Colgate," Jenkins answered. "Here's the address." He pushed a scrap of paper across the table, and Conti accepted it. Lee knew the area. It had been home to lots of Russians, Armenians, and Mexicans prior to the plague. Many years had passed, but the neighborhood still retained some of its original flavor, and the Cherkos might have connections there.

"We'll go twelve on and twelve off," McGinty said. "I would prefer eight-hour shifts, but we're shorthanded."

That was always the case and came as no surprise to either detective. Lee stood. "We should hit the street . . . If that's okay."

McGinty nodded. "Go for it. And watch your six."

West 3rd took them most of the way. The apartment house was situated on one corner of a busy intersection. And there was a bank, convenience store, and a parking lot. Lee turned into it and chose a slot that would provide an unobstructed view of Mrs. Cherko's front door. Once the stakeout was in place, all they had to do was wait for Popeye to show, call for backup, and arrest the piece of shit when he came out.

Time seemed to creep by. People came and people went, but there was no sign of Popeye. The only break in the monotony came when Conti made the midday chow run to the convenience store. He came back with a bag full of crusty taquitos—plus two ice-cold soft drinks, both of which were loaded with caffeine. "That's *it*?" Lee demanded. "You spent my money on two thousand calories' worth of taquitos? There weren't any salads?"

"I didn't look for salads," Conti confessed. "Besides, why eat a salad when you have taquitos?" So Lee ate a taquito and left the rest for Conti, who polished them off in five minutes.

Then the boredom set in once again. And it was getting warm.

Very warm. But they couldn't run the AC without running the engine—and that would give them away. So they cracked the windows, but it didn't make much difference. Both were down to body armor and tee shirts by that time, but it was at least eighty degrees inside the car.

Forty-five minutes crawled by. Lee was slumped behind the wheel, willing Cherko to show, when she spotted movement in the outside rearview mirror. "Uh, oh . . . We have company."

Conti was laid out on the backseat listening to a retro band called The Eagles. He jerked the earbuds out as he sat up. "Whacha got?"

"A car prowl . . . And we're sitting in the car this jerkweed wants to break into."

Conti looked out through the tinted window and saw that a male suspect was coming their way with a ball-peen hammer in his right hand. A smash and grab then . . . A low van could be seen behind the man, with its side door open. "I'll take care of it," Conti said as he put on his jacket. Then he got out.

Lee laughed as she watched in the mirror. The would-be thief did a double take as a large man exited the car, produced an elaborate yawn, and began a series of stretches. That was sufficient to send the car prowler back to the van. He entered, pulled the door closed, and the vehicle took off. Unfortunately, that was the only thing that happened until 6:00 p.m., when the second team took over.

It had been a long, frustrating day, and Lee was happy to return home. By the time Conti dropped her off, it was nearly seven o'clock and way past the time when she normally ran. Should she force herself to do it? Or push it off?

Suddenly, she felt the same prickly sensation she experienced when somebody eyeballed her in a club. But she wasn't *in* a club. She was standing in front of her apartment house.

So who is it? Lee wondered as she took a look around. A snoopy neighbor? That was certainly possible. Yet for some reason buried in the reptilian part of her brain, Lee didn't think so. She felt an urge to seek the safety of her apartment.

That aspect of her brain wasn't in charge, however. And rather than run from the things that frightened her, Lee continually forced herself to confront them. So she chose the vacant house on the other side of the street as being the most likely place for a "looker" to hide and walked straight toward it.

If that elicited a response, she couldn't see it. Her combat boots made a thumping sound as she climbed the front stairs and rattled the door. Lee figured that stealth would be pointless if someone was watching and hoped that being assertive would provide something of an edge.

Having failed to gain entry through the front door, Lee made her way along the north side of the house. A narrow ribbon of cracked concrete led her between clumps of overgrown bamboo, past a sad-looking rosebush, and into a yard filled with trash. Lee drew the Glock and held the barrel straight up as she climbed a short flight of stairs to a screen door with a hole in it. It produced a horrible screeching noise as she pulled it open. That revealed a wooden door that had been left partially ajar. Tool marks could be seen where it had been jimmied. Lee stood to one side with her weapon at the ready. "Los Angeles Police!"

There was no response. Lee paused a moment before entering the kitchen. The place had been ransacked more than once judging from the way things looked. It was nearly dark outside, so Lee removed a small flashlight from an inside pocket and held it away from her body as she entered the dining room. The floor was littered with empty beer cans and fast-food containers. A sure sign that one or more homeless people had camped there at some point.

Glass crunched under Lee's boots and a blob of white light roamed the walls as Lee made her way into a Craftsman-style living room. The front windows were covered with blinds. But the streetlights were on, and strips of greenish light were visible through the slats. Was that where the looker had been standing? Staring out through filthy glass? Probably. Assuming her instincts were correct.

As the light tilted up, Lee saw something that made her blood run cold. Because there, written in red spray paint, was the name bonebreaker. She felt a stab of fear and whirled, ready to defend herself. But she was alone. If the Bonebreaker had been there, he was gone.

So what to do? She could let the Bonebreaker team know, in hopes that they might find some sort of evidence in the house, but was a name on a wall enough to justify that? No, Lee decided, it wasn't enough.

It did scare the hell out of her, however, and Lee was happy to leave the house. Five minutes later, she was in her apartment and changing into some sweats. Then it was time to zap her dinner and carry it into the evidence room. It wasn't the first time she had eaten there and wouldn't be the last.

Assuming the name had been spray painted onto the wall by the killer himself, the first question was *why*? *To spook me*, Lee decided. *To elicit fear.* If so, it was working.

What did that mean? That he was stalking her? That she was the next person on his hit list? Maybe. Although there was no clear indication that the Bonebreaker had a list. All of his victims were cops. That much was glaringly obvious. But beyond that, the homicide detectives had never been able to come up with a common denominator. Not age, race, or gender. The Bonebreaker was an equal-opportunity killer.

Lee ate as she reviewed her records, which was to say a bootleg copy of the department's records, looking for mention of precrime warnings or signs. There weren't any. So either the spray-painted name had been put there by someone else, or it represented a new behavior on the killer's part.

Don't jump to conclusions, Lee told herself. *What if there were previous postings? But nobody noticed them?* It was a good question. Because the odds were against anyone's noticing a name spray painted inside an abandoned house. It wasn't a crime scene after all—and the entire city was covered with graffiti. The discovery felt important at first, but after giving the matter some additional thought, Lee realized that it wasn't. The police couldn't monitor all of the city's tags checking for what might or might not be a warning.

No, the discovery wouldn't lead to the killer. But it was another entry in the profile that Lee was trying to construct. Assuming the killer had been there and written on the wall, it might mean that he or she had accepted the name bestowed upon him or her by the media and come to take pride in it. Did that stem from ego and narcissism? That was possible. If so, those characteristics might cause him or her to make a mistake someday. Lee would be waiting.

The sun was up, and it promised to be another hot day as Conti turned the corner and drove down the street. He'd been out the night before, partying with some of his buddies, and wound up in bed with a blonde he barely knew. What he needed was a steady girlfriend. Somebody to spend evenings with—somebody who had a brain. Like Lee? Yes, the girl was smart and hot to boot. She was serious though . . . Haunted even. Could he make her happy? It would be fun to try.

Conti parked the car, made his way up to Lee's apartment, and pushed the button. The doorbell had just started to ring when someone jerked the door open. And there, much to Conti's amazement, stood Cassandra Lee. All dressed and ready to go. "Come in," she said. "The coffee is ready."

Conti followed her in, surrendered the box, and made his way over to the kitchen table. Lee put the burritos in the microwave for thirty seconds before bringing them over. The coffee came next. "No need to thank me," she said. "That's what partners are for."

Conti chuckled, and they ate in a companionable silence. Once she was done, Lee was up and out of her chair. "Let's get going."

"What's up?" Conti wanted to know. "You're kind of hyper this morning."

"This is the day," Lee predicted. "This is the day we're going to nail Popeye."

"So what is this? Woman's intuition?"

"Maybe . . . It's a feeling, that's all."

They couldn't attend the 7:00 a.m. roll call. Not and relieve the second team at six. So Lee drove straight to the corner of Colgate and Fairfax, where she pulled into the parking lot.

A brief radio conversation was enough to bring Conti and Lee up to date. It seemed that though Mrs. Cherko had crossed the street to visit the convenience store, there had been no sign of her son.

The morning passed much as the previous one had. Conti

listened to tunes in the front passenger seat, the temperature continued to climb, and it wasn't long before they started to sweat. Conti was about to go for some cold soft drinks when a low-slung especiale rolled past. The body was sleek and somewhat reminiscent of the production vehicles from the fifties but covered with gray primer. As if the owner was saving up for a custom paint job. Then Lee remembered. The vehicle Mrs. Fuentes described had been gray as well.

The car slowed in front of the apartment house and crept past. Could it be Popeye? Checking the situation out?

"Did you see that?" Lee said as she brought the camera up. "A possible rolled by. Let's see if he comes back."

They didn't have to wait for long. The smoke gray sedan reappeared in the intersection, took a right, and began to creep past the apartment building. Lee continued to click away as the car passed them. "I think Popeye is going to drop in on Mommy," Lee said. "So pull your shit together and . . ."

"Sorry to interrupt," Conti said. "But we have a 211 at the bank. I see what might be a flash mob out front. At least some of them are armed. We're going to need backup."

And with that, Conti was out of the car and drawing his weapon. Lee shouted, "No! Wait!" But it was too late. Conti was striding across the parking lot by then.

"This is 1-William-3!" Lee shouted into the mike. "We have a 211 at Colgate and Fairfax with multiple 417s." Then, knowing what was about to happen, she added: "Shots fired. Request backup."

Lee drew the Glock as she bailed out of the car and began to run. Conti was out in the middle of the intersection by then, waving cars off with one hand while pointing his pistol with the other. "Los Angeles Police! Drop your weapons!"

Beyond Conti, gathered in front of the bank, were a dozen people all wearing black-and-white skull masks. Roughly half of them were carrying long arms, and the rest were waving pistols, as the front door slammed open and a skull emerged carrying a bag.

Conti fired, and one of the perps did a neat pirouette before collapsing. Lee yelled, "Get down!" but Conti seemed determined to smoke another bank robber. He fired, staggered as a volley of bullets hit him, and fell.

Lee was in a cold fury as she made her way through a maze of vehicles and emerged with her gun raised. "Los Angeles Police!" she shouted, as half the skulls turned to shoot at her. A bullet nipped at her left shoulder, another whipped through her hair, and a third creased her side. So Lee shot a perp in the face and felt everything slow down.

It had always been like that for her. According to what she'd read, some ballplayers had it, too . . . *It* being the strange ability to see the round thing coming at them, make the necessary adjustment, and swing the bat just so. And that's how it was for her as the Glock swung from target to target, seemingly firing of its own volition. As people fell, Lee began to advance on the spot where Conti was lying in a pool of blood.

Sirens could be heard by then, but Lee knew the battle would be over by the time help arrived. So it was necessary to put all of her adversaries down before they could shoot anyone else. Suddenly, the Glock clicked empty signaling the fact that all sixteen .9mm bullets had been expended.

There wasn't enough time to reload, so Lee pulled the Smith & Wesson. She was in the process of bringing it up when a sledgehammer struck her chest. She staggered but managed to keep her feet. The revolver jerked twice, and blood misted the air as a skull dropped his weapon in order to grab the holes in his neck.

As he staggered away, Lee dropped a robber with an AK— and took a shot at a perp who was trying to escape. The first bullet missed but the second hit the back of his right knee. He screamed and went down hard.

Then Lee found herself face to mask with a single skull. He was aiming a .45 at her even as she pointed the .357 mag at him. "That's a revolver," he said. "And you're empty. Good-bye, bitch."

Lee pulled the trigger twice and watched both slugs hit his chest. He fell over backwards with arms outflung and lay staring up into the blazing sun.

Lee flipped the cylinder open and pushed the extractor rod. The empty shell casings produced a tinkling sound as they hit the pavement. "This is a fucking Smith & Wesson 627," Lee said conversationally. "And it holds *eight* rounds."

The speed loader made short work of reloading the weapon, which went back into its holster as Lee knelt next to Conti. There was a lot of blood. And when she pulled his shirt open, there was no body armor to be seen. The heat . . . Conti had left the armor at home because of the heat. Lee swore, and Conti opened his eyes. His voice was little more than a croak. "That'll teach 'em," he said. "I'll bet they're sorry now."

"Don't talk," Lee said. "The EMTs will be here in a sec."

"How bad is it?"

Lee pretended to look. "Not bad at all. You'll be up and around in no time."

Conti tried to smile, but it looked more like a grimace. "Good. Will you let me drive?"

Lee nodded. "Yes, Bryce. I'll let you drive."

Conti coughed. Blood dribbled down his chin. *"Bryce?* You never call me Bryce."

"Don't die on me, Romeo . . . Don't do it," Lee said desperately. But Conti couldn't hear. The light was gone from his eyes.

Lee began to sob. And when the EMTs arrived, she was cradling Conti in her arms and rocking back and forth. That was the photo that wound up on the front page of the *LA Times*. The caption read: "Cop kills nine but loses partner." Justice had been served—but the price was high.

Three days had passed since the bank robbery and Conti's death. After being sent to the hospital, where the doctors patched her up, Lee was released. Shortly after that, she was required to undergo the first of what turned out to be three interviews over two days. During that time, all manner of armchair commandos asked her the same questions over and over again.

Then she was sent home to wade through the TV crews camped out in front of her home—and likely to remain there until the official shooting report was made public. Everybody said it was a so-called "good shoot," but every cop knew what could happen after a high-profile gun battle. Especially one where *nine* perps fell to a single officer. That was a big deal.

Members of the media were calling it the West Hollywood Shootout. And while most citizens were supportive—others thought that less force should have been used. "Why not wound them?" one woman inquired. "There was no need to kill everyone." And, since that woman had a seat on the city council, some people listened.

A day later, Lee had reason to be concerned as she stood in front of the living-room window and waited for the car that would take her to police headquarters and a final meeting with the shooting review board. It was raining outside, and judging from the large number of umbrellas, it looked like the press knew what was about to happen.

One of the reporters pointed up the street, and the rest turned to look. Having spotted the car, Lee made her way back through the apartment, opened the door, and locked it behind her. Then it was necessary to make a mad dash down the stairs and through the gauntlet of media. Cold raindrops hit her face, reporters shouted questions, and the crowd was starting to close in when Jenkins appeared. He used his bulk to clear a path for Lee, and she followed him to an open door and the backseat of an unmarked police car. Two yelps from the siren cleared the way. "Sorry," Jenkins said, as the sedan pulled away from the curb. "They'll lose interest soon. Things will return to normal then."

Except for Conti, Lee thought to herself. *Things will never return to normal for him.* "So what's coming down?" Lee wanted to know. "Good shoot or bad?"

Jenkins shrugged. "I'll find out when you do . . . But it looks righteous to me."

Lee looked out at the rain and back again. "And the funeral?"

"It's scheduled for tomorrow."

"I plan to attend."

Jenkins nodded. "I figured you would."

"Then I'm going back to work."

"That depends on what the shooting board says," Jenkins replied.

There wasn't anything else to say, so they didn't. Rain rattled on the roof, and the wipers continued to squeak until they entered the parking garage. "We'll get out here," Jenkins said, as they stopped at the checkpoint. "No point in going all the way to the dungeon."

Lee got out, flashed her ID, and followed Jenkins into the lobby. Other officers were there, and even if they didn't know Lee personally, they knew of her. "Hang in there," a detective said. "It was a clean shoot. And there's no damned way they can say otherwise."

Lee hoped that the optimistic assessment was correct as the elevator carried them up to the seventh floor, where a conference room had been reserved. As Lee entered, she saw that Chief of Detectives Lacy was present, along with Deputy Chief McGinty, a member of the Internal Affairs (IA) team, the lead detective representing Homicide, and the attorney provided by the Los Angeles Police Protective League. He was a morose-looking individual who seemed like a funeral director in his black suit. Would she need his services? Lee hoped not as she took a seat halfway down the table.

The IA rep started the meeting with a lot of legal blah-blah. Lee ignored most of it but a couple of things stood out. Two security guards had been gunned down inside the bank, and three motorists had been struck by stray rounds. All of which served to justify what she'd done even if she hadn't been aware of it at the time.

There was another item of interest as well. Something that hadn't been confirmed until then. "Based on our investigation," the IA cop said, "all of the bank robbers were members of the San Jose Death Heads. They're believed to be responsible for two other robberies, both of which used the same MO. The scumbags appear out of nowhere, take control of the target through the use of overwhelming force, and demand gold instead of numoney."

After that, the homicide detective read the official ticktock of what had occurred from the moment Lee radioed in to the point where backup arrived on the scene. More than that, she illustrated the account with video clips taken by cameras mounted outside the bank and the convenience store. "So," the IA officer said once the narration was over, "it's our finding that all nine shootings were justified."

Lee felt a profound sense of relief as those seated around her offered their congratulations. Then, as the chatter died down, the homicide detective cleared her throat. "There is one thing though . . . Something none of us could understand. It isn't material to the finding, because this investigation is about what happened, not what was going on in Conti's head. But I'm curious . . . Why would an experienced officer like Conti go out into the intersection all alone? Why didn't he wait for *you*? Or for backup?"

Lee was looking down at her lap. She wondered the same thing—and hours had been spent thinking about it. The answer, in her mind anyway, was that Conti had been trying to impress her. Trying to do something she wouldn't forget. Lee wasn't about to say that, however. No damned way. As her eyes came up, she discovered that a roomful of people were staring at her. "It's a fair question . . . But I don't know."

There was a moment of silence followed by the scrape of a chair as the chief stood. "All of the discussion that took place here is confidential and not for distribution. A press release will be sent out shortly. All media inquiries should be referred to the Public Affairs Office. That will be all."

A thick layer of clouds hid the California sun as officers on motorcycles led a procession of patrol cars along East Cesar Chavez Avenue to the Evergreen Cemetery. First came a contingent of three police cruisers with lights flashing. They were followed by the hearse, a limo carrying members of the Conti family, and the black sedan Lee was riding in. At least a hundred patrol cars brought up the rear. Many wore LAPD markings, but there were representatives from towns and cities that were hundreds of miles away as well. Because all of the cops were part of one big family.

As Conti's partner, Lee had been invited to ride with Chief of Police Corso. He had carefully combed black hair, movie-star good looks, and knew how to say the right things. Lee figured he was more politician than cop. Was that *his* fault? No, that's what the job demanded. Someone who could fight for money, deal with citizen groups, and set the tone.

At that particular moment, the chief was on his cell phone dealing with the fallout from a police brutality case. Most of the people in the department figured the officer in question was guilty as hell. But the fact that the victim was a mutant meant that members of the public felt a lot of sympathy for the cop. And that had political ramifications.

Lee looked out through the window. The first time she'd been part of such a procession, it was to honor her father. She'd been all alone that day and wondering if her mother Alala was still alive. Lee thought she could remember a smiling face looking down at her but wasn't entirely sure. Was that a *real* memory? Or one created to fill a need?

Lee's thoughts were interrupted as the chief said, "Asshole," and put the phone in his pocket. He made a face as Lee turned to look at him. "Sorry . . . That was a mutant lover who writes for *Humanist Magazine*. He's working on a story about how bigoted the LAPD is."

Lee remembered the brown eyes she'd seen through the mesh—and how Conti had given the woman money to get home. "That isn't fair," she said. "But there was no call for Patrolman Hanity to beat the shit out of that mutie, either."

The chief's eyes narrowed. Lee's comment verged on being a criticism, and he didn't like criticisms. "Yes, well, there is that. But it would be a good idea to reserve judgment until after the investigation is complete."

Lee wanted to push back but knew it would be stupid to do so. So she settled for a "Yes, sir," and let the matter go.

The motorcycle cops slowed as they entered the cemetery. That forced the rest of the procession to do likewise as the vehicles followed a winding street to the spot where the advance party was waiting. Arrangements had been made so that vehicles could park at the curb. Even so, it took twenty minutes for people to exit their cars, walk to the gravesite, and take their assigned places. Lee was supposed to stand near the family and the open grave. Conti's mother came over to speak with her. "My son admired you . . . He talked about you all the time."

"And I liked him," Lee replied. "I'm going to miss him."

Most of Mrs. Conti's hair was white. She had high cheekbones, a straight nose, and well-shaped lips. But there was something hard in her eyes. "Thank you," Mrs. Conti said. "Thank you for killing them."

Lee didn't know what to say. She swallowed the lump in her throat. "He was my partner."

Mrs. Conti leaned in to kiss Lee on the cheek before turning away. She smelled of lavender, and her lips were ice-cold. Lee had been able to hold back the tears until then. But now they flowed as the bagpipes wailed, final good-byes were said, and the coffin was lowered into the ground.

The crowd began to break up after that. Some people stood in groups chatting—while others streamed back to their cars. Many paused to offer Lee their condolences and, having been Conti's partner for such a brief period of time, she felt awkward accepting them.

So Lee left the gravesite and was on her way to the chief's car when she spotted McGinty. Like Lee, he was in full uniform, and rather than heading for the street, he was headed somewhere else. To visit a grave? If so, whose?

It was none of her business, of course, but Lee was curious, and walked parallel to the deputy chief, using a row of monuments as a screen. When he stopped, she did as well, and waited for him to leave. Was Chief Corso in his car? Waiting for her? If so, he would be annoyed.

But Lee forced herself to hold on, felt a sense of relief when McGinty turned away, and hurried over to examine the marker. The name alma kimble was engraved in the red granite. Along with the years 2016–2038. Who, Lee wondered, was Alma Kimble? A friend perhaps? Then she remembered the photo of her father, McGinty, and a girl. Was *she* Alma Kimble?

That was when Lee realized that her curiosity was related to her father, not McGinty, or the girl. After her mother ran away, Frank Lee raised her. Yet for all the years spent with the man, Lee felt as if she barely knew him. So maybe the girl was important, and maybe she wasn't. Time would tell.

Lee hurried out to the street and followed it down to the point where the chief's car had been. It was gone, as were many other vehicles by that time, but a cruiser stood waiting. A fresh-faced patrolman came forward to greet her. "Detective Lee? The chief told me to wait for you. He's meeting with the mayor in half an hour. Something about mutants."

Lee thanked him and went around to sit on the passenger side of the car. The clouds were lower, and it started to rain.

THREE

Something was wrong. Lee knew that the moment she woke and saw the stripes of sunlight on the wall. She turned to the alarm and realized that fifteen minutes had passed since she first turned it off. It had been like that ever since the funeral.

Lee rolled out of bed, made her way into the bathroom, and brushed her teeth. There wasn't enough time for a shower, so she put on some extra deodorant and hurried to get her clothes on. Then, after a quick stop at Maria's, she was back in the car.

The LAPD headquarters building swallowed the car whole, an officer waved her through the checkpoint, and she was in the elevator less than five minutes later. Then, by fast walking down the hall, Lee was able to make roll call with a full minute to spare. She was two bites into the burrito when McGinty entered the room. He paused and shook his head. "Eat *before* you come to work, Detective Lee. It smells like a taqueria in here."

That produced a round of sniggers from the other detectives, to which Lee responded with a raised finger. "All right, that's enough bullshit," Jenkins said, as the daily briefing began.

Lee had finished her breakfast and was chasing it with some coffee by the time her turn rolled around. "So," Jenkins said, "let's talk about Popeye. How's it going?"

Lee had been back to work for two days by then, was working solo, and hoped to continue doing so. With that in mind, she struck a positive tone. "I'm working three strategies . . . All of the patrol units are on the lookout for him, I'm canvassing body shops that might have done some work on Cherko's ride, and I'm running an ad similar to the one that Mr. Fuentes ran."

"Nice," Jenkins said approvingly. "But let's get something straight. No lone-wolf bullshit. If Popeye bites, you tell me, and I'll give you some support. This guy is a stone-cold killer."

The last thing Lee wanted to do was share a bust, but if that was the price for maintaining her independence, then she would pay it. "Yes, sir. It would be nice to see some of these slackers do some work for a change."

That produced the predictable storm of protests, all of which led to a rebuke from McGinty and a report from someone else. Mission accomplished.

Once Lee was back on the street, she began the slow, methodical process of visiting body shops in hopes of finding the person or persons who had been working on Popeye's whip. Would they tell her the truth? Maybe not . . . Especially if he owed them money. But even if they failed to come clean, Lee hoped her efforts would put additional pressure on Cherko. The kind of pressure that might cause him to make a mistake.

That's what Lee had in mind as she entered a body shop called Honest Al's. Never mind the fact that "Honest" Al Nurri had done three years for grand theft auto. A power tool chattered as she entered the shop's brightly lit interior. Cars were lined up on both sides of the garage and appeared to be in various stages of repair. Many would have been sent to a junkyard back before the plague. But so long as most of Pacifica's industrial capacity was busy producing the military hardware required to protect the country's eastern border, the manufacture of new cars would have to wait.

"Can I help you?" The voice startled her. Lee turned to find that a man in paint-splattered overalls was standing three feet away. The background noise was so loud that he'd been able to approach undetected.

"I'm looking for Mr. Nurri," Lee replied.

The man had dark hair, a two-day growth of beard, and hungry eyes. They looked her up and down. "My name is Feo," he said. "I'm the manager here. Maybe I can help."

"And maybe you can't," Lee said as she flashed her ID. "How long has it been since the city's safety inspectors took a tour of this dump anyway? Maybe I should give them a call."

The greasy smile disappeared from Feo's face. "There's no need to get your panties in a knot. I was trying to help. Follow me."

Feo led Lee back through the shop to an office in the back. It was glassed in by windows salvaged from a teardown somewhere. Feo entered through an open door, and Lee followed him in. "Sorry to bother you, boss," Feo said. "But Detective Lee wants to talk to you."

Nurri was a small man with a partial head of hair, eyes that peered over wire-rimmed glasses, and a dark complexion. He was wearing a gold ring, a gold watch, and a gold bracelet. His sport shirt boasted an upscale logo, and he made no effort to rise. "Thanks, Feo. I'll take it from here."

As Feo left the room Nurri brought his fingers together to form a steeple. "So, Detective Lee . . . What can I do for you?"

"I'm looking for a car," Lee replied. "*This* car." She dropped a flyer onto Nurri's cluttered desk. The photo had been taken on the day of the West Hollywood Shootout. Her name and phone number were printed at the bottom.

Nurri scanned the flyer and shook his head. "I haven't seen the car, but maybe my employees have. I'll put this on the bulletin board. Who does it belong to?"

"A guy named Cherko, street name Popeye. Do you know him?"

Lee thought she saw a glimmer of recognition in Nurri's eyes when she said, "Popeye." But there was no way to be sure. "Nope," Nurri said, "I've never heard of him."

"Okay," Lee replied. "Put the flyer up and call me if you see the car. It's the kind of gesture that your parole officer will appreciate."

Lee watched the words hit home and smiled sweetly. "It's been a pleasure, Mr. Nurri . . . Let's stay in touch." And with that, she left.

It felt good to step out of the noisy body shop into warm sunshine. But as Lee paused to put her sunglasses on she felt an unexpected chill. As if something evil was looking at her. *Popeye?* No, that didn't seem likely. But there was an even scarier possibility. What if the Bonebreaker was following her? Tracking her the way a hunter tracks his prey?

Lee felt a rising sense of fear and struggled to bring it under control. Then, starting from the left, she began to scan the buildings on the other side of the street. They were low, one-story affairs for the most part, all part of a ramshackle strip mall, at least a third of which was empty. She could go over and look around—but if someone was watching, they would fade.

So Lee returned to the car, performed a 360, and got in. She kept a sharp eye out for a tail but didn't see one. Maybe it was nerves then . . . Plus an overactive imagination.

There were fifteen body shops on Lee's list, and she managed to visit ten of them before it was time to go home. But Lee *couldn't* go home. Not until she put in some time on job number two.

Her task on that particular evening was to visit Dr. Nathaniel Seton at his home in the community of Venice Beach. Seton had been the LA County Coroner prior to his retirement three years earlier. So he hadn't performed the autopsy on her father, but he had done autopsies on victims four, five, and six. Something Lee knew, having read all of his carefully written reports.

But what brought Seton back to her attention was an article that had appeared in the Sunday edition of the *LA Times* online. Although the story wasn't about the murders so much as Seton's collection of torture devices. One of which was described as ". . . a contraption inspired by the serial killer known as the Bonebreaker."

That sentence was more than sufficient to capture Lee's interest. So she called the doctor, introduced herself, and made an appointment to see him. But first she would need to get some dinner, and Venice Beach was a good place to do that.

The 110 took her to the Santa Monica Freeway. Then she turned south onto the San Diego Freeway, took the exit at Sawtelle Boulevard, and headed west. Venice Beach had been a separate city until 1926, when it became part of LA. Then oil was discovered, and the area entered a long period of decline prior to becoming a hip place to live during the late twentieth century. And it was still known for its canals, beaches, and oceanfront walk.

Lee took a right onto Abbot Kinney Boulevard. She'd spent

a lot of time in the area while part of the Pacific Division. And there, on the right side of the street, was a takeout joint called Guido's Pizzeria—home of the BIG Slice.

Lee pulled over, got out, and locked the car. A short walk took her to the front door and the familiar odors within. Most of the restaurant's business consisted of takeout, but there were six miniscule tables, two of which were available.

Lee chose the one that put her back to the wall and provided a clear line of sight to the front door. Then it was time to fire up the tablet and check her trap. The mailbox was registered under a fictitious name—and three messages were waiting in it. The first was an ad that promised to make her "bigger and better" for her girlfriend. The second was a formulaic response from a parts house. And the third was an invitation to attend a law-enforcement convention. So nothing from Popeye. Not yet anyway.

"Can I help you?" Lee looked up, hoping to see a face from the old days. No such luck. The bored-looking teenager had been in middle school back then.

"Yes. A slice of pepperoni, please. And a Diet Coke."

"Got it," the young woman said, and continued on her rounds.

Lee was working her way through a long list of routine e-mails when the waitress returned. "Here you go . . . One slice of pepperoni and one Coke," the girl said. "Will there be anything else?"

Lee said, "No thanks," and watched two cops enter the restaurant. It was a big police department. Too big to know everyone, but she'd been a street cop once and missed the simplicity of it.

The pizza was good, *very* good, and by the time she finished the slice, it was time to go. Lee paid the bill, returned to the car, and circled it prior to getting in. As the engine started, the radio came on. It seemed that 2-Adam-5 was in hot pursuit of a stolen vehicle, and the watch commander was ordering them to break it off. *That'll piss 'em off*, Lee thought as she entered an area called Toledo Court.

It consisted of mostly one- and two-story structures that usually had garages out back. Seton's house was a modest affair which, unlike the neighboring structures, had bars over the windows and was surrounded by an unkempt garden.

There weren't any open slots on his street, so Lee had to turn a corner before finding a place to park. It was dark, and Lee didn't see any other pedestrians as she walked back. Cracked concrete steps led up to what looked like a sturdy door. The dark brown paint was flaking away to reveal the red below.

Lee pressed the doorbell button, but there was no response. So she waited for a bit and knocked. Then she heard the clump, clump, clump of footsteps followed by silence. There was a peephole, and Lee figured that Seton was looking at her.

The door opened to reveal a man with closely cropped white hair. He was dressed in a shirt, a tie, and a jacket. For her? Or was that the outfit he wore around the house? "Dr. Seton? I'm Cassandra Lee. Thank you for agreeing to see me."

"You were on television," Seton said levelly. "You shot nine people, including seven men and two women. Your partner was killed."

The information was delivered without a hint of emotion, and as Lee looked into Seton's pale blue eyes, she wondered how many flat one-dimensional reports the man had written during his years as the county coroner. Hundreds certainly— maybe thousands. "Yes, sir. Detective Conti was a good man."

"Come in." It was more like a command than an invitation. Lee could tell that Seton was single as she entered the living room. No woman she was acquainted with would tolerate the mismatched shelving units that lined the living-room walls or want to live with the items displayed on them. There was an entire row of skulls, assorted bones, and lots of jars. One was filled with eyeballs. "Follow me," Seton instructed. "We can talk in the kitchen. There's no place to sit here."

The kitchen was small and in desperate need of a makeover. There was barely room for a tiny table and two chairs. They sat, Seton offered to make tea, and Lee declined. Then without the slightest attempt at small talk, the ex-coroner cut to the heart of the matter. "The Bonebreaker killed your father, and you are looking for him."

"Yes."

"But you aren't authorized to do so."

"No."

The pale blue eyes stared at her. They blinked. "Everything I had to say is in the official records."

"I know," Lee said. "I read them. More than once."

"So?"

"So I read that you have a collection of torture devices. One of which is a cage called 'the Bonebreaker.'"

Seton nodded. "Yes. After performing autopsies on three of the victims I came up with what I believe to be a replica of the device that the Bonebreaker uses on his victims."

Lee frowned. "How is that possible?"

Seton looked at her the way a demanding teacher might regard a slow pupil. "Inference is the act of reaching a logical conclusion based on factual knowledge. So by looking at the size and depth of an elephant's footprint, one may infer how large the animal is. In this case, I was able to look at the victims' bodies and deduce the manner in which they were tortured."

"I see," Lee said. "May I see the replica?"

"Of course," Seton said as he stood. "I invited the detectives in charge of the Bonebreaker case to look at it, but they never got back to me."

Lee knew that the detectives in question were on the receiving end of crap from all sorts of whackos and probably consigned Seton's message to the "We'll check it out someday" pile. Still, the man had been a coroner . . . So the failure to respond was careless to say the least.

Seton led Lee through the house and into what had once been a garage—but had since been converted into a private museum and workshop. During the next fifteen minutes Seton introduced Lee to more than a dozen medieval devices, including a head crusher, a breast ripper, and a knee splitter. Seton explained that all of the "tools" had been purchased in Europe and brought to California by a collector prior to the plague. Subsequent to the collector's death, Seton had been able to purchase the entire lot from the man's wife. Since that time, more items had been added, including some he'd made himself, the full-scale rack being a good example of that.

And there, next to the rack, stood what looked like a very complicated cage. "Here it is," Seton said proudly. "You'll notice that it's made of wood. But it's possible that the one the Bonebreaker uses is made of metal. Go ahead," Seton suggested. "Step through the opening and sit down."

Lee stepped between a couple of uprights into the small area within. There was barely enough room to turn around and sit on a sturdy chair. "Good," Seton said. "You'll notice that there are four sets of two uprights. Stick your arms and legs through the gaps. That's right . . . The uprights function in a manner similar to the squeeze chutes that farmers use to restrain cattle."

Lee felt a sudden stab of fear, and was about to pull her limbs free, when Seton threw a lever. There was a series of loud clacking noises as a system of cables, pulleys, and ratchets caused the vertical pieces of wood to close in on Lee's arms and legs. She tried to pull them free but couldn't do so.

Seton nodded grimly. "You see? Let's say the Bonebreaker forced you to enter the cage at gunpoint. Or maybe you were drugged. It wouldn't make any difference. You'd be helpless either way."

Lee fought to control a rising sense of panic. She'd been stupid. Very, very stupid. No one knew where she was—or what she was doing. She couldn't access her weapons, and it was quite possible that the Bonebreaker was standing in front of her. And that made sense. Seton had been *inside* the system, where he could monitor the efforts to find him and laugh at how stupid the police were. *She* was. Yes . . . They would find the car. But it was more than a block away. Would they make the connection? The odds were against it.

"Now here's where it gets interesting," Seton continued. "Notice where the clamps are. At your wrists and ankles. That's important because much of what you've heard is wrong. The first thing the Bonebreaker wants to do is destroy a victim's joints. You remember the knee splitter? Same idea."

Lee was breathing faster, there were tiny beads of perspiration on her forehead, and her eyes were darting back and forth. "Take your knees for example," Seton said. "Imagine the pain associated with having your anterior cruciate ligament, the posterior cruciate ligament, *and* the medial collateral ligament all ripped apart at the same time!

"It would be excruciating, not to mention debilitating, making it impossible for you to flee even if the Bonebreaker left the front door open. As for *two* knees . . . Well, you would be reduced to little more than an animal begging for mercy."

Talk to him, Lee thought to herself. *Stall. Try to reason with him.* "But why?" Lee inquired. "Why would someone do that?"

Seton frowned. "To punish them, of course. Now pay attention because this is important. The easiest way to break a joint is through the use of lateral force. See the way your joints are exposed? If I were to swing this hammer, and hit any one of them from the side, that would do the job."

Lee hadn't seen Seton go for the hand sledge, so it must have been nearby. She saw him grasp the wooden handle with both hands, pull it back much as a batter would, and prepare to swing at her left knee. That was when she closed her eyes and took a deep breath.

But the blow never came. Lee heard a rapid clacking sound, felt the viselike jaws release their grip on her limbs, and opened her eyes. "So," Seton said. "The rest is easy. Having immobilized his victim, the Bonebreaker can proceed in any way that he wants to. Since you read the reports, you know that tourniquets were used on some of the victims to keep them from bleeding to death while their arms and legs were being sawed off. Then the Bonebreaker would release all of the tourniquets at once. You can imagine the spectacle! Blood would spurt in every direction, and if my guess is correct, the Bonebreaker takes a great deal of pleasure in that.

"The flensing and boiling would be carried out later. And it wouldn't be until all of the flesh had been removed from the bones that the killer would ritualistically break them."

Lee did her best to respond. But she was so shaken, so nauseated, that it was all she could do to maintain her composure long enough to thank Seton and leave. The experience had not only been extremely frightening—it had shaken Lee's belief in her own competency.

Looking back, it was easy to see where she'd gone wrong. Just because Seton had once been in a position of authority, she'd been stupid enough to trust him. It was a mistake she would avoid in the future.

So was he the one? Had she been face-to-face with the Bonebreaker and managed to slip through his fingers? No. He had allowed her to leave . . . And the Bonebreaker wouldn't have done that.

The trip home was spent thinking about Seton's cage and wondering if her father had been tortured in one like it. She made a note to reread the autopsy report to see if his injuries were consistent with those that Seton described.

When morning came, and the alarm went off, Lee attempted to slap it and failed. And that was because she had placed it on top of the dresser rather than on her nightstand. The sound was loud enough to penetrate the pillow she had pulled over her head.

So after half a minute of nonstop beeping, she got up, turned the alarm off, and padded into the bathroom. She emerged fifteen minutes later, feeling refreshed and curious. Was a message from Popeye waiting for her?

Lee found the tablet sitting next to the Smith & Wesson. She pushed the power button and went looking for clean clothes. That wasn't easy because her laundry was piling up.

Once she was dressed, Lee went online and checked the "bait box." There it was: "I have the following items to sell," the e-mail said, followed by a list of parts. The message was from a person named, "Henry Peters."

Lee brought up a copy of the message Cherko had sent to Mr. Fuentes and read it. The two e-mails were virtually identical. The only difference being Gary's name and that of the sender. "Peter Henry" rather than "Henry Peters."

Lee uttered a whoop of joy and sent her response along with a blind copy to Jenkins. Then it was a mad rush to get in the car and drive downtown. Jenkins had offered to give her some help, and she was going to accept it.

* * *

Popeye was extremely tired and had been for days. But he couldn't sleep. The primary reason for that was a substance called speed, clavo, ice, glass, jib, crank, tweak, and half a dozen more. All of which were slang terms for methamphetamine or meth. It was a highly addictive drug, which, in spite of all the efforts by law-enforcement personnel, was still available throughout the nation of Pacifica.

Taken in low doses, meth could increase concentration and boost the user's energy level. That was the good news. The bad news was that people who were addicted to crank were subject to headaches, heart irregularities, elevated body temperature, diarrhea, constipation, blurred vision, dizziness, twitching, numbness, and insomnia. Which was why Popeye hadn't been able to sleep.

Black plastic had been taped to the windows in order to keep the room dark, but daylight still found its way in through tiny holes and projected gold dots onto the wall to his right. Popeye looked to see if Gina was awake and saw that she wasn't. How old was she anyway? Fifteen? Something like that. She looked even younger in her tee shirt and pink panties.

But regardless of that, Popeye knew that the teenager would wake up hungry. Not for Cheerios, but for clavo, which she would proceed to shoot up. And it was his job to go get it. That required going into the world that lay beyond the black plastic. A place where, according to Honest Al Nuri, a pig bitch was looking for him. *Well fuck her,* Popeye thought to himself as he crawled off the mattress. *I have some medicine for that disease.*

Popeye was careful to slip his feet into some flip-flops before beginning the journey to the bathroom. The floor was covered with pieces of cast-off clothing, drug paraphernalia, and rat droppings. They would move soon and leave the garbage behind.

Popeye flipped the lights on as he entered the bathroom and turned to examine himself in the mirror. His eyes were red, there were open sores on his cheeks, and when he opened his mouth, it was like looking into a black hole. Like so many meth addicts, Popeye had a condition known as "meth mouth." About a third of his teeth were missing, and the rest were in bad condition. According to the dentist he'd seen the year before, the problems were the result of dry mouth, poor oral hygiene, and the consumption of too many carbonated beverages. *Fuck him,* Popeye thought to himself as he lit his pipe and took a seat on the throne.

The fatigue seemed to melt away as the vapor entered Popeye's lungs. Then his thoughts began to quicken. Another fucking mutant was in town. A subhuman piece of shit who wanted to buy parts, take them into the red zone, and sell them to freaks. So the deal was a two-fer . . . Meaning a chance to whack a mutie *and* score some scratch. Gold, preferably, so he could buy tweak at a discount. That would make Gina happy, and everything would be jam. Popeye laughed. Life was good.

After inhaling his breakfast and donning a new set of dirty clothes, Popeye placed a series of phone calls. Then he made his way out into the filthy hallway and turned to lock the door behind him. After descending three flights of stairs, Popeye paused to peer out through a filthy window. Everything appeared to be okay, so he readied the long-barreled pistol and stepped out through the door. Nobody shot him. And that was a good thing. The cool morning air was only slightly tainted by the stink associated with a nearby Dumpster.

After restoring the pistol to its shoulder holster, Popeye placed a pair of wraparound shades over his eyes as he crossed the parking lot. It was home to three beaters and a couple of bikes. But the star of the show was crouched in one of the semiprotected end slots. Stella had been a '36 Caddy once. Well, most of her had, back before a previous owner wrecked her.

Then an enterprising fabricante married the original vehicle to a '34 Buick and threw in some personal touches as well. The result was the sleek, low-riding bitch that Popeye called Stella. She was, along with Gina, everything that he had in the world and therefore precious to him. That was why the lady was dressed in gray. Not because he couldn't come up with enough scratch for some shine—but because a fancy paint job was bound to attract trouble.

While at rest, Stella's curvaceous body came down over her expensive wheels to touch the ground. Not only was that a cool look—it made Stella very difficult to steal. Popeye removed a remote from his pocket and thumbed a button.

Hydraulics whined as the car rose, a spoiler appeared, and the lights blinked. Popeye never got tired of slipping in behind Stella's steering wheel, turning the key, and hearing the huge V-8 rumble into life. Feeding the bitch was almost as expensive as "feeding" Gina but worth every penny. And, thanks to California's offshore oil wells, the citizens of Pacifica would be using internal combustion engines for a long time to come.

After making his way onto I-5, Popeye followed the freeway north to Glendale and the LA Zoo. The instructions to the mutie were simple. She was to meet him out front of the main gate at twelve noon. He wasn't interested in any of that nighttime shit, when it was impossible to see who or what was hiding in the bushes.

Then, once he was close enough, Popeye would cap the freak and take her scratch. With that accomplished, it would be back to the city, score some crank, and party with Gina. While he drove, Popeye was listening to a premix of the single his band was going to release in a week or so. It was a solid rap titled "Mutant Massacre." He was chanting the lyrics as he left the freeway and made his way onto Zoo Drive. Except that it wasn't a zoo anymore and hadn't been since 2039, when some of the animals contracted the plague, word got out, and a mob took the place apart. Elephants, zebras, you name it. The cits killed *everything*, including seven staff members. And that, to Popeye's way of thinking, was the best way to deal with mutants.

After pulling onto the outer edge of a vast parking lot, Popeye stopped and put Stella in park. Then he opened the door and got out. It was necessary to remove the sunglasses in order to use the binoculars. As Popeye panned from left to right, he saw a burned-out car, a pile of rubble from some construction site, and an old travel trailer. It was riddled with bullet holes and had clearly been used for target practice. A momentary breeze came up and sent pieces of litter skittering across the broken concrete before dying away.

Then, as Popeye's gaze slid over a bloated dog carcass, there was a hint of movement. He brought the binoculars back a hair and adjusted the focus. The main entrance appeared. And there, framed inside of it, was a figure dressed in black. Fabric billowed as the breeze came up again, and Popeye knew he was looking at a burqa-clad female. What did she have? Three arms? Anything could be hidden under the baggie. He glanced at his watch. It was 11:58. The freak was right on time.

But, conscious of the fact that there was more territory to examine, Popeye continued the scan. Once that effort was complete, he turned his attention to the sky. The LAPD had drones. Everyone knew that. But when Popeye looked up, all he could see were a pair of white claw marks on the otherwise blue sky. Fighters probably—on patrol.

Satisfied that everything was as it should be, Popeye got into Stella and sent a text message. The reply came quickly. So Popeye put Stella in gear and guided her between various obstacles until he was about a hundred feet away from the woman in the black burqa. Then he got out, went to the trunk, and removed a large duffel bag. It was loaded with rocks to give it heft and chunks of Styrofoam to bulk it out. With the Colt in one hand and the bag in the other, Popeye began to walk.

Lee's vision was limited to the horizontal eye slit. But she could still see quite a bit, however, including the way the air shimmered over the hot concrete and Popeye's emaciated figure as he came toward her. He was holding a long-barreled pistol down along his right leg. That ran counter to the ostensibly friendly manner in which the criminal had approached Mr. and Mrs. Fuentes. It looked as if Popeye had grown more cautious and less inclined to pretend.

Lee's line of reasoning was interrupted by the loud rumble of engines as three customized motorcycles entered the parking lot from different directions and started to converge on her. That, too, was different from Popeye's previous MO and a reason for concern. "Uh-oh," a male voice said in her ear. "Cherko brought backup."

Mick Ferris was in charge of the six-person SWAT team that was deployed on the roof of the building behind Lee. Their positions had been carefully chosen and were well camouflaged.

Initially, Lee had assumed that the snipers would be largely superfluous. Now she was glad to have them. "So it would seem," she said, as her heart began to pound. "Wait for me to identify myself—then go with the flow."

Lee had a reputation as a loner and a bitch. But Ferris had to give the detective credit. He could see her through the telescopic sight on his .308 caliber Remington 700P rifle. And as the motorcycles came to a stop, and the riders got off, Lee stood her ground. Of course, that was what one would expect of a cop who had smoked nine bad guys in a single gun battle. Still, standing there all alone took some major ovaries. He whispered into his mike. "You heard her . . . From the left . . . Tanaka, Hoover, myself, and Ramirez. Oko will cover our six— and Miller has the overlook. Stay sharp."

Popeye came to a stop. The fact that she was still there came as a surprise. He had expected her to run. Then the other band members would run her down. The breeze ruffled the burqa and the duffel produced a puff of dust as it hit the ground. "You want parts, and I have parts," Popeye said. His crew were flanking him by then. Skitch and Kat stood to his right, with Zeeb on the left. It was the same lineup they used onstage.

Lee pushed her badge out through a slit in the fabric. "LAPD! Drop your weapons! You are under arrest!"

Light reflected off the stainless-steel Colt as it came up. But the process was still under way when Ferris put a bullet into Popeye's skull. Maybe the bastard was wearing armor and maybe he wasn't. It paid to be careful. There was a sudden spray of blood as the bullet exited through the back of Popeye's skull. His body hit the pavement and lay with arms spread.

The woman to Lee's left was dressed in leathers and sporting a pink crew cut. She was armed with a sawed-off shotgun which discharged into the air as a third eye appeared between the two she already had.

Then it was over as the others dropped their weapons, raised their hands, and were ordered to lie facedown on the ground. Lee kept them covered while members of the SWAT team came to join her. Then it was time to remove the baggie as Ferris appeared at her side. "Two scumbags down and a quarter million left to go," he said.

"That's a lot."

Ferris nodded. "There's a lot of Popeyes out there."

"Yes," Lee agreed as she looked down at the body. "But this is the only one that Mrs. Fuentes cares about."

FOUR

Lee was staring at a computer screen in a small, nearly featureless room at the *Los Angeles Times* building. It was Sunday, and the newspaper's so-called morgue was closed. But after plying the weekend crew with coffee and doughnuts, Lee had been allowed to use the facility anyway.

Material from the last few years was available online. But the older stuff, meaning stories written immediately after the onset of the plague, could only be accessed via terminals in the morgue. Unfortunately, there wasn't much of it. Many of the reporters were terminally ill as they wrote about besieged hospitals, desperate mobs, and acts of unexpected kindness. As a result, there were days when the paper was only a few pages long and a period of weeks during which nothing was published at all.

Tears streamed down Lee's cheeks as she skimmed page after page. The plague and its effects on LA was an enormous story, so she knew the chances of finding some mention of Alma Kimble were slim, but the photo of the girl standing between the two policemen continued to haunt her. And like any detective, Lee was used to following up on leads no matter how tenuous they might be.

So Lee continued to read, looking for any mention of the mysterious woman. And finally, after an hour and a half of sifting through old editions of the paper, she hit pay dirt. It wasn't as complete as she'd hoped for—but the brief obituary was better than nothing. It appeared in a special edition of the paper called *The People We Lost* and had clearly been written by a relative. "Alma Kimble, age 22. Alma got sick so she shot herself rather than run the risk of becoming a mutant or dying of the plague. May God forgive and keep her."

Lee was still in the process of absorbing that when her phone rang. She checked the screen and saw the name, "Roscoe McGinty." One of the two men pictured with Alma shortly before her death. Was that a matter of coincidence? Or a cosmic echo? The phone rang again. Lee thumbed the screen. "Yes, sir."

"Sorry to bother you on a day off," McGinty said, "but I need your help—and I'd like to brief you before we meet with the victim's family."

"Okay," Lee responded. "Where would you like to meet?"

"I'm in Beverly Hills," McGinty replied. "At a restaurant called Maximo's."

Lee was about to ask "What victim?" when the line went dead. So all she could do was thank the Sunday editor, return to the ground floor, and go out to where her motorcycle was parked. It was a replica of a 2002 Harley Davidson Road King—Police Edition. Though not the real deal, it had all of the original bike's distinctive features, including the huge headlamp, the teardrop-shaped gas tank, and the simple saddle-type seat. A pair of metal panniers completed the look. There was no windscreen; nor did Lee want one. The bubble-shaped visor attached to her helmet was enough protection.

The bike started up at the touch of a button, produced the throaty roar that Lee loved so much, and pulled away from the curb. Traffic was heavy, but based on the stories her father liked to tell, it was nothing compared to the old days. Back before half the population died.

The Hollywood Freeway took Lee to the Silver Lake Boulevard off-ramp, and it wasn't long before that morphed into Beverly Boulevard. Maximo's was half a mile to the west.

Lee spotted the restaurant's sign, slowed, and turned into a pristine driveway that led past the white stucco building to the lot in back. A valet came out to greet her. He was dressed in a red bolero-style jacket and black trousers. Lee braked, toed the bike into neutral, and removed the helmet. "I'll park it myself. Where should I put it?"

The valet had been expecting to see a man, and his expression changed subtly. "Yes, ma'am. Slot five is available."

Lee nodded, put the Harley in gear, and rode it over to a slot that was sandwiched between a low-slung red sports car and a black limo. She'd never been to Maximo's, but it didn't take a genius to figure out that the restaurant was popular with the city's movers and shakers.

She left the helmet sitting on top of the gas tank and crossed the lot to a door sheltered by a red awning. Once she was inside, a woman in a black cocktail dress came forward to greet her. There was a frown on her face. "Yes? Are you looking for work? The manager will be in tomorrow."

That was when Lee remembered the way she was dressed. The outfit consisted of a waist-length leather jacket, a tee shirt, ripped jeans, and her combat boots. Not the sort of ensemble the staff and customers were used to seeing. "No," Lee replied. "I'm employed. Has Deputy Chief McGinty arrived? He asked me to meet him here."

The frown was magically transformed into a smile. "Of course! You're Detective Lee . . . Please follow me."

Lee followed the hostess into a large dining room. The tables were covered with white linen and set with gleaming silverware. An elaborate buffet occupied most of one wall, and it appeared that Sunday brunch was well under way.

As Lee followed the hostess between two rows of tables, she got the impression that the restaurant's well-dressed clientele had come for more than the food. They were there to see and to be seen. Heads swiveled, and there was a sudden buzz of conversation as Lee approached the table where McGinty was seated.

McGinty saw heads turn as Lee entered the room. Part of that had to do with the way she was dressed. She looked like a biker babe—but a babe with a difference. Lee's hard-edged charisma had very little to do with her looks. It came from somewhere deep inside. So why did he dislike her? No, it wasn't dislike so much as a feeling of discomfort that stemmed from the fact that she was Frank's daughter. That wasn't fair, of course, but what was.

Lee saw that McGinty was looking at her. He was dressed in a blue blazer, an open-collared dress shirt, and khaki slacks. Somehow, Lee got the feeling that her boss was no stranger to the restaurant or to the people who frequented the place. That was something of a revelation since the possibility that McGinty had an existence separate from the LAPD hadn't occurred to her. McGinty stood. "Thank you for coming on such short notice."

All of Lee's internal alarms went off. McGinty was being nice. *Why?*

"Let's order something to eat," McGinty suggested. "Then we can talk."

Lee eyed the menu, saw the prices, and hoped McGinty was going to pick up the tab. She took a pass on the fifty-dollar brunch and ordered an open-faced crab melt for thirty bucks. Crab and cheese on a toasted muffin . . . What could go wrong?

All of the waiters were dressed head to toe in gray hazmat suits and spit masks. Not because they were contagious. Far from it. But as a way to assure customers that every possible measure had been taken to protect their safety. McGinty ignored the buffet in favor of orange-scented red beet risotto, with blackberries, mascarpone, and juniper balsamic vinegar. "Okay," he said, once the waiter had left. "Are you familiar with the Church of Human Purity?"

Lee frowned. "I've seen the commercials . . . But that's it."

"Well, as the name might suggest, the church is focused on the concept of purity, both spiritual and physical."

Lee eyed him across the table. "So mutants need not apply?"

McGinty made a face. "Exactly. According to the church's founder, a man named Bishop Screed, the plague was sent by God to cleanse the planet of evil."

"So the good people lived?" Lee inquired cynically. "And the bad people died? Including millions of children?"

"I am not a member of the church," McGinty said, "but yes. That's my understanding."

"So Bishop Screed would see a scumbag like Popeye as a *good* person?"

"Cherko wasn't around at the time of what Screed calls the cleansing. But it's my understanding that the bishop sees the plague as a fresh start. That doesn't mean people will choose good over evil."

Having just finished reading dozens of accounts, Lee knew that millions of good people had died during the plague, and she spoke without thinking. "What about Alma Kimble? Was she evil?"

McGinty's head jerked as if he'd been slapped. "Alma? What do you know about her?"

Lee was sorry she had spoken by that time but couldn't see a way out. "I have a picture of her standing between you and my father; I know she's buried at the Evergreen Cemetery; and I know she committed suicide."

McGinty stared at her. "Suicide? What makes you think so?"

Lee was telling him about the obituary when the food arrived. McGinty leaned forward once they were alone. Lee could see the anger in his eyes. His voice was low and intense. "You're a good detective, Cassandra. That's why you're here. But you are obsessed as well. No, don't try to bullshit me. I know that most of your spare time is spent looking for the person or persons who killed your father. But once you start searching for the truth, there's no telling where that journey will lead. Alma was a wonderful girl. I was deeply in love with her. And your father? Well, he wanted her . . . But only as a plaything—and because Alma was important to me."

Lee started to speak, but McGinty shook his head. "No. You wanted the truth, and you're going to have it. Now, where was I? Your father wanted Alma, too. And, for reasons I will never fully comprehend, she wanted him.

"Then the plague struck, and she became ill. Very ill. The symptoms were consistent with *B. nosilla*. Millions died, but some people caught the plague and made a full recovery. Others weren't so lucky. They became ill, survived, and became mutants.

That possibility terrified Alma. I told her it didn't matter. I told her I would love and care for her no matter what happened.

"But when I returned to my apartment one night, I found an envelope taped to the door. The letter was from Alma. 'Dear Ross,' it said. 'I can't face what could happen, so I'm going to a place where the plague doesn't exist. Thank you for everything. Love, Alma.'"

Lee could see the pain in McGinty's eyes. "I was a cop . . . So I knew where to go. And they let me inside. Because I told them it was part of a criminal investigation I was allowed to see the body. There were so many dead people waiting to be buried that they were stacked inside a supermarket freezer. It took fifteen minutes to dig Alma out. And once they did I saw the bullet hole. It was dead center in the back of her head."

At that point, he just looked at Lee—waiting for her to process the information. Lee frowned. She knew that a self-inflicted wound would have to be at an angle. "Dead center?"

He nodded. "Yes."

"So someone else shot her?"

"Yes. Your father shot her."

Lee was shocked. "I find that hard to believe."

"Believe it," McGinty replied grimly. "I went to him . . . I asked, 'Did you shoot Alma?' And he said, 'Yes.' He said that she asked him to. So I hit him . . . That led to a fight, and I lost. I requested a different partner, got one, and that was the end of it. So, Cassandra, that's the *real* story about who Alma Kimble was . . . And, I'm sorry to say, it's the real story about who your father was as well. A cold-blooded son of a bitch who didn't care about anyone other than himself."

Lee didn't want to believe that. But even if it was true, that didn't mean her father was a monster. It sounded as if Alma *wanted* to die—and knew McGinty would refuse to help. So perhaps her father *was* in love with Alma. Maybe he loved her so much that he'd been willing to kill her. Or was that a bunch of self-serving crap? There had been something remote about him . . . A coldness that Lee rarely allowed herself to consider because to do so would be disloyal. "I'm sorry," she said, and discovered that she meant it.

McGinty looked away and swallowed as if to control his emotions. There was a crooked smile on his lips as his eyes came back into contact with hers. "Me too," he said. "Enough of that. Let's eat."

The cheese on Lee's crab meat had congealed by then, but the meal was good anyway. McGinty ate half of his food before pushing the plate to one side. "Let's get back to the case at hand," he said. "A crime was committed, and it doesn't matter what Screed and his followers believe. Our duty is to solve it."

Lee paused with a fork halfway to her mouth. "And the crime is?"

"Kidnapping," McGinty said grimly. "Bishop Screed's daughter Amanda was abducted in broad daylight on Rodeo Drive. We're searching for her but no luck thus far. And, because Screed's followers have a tendency to vote as a block, the mayor is involved. She called Chief Corso and asked for you. 'I want the cop that killed the bank robbers.' That's what she said."

Lee's eyebrows rose. "And Corso went along?"

"Of course he did," McGinty replied matter-of-factly. "Corso wants to keep his job and, more than that, he might want to run for office later on. If he does, a good relationship with the present mayor could come in handy."

Lee knew that people at McGinty's level and above had to play politics to survive and didn't envy them. "Were there any witnesses?"

"Yes," McGinty replied. "But before you talk to them, you should speak with Screed . . . To shut him up if nothing else. And why not? You would talk to him anyway."

That was true, but Lee would have preferred to speak with people who might help solve the case first. "Has Screed received a ransom demand?"

"No, not that I know of. The bishop should be home from church by now. So let's drop in."

Lee was thrilled to see her boss pick up the check. Their eyes met as he put his wallet away. "The stuff about Alma . . . That's between the two of us, right?"

Lee frowned. "Alma who?"

McGinty chuckled. "You're a pain in the ass—but I like your style."

Lee followed him out into the parking lot, where he went over to the red sports car that was parked next to her Harley. As she took the helmet off the tank, he said, "I should have known. Follow me."

So Lee followed him into Beverly Hills. It had been a city prior to the plague, but half of the original structures had been destroyed during the riots of '38 and '39. A time when those who needed food and medicine tried to get it any way they could.

Fires were set, which because of a drought, had plenty of fuel to feed on. The result was that a great deal of what the rioters hoped to steal went up in flames. And there was so much destruction that the surviving citizens petitioned to become part of Los Angeles. After the request was approved, the Beverly Hills Police Department became part of the LAPD.

Most of the mansions had been rebuilt, but they were different now. The new homes were protected by high walls, surveillance systems, and rent-a-cops. A series of left- and right-hand turns led to a wide street lined with homes on double or even triple lots acquired during the days that followed the riots. A period when previously expensive real estate could be purchased for pennies on the dollar.

One such mansion towered over its neighbors and was meant to be seen. It consisted of a bell tower attached to a building that was reminiscent of a Spanish-style mission. It was fitted with a red-tiled roof, adobe walls, and narrow gun-slit-style windows.

Lee could see why it would have been difficult to abduct Amanda Screed from her home. The property was surrounded by a high wall topped with functional iron spikes. Pole-mounted cameras were in evidence as well, and some of them panned as the car and motorcycle came to a stop in front of a wrought-iron gate.

As the guards came out to speak with McGinty, Lee took the opportunity to examine the arch over the gate. It, too, was made of ornamental iron and featured two angels. They were facing each other and blowing horns. A reference to Los Angeles? Or to Screed's church? Lee didn't know. But one thing was for sure . . .

The religion business was doing well.

The gate made a whirring sound as it opened, and the Harley roared as Lee followed McGinty into the compound. A curved drive led them up to a portico, where McGinty stopped. Lee did likewise, put the kickstand down, and placed her helmet on the gas tank.

Then it was time to follow her boss up some steps to a metal-strapped door. It opened to reveal a woman with blond hair and a youthful face. She was holding a small dog in her arms. Her eyes were red as if from crying. "Hello, I'm Cathy Screed. Please come in. My husband is in his study."

Mrs. Screed led them down a long hallway. The high ceiling was supported by dark beams, ornate light fixtures dangled over their heads, and a wall of windows let lots of light in. Eventually, they arrived at a pair of double doors that provided entry into the ground floor of the bell tower. As Lee glanced upward, she saw that a mural covered the ceiling high above where a kindly-looking God could be seen looking back at her. He was unmistakably Caucasian and surrounded by a lot of wind-whipped hair. Below were shelves of books, all of which could be accessed from a circular walkway. That struck Lee as a silly conceit since all of them would fit on her tablet with memory to spare.

The ground floor was equally opulent. It was dominated by stained-glass windows, an enormous desk, and a fancy chair. A man Lee assumed to be Bishop Screed was sitting with his back to the double doors. He had wispy, ginger-colored hair that was just long enough to hang over the collar of his shirt.

Mrs. Screed called the bishop's name, and when he turned, Lee saw that he was talking on a cell phone. Her first impression was of a man with a high forehead, close-set eyes, and a long nose. It pointed to a slitlike mouth that was turned down at the corners. Screed was dressed in a white suit, pin-striped shirt, and a dark tie. He said, "Thank you, Henry. I won't forget this," and ended the call.

"That was Henry Colmer," Screed said as he stood and circled the desk. "He's leading the effort to create a reward for information leading to the arrest and conviction of the mutants who abducted Mandy. Thank you for coming, Deputy Chief McGinty . . . Especially on a Sunday. And this must be Detective Lee. It's a pleasure to meet you. The mayor said she would get you assigned to the case, and I can see that she's a woman of her word."

As they shook hands, Screed brought his left hand over and placed it on top of the other two as if to lock the arrangement in place. Lee was thankful when he let go. "We'll do everything we can to find your daughter," she promised. "You mentioned mutants a moment ago . . . Is there some reason to believe that mutants took her?"

"*Yes*," Screed said emphatically. "But let's go over to the conference table. You'll be more comfortable there."

The oval-shaped table was located off to one side and surrounded by eight high-backed executive-style chairs. Once the group was seated, Cathy Screed spoke first. Her eyes darted from face to face. "Mandy had just left a store called Cisco's when a van stopped and four men jumped out. Two of them went for our daughter and began to drag her to the vehicle. Mandy's bodyguards rushed to help but were attacked from behind."

"Excuse me," Lee said. "Are you saying there were more than four kidnappers?"

"That's what we were told," Bishop Screed answered. "Mutants attacked the bodyguards from behind and hit them with clubs. Once Mandy was in the van, it took off. The men with the clubs ran."

"And they got away," McGinty put in.

"Yes," Cathy Screed said. "Mandy's bodyguards gave chase but weren't able to catch up."

"But they *saw* them," Lee said. "So we should have descriptions."

"Sort of," Screed replied. "All of the kidnappers were wearing spit masks that concealed their faces. But we know they were mutants."

"How so?" McGinty inquired.

"I just told you," Screed said irritably. "They were wearing spit masks."

"*Anyone* can wear a spit mask," Lee countered. "Half the people on the street wear them."

"True," the bishop conceded. "But if norms kidnapped Mandy, they would send a ransom note. And we haven't received one."

Lee couldn't help but ask the obvious question. "I'm not sure I understand what makes norms different from mutants in that regard."

Screed frowned. "Perhaps we were mistaken. Maybe you aren't the right detective for this case. The answer is obvious. The perverts took Mandy because of her purity. They intend to use her as a surrogate mother."

Cathy Screed began to sob, stood, and hurried out of the study. "There," Screed said as he glared at Lee. "See what you've done? The mayor will hear about this." And with that, he, too, left the room.

Lee looked at McGinty. "It looks like we're off to a good start."

McGinty sighed. "The bishop has a point, you know . . . Female norms *have* been kidnapped and taken into the red zone for use as surrogate mothers. Let's say you're a mutant, you're wealthy, and you hope to produce a normal child. A paid or forced surrogacy is the only way to accomplish that . . . And given the risk of contracting *B. nosilla* while in the red zone— very few norms are willing to go there for money."

Lee had heard of such kidnappings but believed them to be rare. The people who ran the Republic of Texas wanted to prevent such crimes lest they be used as an excuse to declare war. The Aztec Empire made no secret of its desire to take large chunks of Arizona and Texas back—so the last thing the Republicans needed was a conflict with Pacifica. "Yes, sir," Lee said. "The surrogate thing is a possibility. But first things first."

"Such as?"

"Such as talking to those bodyguards. Plus it seems safe to assume that the surrounding stores are equipped with security cameras. So I'll want to review any footage they have. When did the kidnapping take place?"

"Yesterday," McGinty replied. "At 3:36 p.m."

"So detectives responded? If so, I'll need to read their reports."

McGinty nodded. "One thing though . . ."

"Yes?"

"Detectives Yanty and Prospo were assigned to the case. They won't like being taken off it by the chief—and they won't like being replaced by you."

Lee frowned. "*Me?* What did I do?"

McGinty stood. "You're a publicity hound . . . That's the way they're likely to see it."

Lee rose as well. "So what am I supposed to do?"

McGinty shrugged. "Do what you always do . . . Solve the case."

Time was of the essence. Each passing minute increased the possibility that the kidnappers would harm Amanda, or if Screed was right, take her out of the country. So rather than go home from Bishop Screed's house, Lee went straight to LAPD headquarters. Yanty and Prospo were there and agreed to review the evidence they had gathered the day before. And in spite of any negative feelings they may have had, the other detectives behaved professionally, and once the briefing was over, Lee thanked them for doing a great job.

The sun was rising as Lee finished watching the last security-cam video, called Jenkins to let him know what she was up to, and went downstairs to get her bike.

Once she arrived home Lee took a much-needed two-hour nap. Then she got up, took a shower, and put on some clean clothes. She was down in the garage and about to put her helmet on when Lee felt the strange sensation again. Her eyes went to the vacant house. Was he in there? Watching her through the blinds? Or was she paranoid?

It was tempting to walk over and try to catch the peeper, but she didn't have time for that. So Lee got on the motorcycle and drove away. After a burrito at Maria's, Lee made her way onto the Harbor Freeway, and from it to West Pico Boulevard. And that is where the so-called staircase to heaven was located.

The nickname stemmed from the fact that the four buildings located on the site of the old convention center were of different heights and "stair-stepped" up to the largest, which was about twenty stories tall. All of them were sheathed in solar panels, which meant that the Purity Center was largely self-sufficient where electricity was concerned.

The complex was also well protected. Lee had to show her ID before being allowed to cross the moatlike hundred-foot-wide "water feature" and pass through the twelve-foot-high "peace wall" designed to protect the inner church from the sort of debacle that had taken place on the site back in 2038.

During the days subsequent to the plague, hundreds of thousands of people poured into LA seeking the sort of medical attention they hadn't been able to obtain in the suburbs or rural areas. It wasn't long before the hotels were full, and people were camping in the parks. So in an attempt to corral them, the authorities sent thousands of refugees to the city's convention center. Within a matter of days, the facility was filled to overflowing with more than twenty thousand desperate people. Then the food ran out, sanitation broke down, and *B. nosilla* began to spread.

More than a thousand brave volunteers went to help, and thanks to their efforts, plus those of people outside, the situation was brought under control. But half of those in the convention center were dead by that time and convoys of trucks were required to transport the bodies to the emergency landfill in the Angeles National Forest.

What happened after that was still a matter of debate. Some people believed that the convention center was destroyed by an accidental blaze. An open fire perhaps—used to prepare food. Others claimed that dozens of fires were set inside the complex in a misguided effort to purify it. Whatever the truth, the convention center was reduced to rubble—and might have remained that way if Bishop Screed hadn't offered to lease the land in 2040.

There were hundreds of other projects that the mayor and city council considered to be more important, and they needed money, so the lease was approved. The complex took three years to complete. The result was part church, part corporation, and part fortress.

Lee was forced to brake next to a tidy-looking shack as a

uniformed security guard emerged to check her ID. He had a jowly face, a midriff bulge, and an unctuous manner. "Yes, Detective Lee . . . I was told to expect you. Please surrender your weapon, and I will return it as you leave."

"Sorry," Lee said sweetly, "I can't do that. What I *can* do is arrest you for interfering with a police officer, call for backup, and request a search warrant. Then we'll come in and take this place apart brick by brick. How does that sound?"

All of the blood seemed to drain out of the guard's face. "Excuse me," he said. "I need to check with my supervisor." After retreating into the glass-enclosed shed, the man could be seen talking on a phone. He returned moments later. He made no apologies. "Please follow the signs to visitor parking and use slot seven. Have a nice day."

"You too," Lee said, and took her foot off the brake. She followed the signs to slot seven, where a young woman wearing a white sailor's hat and a blue uniform stood waiting. She had almond-shaped eyes, perfect skin, and pursed lips. "Good morning, Detective Lee. My name is Cindy, and I will be your guide."

"Thanks," Lee said as she got off the bike. "I have an appointment with Mr. Harmon."

"Yes," Cindy acknowledged. "I know. Mr. Harmon is waiting in the security center. Please follow me."

As Cindy led the way, Lee made note of the fact that the other woman was wearing heels. Who insisted on that? she wondered. Bishop Screed? His wife? Not that it mattered.

Cindy used a keycard to open a door, and her heels made a rapid clicking sound as she escorted Lee through a maze of passageways to a lobby and a bank of elevators. There were plenty of people in the hallways. Most of the men wore white shirts, blazers, and khakis. And the women were dressed in plain blouses, knee-length skirts, and high heels.

None of the elevator passengers were willing to meet Lee's eyes or even speak with each other in her presence. The lift took them down to the third subbasement, where they followed a hallway to a pair of double doors and a sign that read: security.

Cindy's card was sufficient to get them in, but a chest-high reception desk barred further progress. The man seated behind it was dressed in a uniform identical to the one the jowly gate guard had been wearing. There was no need for Cindy to introduce Lee because the receptionist knew who she was. "Mr. Harmon is waiting for you." The words were said in a way that seemed to imply that Lee was late.

"I'm glad to hear it," Lee replied levelly. A section of the wall-like reception desk swung out of the way to reveal another uniformed guard. Lee turned to thank Cindy, but the woman had disappeared.

"Please follow me," the guard said, and led Lee through a maze of cubicles to a conference room. A man in a gray business suit stood and extended a hand. He had a beefy look, like a wrestler or professional bouncer. A haze of blue stubble covered a square jaw. "I'm Hal Harmon, Chief of Security for the Purity Center."

"It's a pleasure," Lee said, and hoped it would be as a huge paw engulfed her hand.

"This is Edward Tavez," Harmon said, gesturing to one of two men seated at the table. "And that's Oliver Sims. They were with Miss Amanda the day she was abducted."

Both men sat with their eyes on the tabletop and only looked up when their names were mentioned. Lee saw that both had cuts, scratches, and bruises. "They feel badly about what happened," Harmon said lamely.

"I'm sure all of us do," Lee replied. "And we have a common interest in finding Amanda. With that in mind, I'm going to ask you some questions and record your answers."

After removing a small device from her pocket, Lee thumbed the record button and placed it in the middle of the table. Then she gave the date, time, and names of those present.

With that out of the way, Lee asked the bodyguards to take her through the kidnapping. Had that been the first interview they would have been separated, but that stuff was on tape, and Lee wanted to see how they would interact. And there was Harmon to consider. Had the security chief been leaning on them? Was that why they were so subdued? Or were they genuinely upset?

Lee questioned the bodyguards for more than half an hour and was impressed by the extent to which their answers matched what they'd said before. That was consistent with the sort of recall one would expect from professionals, but it could be the result of practice as well.

But regardless of that, one thing was for sure . . . The bodyguards were lying. "Okay," Lee said as she eyed the bodyguards. "Here's the problem . . . Although some of what you told detectives Yanty, Prospo, and me is true, some of it is pure, unadulterated bullshit.

"I've seen video from all of the surrounding security cameras. It shows the van pulling up and four men jumping out. Two of the kidnappers grab Amanda and start to drag her away. Two of them attack you. Meanwhile, two additional assailants approach you from behind. All of that matches up. But here's the problem. Once the four kidnappers have Amanda in the van, they pile in. Then, as the vehicle pulls away, the others run. You claim to have chased them for a couple of blocks. The video shows you giving up after a hundred feet."

Harmon frowned. "What difference does it make?"

Lee shrugged. "What if Mr. Tavez and Mr. Sims didn't *want* to catch the kidnappers? That would explain why they failed to use their guns."

Harmon turned to look at the men in question. There was a thunderous look on his face. *"Well?"*

Tavez looked miserable. "We couldn't fire on the first four . . . Not without running the risk of hitting Miss Amanda. As for the other attackers, there were shoppers beyond them—and they were zigzagging back and forth. So we chased them and gave up. It was as simple as that."

The answer came across as at least partly true . . . But Lee was going to request that both of them be placed under surveillance. If they had played a part in the kidnapping, there was a good chance that they would contact the rest of the gang before long.

A guide who looked a lot like Cindy was there to escort Lee to her bike and waved as she rode away. Getting out of the Purity Center proved to be just as difficult as getting in had been. Once free, Lee made her way onto the Harbor Freeway headed north.

There hadn't been a lot of time to reflect since the meeting with McGinty the day before. As a result, Lee was still trying to absorb what she had learned about Alma Kimble and the role her father might have played in the young woman's death.

It was natural to feel affection for one's father, but the bond between them had been made even stronger by the absence of Lee's mother. So she had grown up not only loving her father but nearly worshipping him. Now she was starting to wonder how well she knew the man. Was Frank Lee the kind of person who would take a girl away from a friend just because he could? And kill her the way a farmer would dispatch a sick animal? And even if he had, was that wrong? Given the circumstances?

The answer to all three questions should be an emphatic "no." So why was she considering the possibility that McGinty was right? Was it because she had always sensed a certain remoteness in her father? Always felt that he was playing a part where she was concerned? *That isn't fair,* Lee thought to herself. *He worked his butt off to support you—and to put you through college. If he was a bit stiff, if he was a little cold, so what? Get over it. He did the best he could.*

Lee's thoughts were interrupted as a call came through her headset. "1-William-3."

"This is Three."

"Deputy Chief McGinty would like to meet with you as soon as possible."

"I'll be there in ten minutes."

"Copy."

Lee sighed. What did McGinty want? An update most likely. So he could feed the food chain. So she would provide it. Then she would go home and get some sleep. At least six hours' worth . . .

After parking the bike, Lee took the elevator up to the sixth floor and arrived at McGinty's office shortly thereafter. The door was open, and he looked up. "Come in and take a load off. You look tired."

"I *am* tired," Lee confessed as she sat down. "I just returned from the Purity Center."

McGinty listened as Lee told him about the bodyguards, the fact that she caught them in what appeared to be a minor lie, and the need to keep them under surveillance for a while. She had just finished her report when someone knocked on the door.

Lee turned to find that a large man was framed in the doorway. The first thing she noticed was the cowboy hat he wore. It was gray, and there were sweat stains around the crown. Not an urban wannabe then . . . The real thing.

Most of the man's face was hidden by a stylized spit mask. The rest of his clothing consisted of a white shirt, a bolo tie with a silver slide, faded Levi jacket, matching jeans, and some beat-up boots. McGinty cleared his throat. "This is Deputy Ras Omo. He's on loan from the Maricopa County Sheriff's Department. Deputy Omo, this is Detective Lee."

Lee stood. A deputy straight out of the red zone! A mutant then . . . That meant the mask was required by law. But what was wrong with him? He looked normal enough. Omo offered his hand and she shook it. "Welcome to LA," she said. "What brings you out west?"

McGinty chose to answer for him. "Deputy Omo is here to work on the Screed kidnapping. He's your new partner."

Lee frowned. "You know what happened to Conti. I don't want a partner."

McGinty made a face. "The chief and I don't give a shit what you want . . . Go home, get some sleep, and come back by tomorrow morning. Then you're going to go out there and find Amanda Screed. Maybe she's here in LA. But if they took her into the red zone, you're going to need a whole lot of help from Deputy Omo here . . . So be nice to him."

Lee looked from McGinty to Omo and back again. Then she said, "Yes, sir," and left the office.

Omo watched her go. Maybe she was okay. Or maybe she was a mutant-hating bigot. That's how it looked. One thing was for sure however . . . Cassandra Lee was interesting. And she had a nice butt. Omo smiled, but no one could see it.

FIVE

Lee had been too tired *not* to sleep well. So she felt rested as she entered the conference room for morning roll call. That didn't mean she was in a good mood, however. Far from it. She was still pissed off about McGinty's decision to assign her a partner, and a mutant partner at that.

And there, sitting at the long table, was the man in question. Except there was something different about Deputy Omo now. Lee couldn't put her finger on the change at first, but then it came to her. The countenance on the spit-mask face he'd been wearing the day before had been smiling. But the latest version was neutral. Was she looking at his "professional" face then? Yes, she thought so. Nonverbal communication was an important part of any conversation. And, since Omo was limited to a single expression, he was forced to choose one in keeping with the occasion. It would be different in the red zone however . . . A mask wouldn't be necessary there.

Unless there was something wrong with Omo's face. Something he didn't want other people to see . . . That's what was going through her mind as she said, "Good morning," and sat down next to him. The other detectives were doing their best not to look at Omo, trying to conceal the fear they felt, but it was difficult. Some mutants were carriers. And *B. nosilla* could kill you.

After running through all of the usual nonsense, McGinty went around the room. It seemed that 1-Charles-5 was working on a big drug case, 1-Zebra-7 was searching for the so-called Red Light Bandit, and 1-Tom-12 was on a stakeout. Each team delivered a short report.

Then McGinty turned to Lee. "I have some news for you . . . Edward Tavez committed suicide last night."

Lee remembered the bodyguard named Tavez and the sadness in his brown eyes. "How did we get the news?"

"Yanty and Prospo had the Tavez residence under surveillance. They heard a noise. Mrs. Tavez emerged from the house screaming moments later."

"Damn," Lee said. "That's too bad. So we're sure it was a suicide—not a hit?"

McGinty frowned. "Why would someone want to kill Tavez?"

"I don't know," Lee admitted. "It was a passing thought, that's all."

"Did Tavez leave a suicide note?" All of the detectives turned to look at Omo. But there was nothing to see other than the expressionless mask.

"Yes," McGinty answered grimly. "He did. It was four words long. 'The mutants have her.' That's what it said."

"So Tavez knew more than he admitted," Lee mused. "Sims and he were on the take."

"And Tavez felt guilty about allowing the kidnappers to take her," Jenkins agreed. "Which is why he killed himself."

"Where's Sims?" Lee inquired.

"The bastard is missing," McGinty said darkly.

"How can that be?" Lee demanded. "He was under surveillance."

Jenkins shrugged. "Our team was out front. He slipped out through the back door, climbed a fence, and ran."

"Someone told him about Tavez," Omo suggested. "And he knew we would come looking for him."

"That's the way it looks," McGinty agreed. "We issued a BOLO (be on the lookout) for him. Who knows? Maybe we'll get lucky."

"It looks like Bishop Screed was right," Lee said. "A gang put the grab on Amanda, and they're going to take her east."

"Or already have," Jenkins said glumly.

"And that's why we asked for assistance from the Maricopa County Sheriff's Department," McGinty reminded her. "In case the trail led into the red zone."

And to cover your ass, Lee thought to herself. *So you could tell Screed you were taking the case seriously.* But regardless of the reason, McGinty had sent for help, and that was a good thing. Or would be if Omo was competent. "All right," Lee said. "Is that all? If so, we'll hit the street."

They were in the elevator down to the parking garage when Omo said, "Let's take my rig."

Lee didn't want to surrender control if that could be avoided. She frowned. "Why?"

"Because I've seen your unmarked cars," Omo replied. "And most of them have the letters TIACC woven into the graffiti that covers them."

"TIACC?"

"This is a cop car," Omo answered, and Lee felt a sudden sense of embarrassment. Was Omo correct? Probably. And she hadn't noticed. The graffiti that covered most of the police department's vehicles was so ubiquitous, she didn't see it anymore.

She followed Omo out of the elevator onto the top level of the underground parking facility. And there, in a slot marked visitor, was a vehicle unlike any cop car she'd ever seen. The SUV-style especiale was surrounded by roll-cage-type tubing that protected the vehicle's grill, sides, and tail end. A set of four humungous off-road tires kept the truck up off the ground.

Something else made the especiale look different as well . . . And that was the magnetic sign attached to the driver's side door. It consisted of the letter M for "Mutant," which was red on a field of white. The signs were issued to any mutant who entered Pacifica. And they, like the masks they were forced to wear, made them that much more visible.

Omo thumbed a remote. Lights flashed, the engine started, and the doors popped open. "For fast getaways," Omo explained, thereby raising more questions than he answered.

Lee went around to the far side of the truck, pulled the door open, and discovered that she had to climb in order to get in. Once inside, Lee found herself sitting in one of two bucket seats that were screened off from the back. A lever-action shotgun was racked above the windshield. Lee recognized it as either a retro Winchester 1887 12-gauge or a good reproduction thereof. It was held in place by two quick-release clamps. Omo followed her gaze. "It belonged to my daddy, and to *his* daddy before that. I call it The Equalizer."

"Copy that," Lee said, as they drove up the ramp and stopped next to the security kiosk. A uniformed officer asked to see Omo's ID and stared at it. That was when Lee realized the officer was looking at a picture of a man wearing a mask. She leaned over to show her ID.

"He's for real," she said. "You can check with Deputy Chief McGinty if you need to." That did the trick, and the officer waved them through.

A four-armed hula girl was fastened to the center of the dash. She swayed seductively as the truck entered traffic. Was Omo making fun of mutants? Or was the hula girl an unapologetic statement of who he was? There was no way to be certain. "This is your turf," Omo said. "Where do we start?"

"In Beaumont," Lee answered. "Do you know how to get on I-10 eastbound?"

"I do," he said. "So we're going to drop in on the freaks."

Lee looked at him. That was when she realized the extent to which the mask covered the side of his face. She could see the flesh-colored elastic cords that held it in place.

Why had Omo chosen to use such a pejorative name. In an effort to shock her? To show how tough he was? Or to put her at ease? All of the possible explanations seemed equally believable. "Yeah," she said. "We're going to visit the TA. Assuming a gang of mutants snatched Amanda, they might be hiding there waiting for a chance to enter the red zone. Or, if they passed through, the locals might be aware of it."

"You mean one of the freaks."

Lee sighed. Beaumont was only an hour and a half away, but it was going to be a long trip. "Look, Cowboy, you're a mutant, and there are a lot of norms who hate mutants. I'm sorry . . . But let's get something straight. I'm not one of those people."

Omo glanced at her. "I believe that you believe that. As for the truth? Who knows? We'll see. Tell me something . . . Have you been to the TA before?"

Lee shook her head. "No."

"Okay, then . . . Here are some things to keep in mind. There's no such thing as normal where mutants are concerned. Everyone looks different, and nobody looks the way God intended them to. So beauty's in the eye of the beholder."

Lee started to speak, but Omo raised a hand. "Hear me out . . . There's more. You're pretty. A mask will hide that to some extent, but not entirely. And when mutant women compare themselves to you, they will come up short and hate you for it. And the men? The men will want you for all sorts of reasons, many of which aren't very pretty. So keep your guard up. You'll be sorry if you don't."

Lee was thinking about that when Omo glanced at the driver's side rearview mirror. "Uh, oh . . . Man with a gun! Duck!"

Lee ducked and had her hand on the Glock when she heard the roar of a motorcycle and a series of thumps. White goo covered most of the driver's side window. A motorcyclist flipped them the bird as he raced away. "What happened?" Lee inquired as she sat up.

"We took some hits from a paintball gun," Omo replied calmly. "That's what happens when you ride around with a huge M on the side of your truck."

"Yeah," Lee said soberly. "That would explain it. I'm sorry."

It took awhile for the adrenaline to fade away. But once it did, Lee managed to sit back and relax. It was a sunny day, and there was plenty to see. Some if it was pretty, like the well-watered circles of green cropland and the tidy farmhouses that sat adjacent to them.

But there were vast glittering tracts of solar panels, too . . . They weren't very pleasant to look at but were an important source of power for the city of Los Angeles.

Other areas hadn't fared so well. Lee could see them from the freeway, ghost towns really, where rank after rank of nearly identical homes had succumbed to a combined assault by the forces of sun, wind, and rain.

It was just before noon when they arrived in Beaumont. The

city had been home to more than 125,000 people back before the plague but was a third that size now. Due to the fact that the community sat astride a main east–west highway, it had been chosen as the location for a so-called Transit Area or TA. Meaning a place where legal transients could pause as they traveled to and from the red zone. Had Omo stayed there on his way to LA? Probably. And that's why he felt qualified to lecture her on what the facility was like.

The TA was confined to the area south of the freeway that had once been known as the Sun Lakes Country Club. A spot chosen during the early days of the plague because the golf course could be fenced off for use as an internment camp.

But "improvements" had been made since then. And as Omo turned off I-10, and onto Highland Springs Avenue, Lee could see the guard towers in the distance. There were four of them, all connected by a twelve-foot-high concrete wall topped with razor wire. As the truck drew closer, Lee decided that the TA looked more like a prison than a rest stop.

As Omo turned left onto an access road, the wall was straight ahead. The only way in or out was a massive gate flanked by gun emplacements. "They lock that thing at 6:00 p.m.," Omo told her. "So we'll need to exit by then or stay the night."

The truck came to a stop behind a line of other vehicles. All were of uncertain lineage and all bore a telltale "M." As they were cleared, Omo was able to creep forward until he was level with the security shack. The security personnel wore army uniforms and carried automatic weapons. A corporal stepped forward as the truck came to a halt. She had a snub nose, freckles, and a cleft chin. "ID please."

Both officers surrendered their badge cases. The corporal scanned them and made eye contact with Lee. "No offense, ma'am. But it's dangerous in there."

"So I hear," Lee said. "But that's where I need to go."

"Yes, ma'am. If you say so. The gate will be locked at 1800 hours—and no one will be allowed to leave until 0600. Any questions? No? Here are your passes. Park in the lot."

Omo handed one of the passes to Lee. "Fun place, huh?"

The parking lot was surrounded by a six-foot-high chain-link fence and half-filled with a wild assortment of cars and trucks. The heat fell on Lee like a hammer as she left the air-conditioned truck. It would have felt good to remove the cotton jacket, but she couldn't do that without revealing her weapons.

She was busy placing a formfitting, self-adhesive mask over her face as Omo rounded the front of the truck. He was wearing his cowboy hat, Levi's, and boots. He nodded. "Remember . . . You're going to stick out like a sore thumb. And we're cops . . . They can tell, and word of that will spread fast. Okay . . . Let's do this thing."

As they followed a couple dressed in black robes through the gate, Lee heard a keening noise that might have been music, followed by the distant chatter of a power tool and grunting sounds from the animal pens located on the left.

Now the reality of the situation struck her. She had entered Freak Town. And mutants were all around her, some of whom were carriers. Yes, she was wearing a mask. But *B. nosilla* was in the air. And *B. nosilla* could kill her. She struggled to control her fear.

"There are two classes of people here," Omo said, as they passed an open-air bar. "Transients and the people who live here full-time. They make their livings by providing services to travelers."

The throat-clogging stench of animal feces hung heavy in the air as they passed a pen filled with goats and entered a maze of passageways. The buildings, if they could be dignified as such, were ancient "high-cube" shipping containers. They stood a little over nine feet tall, were forty-eight feet long, and came in a wild selection of sun-faded colors. Light red, blue, and green were the most common. With few exceptions, one end of each container was left open so that hardworking fans could push at least some of the hot air outside.

A complex network of crisscrossed ropes ran back and forth above the passageways and supported a wild assortment of laundry along with overlapping sheets, faded curtains, and plastic tarps. All of which combined forces to provide the warren of passageways with a modicum of shade.

As the path narrowed, Lee began to pay more attention to

the residents. An elderly woman with an eye at the center of her forehead glared at Lee from a tiny taqueria. A three-armed man shuffled past. He had a dusty suitcase strapped to his back and was staring at his feet. A child with a metal nose appeared out of the shadows. She tugged at Lee's sleeve. "You're beautiful," she said brightly. "Are you real?"

"She's real," Omo said gruffly. "Now run along." The girl vanished into a side passage.

"So," Omo said. "I assume you have a plan."

"Yes," Lee answered. "An informer named Izzi Tubin lives here. He runs a bar called Hyundai 461."

"That's the name and number on the side of his container," Omo said. "I've been there. Follow me. I think I can find it."

Lee followed Omo down a long passageway past a shop selling tie-dyed shirts and a small pharmacia to the courtyard beyond. A dry fountain marked the center of the open area. It looked like something left over from the country club.

Eight containers were pointed at the fountain, and most of them were open. "There," Omo said, "on the other side of the plaza. That's what we're looking for."

A dog with two tails lay panting in a patch of shade and could barely muster the energy required to track the visitors with its eyes as they walked past. The sound of Salsa music grew louder as they entered the bar and followed an open pathway back through a maze of small tables. A man with a tumor growing out of the left side of his head was seated at one of them. He was smoking a joint and reading a tattered book. As Lee passed the man, she felt a breeze ruffle her hair. It was driven by the enormous floor fan that whirred loudly as it panned back and forth.

A long bar ran down the left side of the room, with a line of booths on the right. Omo bellied up to the bar, and Lee did likewise. The bartender was wearing a blue bandana and had a mouthful of crooked teeth. Some of them looked like fangs. His eyes were a beautiful green color, however—and they flicked from Omo to Lee and back. "What'll it be?"

"A couple of beers," Omo said. "*Cold* beers if you've got 'em."

The man nodded, turned to the water-filled cooler behind

him, and chose two brown bottles. He popped the caps, inserted straws, and pushed them forward. *B. nosilla* was an airborne disease so they should be safe. Lee sure as hell hoped so.

"Thanks," Lee said as she gave the bartender a ten. "Keep the change. Is Mr. Tubin in? I'd like to speak with him."

The bartender turned and walked back toward the far end of the container. Lee's throat was parched. So she stuck the straw in through the drink valve in her mask and sucked some cold beer into her mouth. The liquid felt great going down. The bartender returned. "Mr. Tubin will see you. Go straight back."

Lee said, "Thanks," and followed Omo back to a table covered with rows of playing cards. And there, sitting behind the game of solitaire, was a man with two horns protruding from his forehead. The rest of his face was fleshy but normal. "*Two* cops," he said disgustedly as he looked up at them. "One is too many."

Lee sat without asking for permission. Omo did likewise but positioned himself to watch the front door. "My, my," Lee said disapprovingly. "You have a very negative attitude for a man who sells information to the LAPD on a regular basis. Hmm . . . Maybe an award for good citizenship is in order. What would your friends make of that?"

A pair of very large hands swept the cards into a single pile. "What do you want?" Tubin demanded.

"That's better," Lee said sweetly. "We're looking for a girl. *This* girl," Lee said as she pushed a photo of Amanda Screed across the table. "She was snatched off Rodeo Drive in LA. The kidnappers might try to take her east."

Tubin ran a snakelike tongue over blubbery lips as he eyed the picture. "She's pretty."

"Yes," Omo said. "She is. Have you seen her?"

"No."

"Have you heard about her? Or heard about a snatch?" Lee inquired.

"No," Tubin reiterated. "But there is a man who might know . . . A norm who smuggles packages in and out of the red zone."

"He lives *here*?" Omo inquired. "In the TA?"

"No," Tubin replied. "But he spends time here. He's one of the few norms who do."

"What's his name?" Lee wanted to know.

"I don't know," Tubin replied. "But they call him Wheels."

"Okay," Omo said. "Where does Wheels live? We'd like to speak with him."

Tubin eyed Lee. "That'll cost a hundred nu."

Lee looked at Omo. He nodded. "Okay, but with the following understanding . . . If you warn Wheels, or if we walk into a trap, you're going to be one dead son of a bitch. Do you read me, freak?"

Lee was surprised by both the threat and the use of the "F" word, but Tubin wasn't. He scowled. "You know my rep . . . That's why you're here."

Lee placed two bills on the table. Tubin chose a pencil from the clutter at his elbow, licked the lead, and wrote something on a napkin. Omo accepted it, and the money disappeared. "You're bad for business," Tubin said. "Get out of my bar."

So they left, and after asking strangers for directions, wound up in front of a stack. "There it is," Omo said. "The one on the top is Maersk 213."

A set of metal stairs had been welded to the outside surface of the three-container stack. They led up to a catwalk and a series of doors. "It looks like someone divided the container into rooms," Omo said. "We're looking for number eight."

Their boots made clanging noises as they followed the stairs up to the catwalk. Washing had been hung out to dry along the rail that bordered the catwalk, most of the doors had been left ajar so that fans could blow the hot air out, and Lee could hear the faint tinkle of music coming from one of the compartments. A cat watched them from a doorway, and a man wearing a sombrero sat dozing in the sun. "Here we go," Omo said, "numero ocho."

Lee saw that a huge number eight had been painted on the door with two eyes in the upper circle. But, unlike the rest of them, the door was closed. And that signaled *what*? That Wheels wasn't home? Or that he had a penchant for security?

Omo held a finger up to the point where his lips would be and produced a picklock. Lee frowned, but he ignored her. The pick went into the keyhole, Omo went to work with it, and presto! The door gave slightly. Lee stood to one side as Omo toed it open. Nothing. No shouts of outrage—and no shotgun blast. Illegal as hell—but a clean entry.

Lee looked around to see if their activities had attracted any attention and was pleased to see that they hadn't. None she could detect, at any rate. Lee followed Omo inside and was careful to secure the door. It was hotter than hell, but if Wheels returned, she didn't want to tip him off.

The room was equipped with a wall-mounted sink, a filthy toilet, and a small refrigerator. The motor was running full out. A bed with rumpled sheets completed the furnishings. The walls were hung with photos of fast cars, naked women, and a fly-specked mirror. "What a dump," Omo said as he looked around. "So what do you think? Shall we wait for Mr. Wheels to return home?"

"We shouldn't be here," Lee said. "Entering someone's home without a warrant is against the law."

Omo laughed. "Give me a break. You threatened to expose an informer twenty minutes ago, and now you're Miss Goody Two Shoes. Besides, have you seen any law around here? They lock the gate at night and let the freaks fight it out."

Lee knew Omo was right. "Okay, point taken. We'll stay for a while. If we can hack the heat."

Omo opened the refrigerator. "Well! Look what we have here . . . Plenty of cold beer. And a six-pack of Coke. That will help."

"I'll take a Coke," Lee said.

"Coming up," Omo agreed, and brought two cans over to a tiny plastic table. It had been white once—but that was long ago. Now it was gray and covered with stains. Omo took his jacket off and draped it over a chair. That was when Lee saw the guns. One under each arm. What are you carrying?" she inquired. "Colt .45s?"

"Nope," Omo replied. "Pythons with six-inch barrels."

"Lord . . . How long does it take you to drag one of those hog legs out into the open?"

"About an hour. So give me plenty of notice if the shit is about to hit the fan."

Lee laughed and realized that she was starting to like Omo.

Don't do it, she told herself. *Not if you want him to survive. Remember what happened to Conti.*

Time started to slow after that. So as the hours dragged by, they sipped drinks and told each other about their families. Omo's was *huge*, and from the sound of things, closely supervised by his mother.

Lee told Omo about her father without going into his death, her days as a street cop, and the climb to detective. "So you like it," Omo said. "And you're good at it."

Lee shrugged. "Yes, and no . . . I think what I do makes a difference. But I detest all of the bureaucratic bullshit." That was when they heard voices, and a key rattled in the lock. Both got up off their chairs, and Omo flipped the wall switch.

The darkness was only momentary, however, because as the door opened, the lights came back on. That was when Omo grabbed the man and jerked him into the room. A woman stood in the doorway. She was about to run when Lee got a grip on her long black hair. The suspect cried out in pain as the detective pulled her into the metal box and kicked the door closed.

The man was on tiptoes by then with one of Omo's pistols up under his chin. He had long, stringy hair, eyes like black marbles, and was sporting a military-style mask with a replaceable filter cartridge on one side. His voice was muffled. "Who *are* you people?"

"I'm the guy with the gun," Omo answered evenly. "Now let's talk about *you*. Are you the scumbag they call Wheels?"

Just then the door opened and a man carrying a case of beer entered. He had a very prominent supraorbital ridge, a barrel-shaped chest, and a gravelly voice. "Wheels? Vicki? What's going on here?"

"Stomp 'em!" Wheels shouted. "They're trying to rip me off!"

Lee had released Vicki and was reaching for the Glock when the giant threw the case of beer at her. The natural reaction was to catch it, which she did, but the weight knocked her over.

Omo let go of Wheels in order to confront the new threat, and the norm made a run for it. Vicki was right behind him, and both of them managed to escape. That left the police officers to cope with the giant. He raised an enormous pair of hands as they pointed their weapons at him. "Okay, no problem . . . I'm out of here."

"Oh, no you don't," Omo said. "Where will Wheels go?"

The giant frowned. "Who knows? He might go anywhere."

"Okay," Lee said. "Shoot him in the knee . . . That'll make him talk."

The giant was visibly alarmed. "No! Don't do that . . . He likes to hang out in the Blue Pig."

Omo was holding one of the Pythons in his right hand. He pulled the hammer back to full cock. The clicking sound seemed unnaturally loud. "And if Wheels isn't at the Blue Pig?"

"Then he might show up at Pancho's or the Road Kill."

"Sit down," Lee said, and waved the Glock toward a chair. "Find his cell phone, Ras . . . Then rip some sheets. We'll tie big boy to the chair."

It took the better part of fifteen minutes to secure the mutant to the chair and give him some parting advice. "You'll work your way free," Omo predicted. "After you do, go home and get a good night's sleep. Because if we run into you on the street or in a bar, it's going to hurt real bad. Do you understand me?"

The giant looked like a mummy. A strip of cloth covered his mouth. All he could do was grunt and nod. "Good," Omo said. "Have a nice evening." And with that they left.

It was still early, and people were collecting in the bars. Lee heard the distant thump, thump, thump of bass as they arrived on the street. "So what do you think?" Omo inquired. "Should we get while the getting's good? Or go barhopping?"

Lee checked her watch. It was 16:45 military time. So they could spend an hour looking around and still get out before the gate closed for the night. "Let's go for it," Lee said. "There's a good chance that our extralarge friend was lying. But who knows? Maybe we'll luck out."

"Right," Omo agreed. "But let's buy a scarf for you first. Something you can wrap around your face."

Lee knew he was right. She was wearing a mask, but a strip of cloth could be used to disguise her even more. So they stopped at a stall where Lee bought a long black scarf. It hid everything but her eyes. "That's better," Omo said approvingly. "We're ready to go."

Omo was familiar with the TA but no expert. So they asked the vendor for information. He was about twelve years old and on crutches. "The Road Kill is closest," he informed them. Lee gave the boy a one-nu tip and followed Omo through the area where the TA's moneylenders were shutting down for the day.

The Road Kill was only a few minutes farther on and marked by an internally illuminated sign. It was early yet, so there were plenty of tables, and car seats to sit on. In keeping with the name, the decor consisted of auto paraphernalia ranging from wall-mounted grills to preplague license plates. Some of the customers turned to look at the pair but no more than usual.

Lee and Omo sat at a table fashioned from a car door and began to scan the crowd. Wheels was nowhere to be seen. So they bought beers, and pretended to chat, but to no avail. "What do you think?" Lee inquired, once fifteen minutes had passed. "Should we stay here? Or move on?"

"Let's move on," Omo replied. "We'll try the Blue Pig. If we come up empty there, we'll head for the gate."

The Pig, as the locals referred to it, was a five-minute walk. It was a barbecue joint and, judging from the odors that wafted through the air, a good one. It had been a long time since her last meal, and Lee felt her stomach start to rumble as they entered. She couldn't eat there though—not without running a considerable risk.

Omo saw a spot against the north wall and hurried to claim it. The table was flanked by a couple of stools, and he chose the one that would give him a good line of sight to the door. Lee felt her stool wobble as she sat on it. A quick scan of the room produced no results. Wheels was nowhere to be seen. "Can I help you?"

The waitress would have been too short for the job had it not been for the drywall stilts she was wearing. "Yes," Lee responded as she eyed a well-worn menu. "I'd like a Coke and a brisket sandwich to go."

"Got it," the waitress said, without bothering to write the order down. "And you, sir?"

"I'll go with the pulled pork," Omo said. "Also to go. And a Corona."

"Perfect," the waitress said, and walked away.

The food arrived fifteen minutes later but would have to wait until Lee could eat it alone. There was no sign of their quarry as Omo paid the bill, and Lee checked her watch. They had fifteen minutes in which to exit the TA. "We'd better get going," she said, and Omo nodded.

It was dark by then, but Lee thought it best to rewrap the scarf anyway, and was in the process of doing so when she saw a couple emerge from a side passage. When they passed through a pool of light Lee felt something akin to an electric shock. "It's Wheels!" she exclaimed. "And Vicki."

That was enough to send Omo charging forward. But the lunge came up short as Vicki stepped in to block his way. Omo hit her, tripped, and went down. His doggie bag fell and was lost in the shadows. Lee rushed to help him up. "Come on! The bastard is getting away!"

And the bastard *was* getting away. He shoved an old man to one side as he ran up the path and disappeared around a curve.

Omo was on his feet by then, but Lee was the faster of the two and took the lead. A woman stepped out of her front door and staggered as Lee brushed past. Her dog gave chase, yapping as it ran, determined to nip at Lee's heels. Omo came up from behind to give the animal a kick. It produced a yelp and scampered away.

That was when Lee realized where they were. The gate! Wheels was running for the gate! With what? Five minutes left before it closed?

A siren wailed. "Three minutes!" Omo shouted. "We have *three* minutes!"

Lee forced herself to run faster, and could see the gate in the distance, when a herd of sheep poured out of a pen to block the way. And by the time she was able to get clear, the gate was closed. Wheels was gone.

SIX

Now that they were trapped in the TA, all Lee and Omo could do was book a room in a hotel, lock the door, and take turns trying to sleep on the grungy bed. There was a TV, so that helped a bit, but the hours dragged by. Lee heard the muted rattle of gunfire at one point but wasn't tempted to investigate. The last thing the police officers needed to do was get in the middle of a local dispute. Lee had been asleep for an hour or so when Omo spoke her name. "Cassandra . . . It's time to get up."

She thought it was her father at first, getting her up for school, then Lee remembered where she was. So she sat up and swung her boots over onto the floor. There was a bad taste in her mouth as she went over to the rust-stained basin to finger-brush her teeth. Then, after checking to be sure that she had everything, Lee went to the door where Omo was waiting. Had he grown some stubble? The mask made it impossible to tell. "Okay," Lee said. "Let's get out of here."

They arrived at the gate five minutes before it opened. A crowd of people had gathered there, and they surged into the open as the double doors swung out of the way. The police went straight to Omo's truck and got in. "I need some coffee," Omo said. "And some breakfast."

Lee nodded. "I'm in."

They drove into town and chose a restaurant located just

off the highway. There were lots of big rigs in the parking lot, and Lee chose to interpret that as a good sign. Heads swiveled as they entered, and Lee knew what the other customers were thinking. Were the newcomers norms? Wearing masks for some extra protection? Or were they mutants? After they sat down, the eyeballs drifted away.

There weren't any breakfast burritos on the menu, so Lee had to settle for an omelet and a side of crisp bacon to go. While they were waiting, she sucked coffee through a straw, and that made her feel better. Once their orders arrived, it was time to pay and return to the parking lot. They couldn't eat together, so Lee left him to eat in the truck, while she took her breakfast over to a retaining wall, where she could safely remove the mask and chow down.

The food tasted good, and once breakfast was over, it was time to apply a new stick-on face mask and return to the SUV. They were back on the road by eight.

Lee fell asleep at some point and awoke with a crick in her neck. By that time, they were entering LA. "We were going to share the driving."

"I never agreed to that."

"But I *said* it."

"And *I* ignored it."

Lee laughed. "You're a pain in the ass."

Omo nodded. "Yup. That's what they tell me."

The trip had been a bust as far as the case was concerned. But after spending some time with her new partner, Lee had to admit that he was okay. And that was a pleasant surprise.

After entering the parking garage at police headquarters they went straight to McGinty's office. They arrived to find that the chief of police had beaten them to it, and McGinty's door was closed. "In spite of our best efforts, we haven't found Amanda," Jenkins said, as the officers sought refuge in his office. "So the bishop complained to the mayor, the mayor called the chief, and he's talking to the boss. Fun times."

"Maybe *you're* having fun," McGinty said as he entered the room. "But I'm not. Chief Corso wants to know when I'm going to put someone competent on the Screed case."

Jenkins frowned. "Did you remind him that both he and the mayor specifically requested Lee?"

McGinty grinned. "Yeah, I couldn't resist. You should have seen his eyes bulge . . . I thought he was going to explode! Of course, that triggered another five-minute shitstorm, but it was worth it. How was the trip to the TA? "

Lee provided them with a rundown. "So," she concluded, "we never got to talk with Wheels. Maybe he's involved somehow— or maybe he runs every time he sees a cop."

McGinty sat in one of the guest chairs. "Fortunately, while the two of you were drinking beer in the TA, we caught a break."

Lee sat up straight. "What kind of break?"

"Sims was arrested for a DUI last night. He's on ice at the MDC."

"Did he lawyer up?" Lee inquired. "Or can we talk to him?"

"You can," McGinty replied. "But I'd get over there right away if I were you. The guy who runs security for the Purity Center is looking for him. That's what all the messages on my phone say. Unfortunately, I've been too busy to call him back."

McGinty was stalling. Lee remembered Harmon and wondered what the security chief's motives were. Did he hope to help Sims? Or to shut him up? Because if Tavez and Sims were on the take, he could be as well. "Thanks, Chief," Lee said. "We'll get over there right away."

The Metro Detention Center was a short walk from the headquarters building. Once inside, there were multiple layers of security to wade through. The officers had to show ID in order to get beyond the reception desk, then they had to show it again once they arrived at a checkpoint, and that's where they were required to surrender their weapons. The clerk's eyebrows rose as four handguns went into a wire basket.

After logging in, the police officers had to pass through a metal detector and a health screening before being shown into one of the interview rooms. The walls were covered with puke green paint, and the space was furnished with two innocuous cameras, a table that was bolted to the floor, and some mismatched plastic chairs.

Sims had been sent for. So all Lee and Omo could do was

wait, knowing that anything they said would be recorded and might be played in a courtroom. That's why they said very little until the door opened, and a corrections officer escorted Sims into the room. "Cuffs on?" the guard inquired. "Or cuffs off?"

"Off," Lee said.

The officer nodded, unlocked the cuffs, and gestured to a wall-mounted phone. "Dial five when you're done." And with that, he left the room.

Sims had short black hair and there was two days' worth of stubble on his receding chin. His eyes flicked from Lee to Omo. It was easy to read his mind. He was thinking about the mask. What was he looking at? A mutant? Or a paranoid norm?

"Take a load off," Lee instructed. "Sorry about the DUI charge . . . That sucks."

Sims mumbled something unintelligible as he sat down across from the police officers. "Speak up," Omo said crossly. "Detective Lee can't hear you."

Even though they hadn't discussed strategy prior to the interview it was clear that Omo planned to play good cop–bad cop with himself in the role of bad cop. And that made sense given the mask. "Okay," Sims said. His voice was louder now.

"That's better," Lee said approvingly. "I was sorry to hear about Tavez . . . That's why we're here. You guys were partners just like Deputy Omo and I are. So you know who killed him."

Sims looked startled then worried. *"Killed him?* Edward committed suicide."

Lee nodded. "That's what everybody believed until the coroner's report came back. Now we know Tavez was murdered because of the angle at which the bullet entered his skull."

The lie was perfectly legal since it hadn't been given under oath, and Omo played along. "I think we're looking at the guilty party right now . . . Maybe the two of them got into an argument over money."

"I think Deputy Omo is onto something," Lee said thoughtfully. "The kidnappers paid you to let them take Amanda. You got into an argument with Tavez, he ran his mouth, and you popped him."

"No!" Sims said. "That isn't true."

Omo shrugged. "Okay, convince me. Who, other than yourself, would want Tavez dead?"

"Oh, shit!" Lee said. "I've got it! The kidnappers killed Tavez to cover their trail!"

"That could explain it all right," Omo said gravely. "Of course, that means they'll have to grease Mr. Sims as well. Maybe they'll do our work for us. "

All of the blood seemed to drain out of Sims's face. "I don't believe that," he said weakly.

"You don't *believe* it," Lee said, "but you agree that it's possible."

"I have an idea," Omo said brightly. "Sims will make bail pretty soon. We'll tail him. Then, when the muties kill him, we'll be there to make the arrest."

"I like it," Lee said approvingly as she pushed her chair back from the table. "Good thinking, Deputy Omo. Our work is done. Case closed."

"Wait," Sims said desperately. "Maybe we can do a deal."

"We don't do deals," Omo said ominously.

Lee scooted her chair forward. "Don't be such a dick, Ras . . . Sims is trying to work with us. The least we can do is hear him out. Go ahead, Oliver. What have you got in mind?"

A sweaty sheen could be seen on Sims's forehead. He swallowed nervously. "I give you a name, and you get the prosecutor to up the charge."

"Now that's clever," Omo said admiringly. "Sims sends *us* after the guy that did Tavez . . . And he stays where the muties can't touch him. This norm ain't as dumb as he looks."

Lee nodded. "Okay, I get it. That could work. So give us the name, and we'll have a chat with the prosecutor."

Sims looked from Lee to Omo and back again. "You promise?"

Lee smiled sweetly. "We promise."

Sims swallowed. "Okay, then . . . I'm not saying that any of the money stuff was true. But there's a guy who works for the traffickers. A guy named Wheels."

Lee shrugged. "I've never heard of him. And when you say traffickers, are you talking about drug traffickers or human traffickers?"

Sims looked away. "Human traffickers. They take normal girls into the red zone and use them for . . . You know."

"They use them as surrogates?" Lee demanded.

"Yeah," Sims said weakly. "Anyway, because Wheels is a norm, he can drive back and forth without getting pulled over."

"Tell me something," Omo put in. "How would a nice guy such as yourself come to know a scumbag like Mr. Wheels?"

Sims looked down into his lap. He was silent for a moment. And when he spoke, his voice was barely audible. "He's my brother-in-law."

"So he's the one who shot Tavez?" Lee inquired.

"No," Sims said miserably. "But he would know who did."

Lee looked at Omo, and the mutant nodded. "We need his name Mr. Sims. We need his *real* name and his address."

After leaving the metro, Lee and Omo returned to LAPD headquarters where they met with McGinty. He listened, made some suggestions, and placed a call to the prosecutor's office. That led to a second meeting. The DA was reluctant at first, but came around once the extent of the mayor's involvement was clear, and agreed to bump the charges against Sims up to reckless driving and racing. The hope was that the revised charges plus a request for high bail would keep the ex-bodyguard on ice for a few days. Then, if all went well, he would face charges of aiding and abetting a kidnapping.

But in order to get the evidence required to file those charges against Sims, the police had to find Willy Conroy, AKA Wheels, and get some information out of him. The good news was that they had an address. But would Conroy be there? And if so, would some of the traffickers be present as well? Either way, it could be a difficult situation.

So to avoid mistakes and minimize the possibility of a firefight, every effort would be made to check the location out prior to the raid. That included drive-bys in unmarked cars, overflights by drones, and a tap on the subject's phone. As those arrangements were being made, Lee and Omo went off to grab a few hours of much-needed sleep prior to the raid.

They were back six hours later and meeting with Lieutenant Mick Ferris half a mile from the house where Conroy lived. His SWAT team and various support units had gathered in a parking lot and were ready to move in. It was dark by then, which could be an advantage or a disadvantage depending on how things went down. Ferris placed a laptop on the hood of a squad car. "Here are the daylight photos the drone took," Ferris said as he swiped a picture onto the screen.

The images were crisp and sharp. Lee figured they had been taken at a very low altitude. That suggested one of the smaller drones, some of which were no larger than a model airplane. She saw a house with peaked roof, a driveway that ran along the south side of the property, and what looked like a prefab building out back. She figured it was large enough to hold three or four vehicles. Just right for a transporter like Conroy. "How many people are there?" Lee inquired.

"Good question," Ferris replied. "We shot some infrared stuff about an hour ago and saw four heat signatures. Conroy has a wife and two kids, so that would make sense."

"Unless the family is somewhere else," Omo mused. "Then we could run into trouble."

"Exactly," Ferris agreed. "So it's important to be careful."

It took ten minutes to load up. Once all the units were ready, a patrol car led the way. Its assignment was to block the north end of the street, while the SWAT team's armored "war wagon" stopped in front of the house, and another black-and-white sealed the intersection to the south. Other cars were scheduled to swoop in via the alley behind Conroy's shop. Their job was to prevent Conroy or other members of the gang from slipping out the back.

Lee and Omo were supposed to follow the armored car in but stay out of the SWAT team's way. Both were dressed in LAPD body armor and wore their badges where they could be seen. An aid car was parked two blocks away, ready to respond if there were casualties or if Amanda was found.

Lee was at the wheel and followed the war wagon onto the street where Conroy lived. She pulled over to the curb as the armored car pulled in to block the driveway. Once the boxy vehicle stopped, doors flew open, and the SWAT team boiled out. There were two teams. One raced up onto the front porch while the other ran back along the side of the house to secure the shop.

Lee and Omo drew their weapons and followed team one up to the front door. The first officer was equipped with a battering ram and the second was armed with an assault rifle. "Los Angeles Police Department!" Ferris yelled through a bullhorn. "Open up! We have a search warrant."

There was a short pause. Then the door swung open to reveal a little girl. She appeared to be eight or nine years old and was clearly terrified. The first officer took her by the arm and pulled her out onto the porch. That allowed the SWAT team to surge inside.

Lee knelt next to the girl. She had mousy hair, freckles, and a double chin. "Hi. My name is Cassandra. Don't worry, no one will hurt you. Are you Lisa Conroy?"

The girl nodded.

"Okay," Lee said. "We're looking for your father. Where is he?"

"He's in the back," Lisa said. "Working on his van."

"Good," Lee said. "Thank you. Where is your mother? And your brother?"

"Inside," the girl answered, and pointed to the house.

"Got it," Lee said. "Now, this is very important . . . Does anyone else live here?"

Lisa shook her head. "Not right now."

"But they have in the past?" Omo inquired.

Lisa looked at the mutant. "Sometimes," she said.

Lee noticed that the little girl was willing to speak with Omo. Most children raised in the green zone had been taught to fear mutants. But maybe she didn't realize that Omo was one . . . Lots of people wore masks. "Who were they?" Lee inquired. "Who were the people who stayed here?"

"Mommy and Daddy help runaways," Lisa explained.

Lee felt her heart start to beat faster. "That's very nice of them," she said. "Were the runaways boys? Or girls?"

"Girls."

"So where do the girls go after they leave here?"

"They go to homes. Places where nice people take care of them."

"I see," Lee said. "What about *this* girl . . . Did she stay here?"

Lisa examined the photo. "Yes, that's Mandy . . . She tried to run away, and Daddy caught her. She cried when Daddy hit her."

Amanda Screed had been nothing more than an objective up to that point. A spoiled rich girl Lee was supposed to find. Now, as Lee listened to Lisa, the kidnap victim was starting to become a real person. A young woman who had been snatched off the street, held prisoner, and had enough guts to make a run for it. Now Lee felt a burgeoning sense of sympathy and an even stronger desire to find the missing woman. "How long?" Lee inquired. "How long ago did your daddy take Mandy away?"

Lisa frowned. "I don't know . . . Three or four days maybe."

Lee stood. There hadn't been any gunshots, and that was a good sign. She took Lisa's hand and led her over to where a uniformed officer was standing. "This is Lisa . . . Please place a call to Family Services. Tell them there's a brother, too . . . A boy named Neal."

The officer nodded and smiled. "I'll take care of it."

Lee thanked her, and with Omo in tow, made her way past the war wagon to the backyard, where lots of people were milling around. Ferris was present and that meant the SWAT team had cleared the house and gone out through the rear door. He saw the officers and came over to speak with them. "We've got them. That includes Conroy, his wife, *and* the boy. Conroy was hiding in the attic."

"Nice job," Lee said. "I spent some time with the daughter. She's out front and confirms that Amanda was held here. And the mom was in on it."

"Yeah," Ferris agreed. "There's no way Conroy could have been holding women here without his wife's knowledge. Come on . . . There's something I want to show you."

Lee and Omo followed Ferris into the brightly lit shop. A messy workbench ran the length of one wall, an engine dangled from a chain hoist, and the floor was stained with grease. An especiale was parked under the motor and next to a white cargo van. One of thousands that looked just like it except for one thing: This vehicle was equipped with four-wheel drive.

As Ferris led them to the back of the garage, Lee saw the cages. There were three of them, all made out of chicken wire stapled to wooden frames. But these coops weren't made for chickens as could be seen from the cots, jury-rigged toilets, and the leg irons that lay on the floor. Lee felt a combination of shock and disgust as she turned to Omo. "Come on. Let's say 'hi' to Wheels."

Conroy and his wife Mona were outside. They had been separated, and a couple of uniformed officers were getting ready to take Wheels away. Lee recognized the long, stringy hair and the beady eyes. A sneer appeared on his unshaven face as Lee and Omo approached. "Oh look . . . *More* pigs. The same ones that tried to bust me in the TA."

Lee ignored Conroy and addressed the officers instead. "Did you read him his rights?"

The cop nodded. "Yes, ma'am."

"Take good care of him."

"I'll remember you bitch!" Conroy yelled, as the officers took him away.

"I think he has a crush on you," Omo observed.

Lee smiled. "Tell me something, Ras . . . Can we trace calls into the red zone?"

"I don't know," Omo replied. "There hasn't been any attempt at cooperation for a long time."

"But they sent you."

"Yeah . . . Things have improved, and they're worried about the Aztecs. Why do you ask?"

"When they let Conroy use a phone, he will call an attorney. Then he'll try to warn the people he works for."

"And you want to know who they are."

"*We* want to know."

Omo nodded. "That makes sense. I'll get on it."

"Thanks. I'll call McGinty and try to buy some time. Maybe we can push the calls into tomorrow."

Lee took Omo back to LAPD headquarters to get his truck. Where was he staying, she wondered. In Freak Town? Probably . . . Since a regular hotel wouldn't accept him. Omo hadn't complained—but he rarely did.

It was well past midnight when Lee arrived home, parked

out front, and gave her motorcycle an affectionate pat as she walked past. Then it was up the stairs to the top landing. And that's when she saw that the area around the locks was badly splintered, and her front door was ajar. The bottom fell out of Lee's stomach as she drew the Glock. "Los Angeles Police! Drop your weapons and come out with your hands in the air!"

Lee waited. There was no reaction. So she toed the door open. It was dark inside the apartment, but no one fired at her. She tried again. "Los Angeles Police Department! Come out with your hands up." Still no response.

Lee held the Glock in one hand as she entered. That left her other hand free to turn the lights on. Everything *looked* normal so she stopped to listen. The refrigerator hummed, and a dog barked somewhere nearby, but there were no other sounds.

Lee went from room to room. The apartment was empty. The TV had been left untouched. That seemed strange. But how about the small stuff? Jewelry and the like? There was only one way to find out. She returned to the kitchen where she closed the door and wedged a chair under the knob.

Then Lee took a careful inventory of the front room, but as far as she could tell, none of her belongings had been taken. Her father's bedroom was next. The hollow-core door had been forced, but that was to be expected. Any burglar worth his or her salt would see the padlock and assume that the good stuff was inside. *Boy, were they disappointed,* Lee thought to herself as she entered the room.

Still, there was the possibility that the intruder had taken items that belonged to her father. His badge, his cuffs, or something like that. She circled the room. Some items had been moved—but all of them were there. Or so it seemed until she came to the worktable.

Her papers had been shuffled around and that made the task more difficult. So she put everything back the way they had been to the extent that she could. And that was when Lee realized that something *was* missing. The picture of Roscoe McGinty, Alma Kimble, and her father was gone.

What felt like cold ice water entered her veins. McGinty had broken into her home! Something he could do since he knew she was participating in the raid. No, that was absurd. But who else would take the photo and only the photo? The obvious answer was the Bonebreaker. As for why, that was unknowable.

Lee continued to search her apartment. But nothing else was missing. Should she report the burglary? As well as her suspicions? According to McGinty, people were well aware of her efforts to solve her father's murder. And they weren't likely to see a connection between the missing picture and the serial killer. More than that, they might decide that she was crazy and place her on administrative leave. That would be disastrous. Because having seen the chicken-wire cages, Lee was all the more determined to find the traffickers and bring them in. So no, she wasn't going to report the burglary, but she was going to get a better door.

Lee fortified her front door as best she could and went to bed. She would call a carpenter and a locksmith in the morning. And, if she was lucky, Wheels would lead her to the traffickers. She took the positive thought to bed with her, but it wasn't enough to stave off a succession of bad dreams.

When morning came, Lee put in a call to a carpenter she'd used in the past and asked him to replace both doors. And because Lee would have to leave the apartment unlocked, he agreed to come right away. Once he was done, she would contact a locksmith.

So in spite of recent efforts to show up on time, Lee arrived late. McGinty gave her a dirty look but continued the briefing. Once McGinty finished talking about the case that Murphy and Dunbar had been working on, he turned his attention to the Screed kidnapping. "By now all of you know that last night's raid was a success. With help from the SWAT team and the patrol division, we managed to nail one of the people responsible for the Screed kidnapping."

That produced a chorus of congratulatory comments, and McGinty nodded. "Unfortunately, our efforts to trace the suspect's calls into the red zone weren't successful. Even though the Maricopa County Sheriff's Department has been cooperating with us, a lot of their communications infrastructure was destroyed after the plague hit. And the new stuff isn't fully compatible with our equipment. We were able to record Conroy's calls, but he played it smart. Once a person answered, he said, 'This is Wheels. The LA police put me in the can—and I could use some help.' Then he hung up."

Lee felt a profound sense of disappointment. She'd been hoping for a breakthrough. "Okay," she said. "We'll go to work on *Mrs.* Conroy then."

McGinty nodded. "You do that. Now, let's talk about the Compton sniper."

Once the meeting was over, Lee and Omo left for the MDC where Mona Conroy was being held. Once they were outside, Omo looked her way. "Are you okay?"

"Sure, why wouldn't I be?"

Omo shrugged. "I don't know. You seem worried."

Lee thought about that. She *was* worried. And with good reason in the wake of the burglary. It wasn't fair. Omo could see her nonverbals, but she couldn't access his. "I'm afraid that Amanda is somewhere in the red zone by now," she replied evasively. "The clock is ticking."

"I'm sorry the trace didn't work," Omo said glumly.

"Don't worry, Cowboy," Lee said lightly. "We'll get them. By the way . . . The good cop–bad cop thing worked with Sims. But let's try good cop–good cop with Mrs. Conroy. Odds are that she's scared enough already."

Omo nodded. "Got it."

As before, it was necessary to pass through multiple layers of security before being shown into an interview room. Mona Conroy was there waiting for them. She might have been pretty once, but the intervening years had been less than kind. Mona had bleached blond hair, dark roots, and china blue eyes. They had the furtive look of a dog that has been beaten and always expects the worst. "I'm Detective Lee, and this is Deputy Omo," Lee told her. "I spoke with Lisa last night, and she's a cutie."

Mona's lower lip quivered. "They took her away."

"Yes, they did," Lee agreed as she sat down. "But it's my hope that you'll be reunited with your children soon."

"They need me," Mona said pitifully.

"We understand that," Omo said sympathetically. "But here's

the problem. It looks like your husband took part in a series of kidnappings. And you were in on it."

"I didn't want to," Mona said earnestly. "He made me do it."

"And I believe you," Lee said soothingly. "Unfortunately, in the eyes of the law, you were an accessory. That means you can be charged, tried, and sent to prison. But, if you help us find Amanda Screed, or any of the other women who were taken, that could be helpful. The prosecutor might cut you some slack."

"He *might* cut you some slack," Omo added for the sake of the camera. "We can't promise anything."

"No we can't," Lee agreed. "But it's worth a try. Deals get done every day."

"Willy would beat me," Mona said pathetically.

"Willy is going to be in the slammer for a long time," Lee predicted. "And we will protect you."

Mona hung her head. Lee felt sorry for the woman. Eventually, the blue eyes came up to meet hers. "What do you want?"

"We want to know where Willy took the girls," Omo said. "And who he delivered them to."

"The first part is easy," Mona replied. "He took them into the red zone. To someplace outside of Phoenix."

"Okay," Lee said. "Who was he working for?"

"He mentioned a man named Vincent Rictor," Mona replied.

Lee wrote the name down. "Good. That's a start."

The interview continued for thirty minutes after that. A picture began to emerge. Conroy would get a phone call, prepare the van for a trip, and disappear. Often for a week or more. Then he would return to the house with one, two, or even three girls chained to the van's floor.

When that occurred, it was Mona's job to feed the prisoners, empty their potty buckets into a toilet inside the house, and guard them when her husband went off to spend time at the local tavern. And that was the situation the night Amanda escaped. She had been one of two prisoners at the time. After using some of her own feces to lubricate an ankle, and bending her foot in a manner that most people couldn't, she'd been able to remove the ankle bracelet.

And if Amanda had chosen to leave the garage at that point,

she would have gone free. Instead, she made use of Conroy's tools to break into the neighboring cage and was trying to free a girl named Shelly when their captor returned.

Conroy was drunk. He beat Amanda, put her back in her cage, and tightened the ankle bracelet. Then he entered the house. Mona was watching TV. "He called the children into the living room," Mona said miserably, "and he told them how stupid I was. Then he forced them to watch while he beat me."

Lee was experiencing all sorts of emotions by that time. Admiration for Amanda, a fierce desire to punish Conroy, and concern for Mona's children. "I will tell the prosecutor everything you told me," she promised. "You should have reported your husband to the police. But, if you continue to cooperate, there's a chance that you'll get off without doing any time. We'll see."

The police officers left after that. "So," Omo said, as they arrived on the street. "What now?"

"Rictor," Lee said. "Can you get somebody to pull his package? There's bound to be one."

"I'll get to work on it."

"Good. Then we need to find Amanda. We need to find *all* of them."

After they returned to the sixth floor of LAPD headquarters, Omo borrowed a desk while Lee went to get coffee. She returned to find her partner staring out a window. She put a cup and a straw on the desk next to his elbow. "So? What did you learn?"

"Rictor had a record all right—and it's as long as your arm. He was wanted for murder among other things."

"*Was?*"

Omo turned to look at her. That particular mask had a sardonic expression. "Somebody shot Rictor last night. He's dead."

SEVEN

After grabbing some sleep, Lee had been ordered to attend a high-level meeting with the chief of police. And that was a rare event indeed. It made sense, however, since Bishop Screed was still throwing his weight around—and there was every reason to believe that Amanda was alive.

Lee felt nervous as she followed McGinty and Omo into the large conference room located adjacent to Chief Corso's executive-style office. The walls were decorated with artistic black-and-white photos of the "new" LA, planters were full to overflowing with carefully arranged greenery, and the glossy-looking redwood conference table could easily seat twenty people. Corso was ten minutes late and clearly in a hurry. "Okay," he said as he claimed the seat at the head of the table. "I'm taking flack on the Screed case . . . Bring me up to speed."

McGinty provided Corso with a good summary of what had taken place over the last few days, and Corso nodded. "Good job. But here's the deal . . . In spite of all the progress that has been made, Bishop Screed feels that things are moving too slowly."

McGinty started to protest, but Corso raised a hand. "I know . . . That's grade-A bullshit. But that's what he told the mayor, and she's buying it. So I want you to put some new people on the case, send them over to kiss Screed's ass, and do whatever they can to find any traffickers who may be lurking here in LA."

Lee thought she'd seen every expression McGinty had to offer. Especially those that conveyed irritation, annoyance, and anger. But she was wrong. McGinty's face turned beet red and it looked as if his head was going to explode. Corso laughed. "Don't blow a gasket, Ross . . . There's more. You may find this hard to believe—but I still consider myself to be a cop. And I want to find *all* of the missing women. So I'm directing you to send Lee into the red zone along with Deputy Omo. I called Sheriff Arpo earlier this morning. And, while I'm not sure he's real happy about the prospect of having a norm on his staff, he agreed."

The statement was followed by a moment of silence as McGinty took it in. Then, bit by bit, a smile appeared on his face. "Yes, sir! Thank you, sir."

Corso smiled. "Be sure to warn him about Lee here . . . Personally, I feel sorry for the poor bastard."

It was a sunny day, warm air was buffeting her face, and Lee felt good. Thanks to the unexpected orders from Chief Corso, she and Omo were headed east. That meant she could put McGinty and the LAPD's rules behind her for the moment. Plus there was the very real possibility that they would find Amanda.

There was the red zone to think about, of course, but she had plenty of masks and nostril filters with her. So everything would be fine. That's what Lee told herself even if she didn't entirely believe it. The red zone was up ahead somewhere.

As they passed through Beaumont, Omo glanced at Lee and back again. The side window was open. The slipstream ruffled her hair and produced a gentle rumbling sound. *What's she thinking?* he wondered. There was no way to tell. Because in spite of the way Lee ran her mouth, she kept most of herself hidden.

And you're no different, Omo told himself. *She's going to find out. So tell her.*

But Omo didn't want to tell her. Because if he told her, then she'd view him differently. Or would she? Maybe her opinion was low already. *And what difference does it make?* Omo asked himself. *She's a norm, for God's sake . . . And you're a freak. It's impossible to lose a chance you never had.*

It was almost 1:00 p.m. when they entered the outskirts of Indigo. It had been a railroad town once, but that was long ago. Now it was a farming community with a reputation for producing excellent grapes, citrus, and dates. "There's a roadside stand up ahead," Omo said. "How 'bout some lunch?"

"I'm hungry," Lee answered. "And a break would be nice."

Omo pulled off the highway and onto a frontage road where a row of cars was parked in front of an open-air market. They were out of the truck and walking toward an arched entryway, when Lee saw the sign: no mutants allowed. Omo came to a stop. "You go ahead," he said. "I'll wait here."

"You're a police officer. They can't keep you out."

"There's no point to forcing the issue," Omo replied. "I'd like a cold drink, a hunk of cheese, and some fruit. I'll give you some money."

Lee waved the offer away. "There's no need. I have this."

Lee entered the market, purchased the items Omo had requested, and returned to the truck. "There's a rest area up ahead," he told her. "Let's eat there."

The rest area was only half-full, which meant Omo could park in a patch of shade. Some picnic tables were located nearby, so they took the food over to one of them. "How are we going to do this?" Lee inquired.

Omo pointed at a table twenty feet away. "You sit there— and I'll sit here. Phone me. There's something we need to talk about."

Lee looked at him. "Is this about a divorce? If so, I want your truck."

Omo laughed. "No . . . It's just that there's some stuff you don't know. Call me."

So Lee went over to the table and laid out her lunch. She dialed the phone, looked at Omo, and saw that his back was turned to her. He answered right away. "Hi there."

Lee popped a section of orange into her mouth. It was cold and juicy. "So, what's up?"

Omo took a sip of Coke. "We're headed for Phoenix. And once we arrive, you'll learn the truth. So I might as well tell you now."

"Wait!" Lee said. "Don't tell me . . . Let me guess. You collect Roy Rogers stuff."

"No."

"You communicate with the dead."

"No, but that would come in handy sometimes."

"You're a part-time ballet dancer."

"Nope. I like Salsa though."

"Okay, I give up. What is this dreadful secret?"

"I shot my partner."

Lee turned to look at his back. "You *what*?"

"I shot my partner," Omo repeated. "A perp had an arm around his throat and was using him as a shield."

"So you shot the poor bastard?" Lee asked incredulously.

"I shot *through* him," Omo explained. "The bullet passed between his left arm and chest. It hit the perp and killed him instantly."

"Shit," Lee said. "I *love* it! Did they give you a medal?"

"Nope," Omo answered soberly. "My boss gave me a negative performance rating—and I was sent to LA by way of a punishment."

"I don't understand," Lee said. "Your partner was okay."

"Yeah, but he shit his pants when the bullet creased his side."

Lee began to laugh. "I thought you were the departmental hotshot! The perfect guy to serve as an ambassador to the LAPD."

Omo shook his head. "No way. Sheriff Arpo doesn't like Pacifica, or norms for that matter."

"Then who set the loan up?"

"Maria Soto serves as president of the Maricopa Board of Supervisors, and she swings a big stick. So when McGinty contacted her, she asked Arpo to send a deputy to LA. He chose me in the hope that I would get lynched or something."

"And you're telling me this because?"

"I'm telling you because we aren't likely to get a whole lot of support from the sheriff. Not unless it suits his purposes somehow."

"And Soto?"

"She hates traffickers," Omo replied. "So she'll support what we're doing. But she has zero authority over the sheriff's department and the way Arpo runs it. So we can't expect much help from her."

Lee took a sip from a can of lemonade. "So you're known as the departmental screwup."

"Yes. I'm afraid so."

"Well, don't worry about it, Cowboy," Lee said. "We'll find a way. And Ras . . ."

"Yes?"

"If a perp has *me* by the throat, shoot the bastard."

They were halfway back to the truck when Lee felt the now-familiar prickling sensation. She paused to take a long, slow look around. There were people, some of whom were near the market, and some of whom were seated at tables. Any one of them could have been eyeing her. "What's up?" Omo wanted to know.

"It's a feeling, that's all," Lee replied. "Like we're being watched."

"People stare at me all the time," Omo said. "I'm a mutant."

"Yeah, that could explain it," Lee agreed. But she didn't think so. Omo was understandably self-conscious, but he *looked* normal because plenty of norms wore masks.

Once they arrived at the truck, Lee insisted on performing a 360. Something she should have done before leaving LA. Omo joined in, and he was the one who found the black box. A simple magnet held it against the inside surface of his back bumper, and while there wasn't any sort of label on the device, Lee knew it was a tracker. What else *could* it be? So she walked over to a tractor-trailer rig and let the magnet attach itself to the truck's frame.

Would the trick work? Not if they were under surveillance. One thing was for sure, however . . . Someone was following them. The question was not only *who*, but *why*.

It took about an hour and a half to reach the outskirts of Blythe. It was located on the border between Pacifica and the Republic of Texas. It had long served as a stopover for weary travelers and still did. But unlike the sun-baked tourist city of preplague days, Blythe was now called *Fort* Blythe, and served as a very important border-control point. There were only a dozen locations where people could legally enter or exit Pacifica, and Fort Blythe was one of them.

A series of successively lower speed limits forced the truck to slow down—and Lee could see the many ways in which the military had put its stamp on the community. There were lots of signs directing incoming troops to various operational areas, bases, and firing ranges.

To the left and right, Lee could see a vast sprawl of identical prefabs all shimmering in the midday heat. And there were water towers, too . . . Not to mention vehicle parks and airstrips for a variety of planes and drones. The whole thing had an ominous feel.

"How do you want to play it?" Omo inquired. "Would you like to spend the night here? And leave in the morning? Or tackle the border crossing now?"

"How long will it take us to reach Phoenix?"

"A little over two hours."

Lee thought about Amanda. Time was critical. "Let's go for it. The sooner we arrive, the better."

"Right," Omo said. "That makes sense."

A few minutes later, Lee saw a sign that read, border crossing ahead. mutants right lane only.

Omo turned the wheel in that direction. An off-ramp delivered them into a single-file line of vehicles. There were at least fifty of them. Many sat with windows open and their engines off. "This could take awhile," Omo predicted as he turned the truck off.

They were inside the security lane at that point, and there were concrete barriers on both sides. That made it impossible to turn around and leave. Steel pylons were located every hundred feet or so, each of which supported a sensor package.

That was to be expected. But when the hummingbird-style drone dropped down to hover in front of the windshield, Lee felt a stab of fear. The device hung there for a moment, scanned the interior, and darted away. Lee looked at Omo. He nodded. "You think *that's* scary? Getting in is worse."

It took forty minutes to get through the line. A barrier dropped in front of the truck as it stopped between a pair of what looked like concrete pillboxes. Soldiers took up positions on both sides of the vehicle. They wore full-face respirators, body armor, and were armed with submachine guns. "Step out of the vehicle," the man on Lee's side said, "and place your hands on top of your head."

Lee did as she was told, then a third soldier appeared. He, or she, ran a wand up and down the detective's body. It beeped intermittently as it sensed the pistols, backup ammo, a pair of cuffs, and a flick knife. "She's armed," the soldier said.

"Of course I am," Lee said. "I'm a police officer. If you will allow me to lower my hands, I will show you my ID and a Priority One government passport."

"Unload her," the first soldier ordered, "and stay out of the line of fire."

Lee was forced to submit as the second soldier took her weapons and went through her pockets. "Look at my ID," she said through gritted teeth. "I'm a member of the LAPD."

"Yeah?" the first soldier said skeptically. "If you're a cop, who's the freak?"

"His name is Deputy Ras Omo, and he's a member of the Maricopa County Sheriff's Department on loan to the LAPD. Please treat him with the same respect due me."

That was too much for the private, who laughed as he brought the clip-on mike up to his lips. "Grimes here . . . Ask the sarge to come out. We have a couple of yo-yos here. One is a norm, and the other is a freak. They claim to be police officers."

What happened next was both predictable and annoying. A sergeant came out, examined Lee's papers, and put in a call for an officer. Lee couldn't see what was happening to Omo, but heard snatches of commentary like, "This takes the fucking cake. A freak with a badge."

But once a businesslike lieutenant arrived on the scene, things took a positive turn. After examining Lee's credentials, she ordered the soldiers to return the detective's belongings. The officer's name was Snyder. She had overplucked eyebrows, a long nose, and thin lips. "Sorry, ma'am . . . We get all sorts of scam artists, many of whom have fake IDs."

"I understand," Lee said. "And Deputy Omo?"

"He's free to leave as well," Snyder replied.

"Good. Please pass the word. I don't want to take a bunch of crap going the other way."

Snyder shook her head sadly. "I don't know where you're headed, ma'am, or why, but there's very little chance that you'll come back. Have a nice evening."

Once they were back in the truck, the barrier was lifted, and Omo could put the four-by-four in gear. From there, it was a short drive over a bridge and into the red zone.

Given what they'd been through a few minutes earlier Lee was expecting another hassle. She was wrong. A sun-faded sign read, welcome to the republic of texas, and a man in a tan uniform was sitting out front of the nondescript building on the right. He waved as the truck passed by. "That's it?" Lee demanded. "The government doesn't keep track of visitors?"

"Why bother?" Omo said. "The chances are that you're the only norm who crossed the border today. The only one who did so legally, anyway. Plenty of drug smugglers, human traffickers, and other assorted riffraff go back and forth out in the boonies. As for my people . . . There's no need for a passport. We *look* like what we are."

Lee thought about that as they passed through the town of Ehrenberg. It, too, had been militarized, and both sides of the highway were lined with installations. She saw tanks parked in revetments, rows of prefab buildings, and lots of activity. So even though the mutants were pretty laid-back where the border crossing was concerned, they were ready for trouble if it came their way.

Lee knew there were some politicians, people like Maria Soto, who favored a peaceful coexistence. But other mutants, and Sheriff Arpo might be one of them, had a deep and abiding hatred for Pacifica. Both because it belonged to norms and because they wanted what the long, narrow country had to offer. That included unfettered access to the sea, a high-tech industrial base, and oil.

But past efforts to take what they wanted had failed, including the disastrous War of 2052, when the Republic of

Texas sent its air force to bomb San Diego and were attacked in return, evidence of which could be seen as the police officers passed through the desert east of Ehrenberg. That was where the Republic of Texas's Second Armored Division had been assembled waiting to push cross the Big River. But the division had been decimated by Pacifica's air force, some of the planes flying down from locations as far away as Seattle.

Now, many years later, the sand-drifted remains of the Second Armored Division's vehicles still littered the desert. And the Republicans had to focus on the southern border, where the Aztecs were threatening to invade.

Lee's thoughts were interrupted as Omo took an off-ramp that led to what had once been a weigh-in station. She could see a line of vehicles up ahead, yet there was no apparent reason to stop. She glanced at Omo. "What's up?"

"It's a convoy," Omo replied. "We'll pay a fee. Then, once they have twenty vehicles, mercenaries will escort us into Phoenix."

"And if we go it alone?"

Omo shrugged. "There's a pretty good chance that we'll make it. But bandits prey on lone vehicles—so why take the risk?"

"That makes sense, I guess," Lee said. "But why doesn't the government crack down on the bandits?"

"People out this way don't like to pay taxes," Omo answered. "And they don't approve of government in general. 'We trusted the government to protect us back in '38, and look how that turned out.' That's what they say. So those who need extra protection pay for it."

"And those who can't afford to do so?"

"They're SOL," Omo said as he brought the truck to a halt behind a heavily laden truck. "I suggest that you wear a mask."

Lee knew he was correct. From that point forward, she would need to protect herself from *B. nosilla*. "How about you?" she asked. "Are you going to remove your mask?"

Omo was silent for a moment. He stared straight ahead. "No."

"Why not?"

Omo's voice was tight. "I want to protect you. And . . ."

"And what?"

"And I don't want you to see."

There was a lump in Lee's throat, but she managed to swallow it. "It's that bad?"

"Yes," Omo said flatly. "It's that bad."

"I don't care."

"You would," Omo said bleakly. "You wouldn't *want* to care, but you would."

The conversation was interrupted as a man wearing what looked like homemade body armor rapped on the driver's side window. Omo rolled it down. The mercenary's lower jaw was so misshapen that it was difficult for him to speak. "Cost one eagle. Pay now."

Omo gave the man a gold coin. Then there was nothing to do but wait for two additional vehicles to show up. Once they did, a pair of especiales came roaring out of the desert to take up positions at both ends of the convoy. They were armed with . 50 caliber machine guns and protected by sheets of dented steel. "What's to prevent the mercenaries from being bandits one day and escorts the next?" Lee inquired.

Lee couldn't see Omo's expression but sensed that he might be smiling. "Nothing," he answered wryly. "Nothing at all."

The convoy left shortly. It was getting dark by then—and Lee fell asleep not long thereafter. As Omo glanced Lee's way, he saw that her mask was slightly askew, thereby revealing the curve of her cheek. Her face was as beautiful as his was ugly. And like most men, he wanted her.

But Omo knew his desire was something more than a sexual attraction. There was a magnetism about her. An attraction rooted in her moral clarity, her wry sense of humor, and her unblinking bravery. He had watched the bank-gunfight video multiple times. And each time Omo did so, he paused the video in order to stare at the final scene. The one in which Lee was cradling Conti in her arms and crying.

Had she been in love with him? There was no way to be sure. Omo knew one thing, however. Had he been a norm, he would have done anything to win Lee's love and respect. But that could never be. All he could do was to protect her from evil—and that would be no small job where they were going. The engine hummed, a pale moon rose, and a pair of red eyes led him home.

Lee awoke with a start as the truck lurched through a deep pothole. And when Omo glanced her way, his mask had a greenish hue thanks to the light from the dashboard. "Sorry about that," he said. "But the streets in the Maryvale Village area don't get much maintenance."

"Maryvale? I thought we were going to Phoenix."

"Maryvale is west of Phoenix," Omo explained. "It was a run-down area *before* the plague, and it's even worse now."

Lee looked out the window. At least half the streetlights were out, and canyons of darkness lay between the widely separated homes, most of which were surrounded by high walls. Some appeared to be quite sturdy, but most of the protective barriers were made out of junked cars, rusting refrigerators, and piles of rubble. Anything that would keep intruders out or slow them down. "Okay," Lee said. "We're in Maryvale. But *why*?"

"Because you have to stay somewhere," Omo said simply. "And there aren't any hotels that cater to norms. So you're going to stay with my family. You'll be safer that way."

Lee felt mixed emotions about that. She was glad that Omo cared—but concerned as well. "Did you talk to your family about this?"

"Yes," Omo answered. "My father passed away a few years ago, but Mama is very excited. There are four houses in our compuesto, and one of them is a small casita. Mama began cleaning it yesterday."

The four-by-four turned a corner, lurched through a drainage ditch, and came to a stop in front of a metal gate. It was set into a wall made out of concrete blocks. Lee figured that the amount of work that had gone into the wall was a good measure of how important it was.

Omo spoke into his phone, and the metal gate swung open. That was when Lee saw two men, both of whom were armed with assault weapons. "About twenty-five members of my family live here," Omo explained. "At least two of them are on guard at all times."

Omo drove into what might have been a front yard many years before but had long since been converted into a parking lot. Lee saw a dusty sedan, a bulldozer on a flatbed truck, and an unidentified vehicle that was sitting on blocks.

Lee opened the door and stepped out into the spill of light that fell from above. That was when a woman with thick black hair and a limp came out to greet her. It appeared that one of her legs was shorter than the other as evidenced by the built-up shoe on her left foot. "Welcome!" the woman said. "Please call me Momma. Everybody does. Come . . . Meet the family. Then Ras will take you to the casita."

Lee was led up a path and into a large, ranch-style house. The interior was decorated southwest style and felt very homey. Lee was introduced to more than a dozen people, including Omo's brother Jorge, an uncle named Gary, and a cousin named Tina. All of them were polite but curious. And that was understandable since most had never been face-to-face with a norm before.

The question-and-answer session might have gone on for an hour or more if Omo hadn't intervened. "Okay, everybody . . . Cassandra will be here for a while, so there will be plenty of chances to get acquainted. But we've had a long day, and she's tired. So say good-bye."

There was a chorus of good-byes, and Lee was grateful for the chance to escape. But before she left, Lee went over to thank Mrs. Omo for her hospitality. The older woman smiled. "You are very welcome, my dear. Ras speaks very highly of you. He says you're one of the good ones."

Lee knew what that meant. "Good ones," as in good norms, of which there were very few. Or that was the way Momma and her family saw it. And the way *most* mutants saw it for that matter. Lee smiled but knew Mrs. Omo couldn't see it. So she took Momma's hand and gave it a squeeze. "Your son is a good one, too . . . Thanks. And good night."

* * *

Momma felt a profound sense of sadness as her son held the door open for Lee. Momma could tell that Ras was smitten and understood why. The chica normal was very beautiful, and if even half of what she'd been told was true, very brave as well.

But Lee would hurt Ras as surely as the sun would rise in the morning. Not because she wanted to—but because she couldn't help herself. But could she stop it? No, not in a thousand years. Ras was like a moth drawn to a flame. She sighed. It was time for bed.

They went to the truck, where they retrieved Lee's bags. If Omo was surprised by how heavy the case full of food was he gave no sign of it. A path led between two houses to a tiny building that sat all by itself. The front door was unlocked and opened onto a space that was part kitchen and part living room. After dropping the bags by the door, Omo gave Lee a quick tour. There was a room just large enough for a bed and dresser and a spotless bath beyond that.

"It's lovely," Lee said. "Please tell your mother how much I appreciate being allowed to stay here. Which house do you live in?"

"I don't live here," Omo replied. "I have a place closer to work. By the way, we're supposed to meet with Sheriff Arpo at eight thirty in the morning."

Lee took the mask off and wondered how Omo could wear one all day. The answer was obvious. To leave his face exposed would be painful in other ways. "Why does everyone have to start work so early?" she inquired plaintively.

Omo laughed. "To torture you. Be ready at seven thirty. I'll bang on the door." Then he was gone.

Lee spent the next half hour unpacking. After checking the door to make sure it was locked, Lee removed her clothes and stepped into the shower. The Smith & Wesson went with her. It was made of stainless steel, which made it the perfect weapon for such a situation. There was a small window in the shower, so she placed the pistol on the sill.

The water was only lukewarm, but the air was warm, so Lee didn't mind. She emerged from the shower ten minutes later, made use of the pink towel Momma had left for her, and padded into the bedroom. The ceramic tiles felt cool under her bare feet.

After donning a tee shirt and panties, Lee checked her phone. She was delighted to discover that she had a signal. Not from a local tower but by one of Pacifica's communications satellites. There was an e-mail from McGinty. "Please confirm when you arrive."

Lee sent a brief reply, checked the door one last time, and drank some water from the pitcher in the fridge. And that was safe because *B. nosilla* was an airborne disease. In fact, had it not been for the need to wear a mask while in the presence of mutants, Lee could have eaten their food. That's what she'd been told anyway.

Then, with the Smith & Wesson for company, Lee went to bed. The sheets were crisp and a single blanket was sufficient to keep her warm. As Lee lay there, she heard the pop, pop, pop of gunfire from somewhere not too far away. That was followed by a resonant boom about thirty seconds later. The explosion was off in the distance—but served to remind Lee of the surrounding dangers. What was it? A bomb? There was no telling. Silence returned, and sleep pulled her down.

Lee awoke to the bang, bang, bang of a gunfight. No, someone was pounding on the door. Conti! No, Conti was dead. Lee grabbed her phone, saw that it was 7:31, and swore. According to the indicator, no alarm had been set. She rolled out of bed and made her way to the front door. "Who is it?"

The response was muffled. "Omo." A glance through the peephole verified the claim.

"I'll unlock the door. Give me twenty seconds and come on in."

Lee turned the bolt and made a quick retreat to the bedroom. After hurrying through the usual routine Lee put on a tee shirt, jeans, and a cropped bolero jacket. It was made of cotton and barely long enough to hide her weapons. Then it was time to pull on a pair of low-cut cowboy boots and grab her purse. "I like the outfit," Omo said. "It's very western. All you need is a hat. I know you like breakfast burritos—so I brought you one." He pointed to the kitchen counter.

Lee said, "Thanks. I'll eat it on the way. Sorry I'm late."

"We aren't late," Omo countered. "The appointment is for nine thirty."

Lee laughed. "You bastard!"

"Don't let Momma hear you swear," he cautioned. "You'll ruin the good impression you made last night."

The burrito wasn't as good as the ones Lee normally ate in the morning, but she said it was, and Omo was clearly proud of himself. The sun hadn't been up for very long, but the desert heat had already started to build as they went out to the truck. Lee noticed that the M for mutant sign had disappeared as she got in, and Omo drove out through the open gate. Gary waved, and Lee waved in return.

It was a bumpy trip from the family compound to the highway. The area looked even more desolate in the naked light of day than it had the night before. Now Lee was coming to realize that the Omo family was relatively well-off. Most houses, hovels really, stood protected by nothing more than their abject poverty. It's difficult to steal what people don't have. That plus a legion of grubby children, skinny dogs, and foraging chickens made for a sad picture.

Occasionally, the truck passed craters. They weren't that large—but they were distinctive. So she asked about them. "What's with the craters?"

"The Aztecs fire rockets at us," Omo answered. "Most do no harm. But they get lucky every now and then."

Lee knew there was tension between the Republic of Texas and the Aztec Empire but hadn't heard about the attacks. "Rockets? What the hell for?"

"This area, like parts of New Mexico and Texas belonged to Mexico at one time," Omo explained. "After the plague hit, and northern Mexico became the Aztec Empire, the folks down there decided to take their land back regardless of the wars, treaties, and land purchases made in the past. That's one of the reasons our government has to cooperate with Pacifica to some extent. A lot of our troops are tied up trying to keep the Tecs from coming north."

Lee remembered the explosion she'd heard the night before.

Was that an incoming rocket? Quite possibly.

Highway 10 took them into the city. A lot of people were poor but there was plenty of traffic. Omo turned onto Interstate 17 and followed that south to West Jefferson. From there it was a straight shot to the sheriff's office. It was huddled in a rather nondescript cluster of midrise buildings circa 2035.

After flashing his badge, Omo was allowed to enter the adjacent parking lot. As he led Lee into the building, she could feel the stares. That was to be expected since they were the only ones who were wearing masks. But it still felt weird.

Then they were forced to stop at a security checkpoint. Both police officers were asked to show their IDs before being allowed to proceed to the next stop, where they were ordered to place their weapons in bins, empty their pockets, and pass through scanners before being allowed to enter the building. Once inside, their belongings were returned.

They took an elevator up to the third floor, where it was necessary to cross a large room in order to reach the corner office. The so-called bull pen was about half-full, and all eyes tracked the pair as they made the long march. Lee thought she knew why. People are people. And the word was out: "Omo's back . . . And he brought a norm with him." That alone was enough to generate curiosity.

The secretary in front of the sheriff's office looked up as the officers arrived. A spiral horn was growing out of the center of his forehead, and his ears had an elfin appearance.

"Ah, Deputy Omo . . . Welcome back. And this would be Detective Lee. The sheriff is on a call at the moment. Please have a seat."

So they sat on some guest chairs, and as Lee looked out into the bull pen, she realized that the atmosphere wasn't that different from the sixth floor at LAPD headquarters. Cops were cops even if these cops were different in some ways. Her thoughts were interrupted as the secretary spoke. "The sheriff will see you now."

Omo went first, and Lee was happy to follow. Arpo was seated on, and partially overflowing, a motorized scooter. It produced a whirring noise as he turned away from the outside window to face his guests. Arpo's face was so full that the surrounding flesh nearly eclipsed the piggy eyes that stared out of deep recesses to either side of his upturned nose.

Lee estimated that the sheriff weighed about four hundred pounds. Because he ate too much? Or because he'd been born with a metabolic disorder? She suspected the latter. Arpo was dressed in a tentlike white shirt, an oversized bolo tie, and black pants. "Well," he said, "look at what the cat dragged in. Deputy Omo and his new sidekick."

Arpo shifted his gaze over to Lee. "Deputy Omo has a tendency to shoot his partners if they get in the way. Something to keep in mind. Please have a seat . . . And welcome to Maricopa County."

Four chairs were arrayed in front of the executive-style desk, and Lee chose one of them. "Okay," Arpo said, "let's get to it. Somebody snatched the Screed girl and, based on the information Deputy Chief McGinty sent me, it looks like she could be in this area. The problem is that Maricopa County is *huge*, never mind the rest of the Republic, which is enormous. So it's going to take some mighty fine police work to find Miss Screed."

The chair made a whining sound as Arpo leaned back toward the window. "And that's a problem," he continued, "because Omo here can't find his ass with both hands."

Lee watched the pink-colored eyes swivel her way again. "But, according to Assistant Chief McGinty, you are one cracker-jack detective. So, who knows? Maybe you can show us country boys how it's done. That would be nice because I'm tired of taking shit from her highness Maria Soto.

"As for Omo here, I'm afraid you're stuck with him. No offense, but it would be hard to find another deputy who'd be willing to work with a norm, so consider yourself to be deputized. Here," Arpo added, as he slid a gold badge across the glass. "People around here aren't likely to take an LAPD badge seriously. Now get out there and find Amanda Screed."

Omo got up, and Lee followed him out of the office. Arpo watched them go. A norm and the departmental fuckup. What a team. But if sending them out on a fool's errand would keep Soto off his back, then so much the better. It was no secret that she had hopes of engineering an alliance with the whack-a-doodles in Pacifica. "A counterbalance," she called it, meaning a way to keep the Aztecs in their box. Arpo felt his stomach start to rumble and cursed it. Every day was a battle—and one that he always lost.

EIGHT

After they left Arpo's office, the police officers had to make the long journey across the bull pen before escaping into an elevator. "Well," Omo said. "That went well."

"You must be joking," Lee replied. "Is the sheriff always like that?"

"No," Omo replied. "He's usually worse."

"That's hard to believe," Lee said, as they left the elevator. "I know you shot your partner, and I can understand why Arpo might object to that, but why continue to harp on it?"

They were outside by then—and headed for the truck. "My ex-partner is Arpo's son," Omo explained bleakly.

Lee looked at him to see if he were joking, but the mask got in the way. "Seriously?"

"Yes."

Lee laughed. "And everyone knows that he filled his pants."

"Yup."

"My God, Ras . . . That's amazing. We'd better solve this case. You need some positive PR."

They got in the truck, and Omo drove it out toward the street. It bounced over a speed bump, and he waved at the parking attendant as they rolled past. "Where are we going?" Lee inquired.

"To have a visit with Vincent Rictor's mother," Omo replied. "I figure there are two possibilities. Rictor might have been shot for reasons completely unrelated to this case. On the other hand, there's the possibility that somebody was in a hurry to shut him up."

"You're pretty smart for a cowboy," Lee said. "Let's do it."

I-10 led them to the Superstition Freeway—and that took them east into the town of Apache Junction. Lee could see mountains in the distance, but other than that, things looked the same. It was clear that Omo knew his way around. After a series of turns, he pulled into the parking area that fronted a seedy strip mall. It was home to a number of businesses, including a pizza joint, a Laundromat, and a beauty parlor called Quik Cuts. "Rictor's mom owns the place," Omo explained. "It'll be interesting to see what she says."

The officers got out of the truck and made their way over to the shop. Omo pulled the door open and waited for Lee to enter. She felt a blast of cold air. AC was expensive, but it was a draw as well and could easily pay for itself. Especially in a beauty parlor. A long mirror ran the length of the left-hand wall, and there were four chairs, three of which were occupied.

One of the customers was wearing a chromed faceplate. Another had folds of loose skin hanging from her face, and the third was leaning forward, staring at the newcomers through thick goggles. "Can I help you?" a woman said as she stepped away from the lady with the loose skin.

"Yes," Lee said. "We're with the Maricopa Sheriff's Department—and we're looking for Mrs. Rictor."

"I'm Mrs. Rictor," the woman said. Her black hair had been teased up into a conical beehive, her brown eyes were set off by fake eyelashes, and her mouth was a slash of pink. "Deputy Haster spoke with me a couple of days ago."

"This is a follow-up visit," Omo said.

"I'd like to see some ID," Mrs. Rictor said. "No offense, but it pays to be careful these days."

Both officers produced their badge cases—but it was Lee's ID that Mrs. Rictor chose to squint at. "You're very pretty. We don't see many norms around here."

"Thank you," Lee said. "Can we talk?"

"Yes," Mrs. Rictor said. "Give me a minute, and I'll be right with you."

After asking one of her employees to take over, Mrs. Rictor led them outside. "Let's go next door," she suggested. "We'll have more privacy there."

"Next door" meant Pizza Pete's. A dingy shop with two employees, three annoying flies, and a single customer. Maybe things would start to pick up at noon. Mrs. Rictor chose a table just inside the open door. If Pete had air-conditioning, it was on the fritz, leaving an ancient fan to push the hot air around.

The proprietor brought Mrs. Rictor an iced tea without being asked. Omo ordered a Coke, and Lee chose coffee. That was a mistake. It was bitter. "So," Mrs. Rictor began. "You're looking for the people who murdered my son."

That wasn't true. Not in the literal sense. But it was a possibility. So Lee said, "Yes, we are."

"Vincent was a good boy," Mrs. Rictor insisted. "He wanted to be anyway. But his friends led him astray. I told Deputy Haster that."

"I read his report," Omo said. "And I've seen your son's criminal record. He robbed a convenience store when he was eighteen, got caught, and spent three years in prison. During his stay he became a member of the D-Dawg gang. A group that specializes in human trafficking."

"That's true," Mrs. Rictor said reflectively as she produced a pack of cigarettes. "They're the ones who led my Victor astray." There had been a resurgence of smoking since the plague. Maybe that was due to less government regulation—or maybe people figured they weren't going to live that long anyway. There was a sudden flare of light as Mrs. Rictor lit the cigarette, took a drag, and directed a stream of smoke toward the door. The fan propelled it outside.

"Did members of the D-Dawg gang kill him?" Lee inquired.

Mrs. Rictor frowned. "Deputy Haster asked me the same question, and I said 'no.' But now, having given the matter some additional thought, I'm not so sure."

At that point, Mrs. Rictor looked around as if to ensure that no one was listening.

"The leader of the D-Dawgs is a man named Manny Hermoza. But everybody calls him El Cabra."

"The goat?" Lee said.

"He has long, floppy ears," Omo said. "They don't use that name in front of him, though."

"No, I wouldn't think so," Lee said. She turned to Mrs. Rictor. "So, what does this Hermoza person have to do with your son?"

Mrs. Rictor shook her head sadly. "My Victor was very handsome. That's how he wound up spending too much time with El Cabra's wife . . . A puta named Carla Lopez."

"Your son told you this?" Omo said skeptically.

Mrs. Rictor looked shocked. "No! Of course not. Victor never spoke to me about such things. I heard it from one of my customers."

That was believable, or so it seemed to Lee, who knew that all sorts of things were discussed in hair salons. "Okay, that could explain it," she said. "If Victor was getting it on with Carla, and Hermoza found out, that could be fatal."

The interview continued for another ten minutes or so but didn't produce anything of value. So the officers thanked Mrs. Rictor and returned to the truck. It was covered with a thick layer of dust. And as Lee approached the passenger-side door, she saw that the word BONEBREAKER had been spelled out in the grime. The sight sent a chill down her spine. Was it some sort of weird coincidence? No, that was absurd. So it was a message. "I'm here. I'm watching."

Lee ran a hand across the name and wiped it away. There was no need to tell Omo. Not yet anyway. She climbed up into the truck. "So?" she inquired. "What do you think?"

"I'm not sure I believe the Carla theory," Omo said as he drove out onto the street. "But the D-Dawg gang is known for selling girls into prostitution. So the Amanda Screed's abduction is consistent with their business model."

"We need to know more about what they're up to," Lee said. "Maybe we could find one of Rictor's friends and put the squeeze on him."

"Maybe," Omo allowed. "But if we lean on someone who tells Hermoza, he'll know we're checking on him."

"Good point," Lee said. "So it'll have to be a person who *won't* spill his guts."

Lee kept an eye on the outside mirror as the truck entered the freeway. Was somebody following them? She couldn't tell.

They returned to the sheriff's department, where Lee made herself to home at an empty desk. Then she spent the afternoon reading all of the files that pertained to the D-Dawgs and human trafficking in general. It was about 4:00 p.m., when Omo came by. "I have the guy . . . Or what I *hope* is the guy," he said.

"Yeah?" Lee said. "Tell me more."

Omo sat in the single guest chair. "His name is Marcus Ford, and he is, or was, a member of the D-Dawgs."

"*Was?*"

Marcus got pissed off at this girlfriend and chased her into a restaurant, where he opened fire with a machine pistol. Three people were killed, two of whom were children."

"So?"

"According to what the folks on the gang squad told me, Hermoza had a little sister who was killed in a drive-by. So members of his gang aren't supposed to spray restaurants with bullets."

"I don't know," Lee said. "Al's in prison. I get that. But a lot of information goes in and out of prisons. If we put the squeeze on him, Hermoza will know an hour later."

"That's why I chose Marcus," Omo replied. "He's on death row. And they're going to hang him tomorrow."

"Okay," Lee said. "But why would Marcus spill his guts to us?"

"Because Hermoza was the one who turned him in."

Lee's eyebrows rose. "You're a fucking genius."

Omo nodded. "That's what I keep telling myself."

The appointment to see Marcus Ford was scheduled for 10:00 a.m. And even though the Florence Correctional Center was only an hour and a half away, Omo wanted to leave the family compound at eight. So Lee went to great lengths to set her alarm for seven, so she would have time to shower, get dressed, and eat before Omo arrived.

That got the day off to a good start. I-10 took them to 60 East, which delivered them to 79, and that led south to Florence. It had been a small town prior to the plague, and now it had a population of only 12,672 people according to the sign at the edge of town. Omo explained that most of the city's citizens were employed by three prisons that were located in Florence. The same number of prisons that had been there *before* the plague. Lee pointed that out to Omo, but he was unmoved. "Yup. That's where bad people belong," he said. "And we have plenty of 'em."

As they approached the complex, Lee saw a tall fence topped by coils of razor wire. Beyond that, some low one-, two-, and three-story buildings could be seen, along with a water tower on stilts. Not too surprisingly, it was as difficult to enter the Correctional Center as it was to leave it. After parking out front, the police officers had to show their IDs in order to pass through a heavily guarded gate. From there it was a short walk to a plain-looking building and a second security check. They had to surrender their weapons, sign a log, and listen to a short safety lecture.

That was followed by a five-minute wait before an Officer Wilkins arrived to take them over to death row. It was in a different building located a short walk away. Once inside, they were shown into a cell-like meeting room, where a second wait began.

About ten minutes passed before the door opened and an orange-clad prisoner entered. Ford's hair was cut so short that he was nearly bald, his skin was brown, and he had modelish good looks. Lee assumed Ford was a mutant but couldn't see any signs of it.

Once inside the room, Ford's eyes darted around as if looking for a way to escape. Then they came to rest on Lee. "Hey, baby," he said. "What's behind the mask?"

"That's none of your business," Wilkins said. "Sit down and shut up unless you're spoken to."

"Or *what*?" Ford demanded defiantly. "Or you'll kill me? Fuck you."

Wilkins drew his nightstick, but Lee raised a hand. "I think we should cut Mr. Ford some slack. Please, sit down. I'm Detective Lee—and this is Deputy Omo."

Ford nodded. "*Mr.* Ford . . . I like that." His hands were

cuffed behind him and remained there as Ford perched on the edge of a chair. A small table was located between him and the police officers. Ford leaned forward and made a show out of sniffing the air. "Pussy! I can smell it. Fuck the last meal crap. I want some poontang." His eyes were on Lee.

The words made Lee angry, but she refused to let it show. Plus the mask hid her face. "I can't help you there," she said evenly, "but I can offer you something else."

"Yeah?" Ford said. "Like what?"

"Like a chance to get even with El Cabra," Omo put in.

Ford's eyes lit up. "Now you talking. The bastard gave me up."

"Yes, he did," Lee said agreeably. "And we want to put him away . . . But we need some information."

Ford nodded. "Name it."

"Tell us about Rictor," Omo said. "We heard he was getting it on with Carla Lopez. Is that true?"

Ford laughed. "Hell no, it isn't true. Carla loves the goat. Besides, she's too smart to put out for a third-rate player like Rictor."

"Okay," Lee said. "So who killed him?"

Ford shrugged. "Beats me."

"Let's go at this a different way," Omo suggested. "You and Rictor were members of the D-Dawg gang. The word is that you were one of Hermoza's enforcers. What role did Rictor play?"

"Rictor was supposed to bring norm bitches to Hermoza," Ford answered.

"So he entered the green zone," Lee said.

Ford shook his head. "No. Rictor would meet up with a guy named Wheels, stash the meat in a van, and take the van to the man."

"Where?" Lee inquired.

"I don't know," Ford replied. "The goat, he don't tell no one stuff they don't need to know, and I didn't need to know."

The interview continued for another fifteen minutes, and Omo was able to extract some useful information from Ford. But he'd been in prison the day Amanda Screed was kidnapped and didn't know whether Hermoza had her or not.

As the session came to an end, and Ford was told to stand,

a shit-eating smile appeared on his face. "I'll be thinking about you tonight baby . . . Me and my hand. And you tell Mr. Goat that on the day he arrives in hell, I'll be there waiting for him."

Ford was led away, and Wilkins escorted the officers back to the reception area. Once they retrieved their weapons, it was back to the parking lot. It felt like a furnace inside the truck, but the interior began to cool as the AC came on. "So, what do you think?" Omo inquired.

"I think we're onto something," Lee answered. "We knew that Amanda was delivered to Wheels by parties unknown—and we knew that Wheels took girls across the border on a regular basis. Now we know who he handed them off to. But where did Rictor take them? That's the question."

The first part of the drive north was uneventful, but that changed as a call came over the radio. "This is Nora-One-One with a code three. We have what looks like multiple missile strikes north of Phoenix. I can see at least a dozen columns of smoke. Over." That was followed by *more* calls and requests for aid units.

"Shit," Omo said. "It looks like the Tecs are at it again. We'd better get up there and lend a hand." Police lights were hidden behind the truck's grill. They began to flash, and a siren began to wail as Omo pulled into the fast lane and put his foot down. Lee wished she was behind the wheel as cars hurried to pull over.

Omo called in and was told to report to headquarters. It wasn't long before they could see the columns of smoke for themselves, and as they neared the building, two cruisers passed them headed in the other direction.

Omo cut the siren and waved at a security guard as he turned into the parking lot. Lee opened the door and dropped to the ground. That was when she noticed the yellow school bus. It was traveling at a high rate of speed and headed straight for the headquarters building! A car spun out of the way as the vehicle struck it. "Ras! Look! The bus is going to hit the main entrance!"

Omo swore and was reaching into the truck when the vehicle hit an officer and tossed her through the air. Then Lee heard a loud crash as the bus hit the checkpoint and kept on going. She figured the bus was loaded with explosives, and was waiting for an explosion, as it screeched to a stop. That was when people dressed in hoods and black combat gear poured out of the vehicle. Omo had the 12-gauge by then and waved her forward. "Come on! Let's stop those bastards!"

Attackers were still spilling out of the bus as they ran. Lee estimated that at least ten of them were on the street, all wearing knapsacks and armed with machine pistols. Most ran toward the entrance, but a few stopped and turned their backs to it. It didn't take a genius to figure out that they were supposed to provide security.

Bullets chewed into the asphalt directly in front of Omo's cowboy boots as one of the pistoleros fired his weapon one-handed. The so-called Equalizer went off with a loud boom, and a load of double-ought buck snatched the terrorist off his feet.

Lee was pretty sure that the attackers were wearing body armor so it was hard to tell if any of the big pellets got through. It didn't matter, though, because a powerful explosion tossed the Tec up into the air two seconds later. The body seemed to hang there for a moment before landing with a meaty thump.

That was when Lee understood why the attackers were armed with weapons they could fire one-handed. The other hand was holding a dead man's switch connected to the explosives stored in their knapsacks. Once they let go, BOOM!

The Glock was out by then . . . And she heard the chatter of a machine pistol as a second attacker pulled the trigger and held it back. But the recoil caused the barrel to rise and bullets were flying over Lee's head as she fired in return. The terrorist was forced to take a step backwards each time a .9mm slug hit his chest protector. Then he tripped on a curb, threw his left hand out in order to break the fall, and blew up.

Another more powerful blast followed that. A shock wave knocked Lee off her feet. She thought she was dead at first, or severely wounded, but managed to stand. That was when Lee realized that she'd been correct . . . The bus had been loaded with explosives and timed to blow. All that remained of it was some blackened wreckage, which was on fire. She was still thinking about that when Omo appeared at her side. "Are you okay?"

"Yeah . . . And you?"

"I think I caught some pieces of shrapnel. Nothing serious though. Come on . . . Some of those assholes got inside."

They ran past a couple of dead deputies and the blazing bus to the checkpoint. It had been obliterated by a bomb blast. All they could do was keep going.

Weapons at the ready, they entered the building. Three civilians lay sprawled in the lobby. All of them had multiple gunshot wounds. Omo swore. "We'll take the stairs."

As Lee followed Omo upward, she heard the muted pop, pop, pop, of a semiauto followed by the rattle of a machine pistol. They arrived on the second floor to find a woman and two children huddled in a corner. Omo flashed his badge, and whispered. "Which way?"

The woman pointed to the hall and hooked her thumb to the left. Omo nodded and told her to stay put. Then, with Lee right behind him, he hurried down the hall with the shotgun at the ready. A female deputy, gun in hand, lay sprawled in the corridor.

By that time, they could see the makeshift barricade that had been thrown up in a futile effort to keep the terrorists out. It was made out of chairs, tables, and a watercooler. Not enough to stop the bomber who blew a hole through it. Chunks of flesh were stuck to the walls, and there was a large patch of blood on the ceiling.

Lee crawled up to the barrier and peered through one of the many gaps. That's when she saw the figure in black standing in front of an office filled with terrified workers. He was lecturing them in Spanish while he kept one arm wrapped around a woman's neck. His right hand was clenched tight. Was he holding a dead man's switch? Lee thought so.

As Omo arrived, Lee pulled him in close. "This guy has a hostage but no machine pistol. I want you to stand up and get his attention. In the meantime, I'll circle around, reach in, and get control of the switch. Once I have hold of his hand, shoot the son of a bitch in the head. *Not* the body because he's wearing armor."

"That's bullshit," Omo whispered in return. "*You* talk to him while I . . ." But Lee was gone by then. She scooted along the barrier to the wall where a small gap offered a chance to wiggle through. Behind her, she could hear Omo speaking in Spanish and stalling for time. Would the plan work? Lee hoped so as she pushed her way through the hole and into the office beyond.

Two of the office workers saw her and Lee held a finger up to her lips. Then she turned to face the Tec and confirmed that he was fully engaged with Omo. They were yelling insults at each other, and Lee knew things wouldn't get any better than that. So she put the Glock away, assumed a crouch, and took off.

The terrorist saw movement out of the corner of his eye, let go of the hostage, and tried to grab the machine pistol holstered on his thigh. But he was too slow. Lee collided with him and got a hold of his fist. Her job was to hold his thumb down and keep it there. Nothing else mattered. She was about to yell "Shoot him!" when one of the big revolvers went off. It was loud in the enclosed space, and the top half of the Aztec's head flew off. Warm blood fell like rain.

The terrorist fell, and Lee went with him, still clutching his hand. The floor came up hard but Lee refused to let go as Omo yelled at people. "Call bomb disposal! Tell them we have live explosives at this location . . . And get out of here."

Unfortunately, all the bomb-disposal experts were out in the field working to defuse rockets that had failed to explode. And that, Omo realized, was part of a very sophisticated plan. The first step was to launch rockets, some of which weren't armed, and wait for the police to respond. Then the ground attack could begin.

All he could do was tell Lee to hang on as he left to check on the floor above. Like the second floor, the third had been attacked, and thanks to the number of deputies who had been drawn away, was only lightly defended. And those who were present lay scattered about. Two were wounded, but the rest were dead.

It appeared as though at least one of the terrorists had been able to penetrate the bull pen, where he or she had blown themselves up. There was a black spot on the floor, the surrounding partitions were down, and blood splatter was all around.

As he made his way back toward the sheriff's office, he could see that Arpo's secretary was slumped facedown on his desk and the wall behind him was riddled with bullet holes. So it was with a sense of trepidation that Omo entered Arpo's office. And the sense of concern deepened when he saw splotches of red on the sheriff's back. It looked as though he'd been hit by bullets that passed through the wall.

The scooter produced a whining sound as the sheriff turned around. He was talking on a cell phone. "Call me when you know how many people we lost," he said to the person on the other end of the call before thumbing the device off.

"That's right," Arpo said as his eyes made contact with Omo's. "I'm still alive. That's the good thing about being fat . . . There's nothing like a layer of lard to slow bullets down."

"I'll call for some EMTs."

"Don't bother," Arpo said. "They're busy. Has the building been secured?"

"Yes, sir."

"And Detective Lee?"

"She killed one of the bombers and managed to disarm another one."

Arpo nodded. "Not bad for a norm. Tell her I said, 'Thanks.'"

"I will."

Arpo raised his eyebrows. "So? What are you waiting for? A fucking commendation? Get back to work." Omo sighed. It seemed that some things would never change. He left the room.

Lee had been clutching the dead man's hand for more than an hour before a bomb-disposal expert finally arrived. Then it was another ten minutes before she could let go. "Thank you," Lee said as she got up off the floor. The Tec had emptied his bowels seconds after his death, and she was sick of the foul odor.

"I'm the one who should thank *you*," the deputy said soberly. "My wife works in this office."

Omo was waiting, and together they made their way down the stairs, past the triage center that had been set up in the lobby, and out onto the street. Cruisers continued to pour in from neighboring counties as they crossed the parking lot. And a good thing, too, since it sounded as if 10 percent of Arpo's officers had been wounded or killed. Other cities had been hit as well including Tucson, Yuma, Las Cruces, Carlsbad, Laredo, and McAllen.

Those attacks had not gone unanswered. According to news reports, the army and air force were launching retaliatory strikes into the Aztec Empire, and a formal declaration of war would be made soon. "So what happens now?" Lee inquired as she entered the truck. "Am I about to lose you?"

Omo shook his head. "Nope. Not yet anyway."

"I'm glad to hear it," Lee replied.

"What?" Omo demanded. "You *want* me as a partner?"

"I didn't say that."

"Yes, you did."

"I'm hungry," Lee said, in a transparent attempt to change the subject. It was midafternoon by then, and they hadn't had lunch.

"I'll take you to dinner," Omo offered. "Assuming that Lonigan's wasn't struck by a missile."

"Lonigan's?"

"My favorite steak house."

"A steak sounds good. But we'll have to use the phone trick again."

Lonigan's was mostly empty due to the missile attack and the relatively early hour. So they were able to get two tables back in a corner well away from everyone else. Conversing by phone was awkward, but necessary, and even with that, Lee knew she was taking a chance.

The ceilings were low, the walls were a dark red color, and the tables were covered with white linen. And somewhere between drinks and their desserts the conversation turned to things other than work. That was when Lee learned about Omo's interest in painting. And by the time they walked out into the cool night air, something was different. "So," Omo said. "Would you like to see them?"

"See what?"

"My paintings."

As always, Omo's features were hidden by a mask. "Your paintings?" she inquired. "Or your bed?"

Omo looked away. "My paintings."

"I'm sorry, Ras. That was stupid."

"No," he said. "I know how men look at you. It must happen all the time."

"That's a crock," Lee said. "Let's go. I want to see your paintings."

It was a short drive to a slightly seedy area and the flat-roofed adobe two-story that Omo lived in. The front of the building consisted of two garage-style doors. One of them rumbled up out of the way as Omo thumbed a remote. "This was a small garage back before the plague," he explained. "I like it because I can park inside, and there's plenty of room on the second floor."

The lights came on as the truck pulled in, and Lee was impressed by how clean and tidy the apartment was. One entire wall was taken up by a shelving, a workbench with nothing on it, and a waist-high metal tool chest.

Omo led the way up a flight of gray wooden stairs to the floor above. What Lee saw as the lights came on was very different from what she had expected. Except for three vertical posts, the room was open. And, thanks to the high ceilings, the space felt even larger than it was.

A simple kitchen was positioned against the right-hand wall and was open to the adjacent sitting area. And, way in the back, she could see a large wardrobe and a bed. But with those exceptions, the rest of the room was dedicated to painting. A huge easel was positioned under a skylight. It occupied a paint-splattered tarp, which, had it been framed, would have been reminiscent of a Jackson Pollock painting.

But there was nothing expressionist about the landscapes that hung on the north wall. As Lee moved closer, she saw beautiful desert scenes, the sun rising over the Superstition Mountains, and a vista of what she imagined to be the Colorado River. "This is beautiful," she said. "It reminds me of Albert Bierstadt's work. I see some of the same reach and luminosity."

"You're familiar with Bierstadt?" Omo inquired eagerly. "That one isn't half as good as his worst painting, but a guy can try."

"I know very little about art," Lee confessed. "I took an art appreciation class in college. That's it. But I do remember Bierstadt. He was a member of the Hudson River School—and something of a romantic."

She turned to look at Omo. "This is entirely unexpected coming from a gun-toting cowboy."

Omo shrugged. "I have to eat . . . And I believe in what I do. People, regular people, need to be protected."

"Which reminds me," Lee said. "How's your family doing? Are they okay?"

"None of the rockets came close," Omo replied. "And Momma says, 'Hi.'"

Lee looked at her watch. It was half past ten. "It's late. I should get back to the casita."

"You can sleep here if you like," Omo offered. "You take the bed, and I'll take the couch. We'll get up early and swing by the casita then."

Lee thought about how tired she was and the half-hour drive to the family compound. "That sounds good. But don't snore. I'll shoot you if you do."

Twenty minutes later, Lee was between fresh sheets listening to Omo snore. Even though the couch was on the far side of the room, she could still hear it. The landscapes had been a surprise. But the art that affected her the most was the row of masks that hung on the west wall. There were seven in all . . . And she had seen some before, including the sardonic smile, what she thought of as the neutral look, and the "what the hell" expression. But it was the first time that Lee had seen the angry face, the laughing mouth, or the Omo with tears streaming down his cheeks. And that was the one that followed Lee into her dreams.

NINE

It was hot in the desert. At least a hundred degrees. So as Manny Hermoza climbed the hill, he began to sweat. He glanced up from time to time to see the shape of a man on a cross silhouetted against the azure sky. But even though the man's name was Jesus, as in Jesus Alvarez, there was nothing holy about the hijo de puta (son of a whore). "Good morning," Hermoza said cheerfully as he reached the top. "Wow! Look at that view! Although I suppose you have by now."

Alvarez had been stripped naked prior to being crucified. His black hair was coated with windblown dust, his bloodshot eyes were barely visible in black caves, and his lips were cracked. Hermoza had heard that many depictions of Christ's crucifixion were inaccurate. But he regarded himself as a traditionalist, so three nails had been used to secure Alvarez. One through each wrist and one to pin both legs at the same time. All the wounds were crusted with dried blood. Did such details matter? They did to Hermoza. He believed in the old saying that "If a job is worth doing—it's worth doing right."

Hermoza removed a small bottle of water from his back pocket and made a show of unscrewing the cap. Then, with Alvarez looking on, he took a long pull. The belch was fake but effective nevertheless. Alvarez ran a dry tongue over his broken lips and winced when Hermoza poured the rest of the water over his head. "Ah," the gang leader said, as rivulets of water ran down his face. "That feels good."

Then, after wiping the rest of the water away with a shirtsleeve, Hermoza looked up at Alvarez. "Enough screwing around, Jesus. You know why I'm here. The Blancos are about to bring some girls in from New Mexico. I know that. What I *don't* have is the when and the where.

"Such information is valuable," Hermoza continued. "I know that. So, as I told you yesterday, I'm willing to pay for it. I offered you one thousand nubucks. That's a lot of dinero for anyone other than a cara mierda (shit face) like you. But, in light of your present circumstances, the price has gone down. Now I'm willing to pay you with one of *these*."

El Cabra made an elaborate show out of removing the enormous Smith & Wesson revolver from its shoulder holster, flipping the cylinder open, and loading a single .50 caliber bullet into one of five empty chambers. "It's all yours," Hermoza said as he pulled the hammer back. "All you have to do is tell me when the Blancos are going to arrive and where they'll be."

Alvarez opened his mouth as if to speak, but Hermoza raised a hand. "Don't lie to me. If you do, I will snatch your wife and give her to my men. And you know what will happen then."

There was a pause, as if Alvarez was thinking about what could happen to his wife, followed by a dry croak. "I'll tell."

"All right, give."

Alvarez swallowed in a futile attempt to moisten his mouth. "They're going to stop at the old Wilcox ranch north of Portal."

"When?"

"Thursday."

It was Tuesday. That meant the D-Dawgs would have to move quickly. "All right, Jesus . . . You'd better be right. If you're wrong, or if you lied to me, I'll be first in line to fuck your wife Friday night."

Hermoza pointed the pistol and Alvarez closed his eyes. The report was loud enough to echo off the surrounding hills. The huge bullet hit Alvarez in the chest, passed through his body, and blew a chunk out of the wooden upright. Blood splattered the desert sand.

Hermoza flipped the cylinder open, ejected the empty casing, and placed a speed loader over the empty chambers. Once loaded, the weapon went back into a shoulder holster. Hermoza looked up at the dead man, crossed himself, and turned away.

Going downhill was easier than climbing up had been even in white loafers. Hermoza could see the white SUV at the foot of the hill. The engine was running, and the interior would be nice and cool. That would feel good. And stealing a shipment of women from the Blancos? That would feel even better.

Lee and Omo were up and out of his house by 6:00 a.m. That would give them time to swing by the casita and make it to headquarters by 8:00 a.m. Traffic was heavy as usual, but they made good time and pulled into the family compound at 6:33.

After parking the truck, Omo went to say hello to his mother while Lee made the short journey to the casita. She had slept surprisingly well given the strange bed and the events of the previous day. So after taking a quick shower and putting on some clean clothes Lee would be ready to go. That's what she was thinking as she approached the front door. It was ajar, and the wood around the lock was splintered. Just like the door to her apartment back in LA.

Lee drew the Glock, toed the door open, and announced herself. "Maricopa County Sheriff's Department! Come out with your hands on top of your head."

Not hearing a response, Lee went in ready for anything. It took less than a minute to confirm that the intruder or intruders were gone. But the word bonebreaker had been written on the bathroom mirror using her own lipstick.

"What happened to the door?" Omo wanted to know as he entered the room. And then he looked past her to the mirror. *"Bonebreaker?* What does that mean?"

Lee sighed. "I'll tell you on the way to work. In the meantime, I suggest that you warn your family. Somebody came over the wall. Probably a single individual—but I can't say that for sure. I'll pay for the door."

"Screw the door," Omo replied. "I want to know why you were holding out on me."

"Because it didn't have anything to do with the Screed case."

"Does this have something to do with the tracker that was placed on my truck?"

Lee shrugged. "Yes, maybe, hell—I don't know."

Omo nodded. "Okay. I'll ask Uncle Gary to get the door repaired—and we'll put more people on the wall. But here's something to consider . . . You weren't home last night. What if you had been? I'll meet you at the truck." And with that he left.

Lee thought about what Omo had said as she showered. Assuming the word bonebreaker had been left there by the serial murderer himself, and that seemed to make sense, had he or she been there to kill her? Or was the break-in part of a continuing effort to intimidate her? If so, it was working.

Omo was waiting when she arrived at the truck. "Uncle Gary is very sorry and hopes that you will accept his apology," Omo said. "He plans to add a man to the night watch. It's difficult, however, since most members of the family work during the day."

"I'm the one who should apologize," Lee responded. "By agreeing to stay in the casita, I put your family in danger. Please tell Momma and Uncle Gary that I will move to a hotel."

"No way," Omo said firmly. "That would hurt their feelings. Come on, let's get going. We can talk about this on the way."

Once they were on the freeway and headed east, Lee told Omo about the Bonebreaker murders, her father's death, and her determination to find the perp or perps. The full briefing included information about the break-in at her apartment and the fact that the name "Bonebreaker" had been written on his truck as well.

Omo heard her out, but then he spoke his mind. "So why keep everything to yourself, Cassandra? Why wall everyone out?"

Lee took a moment to think about that. "There are a number of reasons," she said finally. "First, I'm not supposed to work on the Bonebreaker murders. Second, once you share personal things, people have a hold on you."

Omo glanced at her. "And that includes me."

"Of course it does," Lee answered honestly. "Or did. You were a stranger . . . Why would I spill my guts to a stranger?"

"Plus I'm a mutant."

"That's bullshit, Ras. My last partner was a norm. I didn't tell him either."

Omo was silent for a moment. "Okay, but no more secrets. Right?"

"Maybe," Lee said. "And maybe not. Who's the girl in the photo? The one with the big boobs? I saw the picture sitting on your desk at home."

Omo said, "None of your business," and both of them laughed.

The cleanup was still under way at the headquarters building, but considerable progress had been made. The burned-out bus had been towed away, and additional concrete barriers were being lowered into place with a crane. It took a full fifteen minutes to pass through security, and once inside the building, the bomb damage and bullet holes were still visible.

The bodies had been removed, however, and repairs had begun. "We're going up to the fourth floor," Omo announced. "That's where the gang squad hangs out. They need to know what we're up to—and we need their help."

As they arrived on the fourth floor, Lee saw that it was undamaged. The terrorists had been able to reach the third floor but hadn't gone any higher. Omo led her through a maze of cubicles to an open area. The conference table was littered with cups, printouts, and a variety of personal belongings. Five cops were present, all of whom looked like the sort of people they were supposed to chase. Omo made the introductions. The team leader was a man named Van. He had a bald head, a handlebar mustache, and a pair of world-class biceps that were on full display. Lee couldn't help but notice the webbing between his fingers and wondered how that would affect his ability to fire a gun.

Next came a woman named Fossy. She had purple hair, an elfin face, and arms covered with tattoos.

"The Stick," as Van referred to him, was so thin he looked like a living skeleton. He waved a hand.

A woman called Coco was sitting next to the Stick. She had blond hair, a pretty face, and a snakelike tongue. It flicked in and out from time to time.

Finally, there was Kirby. He was so short that he had to sit on two cushions and was armed with a G-26 or "Baby Glock" rather than a larger weapon. Once the introductions had been made, he looked at Lee and frowned. "Are you the one who saved the people on the third floor?"

"No," Lee said. "I'm the one who held on to the switch while Deputy Omo shot the asshole in the head."

A number of looks were exchanged, and Lee knew, or thought she knew, what the police officers were thinking. Omo was the same man who shot a perp through Arpo's son. Some of them chuckled, and Van extended a hand. "Nice work, Omo . . . You saved a lot of lives.

"Okay," Van continued. "The word came down that the case you're working on could be connected to the D-Dawgs. We'd love nothing better than to nail those assholes. How can we help?"

It was dark, but thanks to a silvery frosting of starlight, Manny Hermoza could see the dirt road below. It was the perfect night for killing Blancos and taking their women. Hermoza planned to take a norm bitch for himself one day and use her to produce a son. A fine, strapping boy who would inherit his father's organization and make it even larger. Carla wouldn't like that, but so what? Hermoza's thoughts were interrupted as a voice came through his earbuds. "They coming."

The lookout was correct. As Hermoza looked to the left, he saw a pair of headlights appear. Strips of duct tape had been used to reduce the amount of light they produced, but a couple of horizontal slits were visible. "Okay," he said into the boom mike in front of his lips. "Now remember . . . Hit the first ride, and the second ride, but stay off the rest. If somebody shoots a girl, I'm gonna roast him like a pig."

After walking the road the day before, Hermoza and his gang had chosen the kill zone laid out in front of him. There was no way to know how many vehicles the Blancos would bring and the length of the intervals between them. So it was impossible for Hermoza to offer anything more than general instructions until some specific information came in. It seemed to take forever but was actually no more than thirty seconds or so. "The last one is coming your way," a lookout announced. "It's a gun truck with a fifty on the back."

"Okay," Hermoza said. "Hold, hold, hold . . . Fire!"

All of the D-Dawgs were lined up along the north side of the road so they wouldn't shoot each other. The RPG men fired first, and both grenades flew straight and true. Light strobed the night as the lead vehicle slewed sideways and veered into a ditch. It was on fire and blew up when the flames found a box of ammo.

It was tempting to sit back and watch the fireworks. But Hermoza knew better than to do so. His job was to stay in touch with the big picture, and thanks to a flood of radio reports, he knew that while the last vehicle in the convoy had been hit, it wasn't blocking the road. And that meant the surviving Blancos could back out of the trap. "They're escaping!" someone shouted, and it was true. But Hermoza had an app for that. "Blow the charges," he ordered. "And when the bastardos get out, shoot them."

Hermoza left cover and took the slope in a series of jumps. The Blancos were firing wildly in hopes of scoring some lucky hits. Then the charges went off, and a curtain of soil shot upward. Clangs were heard as rocks rained down on the SUVs and struck some of the D-Dawgs as well. One man stumbled away, holding his head.

Hermoza was on the road by then, with his pistol raised. The headlights in front of him continued to grow dimmer as the vehicle backed away. He chose a point halfway between the lights and squeezed the trigger. There was a loud boom, and the recoil was so powerful that Hermoza had to pull the hog leg back down before he could fire it again. The second shot was right on the money, and the especiale jerked to a halt as a cloud of steam poured out of it.

At that point, the Blancos had little choice but to beg for mercy or fight back. And, since there was no likelihood of mercy, they came out firing. The D-Dawgs gunned them down. Then, just to make sure, a Dawg named Deuce put two bullets into each head. Hermoza went over to spit on the last one. "How you like that, bitch?" he demanded. The woman didn't answer.

After crushing the opposition, it was time to examine the

145

take. There were three of them, all norms, and all under the age of thirty. The D-Dawgs lined them up so that Hermoza could squeeze their breasts and grade them. "Two B's and a C," he concluded. But that was fine since each bitch was worth eleven pounds of cocaine, five pounds of gold, or one hundred thousand nu. Cocaine was Hermoza's currency of choice.

"This," Hermoza said, "has been a very profitable evening. Collect their weapons, check to see which vehicles can be driven, and load the ladies. Oh, and don't touch them. You'll be sorry if you mess with my merchandise."

"How about the bodies?" a D-Dawg wanted to know.

"Leave 'em for the coyotes," Hermoza answered phlegmatically. "Everybody has to eat."

It was early morning. Two precious days had passed since the first meeting with Van and the other members of the gang squad. And if Amanda Screed was still alive, Lee knew that forty-eight hours would feel like an eternity to her. But it took time to plan, get the necessary warrants, and establish a stakeout. Lee was on the top floor of a two-story residence directly across from aptly named Bandido Bar in south Phoenix. A watering hole where, according to Van, the D-Dawgs spent a lot of their spare time.

Thanks to the low windowsill, Lee could sit on the wooden chair and peer down through dusty blinds at the seedy saloon below. She was hoping that Hermoza would roll up and go inside, giving Kirby a chance to tag his ride. Would that happen? Maybe, but Lee wasn't going to hold her breath.

Still, the stakeout was something. And something beat the hell out of nothing. That's why Kirby was stationed in a parked van waiting to fire his air rifle at vehicles parked near the bar. The BB-sized tags were designed to hit, splatter, and stick. And by tracking the signals they sent, the deputies could determine where the target vehicles went.

Lee's thoughts were interrupted by a series of four knocks. Not two, not three, but four. The door was locked and kept that way at all times. Lee got up, drew the Glock, and went to stand beside the entryway. "Who's there?"

"Omo."

Lee threw the bolt but waited to make sure that Omo was alone before closing the door and locking it. The pistol went back into the holster. "Hey, Cowboy . . . What's up?"

"I brought you some coffee," Omo said as he offered a cup. "And some news. Somebody ambushed a convoy of Blancos out in the desert—and we have reason to believe that the D-Dawgs were responsible."

Lee slipped the face mask up onto the top of her head. Then she took a sip. The coffee was good. "Blancos? Who are they?"

"A gang from New Mexico."

"Okay . . . And we care because?"

"We care because they were bringing girls into the area with plans to sell them."

Lee took a second sip. "Says who?"

"Says one of the Dawgs. He got hit by a falling rock and was left for dead. Once your relief shows up, we'll go over to the jail and talk to him."

Stick arrived shortly thereafter, which allowed Omo and Lee to leave the building. A narrow flight of stairs led down to the back door, which opened onto an alley. After a careful 360, Omo pronounced the truck clean, and they got in.

It was a twenty-minute drive to the so-called tent-city jail located on Durango Street. Various iterations of the encampment had been around since 1993 and the mostly-open-air facility still housed more than two thousand prisoners.

After parking in a lot, they got out of the truck and proceeded on foot. "You can see the guard towers," Omo said. "And the stun fences. But what you aren't likely to notice is the facial-recognition system, the minidrones, and the ringers."

Lee looked at him. "Ringers?"

"People who *look* like inmates but aren't."

There were multiple layers of security to pass through. But finally, after checking their weapons, the officers were allowed to enter. The sun was up, and Lee was starting to sweat as a uniformed deputy led them into a tent. Dupree was waiting. A caplike bandage covered the top of his head and his face, neck, and hands were covered with zits. Some were weeping pus, and Dupree dabbed at them while the visitors sat down. "This is Detective Lee," Omo said. "And my name is Omo. What happened to your head?"

Dupree had beady black eyes. They darted from face to face. "I don't remember."

"It's too late for that bullshit," Omo said. "You were quite talkative when they arrested you, and I've seen the video."

"They'll kill me," Dupree said pitifully.

"Maybe and maybe not," Omo replied. "If you're a good boy, we'll swap you for a prisoner in Texas. The Dawgs don't mean jack shit down there."

Dupree looked hopeful. "Really? You can do that?"

"Yes. *If* you answer our questions."

"Okay," Dupree said as he blotted the right side of his face. "I'll tell you what I know." And that, as it turned out, included the crucifixion and the ambush.

"Was the ambush successful?" Lee demanded.

Dupree shrugged. "I don't know. After the rock hit me, I fell into a ditch and passed out."

"Understood," Lee said. "But let's assume the ambush was successful. Where would the gang take the girls?"

"Only El Cabra and the so-called Big Dawgs know that," Dupree responded.

"But I'll bet that you've heard things," Omo put in.

"They say Hermoza has a ranch," Dupree said. "Maybe he took them there . . . Or maybe he went somewhere else. Pretty soon now, he'll send out invitations, hold an auction, and collect his money. Simple as that." The interview was over.

Manny Hermoza parted his lips, and Deputy Coco Moss sent her snakelike tongue into his mouth. That was followed by a good deal of heavy breathing, mutual groping, and a violent coupling. Once the climax was over, Hermoza allowed himself to roll off his lover's body and lay wheezing beside her. The ceiling fan had only one speed, and that was slow. However slight, the breeze helped to cool his sweaty skin. The motel room was dark except for the light that leaked in around the heavy curtains and the illumination provided by a flickering TV screen. "Damn, woman . . . You know how to fuck."

"Watch your mouth," Moss said as she elbowed her way up against a couple of lumpy pillows. "There's a lady in the room. Pass my cigarettes."

Hermoza didn't approve of smoking. It was bad for your health, and he hated the stink. But Moss had privileges that other people didn't. One of which was to smoke in his presence. So he gave her the pack and a fancy lighter. There was a momentary flare of light and some tinny music. Way down in Dixie? Yes, Hermoza thought so. "So," he said. "You wanted to see me."

"Yeah," Moss replied. "I have some information for you."

"That's what I pay you for," Hermoza said, as a stream of smoke hit the fan.

"We have a visitor," Coco said. "A detective from LA. She's working on a slave-trading case. One of our deputies was assigned to help her."

"So?"

"So they had a chat with Marcus Ford."

"Ford's dead," Hermoza replied mildly. "They hung him."

"They spoke to him the day *before* he died," Moss countered. "And he had plenty to say."

Hermoza swore. "I should have popped the weasel myself."

"And they spoke to Jimmy Dupree. He survived the ambush, and he's sitting in tent city, waiting to be arraigned."

"What did he tell them?"

Coco shrugged. "Not much because he doesn't know much. But the heat is on. I think you should sell those girls and do it soon."

Hermoza considered that. "I have to notify potential customers, give them enough time to respond, and set things up. So I need four or five days minimum. Where is this detective staying?"

"She's staying with Deputy Omo's family. In their compound."

Her hand found him, and Hermoza was pleased to discover that he was ready again. "Brush your teeth."

"Why?"

"Because you smell like an ashtray."

Coco left for the bathroom, and Hermoza smiled.

* * *

Another day had passed and, in spite of all their efforts, very little progress had been made. The tag strategy was a success, in that the police officers knew where many of the D-Dawgs had been, but that didn't help much. Hermoza knew better than to maintain a headquarters location that could be bugged and used against him. He stayed on the move and used disposable cell phones to communicate with the gang.

As Lee's shift came to an end, and Omo arrived to relieve her, she was depressed. Some progress had been made but not enough. The sun was a red smear on the horizon as she drove Omo's truck to the family compound. Cousin Teo pushed the gate open. Lee waved, drove inside, and parked. A short walk took her to the casita. The old door had been removed and a new one had been hung. She opened it and went inside.

After a quick shower, Lee made a dinner that consisted of boiled pasta, a half can of tuna, and some shredded cheese. After washing the dishes, she placed a call to Travis Air Force Base in California. It had taken more than a day for McGinty to capture the right general's attention, convince her of the necessity, and set things up. Unfortunately, the major in charge of the project didn't have any news for her.

So Lee was left to paint her toenails and listen to some R&B. After that, it was time to go to bed. Sleep came slowly, but once it came, Lee went deep. And that's where she was when the attack started. She heard a burst of automatic fire, sat up straight, and was reaching for the Glock when something went BOOM.

Was that the sound of a missile hitting the compound? Or something else? There was no way to be certain as Lee rolled out of bed and started toward the door. The Glock was in her hand, but the Smith & Wesson was sitting on the dresser, so she took that too. She was still in motion when a *second* explosion destroyed most of the casita's east wall. One minute it was there, and the next it wasn't, as a mixture of dust and smoke filled the air.

Then the headlamps appeared. They made excellent targets, and Lee immediately went to work on them. She started on the left and worked her way to the right, being careful to aim at a spot just under each light. Three targets fell in quick succession.

Then she saw something fly through the air, bounce off a wall, and fall to the floor. Even though Lee was alone, she yelled, "Grenade!" as she took a running dive. She couldn't break the fall without releasing the pistols. So she hit hard and was skidding into the kitchen when the bomb went off. There was a flash of light, a loud bang, and the sound of broken glass as the kitchen window shattered.

None of the flying metal struck her, and Lee was giving thanks for that, when a battering ram hit the front door. It struck once, twice, and three times before breaking the lock and causing what remained of the door to hit a wall. Lee was sitting with her back to a cabinet by then. Both pistols were raised and she fired them in alternation. There was a yell, a burst of automatic fire that missed her by inches, and the boom of a shotgun. Not inside but *outside*. That raised the possibility that the Omo clan was fighting back.

Lee struggled to her feet and winced as she put her right foot on a piece of broken glass. She was barefoot and still clad in a tee shirt and panties as she approached the door. Two bodies were blocking the way. She shot both of them in the head before stepping on one. It gave slightly as Lee felt the cool night air embrace her. Uncle Gary nearly took a bullet as he materialized out of the shadows. "Come with me!" he said. "I think they entered the main house."

They were halfway across the yard when the mortar rounds began to fall. Both of them hit the ground as the bombs marched across the compound. One of them hit the house and blew a hole in the roof. Lee jumped to her feet and began to run. "Momma!" she shouted. "We need to get her out of there."

As they neared the front door, a man was backing out, firing short bursts from a machine pistol as he did so. Lee shot him in the back, jumped the body, and approached the door with both pistols extended. "It's Cassandra!" she shouted. "Don't shoot!"

They entered the house to find a very scared twelve-year-old clutching a .410 shotgun. One side of her head was damp with blood. "Cindy!" Lee said. "Are you okay?"

Cindy nodded.

"Momma," Lee said. "Where is she?"

"In the kitchen," Aunt Rosa said as she emerged from a hallway.

Lee followed the woman back into what was left of the kitchen, and that was where Momma's body lay. A splinter of wood was protruding from her chest, and she was holding on to it with both hands. Lee dropped down next to her and felt for a pulse. There was none. Lee started to cry.

"A mask," Aunt Rosa said gently. "You need a mask."

But Lee didn't hear. "I'm sorry," she said. "I'm so sorry! This is my fault."

Somewhere off in the distance, a siren began to wail.

TEN

Omo received word of the attack by radio, asked for a patrol car to pick him up a block from the stakeout, and was forced to sit with fists clenched during the ensuing ride. Based on preliminary reports, he knew there would be casualties, and all of them would be people that he loved. People who had accepted a norm into their communal home because *he* asked them to.

And what about Lee? Was she alive? The possibility that she'd been killed during the attack ate at him. If she was dead, that, too, would be his fault because he was the one who suggested she stay with his family.

Then came the question of who was responsible. The D-Dawgs? They were the most likely possibility. But *how*? Unless they had some knowledge. No a *lot* of knowledge. Including the fact that he was working the case. And maybe they knew about Lee, too . . . Where she was staying and why. That implied a leak. There had to be a leak.

They left the freeway, entered the hood, and it wasn't long before the full extent of the damage became visible. As the driver pulled in behind another patrol car, Omo saw that a hole had been blown in the outer wall. And beyond, he could see the remains of the casita.

Omo left the car and approached the hole. There were lots of bodies, and he half expected to see Lee's among them. But all of the casualties were male—and most had been shot in the head. And that was a sure sign that Lee was alive! Or had been immediately after the invasion began.

Omo stepped over the bodies and made his way through the bedroom and into the kitchen. *More* dead men blocked the doorway. No, one of them was a girl, but not Lee.

As Omo stepped over the bodies, Dan Brody appeared. They'd been partners once, and Brody knew his family. There was a look of concern on the deputy's bulldog face. "Hey, Ras . . . They told me you were here."

At that point Omo knew his worst fears had been realized. He'd seen the same expression on Brody's face before. "Give it to me straight, Dan . . . Who did they kill?"

Brody looked away and back again. "Momma's dead, Ras . . . She died during the mortar attack."

"My God . . . A mortar attack?"

"Yes. From about three blocks away. It didn't make much sense, given that they had people inside the compound, but it looks like someone screwed up."

"Where is she?"

"In the kitchen. Don't go in there, Ras."

"It's that bad?"

"Yes, I'm afraid so."

Omo turned and made his way toward the front door. Momma. The woman who called him "pretty boy" because he wasn't. She'd been larger-than-life, a force of nature, and he couldn't imagine the world without her.

The front yard was swarming with cops, but they stepped out of the way as the deputy wearing the grim mask entered the house. Broken glass crunched underfoot, and light strobed the walls as a tech took pictures.

Once Omo saw the blood-soaked body on the floor, and Lee kneeling next to it, he felt a flood of sadness, relief, and guilt. All at the same time.

Lee was about to say something when Aunt Rosa arrived carrying a mask. She pulled it down over Lee's face and helped her to stand. That was when Omo realized that Lee was clad in nothing more than a tee shirt and panties. He removed his duster and went to drape it over her shoulders. She looked up at him. Her face was filthy. And Omo could see the tracks left by her tears. "We'll find them, Ras . . . I swear we will."

Omo nodded, and, when he spoke, his voice cracked. "And we'll kill them when we do." A light flashed, and the moment was frozen in time.

More than twenty-four hours had passed since the attack on the Omo family compound, and the shooting reviews were still under way, as a new secretary gave Lee and Omo permission to enter Sheriff Arpo's office. All of the bullet holes had been plugged by that time, including those in the sheriff. And once the interior wall was painted, everything would look as good as new.

Arpo was staring at his computer screen with lips pursed as they entered the room. Then, having finished whatever the document was, he removed a pair of wire-rimmed glasses and placed them on the surface of his desk. "Have a seat." Arpo's eyes went to Omo. "I was sorry to hear about your mother's death. Please accept my condolences on behalf of the entire department."

Omo nodded. "Thank you, Sheriff. I'll pass that along."

"Please do. Tell your family that most of the dead attackers were wearing D-Dawg tattoos. So we know who did it. And we'll catch them."

Arpo's gaze shifted to Lee. "The Internal Affairs people tell me that your testimony lines up with the information they have gathered up to this point. But I have to place you on administrative leave."

"I know where Amanda Screed and the other women are being held," Lee said.

When Arpo frowned, his eyes nearly disappeared. "That's bullshit."

"No, it isn't."

"How long have you known?"

"A few hours."

"Okay," Arpo said. "Pass the information to Omo, and we'll look into it."

"No way," Lee said. "I want in on the bust."

"So this is about your rep."

Lee remembered Momma lying on the kitchen floor. "Believe whatever you want."

Arpo looked at Omo. "Is she telling the truth?"

Omo shrugged. "This is news to me. But yes, it's my guess that she's telling the truth."

Arpo sighed. "Okay, Detective . . . What have you got?"

"*These*," Lee replied as she lifted a briefcase up onto her lap. "The files arrived on my phone a few hours ago. The folks in your lab were kind enough to print them out."

Lee placed a dozen sheets of hardcopy on Arpo's desk. "I told the people in Pacifica to look for a place in the desert . . . A house or a collection of houses where multiple vehicles came and went on a frequent basis—and where there was a lot of security. But only places that were no more than an hour away from Phoenix. All of them look good—but I'd put my money on number three. Notice the fancy house, the palm trees, and the huge swimming pool. There's a fence, too."

Arpo put the glasses back on so as to examine the photos. "There are smaller buildings as well," Lee added. "I think structure 'A' is a dormitory for the live-in staff. But 'B'? Judging from the secondary fence, I'd say that's the holding tank. The place where they keep the women before bringing them to market." There was a long moment of silence while Arpo scanned each print in turn. Eventually, he put the last one down. "Were those images captured by a drone?"

Lee shook her head. "No. That would be a violation of the cease-fire agreement between Pacifica and the Republic of Texas. They were taken from orbit."

Both men stared at her, but it was Arpo who spoke. "So your government has one or more spy satellites?"

Lee nodded. "Yes."

"I'm surprised your people were willing to signal that."

Lee smiled sweetly. "I think they want you to know."

Arpo swore under his breath. "Okay, so let's say I'm willing to indulge you. What then?"

"I suggest that you recheck all three locations using your

drones," Lee replied. "Then, if everything looks good, we go in. An air assault would be best."

Arpo looked thoughtful. "I will probably live to regret this decision, but okay, let's go for it. I'll notify Sergeant Van."

"*No*," Omo said as he spoke for the first time. "You know what happened to my family. There's a leak somewhere. Possibly in the gang squad. I say we hold off, notify Van two hours prior to liftoff, and collect the team's cell phones before they board the choppers."

"Van will be furious," Arpo predicted.

"I can live with that," Omo said calmly.

Arpo looked from Omo to Lee. "Is that all?"

"Yes, sir."

"Then why are you here?"

The sun was about to break company with the eastern horizon and the air still felt cool as Lee left the building and made her way out to the rental car. The casita was uninhabitable at that point—and Lee didn't want to run the risk of bringing more sorrow to Omo's family. So after a tearful parting the evening before, she checked into the Desert Springs Motel. It would be more difficult to guard her health, but there was no other choice.

It was a relatively short trip to the Maricopa County Sheriff's heliport in Mesa. Security was extremely tight, and Lee wasn't on the department's roster, so she had to phone Omo and have him sign her in. Once the formalities were complete, he slid into the passenger seat for the short ride to the visitor's parking area. "This car is a piece of shit."

"Good morning to you, too," Lee said. "And don't dis my ride. At least I can get into it without a ladder. How does the drone stuff look?"

"Good," Omo said. "*Real* good. You were right about target three. A large pavilion went up overnight. And it looks like they're placing markers for what could be a temporary parking lot."

Lee pulled into a slot and killed the engine. It clattered before shutting down. "A pavilion *and* a parking lot. What does that suggest?"

"An auction."

"So we need to get in there fast . . . Before the girls are sold."

"Exactly," Omo agreed. "I would have preferred a night assault, but what is, is. The choppers are ready, chase teams are on the way, and we're gearing up."

They were out of the car by that time and walking toward a hangar. "The gang squad is here?"

"Yup, plus the SWAT team. That's a dozen people counting you and me. Two chopper loads. The rest of the task force will arrive on the ground. The sheriff wants us to arrest all of the customers, too. Some of them might be running baby farms."

Lee thought about Amanda and shuddered. *Don't give up,* she thought to herself. *We're on the way.*

As they entered the hangar, Lee saw that the deputies were completing their load outs. All were dressed in desert camos and heavily armed. Lee had just started to think about the need for tactical equipment when Coco Moss showed up with a double armful of gear. "Here you go, hon . . . I think we're about the same size, so I took stuff that would fit me. What's up anyway?"

That was when Lee remembered that none of the people on the assault team knew where they were going or why. And for good reason after the attack on the Omo family compound. It would be necessary to brief them however—or run the risk of a major shit show once they were on the ground. "There will be a briefing soon," Lee told her. "Thank you for the gear . . . I'll take good care of it." Coco smiled and turned away.

Lee took the gear over to a workbench, where she went about the process of putting things on and making all of the necessary adjustments. She was still working on it when a male voice came over the intercom. "This is Lieutenant Riley. Please assemble in front of the office. The mission briefing is about to begin."

Riley was in command of the SWAT team, and by the time Lee and the rest of them came together, he had some easels set up. Lee saw the photos provided by Pacifica, plus the stuff from the sheriff's drones, and some other useful information. That included the plans for the main house as filed with the county.

Riley began by explaining the nature of the mission, including the opportunity to, "Put El Cabra out of business for good." Then he assigned individual missions and concluded with a stern admonition. "Remember, people . . . The chances are good that most, if not all of the perps, will run. Let them go. The choppers will track the bastards, and the chase teams will round them up. Our job is to find and secure the prisoners. Do you read me?"

One deputy said, "Got it, boss." Another said, "Yes, your worship." And a third said, "Duh."

Riley grinned good-naturedly. "Good. Now, security is of the utmost importance, so you're going to surrender your cell phones to Perez here. And that means *all* of them. I know that some of you carry two."

That was enough to elicit some anger. "What are you saying?" a deputy demanded. "That one of us is on the take?"

Riley nodded grimly. "Sorry, but we have reason to believe that such a thing is possible. Look at it this way . . . If the goat knows we're coming, *you* could get killed. And that would be real hard on the wife and kids."

That was sufficient to shut the man up, but there was still quite a bit of grumbling as Perez made the rounds. Lee surrendered her phone and was ordered to pair off with Coco for mutual pat downs. Both of them found extra magazines, cuffs, and other pieces of equipment, but no phones. Everybody laughed as some of the phones in the cardboard box began to ring, chirp, and play music. But that came to an end when word arrived that vehicles were streaming into the ranch. And if the potential buyers were starting to arrive, then it was obvious that the auction would begin soon.

Everything seemed to shift into high gear as they split into two groups of six and hurried to board the helicopters. What were they? Sixty years old? All Lee could do was hope that they, like so many cars, had been continually rebuilt over the years.

After a momentary pause, they were in the air. The lead chopper took off to the southwest and stayed relatively low. Both side doors were open, which allowed the slipstream to enter the cabin and pummel the passengers. Lee couldn't see much from where she was seated. Just gated communities, clusters of homes in what had been the suburbs once, and the fields of rubble that separated them. Once the helicopter cleared the city, fortified homes began to appear. Most were collections of shacks, old trailers, and aluminum sheds.

The rest were surrounded by greenery, security fences, and, in one case, a glittering moat. They belonged to the wealthy. People who chose to live out in the desert and away from the dangers associated with city life.

Ten minutes later, the deck tilted as the chopper entered a wide turn. That was when Lee caught a glimpse of the palm trees, the whitewashed house, and a dusty parking lot. About fifteen windshields glinted in the sun. "Get ready," the pilot said. "We're going in."

The ground came up fast, and the skids hit with a thump. Riley was yelling, "Out! Out! Out!" and his deputies began to exit through the starboard door because that was closest to the objective. Lee had been told to wait until the last member of the SWAT team was on the ground before jumping herself. So she was seated when the pilot said something unintelligible and tried to lift off.

A deputy fell out of the door as something struck the aircraft and exploded. Lee was thrown across the cabin as the chopper crashed and flipped over on its side. Lee's left shoulder absorbed most of the impact, and it ached as she struggled to her feet. She could smell the strong odor of fuel as she fought her way forward. The copilot had bailed out by then, and she arrived just in time to see the pilot climb out.

That left Lee free to do likewise. She could feel the seconds passing as she turned back. The kerosene-like smell of helicopter fuel was thick in the air, and all it would take was a spark to set the fumes off. She was standing on the copter's port side, which meant that the starboard door was *above* her.

Lee jumped, managed to grab the door frame, and pulled herself up as all hell broke loose nearby. There were four guard towers, with a machine gun mounted in each. Snipers had neutralized three of them, but the tower closest to Lee was operational. And it looked like the gunner was determined to hose the chopper down. The 5.56mm rounds made pinging noises as they hit the alloy fuselage, and Lee heard a loud whump as one of them sparked a fire.

A sudden surge of adrenaline helped Lee roll over the door frame and drop to the ground. Then it was time to turn and run. Lee could see what she assumed to be the slave house up ahead. The whole idea had been to land as close to the building as the pilots could.

Lee's legs were pumping hard, but she was out in the open, and the machine gunner could see her. He turned his pintle-mounted weapon to the left, and began to chase Lee with a steady stream of bullets, confident that he would catch up with her.

Lee glanced over her shoulder, saw the columns of dirt jumping into the air, and threw herself sideways. Death missed her by inches, and a single report put a stop to the machine-gun fire. Lee looked up to see a stick figure fall out of the tower and smack into the ground. *Better late than never,* Lee thought to herself as she came to her feet.

Lee was running toward the slave house when she heard the rhythmic bang, bang, bang of a semiauto as well as the sharp staccato of a submachine gun. *Theirs? Or ours?* Lee wondered as she drew the Glock. She was halfway to her destination when the ground opened up in front of her and a man with a machine pistol stuck his head up out of the ground! He saw Lee and opened fire. Fortunately, the bullets went wide as she triggered a response. Lee saw the D-Dawg's head snap back and knew it was a lucky shot. Then, as the body dropped out of sight, she realized that there was a tunnel below. Her thoughts were interrupted by a shout. "Maricopa County Sheriff's Department," Riley said. "Open up!"

That seemed to indicate that one or more gang members were holed up inside the slave house. With plans to use the women as hostages? Yes, and that was the very thing Riley had been most worried about. But the loss of the helicopter combined with a spirited defense had been enough to slow the SWAT team down.

Lee approached the hole in the ground with her weapon held in both hands. Then, ready for anything, she peered down into a vertical shaft. All she could see was a body sprawled below. Lee put the pistol away, turned to descend a series of metal rungs, and dropped into the tunnel.

* * *

Omo was pissed. Nothing was going right. After the first copter took a hit from an RPG, the second diverted to a spot that had been designated as LZ-2. It was closer to the main house than the building that he and the members of the gang squad were supposed to secure. Plus, Omo knew that Lee had been on chopper one and felt a tight knot in his gut.

The moment their helicopter touched down near the main house, the deputies were met with heavy gunfire. They jumped to the ground and began to run. Stick took a hit, jerked spastically, and fell. Kirby screamed a series of obscenities as he ran forward, firing the ancient MAC 11 that served as his main weapon. The deputies used palm trees, planters, and ornate fountains for cover as they returned fire. Van had given up on securing the objective until he could suppress the fire that was coming out of the house. Every now and then, a well-dressed man or woman would emerge from a door or window yelling, "Don't shoot!"

Potential customers? Trying to get clear? Yes, that was how it appeared—and the plan was to let the chase teams round them up. But the attack had gone wrong, and Van was afraid to let anyone get behind the members of his squad. What was to stop a D-Dawg from pretending to be a customer? So Van ordered his team to detain them. "Facedown on the ground!" Fossy yelled. "With your arms spread!"

Six of them were lying facedown next to the swimming pool when someone began to shoot at them from the house. Whether that was an error, an effort to silence potential witnesses, or an act of vindictiveness wasn't clear. Bodies twitched as the bullets smacked into them and two people stood. They had just started to run when Fossy shot them down.

Omo heard a thump as Van fired his grenade launcher. That was followed by the tinkle of broken glass and a muted explosion. The firing stopped.

The team made its way past the pool to the point where sliding doors provided access to the interior of the house. One of them had been shattered by stray bullets. Van pushed it aside and led the squad into a beautifully appointed great room. Omo saw a huge fireplace, a seating area furnished with white couches, and a scattering of what might have been real zebra skins on the tile floor.

He was still taking that in when someone yelled, "Get them!" and a series of menacing growls were heard. Van turned as four gray pit bulls charged into the room and converged on him. He was screaming as the dogs ripped into his flesh and Omo entered the fray. He was carrying The Equalizer, and the dogs disappeared in a spray of blood and bone as the 12-gauge went boom-clack, boom-clack, boom-clack. One dog remained and was worrying at Van's leg. Omo couldn't fire without hitting the officer as well. He was reaching for a Colt when Fossy shot the animal in the head.

Omo was about to kneel next to Van and apply first aid when Manny Hermoza entered the room. His hair was slicked back, diamonds sparkled on his droopy goat ears, and he was wearing a black sport shirt. One of the gang leader's wiry arms was wrapped around the neck of the woman held in front of him—and a huge pistol was clutched in his free hand. "Back off!" he said loudly. "Back through the door and into the pool."

Then Hermoza stopped. A look of surprise appeared on his face. "Coco? Is that *you*?"

Coco did the logical thing which was to shoot at him. Anything to shut the bastard up. But she missed—and Hermoza didn't. There was a loud BOOM, and the left half of Coco's head disappeared.

Omo's Colt was on target by then. It seemed to fire of its own accord, the barrel jerked upward, and the woman screamed as the .45 caliber slug creased her side and entered Hermoza's body. He uttered a grunt and let go of the woman in order to place a hand on the wound. Then he fell face forward onto a white couch.

The woman was Hermoza's common-law wife Carla. She tried to run but didn't get far. Kirby shot her in the left knee and she crashed into a piece of statuary, which shattered as it hit the floor.

Hermoza was dead. But what about Lee? Doors slammed as

deputies entered the room, and somebody called for a medic. Half the battle was over. But gunfire could be heard in the distance.

Lee was forced to step on the D-Dawg's body as she lowered herself into the underground passageway. The tunnel was lit by bare bulbs, which dangled from the ceiling at regular intervals. For the first time since exiting the chopper, she had a chance to call in and keyed her mike. "This is Lee . . . Can anyone read me?" There was no reply. Because all of them were too busy to answer? Or because she was underground? Not that it made any difference.

Moving quickly, Lee made her way south. Or what she thought was south toward the slave house. She was forced to bend over because the ceiling was low. She could hear the sound of gunfire, and it was getting louder. Then Lee saw someone drop into the tunnel ahead of her. She wished she had a silencer but didn't. As the D-Dawg turned, the only thing she could do was drop to one knee and fire.

The noise was extremely loud in the enclosed space. Lee rushed forward as the body fell, put another bullet into the gunman, and peered up through the vertical shaft above him. No one looked down at her, so she began to climb the wooden ladder one-handed.

As Lee stuck her head up through a hole in the floor she saw three men, all of whom had their backs turned to her. They were firing out through shattered windows. "Get back!" one of them yelled. "Get back, or the bitches die!"

Lee took a quick look around. The women the man was referring to were huddled in a corner. All of them were wearing masks, which suggested that they were norms. She knew they could see her and raised a finger to her lips.

Then Lee ducked out of sight and lowered herself into the tunnel below. She kept the pistol pointed upward as she whispered into the mike. "Riley? Anybody? This is Lee. Do you read me? Over."

There was a burst of static. "This is Riley. I read you. What's your twenty?"

"I'm in a tunnel under the room where the girls are being held. I poked my head up while the Dawgs were shooting at you. There are three, repeat three perps, and about eight girls." There was a pause, as if Riley was consulting with someone, followed by another burp of static. "Are you carrying a flashbang? Over."

Lee couldn't remember. She checked. "Yes, I am."

"Okay, climb up there, and get ready. When I say 'now,' toss it into the room. Avoid the hostages if you can—and *don't* fire your weapon. You might hit one of us."

"Got it," Lee replied. "Give me thirty to get in position. Let's move soon . . . They could decide to drop through the hole any moment now. Over."

"Copy that. Make your move."

Lee freed the grenade from her vest, climbed up the rungs, and put the Glock in its holster. "Now," Riley said, and the suddenness of it caught Lee by surprise. She pulled the pin, lobbed the grenade into the room, and closed her eyes. Her hands covered her ears as the device detonated.

That was Lee's signal to draw her pistol. She heard a second bang as a battering ram struck the door, and Riley entered the room, weapon at the ready. "Down! Down! Down!" he shouted, and to her relief the D-Dawgs obeyed. They were still seeing afterimages from the flash and were well aware of the fact that they were outnumbered. Lee knew the SWAT team was amped on adrenaline, so rather than pop up out of the hole, she announced herself first. "Good work," Riley said. "You can come up."

Lee put the Glock away and pushed herself up into the room. Riley and the rest of his people were securing the D-Dawgs, which left her free to speak with the prisoners. All of them wore white dresses, and their wrists were secured with plastic ties. "Hello," Lee said. "My name is Cassandra Lee. I'm a detective with the Los Angeles Police Department. You're safe now . . . Nobody's going to hurt you."

One of the girls said, "Thank God," while another began to sob, and a third started to shake. Lee produced a knife and flicked the blade open. But, before cutting anyone loose, she had a question to ask. "I can't see your faces and probably wouldn't recognize them if I did. Are all of you prisoners? Is somebody hiding among you?"

"No," one of them replied. "All of us are prisoners."

Having watched for any signs to the contrary, and having seen none, Lee began to cut the ties. "Which one of you is Amanda Screed?"

"She isn't here," a voice answered. "I was with her in LA ... A man named Wheels kept us in his garage. But then, after he took us into the red zone, people came to take Amanda away. I haven't seen her since."

Lee felt her spirits plummet. Eight women had been rescued. That was good. But Amanda, the girl she'd been sent to find, was missing.

Momma was dead. Omo's cousin Juan was dead, too, having been shot to death trying to defend the family compound and the casita Lee was sleeping in.

Stick was dead. And so was Van, who had been ravaged by El Cabra's dogs and succumbed to his wounds a few hours later.

Throw in the dozen or so deputies killed by the Aztec terrorists, and that added up to a lot of funerals. So many that Lee had to buy a black dress. It wasn't her fault. She knew that. But it seemed as if death followed wherever she went. And that feeling continued to dog her as she went to the memorial services, fought to maintain her composure, and battled to cope with all of the reports that she was supposed to fill out.

Though appalled by the cost, Sheriff Arpo had been pleased with the raid, and for good reason. Not only had El Cabra and his gang been eradicated, eight young women had been rescued, and the resulting publicity was extremely good for his department. Which was to say good for him and his chances of reelection. And that was reflected in his attitude toward Omo, who had been recommended for a medal.

But while the failure to find Amanda Screed wasn't that important to Arpo, it was a big deal back in LA, where the bishop continued to pressure the mayor. And according to all accounts, the politician was riding the chief like a horse. So when

Lee asked McGinty for more time, he'd been quick to grant it. Especially in light of the successful raid.

Now, Lee and Omo were about to interview Shelly Reston, the girl who had been imprisoned with Amanda in Los Angeles. Shelly and the rest of the hostages had been admitted to a Phoenix hospital, where they were undergoing tests prior to being sent to their various homes. Having been cleared through security, Lee and Omo rode an elevator up to the fifth floor. From there it was a short walk to the wing where the girls were housed. Two deputies were on duty, and one of them knew Omo. She sent them to room 501. The door was slightly ajar, but Lee knocked anyway. A female voice said, "Come in."

As Lee entered, she saw that Shelly was dressed in what looked like brand-new street clothes and sitting in the room's only chair. "Hi," Lee said. "I'm Detective Lee—and this is Deputy Omo. Thank you for agreeing to see us."

Shelly stood. She wasn't very tall and didn't have much meat on her. A mask prevented Lee from seeing her face. "You're the one who came up out of the tunnel," Shelly said. "Thank you."

"You're welcome," Lee replied. "Deputy Omo was there, too . . . He's the one who shot Hermoza."

Shelly extended a small hand. "Thank you, Deputy Omo, he deserved to die."

Omo took her hand and shook it gently. "Yeah, he did. Unfortunately, there are more just like him."

"That's why we're here," Lee interjected. "You were with Amanda Screed . . . And we're trying to find her."

"I hope you do," Shelly said fervently. "She deserves it. When I was down, she would find a way to cheer me up. I owe her a lot."

"Let's go to the lounge," Omo suggested. "We'll be more comfortable there."

The lounge was a small room two doors down. It was equipped with a round table, four chairs, and a TV that was tuned to a Spanish-language station. As they took their seats, Lee noticed the scars on Shelly's wrists and knew that she had attempted suicide at some point. Knowing that the young woman had been through a lot, Lee hoped to keep the conversation low-key. "So you were snatched off a street in LA and imprisoned in Willy Conroy's garage. What happened next?"

"Amanda was already there," Shelly said earnestly. "And two days later, she managed to escape. She would have made it, too, except that she spent too much time trying to free me. Conroy came and beat her up.

"Two days later, he loaded us into his van and took off. There weren't any windows, so we couldn't see out. But he said we were headed for the red zone, and that made sense.

"After what might have been a couple of hours, he stopped so we could pee. I don't know where we were except to say it was someplace out in the boonies."

"Could you see any mountains?" Omo inquired.

"No, it was dark. But Conroy said we were going to use a secret crossing. A dry riverbed that ran east to west. And once we got under way, the ride was extremely rough.

"Finally, we came to a stop. Conroy let us out, gave us some candy bars, and built a fire next to the van. We were in Arizona, or that's what he told us. We waited for a while, lights appeared, and a pickup arrived. The man who got out seemed to know Conroy."

"Did you hear a name?" Lee inquired.

"Yes. It was Lictor or something like that."

"How about Rictor?" Omo asked.

"Yes! That's it . . . Rictor. He paid Conroy and made us get into the back of his truck. There was a camper on it, and he locked the door."

"Okay," Lee said. "What happened next?"

"We drove cross-country," Shelly said. "That's what it felt like. For an hour or so. Then the truck came to a stop, and Rictor told us to get out. He put hoods over our heads. We heard voices. One of them wanted to know which one of us was Amanda."

Lee interrupted at that point. "That's what he said? He mentioned her by name?"

"Yes," Shelly replied. "I couldn't see much through the cloth, but I think one of the men took Amanda's hood off and aimed a flashlight at her face."

"Now that's interesting," Omo said thoughtfully. "Slavers want girls. I get that. But why would someone want a *specific* girl?"

"Why indeed?" Lee wondered out loud. "All right, what happened next?"

Shelly shrugged. "I heard the men talk about money as they took Amanda away. She was crying. Rictor forced me into the truck. Then we drove some more. Finally, as the sun came up, we arrived at a bunch of old trailers. Three D-Dawgs were waiting there. They gave Rictor some money, and he left." Shelly shuddered and looked down. "That's when they did things to me. And told me not to tell."

Lee reached over to touch her arm. "I'm sorry, honey . . . You were brave. Very brave. And you survived. That's the main thing."

Shelly looked up. There was a fierce look in her brown eyes. "Two of them are dead," she said. "And one of them is in jail."

"He'll hang," Omo predicted. "Justice is quite swift around here."

Maybe a little too swift, Lee thought, but kept the opinion to herself.

The questioning continued for another five minutes or so—but it quickly became apparent that Shelly had nothing more of consequence to share. So the officers thanked her and left.

Later, once they were on the road, Omo spoke. "So, what do you think?"

"Rictor got paid," Lee replied. "Yet, according to the reports filed by Deputy Haster, there was no money to speak of on his body or in his home. So where did it go?"

"He pissed it away," Omo suggested.

"Maybe," Lee allowed. "And maybe not. Let's ask his mommy."

ELEVEN

Before visiting Mrs. Rictor, it was necessary to perform some preliminary research. So it was midafternoon by the time Omo parked the truck in front of the nearly empty pizza parlor. From there it was only a few steps to the Quik Cuts beauty salon located next door. The interior was still very cold. A beautician came out to greet them. There were two holes where her nose should have been, and she was clearly surprised to see two people wearing masks enter the shop. "Yes? Can I help you?"

"We would like to speak with Mrs. Rictor," Lee replied. "Is she in?"

The woman shook her head. "No, Mrs. Rictor owns the salon, but she's retired. I'm the manager now. Would you like an appointment?"

"No," Lee said. "Not today. But thank you." And with that, the police officers left.

"Retired?" Lee said, as they returned to the truck. "How nice."

"It's consistent with your theory," Omo said. "I have her address. Let's drop in."

The sun had started to sink into the west by then. So the saguaros threw long shadows as the truck passed small horse farms. Most were barely large enough for a single animal, a shed, and a corral. But some ran to a couple of acres. And that was enough for two or three horses.

As they pulled into the driveway, Lee saw that Mrs. Rictor's ranchita fell into the latter category. Her one-story frame house was painted pink with white trim. Farther back, a nicely fenced corral could be seen, along with an exercise area and a brown horse.

Omo followed the circular drive around a cement fountain that was painted pink to match the house and pulled up about ten feet from the front door. As Lee got out, she noticed that a shiny especiale was parked in the carport. It was a nice ride for a lady who ran a beauty parlor.

Omo led the way to the front door and the sign that read, mi casa es tu casa. He rang the bell.

Lee heard a yapping noise followed by a partially muffled voice. "Stop it, Sugar . . . Behave yourself."

There was a pause, as if Mrs. Rictor was looking at them through the peephole. Omo was hard to forget, so Lee figured Mrs. Rictor would remember him, and was soon proved to be correct. The door opened, and there she was. The hairdo was the same, as were the fake eyelashes and the splash of pink lipstick. This time a white dog was tucked under one arm. It bared its teeth and growled. "Deputy Omo!" Mrs. Rictor said. "And Detective Lee. What a pleasant surprise. Come in."

Omo stood to one side so Lee could enter first. She was expecting some sort of western motif and was surprised by the Italianate furniture and a Tuscan paint scheme. Lee's mask did very little to mitigate the stink of stale cigarette smoke. "Please have a seat," Mrs. Rictor said. Lee chose a chair next to their hostess while Omo perched on an uncomfortable-looking couch. "I saw the news stories," Mrs. Rictor said. "El Cabra was killed. Is that why you're here? Did you find evidence that he was responsible for my son's death?"

"No," Lee replied. "Although that is a distinct possibility. We're here because we have a witness who was present when your son sold a girl named Amanda Screed to a group of men out in the desert. People who *weren't* part of the D-Dawg gang. We want to know who those people were."

For the first time, Lee saw what might have been a look of concern in the other woman's eyes. "Well, as I told you before,"

Mrs. Rictor said, "Vincent fell in with bad company. But I never met any of the people he hung out with. Nor did I want to."

"I'm inclined to believe that," Omo responded. "But I think you know *of* them even if you never encountered them face-to-face. And, after your son died, I think you went to his apartment or some other location and removed a very large sum of money. Dirty money . . . If so, that would make you an accessory to a kidnapping. Or a number of kidnappings."

"That's absurd!" Mrs. Rictor said hotly.

"Is it?" Lee inquired. "You had a mortgage on this house until a week ago. Then you paid it off. Along with the loan for the especiale outside. If Deputy Omo is wrong, where did the money come from?"

Mrs. Rictor looked defiant. "Maybe I saved the money . . . And maybe I'll use some of it to hire an attorney."

"You can if you want to," Omo acknowledged. "Although you won't have much money left by the time the legal process is over. Or you could tell us what we want to know. The money, and where you got it, is a side issue as far as we're concerned."

Mrs. Rictor looked at Lee and back again. "If I tell, you'll leave me alone?"

"Yes," Lee replied. "Unless we come across evidence that you knew about one or more abductions in advance and/or played a role in carrying them out. Then we'll come looking for you."

Mrs. Rictor was holding Sugar in her lap. She was silent for a moment. "All right," she said finally. "I've never heard of Amanda what's her name. But Vincent told me that he did business with a man named Tom-Tom. 'Side jobs.' That's what he called the deals Hermoza wasn't aware of."

"Good," Lee said. "Now we're getting somewhere. Did Vincent tell you anything else about Tom-Tom?"

Mrs. Rictor shook her head. "No, not really . . . Well, there was one thing. My son said that Tom-Tom has two heads. Two people really . . . Sharing one body. And both are named Tom." They questioned Mrs. Rictor about the man with two heads, but she didn't have any details to offer, or if the woman did, she wasn't about to share them.

So they left. Once Lee was in the truck, she fastened her seat belt. "Well," she said. "That was interesting . . . How many two-headed men can there be? We should be able to find him, I mean them, by this time tomorrow."

Omo looked at her. "That wasn't funny, Cassandra . . . I wouldn't be surprised if there were a quarter million two-headed people in the Republic of Texas. And I doubt any of them wanted to be born that way."

Lee heard the pain in his voice and wondered the same thing that had occurred to her so many times before. What was behind the mask? "I'm sorry, Ras . . . That was stupid."

Omo drove her back to the hotel and agreed to meet at the headquarters building in the morning. Maybe, if they were lucky, Tom-Tom had a criminal record. If so, they would be in jail, on parole, or out and about. Even then, there would be a last-known address in the database. And that would provide them with a starting point.

So Lee said good night, got out of the truck, and made her way through the shabby lobby to the one elevator that actually worked. Her plan was to freshen up and call out for some pizza.

After exiting the elevator, Lee made her way down the hall to her room, stuck the keycard into the slot, and saw the green light appear. As she entered, she was vaguely aware of the pine-scented deodorizer in the air, the dull rumble of the TV in the next room, and the fact that the bed was made.

She took the jacket off and threw it on the single chair. The shoulder holster was next, followed by the Smith & Wesson. She didn't undress, though. That would have to wait until after the pizza arrived. She could have a Coke however . . . And went over to the bar-style refrigerator to get one.

Lee opened the door, saw the usual array of cans, and was about to reach for one when she saw something that shouldn't be there. It was a clear plastic bag. And a fairly large one at that. She pulled it out, turned to hold it under the ceiling light, and realized she was holding a couple of bones. For a dog perhaps? Left there by a previous guest? No, there was something about one of them. Lee opened the bag, took both bones out, and instinctively fit them together. A human femur! One which had been broken in half! The Bonebreaker . . .

Lee let go of the bones, whirled, and snatched the revolver off the chair. Her heart beat wildly as she scanned the room. There was a knot of fear where her stomach should have been, and the .357 was trembling. Pistol extended, she entered the bathroom. Nothing.

Lee returned to the room at that point and sat on the bed. Ten minutes passed while she sat there clutching the pistol. But that was stupid, and she knew it. He, assuming the killer was male, wouldn't attack on that particular night. The whole idea was to scare the crap out of her and make her suffer.

So she picked the bone fragments up off the floor, put the Smith & Wesson aside, and went through her suitcase item by item. Had he or she been able to plant a tracker on her somehow? Or was the serial killer working the old-fashioned way—watching and following?

But the search didn't produce anything other than dirty laundry. And when it was over, she still had to get some rest. Sleep refused to come, however. All she could do was lie on the bed and wait for the sun to rise. Once it did, Lee got up, showered, and put the bone fragments in her briefcase. Breakfast consisted of coffee and a sweet roll consumed in the lobby. From there, she went out to the rent-a-wreck, which she subjected to a careful inspection. And that produced what she thought it would. A magnetic tracker that was attached to the frame. She threw the device out the window on her way to work.

People knew her by then, so it was a lot easier to get through security. Lots of men and some of the female deputies liked to flirt with her—and Lee handled that the same way she did back in LA. For the most part, a joke or a change of subject was sufficient to put them off without hurting any feelings.

Once Lee arrived in the bull pen, she went in search of Omo and found him in front of his computer. "Got a minute?" she inquired, and led him to a vacant conference room. The bones rattled as she dumped them onto the wood table. Omo looked up from the bones to her face. "Where did you find these?"

"In the refrigerator in my room."

"Any signs of a forced entry?"

"None."

"He bribed a maid, then . . . Or slipped into the room when she wasn't looking."

"Probably."

"So what are you going to do?"

"What *can* I do? Especially here. Keep working. But I promised to tell you if something took place, and now you know."

"Don't worry, Cassandra . . . We'll spot the bastard. It's only a matter of time."

Lee wasn't so sure, but she nodded anyway. "Right."

Omo picked one-half of the bone up and turned it over. His long, tapered fingers would have been suitable for a surgeon. "What's *this*? Who is Larry Evans?"

Lee took the bone fragment out of his hands and stared at it. The inscription was barely legible, but sure enough, the name "Sgt. Larry Evans" had been scratched into the femur with a sharp instrument. Sergeant Larry Evans was the Bonebreaker's second victim. He'd been killed during the month of April in 2055. His head and torso had been left next to the Hollywood Freeway—but the rest of the body had never been recovered.

Suddenly, the coffee and the roll came surging up her throat and shot out onto the table. Omo managed to grab a wastebasket and get it under her chin before her stomach convulsed for a second time, and the rest of her breakfast came up.

It took the better part of five minutes for the heaves to stop, and once Omo knew Lee was okay, he left to get some paper towels. There was a sink in the room, and, together, they managed to clean up. The smell was pretty bad, though—and Omo's solution was to make a fresh pot of coffee. "Our coffee always smells like vomit," he said. "So no one will notice."

Lee laughed in spite of herself, and they were well clear of the room by the time the vice squad entered to have a meeting. They went outside and circled the building so Lee would have time to regain her composure. She told Omo about Evans, and the deputy shook his head. "You've got to be careful, Cassandra. This guy is toying with you. He'll come for you one day. Maybe you should report this."

"No," Lee said firmly. "Arpo will send me back to LA if we do . . . And McGinty would go crazy. You were on your computer when I arrived. What, if anything, did you discover?"

Omo shook his head. "I couldn't find a single person named Tom-Tom, never mind two of them."

"Damn."

"So we need a plan."

"Yes, we do," Lee agreed. "Here's a thought . . . Something that came to mind while I was staring at the ceiling last night. Rictor sold Amanda to Tom-Tom. So, if we dig into the Rictor murder, maybe we'll come up with information that will lead us to Tom-Tom."

"I don't know," Omo said doubtfully. "That sounds like a long shot."

They were upstairs by then and crossing the bull pen. "Okay, Cowboy," Lee said. "Have you got a better idea?"

"No."

"Well, then . . . Let's get to work. A deputy named Haster was working on the Rictor case. Let's talk to him."

"We can't," Omo replied. "One of the Tecs shot Gus in the face."

That was when Lee remembered the memorial service and realized that Haster had been one of the deputies buried that day. He had a wife, too—and a couple of kids. She felt stupid. "I'm sorry, Ras . . . I forgot."

"There were a lot of them," he said bitterly. "Come on . . . I'll take you over to meet Lieutenant Ducey. She's in charge of Homicide. Who knows? Maybe you can use Haster's desk."

It was a short walk, and Ducey looked up as they arrived. "Hey there, Omo . . . Nice work the other day."

Ducey's black hair had been separated and woven into braids, each of which seemed to have a life of its own. They writhed like snakes as the introductions were made, and Ducey listened to Lee's request. The lieutenant had brown skin, a no-nonsense manner, and was wearing turquoise rings on three different fingers. "Sure, hon," she said. "You can use Haster's desk. We've been shorthanded since he was killed, and truth be told, the Rictor case has a low priority. I mean the guy was a gangbanger . . . Somebody was bound to kill him sometime."

Even though Ducey's comments weren't politically correct, Lee understood. Having written Haster's password on a scrap of paper, she sat at his computer and went to work. Lee was familiar with the general outlines of the case, having read some of Haster's stuff earlier.

But now she was reading the material with a completely different attitude. Rather than skimming, looking for potential connections to the Screed abduction, she was reading Haster's files the way a homicide detective would. As a result, she was paying attention to details such as *how* Rictor had been killed and *where* the body had been found. Both of which had been withheld from the news media as well as the dead man's family. Lots of police departments did that so they could use the information to sort suspects.

And the way Rictor had been killed was very unusual. His body had been found with an aluminum arrow sticking out of his chest. Specifically, a tan arrow with a nock made out of injection-molded polycarbonate. That made it a very sophisticated weapon, which had probably been manufactured in Pacifica or another high-tech enclave.

All of which was interesting but beside the point. The real so-what was the fact that Hermoza and his gang were all about killing people with firearms. Hermoza's .50 caliber handgun was an excellent example of that preference. So it seemed likely that the person or persons responsible for Rictor's death killed him for reasons that had nothing to do with Hermoza or the gang leader's wife. And those individuals might know who Tom-Tom was.

Then there was the matter of where the body had been found. And that was in a remote spot on the Salt River Pima-Maricopa Indian Reservation located ten miles east of Phoenix. There were plenty of photos to look at, and as Lee swiped through them, she saw that the murder had taken place in front of an ancient Airstream trailer.

And, judging from where the body was found, it appeared that Rictor had been standing in front of the trailer when the arrow entered his chest. According to the coroner's report the "... arrow's trocar tip punched through the victim's sternum. Subsequent to impact, two stainless-steel blades were released. They cut grooves through internal organs, resulting in death.

And, if the arrow hadn't been blocked by Mr. Rictor's spine, it would have exited through his back. That suggests that the arrow was fired by a very powerful bow."

So, because the body had been found on an Indian reservation, it was tempting to hypothesize that a Native American had been responsible for Rictor's death. But Lee had taught herself to resist that sort of thinking. All sorts of people used bows for hunting—and all sorts of people had access to the reservation. Still, the murderer *could* have been a Native American, and the same possibility had occurred to Haster. That was why he had contacted the Salt River Police Department and requested assistance.

The SRPD had been created back in 1967 but had fallen on hard times since the plague, when more than half of the department's officers lost their lives. Now the once-proud department was down to three officers, who were forced to rely on support from the sheriff's department where serious crimes were concerned. And one of those policemen, a lieutenant named Bo-Jack, had been scheduled to meet with Haster the day *after* the Tecs attacked.

Lee made some calls, got the number she needed, and was able to reach Bo-Jack on his cell phone. After a brief conversation, they agreed to meet at three that afternoon.

Omo wanted to go but couldn't because of a hearing related to Hermoza's death. So Lee borrowed Omo's truck, performed a 360 on the vehicle, and set off for the reservation.

Lee's route took her up I-17 to I-10, and from there to 202. Lee kept an eye on the rearview mirror and took three random side trips in an effort to identify a tail if there was one. It was something she hesitated to do when Omo was present. He'd be willing, no doubt about that, but Lee saw the battle with the Bonebreaker as a personal problem. And something she didn't want to impose on her partner if she could avoid it.

Having failed to spot a tail, Lee returned to 202 and followed it to 87. That took her to the point where she could access the East Indian Bend Road. It was more of a track than a road and badly in need of maintenance. According to the instructions from Officer Bo-Jack, she was to follow the road west for 5.6 miles. After that, she was supposed to watch for the sign that read, miner's creek, and turn right on the next dirt road.

So Lee set the truck's trip meter to zero and drove into the heart of the reservation. The outside temperature was in the nineties by then—and the land was so desolate that she couldn't imagine how anyone could live there without modern amenities. But people had. And plants still did. As Lee bounced along, she saw stately saguaros, desert hackberry, and white thorn acacia on both sides of the track.

The terrain was anything but flat. As the four-by-four continued west, there were lots of hills and water-cut gullies to deal with. That, plus the washboardlike surface of the road, forced Lee to keep her speed down. And that raised an interesting question. What the hell was Rictor doing out on the Indian reservation to begin with? Maybe Officer Bo-Jack would be able to offer a theory.

Lee passed a dramatic outcropping of rock on the left and saw the barely legible miner's creek sign shortly after. The creek was dry, and she had to slow down to five miles per hour in order to lurch up and out of it. Then it was time to shift down into second as the truck bucked up and over the rise beyond.

The dirt road came up rather quickly thereafter, and as Lee made the turn, she could see fresh tire tracks up ahead. It looked as though Bo-Jack was on time, and she was grateful for that. After winding its way between some rock formations the trail came to an abrupt stop. The Airstream was there, along with some old mining equipment, and a clutch of three palm trees.

A four-wheel-drive truck similar to the one she was driving was parked off to one side and positioned to depart in a hurry if necessary. It had a winch, a light bar on the roof, and a whip-style antenna. The windshield was cracked, and the Salt River Police logo was mostly obscured by a thick layer of dirt.

Lee stopped, put the truck in park, and killed the engine. Her boots produced puffs of bone dry dust as her feet hit the ground. "You're a norm." The voice came from behind Lee, and she was reaching for the Glock as she turned. The man had been able to approach her without making a sound. He raised his hands palm out. "Whoa . . . That was an observation. Not an insult. My name is Bo-Jack." It sounded like a single word the way he said it.

Lee removed her hand from the Glock. Bo-Jack's skin was

covered with slightly iridescent scales, and he was dressed western style. The outfit included a flat-brimmed black hat with a domed crown, a tee shirt that said police across the front, jeans, and a pair of dusty cowboy boots. Bo-Jack didn't appear to be wearing a pistol. But he was carrying a knife in a cross-draw sheath. A five-pointed star was attached to a slider on his western-style belt. Lee nodded. "My name is Detective Lee . . . I work for the Los Angeles Police Department."

Bo-Jack produced a boyish grin. "You're a long way from home, Detective Lee. *Why?*"

Lee gave him the short version. Amanda Screed had been kidnapped, and the trail led to Rictor. So, in an effort to get a lead on where she might be, Lee was looking into the trafficker's death. "I see," Bo-Jack said. "How can I help?"

"Tell me what happened here and why."

Bo-Jack shrugged. "I can tell you what *might* have taken place here . . . But there's no way to be sure."

"Okay, tell me what *might* have taken place."

"You read Haster's reports? And saw the photos?"

Lee nodded.

"Okay then . . . Based on evidence collected immediately after the crime, it looks like Rictor came out here to meet someone. Maybe he was in the trailer poking around when the other person arrived."

"What makes you think it was only one person?" Lee asked.

Bo-Jack smiled tolerantly. "Tracks. When I arrived, there were two sets of vehicle tracks—plus a pattern of footprints consistent with the presence of two people."

Bo-Jack was no fool. That was apparent from both his reasoning and the way he spoke. Lee nodded. "Okay . . . Thanks."

"No problem. So maybe Rictor hears the other vehicle arrive and steps out of the trailer. Then the two of them had words. Or, maybe they *didn't* have words. It's possible that the killer planned to kill Rictor from the git-go. All he had to do was raise his bow, pull the string back, and let fly. Either way, the arrow hit Rictor in the chest. Meeting adjourned."

Lee frowned. "Okay, let's say that's how it went down. Why were they here?"

Bo-Jack shrugged. "The most likely reason is a business meeting. Rictor was a gangbanger—but some people say he did deals on the side."

Lee nodded. "That lines up with what we know."

"So let's say he came out here to do a deal," Bo-Jack said, "but it was a trap."

By that time, Lee had the distinct impression that Bo-Jack was leading her somewhere. "Okay, I'll bite . . . Who would set such a trap? And why?"

"I don't know for sure," Bo-Jack answered carefully, "but revenge is a distinct possibility. Rumor has it that Rictor snatched a girl off the reservation. A sweet young thing named Mary. Not to sell as a surrogate, since she was a mutant, but for the D-Dawgs to enjoy during a big party. Some say the D-Dawgs raped her so brutally that she suffered internal injuries. Then they dumped her next to Highway 87. That's where one of our tribal members found her. Mary told him about Rictor, about what had been done to her, and he rushed her to a hospital. She didn't make it."

Lee stared at him. "Did you arrest Rictor?"

"No," Bo-Jack said bitterly. "He had an airtight alibi. Six members of the D-Dawg gang swore that he was in Tucson that night. As for what the tribal member had to say, well, that was hearsay."

Lee looked from Bo-Jack to his truck and back. "Would you mind if I take a look inside your vehicle?"

Bo-Jack produced the same little-boy smile she'd seen before. "No, ma'am . . . Help yourself."

Lee could feel the sun biting into the back of her neck as she made the short journey to the truck. It was unlocked, and when she pulled the door open, she could see the rifle rack. It was hanging on the wire-mesh partition that separated the front from the back. The top slot was occupied by a scope-mounted military assault rifle. But below that, hanging on a second pair of hooks, was a compound bow. And dangling next to it was a tube half-filled with arrows.

Lee removed one of the shafts and turned it over in her fingers. If Bo-Jack murdered Rictor, which seemed quite likely, why use a bow? One possibility was that arrows weren't like bullets. It would be difficult if not impossible to match one to a particular bow and get that to stand up in court. But she could conceive of a second reason as well. Once the cause of death was known to the public, it would send a message: Kill someone from the reservation and expect to be killed in return. Lee turned and carried the arrow back to where Bo-Jack was waiting. "I'm no expert," she said, "but this arrow looks identical to the one that killed Rictor."

"It's similar," Bo-Jack admitted, "but there are lots of those around. Numar is a popular brand out here. Their stuff is made in Pacifica."

Lee could see the challenge in his icy blue eyes. She knew he was the one who had killed Rictor, he knew that she knew, and odds were that everyone on the rez knew too. And Lee didn't blame him. That was something everyone except his mother could agree on: Rictor needed to die.

"Thank you," Lee said as she gave him the arrow. "One last question. A witness told us that Rictor sold Amanda to a man with two heads—which is to say a pair of conjoined twins collectively known as Tom-Tom. Do you know anyone like that?"

The surprise on Bo-Jack's face was plain to see. "You must be joking," he said. "The Ebben twins would never do something like that."

Suddenly, it was Lee's turn to be surprised. "So you know them?"

"Of course. Everyone on the rez knows the twins. They were born and raised here. They work for the Nickels Corporation."

Lee frowned. "Maybe we're talking about different people— although Tom-Tom is a very distinctive name."

"Could be," Bo-Jack agreed. "Like I said, the twins I'm talking about were born here. Their father thought it would be funny to name both of them Thomas, so he did. They have different middle names, however. But you know how kids are . . . Whenever we referred to the twins as a unit, we called them Tom-Tom."

"So you're the same age as the twins?"

"I'm two years younger."

"But you like them."

Bo-Jack nodded. "They built a medical clinic for the rez. We have our own doctors now—and that's a big deal."

"So where do the Ebben twins live?"

"Down in Tucson," Bo-Jack said. "That's where the Nickels Corporation is headquartered."

"Thank you," Lee said. "You've been very helpful. Take care, Officer Bo-Jack . . . Let me know if you visit LA. I'll buy you a beer."

Bo-Jack brought the arrow up to the brim of his hat by way of a salute and watched her return to the truck. He was still there when Lee turned and drove down the road.

It was late afternoon by then, and Lee was grateful for the fact that she had some daylight left to work with. The road back to the freeway was bad enough during the day. Darkness would make it that much worse.

Once she was on 87, it was a simple matter to backtrack to Phoenix and Omo's home. The garage door opened when Lee pressed the remote, and she saw that the rent-a-wreck was inside.

She parked, closed the outer door, and made her way upstairs. Omo was sitting at the kitchen table, drinking a beer and watching the news. Lee could see what looked like columns of black smoke in the distance and military vehicles in the foreground. The reporter was talking about casualties. "What happened?"

"A battalion of Aztec armor crossed the border and laid waste to the town of Douglas," he answered. "The government is sending troops down to push them back."

"I thought you had troops on the border," Lee said as she sat down.

"We do," Omo replied. "But not enough. Or so it seems. How did the meeting go?"

Lee told him about Bo-Jack and her theory regarding the officer's involvement in Rictor's death. Omo uttered a low whistle. "Wow . . . So what are you going to do?"

Lee raised her eyebrows. "About *what*? All I have is a theory."

Omo chuckled. "Okay, what about some sort of Tom-Tom connection? Any luck there?"

"Maybe," Lee answered cautiously. Omo listened intently as

Lee told him what Bo-Jack had shared with her. Then, when she got to the part about the Nickels Corporation, Omo groaned and covered his mask with his hands. "Oh my God, you must be kidding me."

"Why?" Lee said. "What's wrong?"

Omo dropped his hands. "A man named George Nickels owns the Nickels Corporation. And through it he owns a casino that's believed to be a front for a crime syndicate."

Lee frowned. "What kind of crime?"

"Drugs, prostitution, protection rackets . . . You name it."

"So why is Nickels out running around?"

"Because he owns the local police chief, who, by the way, hates Sheriff Arpo."

Lee swore. "Bo-Jack didn't mention any of that. And he would have to be aware of it, right?"

"Right," Omo agreed. "But it sounds like Officer Bo-Jack's world is centered on the reservation, and Tom-Tom built a clinic there, so he's looking the other way."

Both of them were silent for a moment. Omo spoke first. "So what are you going to do?"

She looked at him. "Hell, Ras, you *know* what I'm going to do. I'm going to Tucson, I'm going to locate Tom-Tom, and I'm going to ask him where Amanda is."

"That's a really bad idea. I don't like Tucson."

"Nobody invited you."

"I have to go."

"Why?"

Omo looked at her. He wanted to tell her the truth, he wanted to say, "Because I love you," but knew that would be stupid. So he offered a joke instead. "You're my partner—and you'd be helpless without me."

Lee laughed. It was music to his ears. "I'm tired," she said. "Let's get something to eat."

"Lonigan's again?"

"Absolutely."

They left shortly thereafter, but the Bonebreaker made no attempt to follow. Why bother? The puercos (pigs) would be back.

TWELVE

Amanda Screed's prison consisted of a spacious living room, a comfortably furnished bedroom, and a bath with separate shower. That meant her quarters were similar to those she had at her parents' house in Los Angeles—except that she couldn't come and go as she pleased. But *why*? The apartment seemed *too* nice in a way . . . Not like the prison it was.

She'd been there for weeks, watching TV, performing calisthenics, and waiting for a chance to escape. In the meantime, she had to "earn her keep," as her jailer liked to put it. And that meant making an appearance at one of the weekly bacchanals that George Nickels hosted.

Amanda had attended three of them by that time. And although she had never been assaulted, she had been ogled, groped, and forced to symbolically kiss Mr. Nickels's feet while his guests clapped enthusiastically. Because watching a norm submit to Nickels not only served to reinforce his status but gave his guests a vicarious thrill.

So it was with a terrible knot in her stomach that Amanda waited for the perfunctory knock on the door followed by one of her jailer's forceful entrances. Eva Macintyre, or "Mac" as the rest of the staff called her, was a large woman who had been born with a snout rather than a nose. She was dressed in a severe blue uniform and carried a stun gun holstered on one generous hip. "So slut," Mac said as she entered the room.

"It's party time. Put this on."

Amanda was sitting on the couch. She stood, and the bundle hit her chest. She opened it to find a two-piece swimsuit calculated to reveal most of her long, lean body. It was yellow with black polka dots. "Go ahead," Mac insisted. "Put it on. You wouldn't want to be late."

Based on previous experience, Amanda knew that if she went into the bedroom, Mac would follow. So she turned her back to the jailer, removed her top, and pushed the white shorts down off her hips. That gave Mac an opportunity to eyeball Amanda's butt, which she clearly enjoyed doing.

Fortunately, the skimpy top went on easily allowing Amanda to step into the bikini bottom and pull it up quickly. Then it was time to fasten the ties. A pair of red high heels completed the look. Mac nodded approvingly. "Good . . . You look like the whore that you are. Now stand still while I put your collar on."

The black leather collar with the chromed spikes was a regular part of the attire that Amanda was forced to wear. It, too, was intended to degrade and humiliate her. Once the collar was buckled into place, Mac added a length of chain, and they were ready to go.

Amanda wanted to cry but refused to do so because Mac would enjoy it. So she held her head high as the jailer led her out into the corridor. Having been held there for weeks, Amanda knew that Nickels's circular, one-story house sat atop a hill from which he could look out upon his empire. That included a twenty-story-tall hotel, the casino that was connected to it, and the surrounding mall.

Amanda's prison and three other so-called "suites" were buried in the hill that the entrepreneur's home stood on. That seemed to suggest that Nickels thought of her as an asset. Something he could trade or sell when it pleased him to do so. Maybe that was why she was kept in comparative luxury.

The good news, if it could be regarded as such, was that she hadn't been handed off to someone for use as a sex toy or surrogate. The bad news was that it could happen anytime.

Mac led Amanda out into the hall and down a sterile corridor to an elevator lobby. There were two lifts. One for visitors and one for freight. Staff were supposed to use the freight elevator, and it took several minutes for it to arrive. As the doors parted, Amanda saw a stainless-steel cart and two kitchen workers. The food served at Nickels's parties was prepared in the hotel's kitchen, transported through an underground tunnel via "hot cart," and brought up via the lift. The men leered at Amanda as she was led into the car. One of them produced a low whistle. "What I wouldn't give for an hour with *that*."

"In your dreams," Mac replied. "But feel free to squeeze her ass if you want to . . . She likes that. Don't you cuddles?"

Amanda didn't want the men to touch her—but knew the comment was an attempt to provoke her. So she gritted her teeth and stared straight ahead as unseen hands kneaded her flesh.

Fortunately, the trip was only thirty seconds long, and the men had to push their cart off as the doors parted company. Mac led Amanda out into a small lobby and from there onto the carpeted path that followed curved windows halfway around the house to the point where the prisoner could see a sweeping view of Tucson. It wasn't entirely dark yet, so hundreds of glittering lights were visible. Most, if not all of them, would have to be extinguished now that the new blackout regulations had gone into effect.

But there wasn't much time in which to admire the view. A fancy bar took up part of a wall. The dance floor was located adjacent to that. And a man in a tux was seated at a grand piano singing retro love songs as about thirty people stood in small groups and chatted. One of them spotted Amanda and said, "Look!"

Heads turned, and Amanda forced herself to meet their eyes as she passed through the crowd. It was obvious that the men wanted to have sex with her. And the women, many of whom had birth defects, wanted to *be* her.

Maybe that would change someday. Maybe the definition of normal would evolve so that people no longer compared themselves to those who hadn't been infected with *B. nosilla*. But that day was still a long way off. Until then, the reaction to norms would be the same. First came a sense of curiosity quickly followed by self-loathing and a feeling of resentment.

Amanda did what she could to steel herself against the insults, but it was difficult. "What a slut," one woman said, as if Amanda had chosen to wear the two-piece. "I wonder what her face looks like?" a man said, and Amanda felt a jolt of fear. What if they removed her mask? It hadn't happened thus far, but it could.

Mac jerked on the chain, which caused Amanda to stumble. The crowd laughed. Then the mutants were left behind as Mac towed her to what Amanda thought of as the throne. The richly upholstered chair was positioned on a platform where everyone could see it. A tiger was sprawled next to it. It growled ominously as Amanda was ordered to take her place on the other side of the platform. Mac secured the chain to an eyebolt and withdrew.

The stage was set at that point, and the entire crowd turned to look as their host arrived. It was impossible to know what Nickels looked like originally, but it was safe to say that he'd been born with numerous mutations, all of which had been addressed with radical surgery.

He stood about six feet tall. And while most of his face appeared to be normal, the lower-left part of his jaw was made of metal. Nor did the modifications end there. Steel rods, pulleys, and a servo had been used to replace his right arm. And, judging from the fact that the right sleeve of his jacket was missing, Nickels *wanted* people to see his artificial limb. Amanda couldn't help but admire that in spite of the hate she felt for the man.

Such was Nickels's importance to those in the room that they nearly tripped over each other in an effort to catch his eye, tell him how good he looked, or otherwise suck up to him. And Amanda had seen that sort of behavior before. It was, she realized, the same way that those who occupied the inner circle of her father's church treated him.

And the adulation was an important part of what made "the bishop" tick. He loved the sense of importance that his position afforded him and fed off it in much the same way that Nickels did. The businessman didn't even glance at Amanda as he took the platform. Neither she nor the tiger were of any importance to him. They were little more than exotic curiosities intended to signal his wealth and importance.

Machinery whined as Nickels sat down, and the guests gathered around. Amanda was reminded of the times when her father met with the church elders. "Good evening," Nickels said gravely, as his piercing blue eyes swept the crowd. "Each of you is here this evening to receive special recognition for your contribution to the corporation's success. Let's begin with Chief Dokey."

That produced a round of applause, and the police chief looked suitably embarrassed as he stepped forward. He was dressed in a business suit, which, although custom-made, couldn't hide the hump on his back. Nickels smiled approvingly. "Nice job, Chief . . . Thanks to you and your people, crime in and around the casino is at an all-time low. Please accept this gift as a token of my appreciation."

That was when the two-headed man stepped forward. Amanda knew that each head housed a separate brain and personality. But for reasons not apparent to her, the conjoined twins were collectively referred to as "Tom-Tom" and typically present for such occasions.

Both of Tom-Tom's heads had some independence of movement and conveyed their own expressions as they came forward to present Chief O. K. Dokey with a stack of so-called pumpkins, which was casino slang for thousand-eagle chips.

That produced more applause, and so it went, as a steady stream of public officials and executives came up to claim their bonuses. Eventually, after all the rest of the guests had been thanked, Nickels summoned one last person. "Frank Grifty . . . It's your turn! Please step forward." Grifty had bright eyes and a monotonous head tic. He shuffled forward to stand just feet from the platform.

Nickels eyed the crowd. "As all of you know, Frank is in charge of the baccarat tables. What you *don't* know is that he's been stealing from the casino."

Grifty tried to bolt, but a couple of burly men were ready and stepped in to seize his arms. "Stealing is very bad for your health," Nickels said sternly. "Especially when you steal from me."

Grifty attempted to speak, but Nickels brought a metal finger up to his lips. "Shhh . . . Don't embarrass yourself, Frank. You knew the chance you were taking, and you took it anyway. So let's behave like grown-ups. These nice gentlemen are going to take you out to the city dump and shoot you in the head. Don't worry, you won't feel a thing. And no, there won't be any severance pay."

The last comment produced some awkward laughter from the crowd. Grifty was led away, the tiger licked a paw, and Nickels came down to mingle with his guests. It was early yet, and the party had just begun.

It was midmorning, and Lee was driving the rent-a-wreck south from Phoenix to Tucson. And, because Interstate 10 wasn't considered to be safe at night, there was lots of traffic during the day. The southbound flow consisted of trucks for the most part—but there were plenty of passenger vehicles, too.

There wasn't much to look at other than the occasional bullet-hole-riddled wreck next to the freeway and lots of desert. If Lee had driven a more boring stretch of road, she couldn't remember when. She glanced at Omo. The deputy was slumped in the passenger seat with his Stetson pulled down over his mask. Lee smiled as she turned back to the road. "I don't need you." That's what she'd told him. It was a lie of course—but he didn't know that. Or did he?

Either way, Omo had insisted that they go to see Arpo, and the sheriff opposed the plan. "Nickels owns Chief Dokey," Arpo said, "not to mention the rest of the department. And Tucson is outside my jurisdiction. That means your badges will be worthless down there. Detective Lee can do whatever she wants so long as her boss agrees. But there will be political hell to pay if I let an active-duty officer work in someone else's territory without their okay."

"So I can't go?" Omo had inquired.

"You can't go on *my* time," Arpo answered. "But what you do while you're on vacation is up to you."

So Omo was using his vacation to escort an LA police detective to a potentially hostile city where he could get shot. *Why?*

Lee felt a lump in her throat. Omo was coming for the same

reason that Bryce Conti had gone out to confront the bank robbers. *For her.*

She felt a tear trickle down her cheek and turned to make sure that Omo wasn't looking. He was snoring gently, and she could see a pistol butt through the opening at the front of his jacket. *I want you to survive,* she thought to herself. *I want you to live. Don't do anything stupid.*

Thanks to the early start, they arrived in Tucson around 9:30 a.m. And, since the twins were employed by George Nickels, the first order of business was to visit their place of employment. That was easy to find as they followed the freeway south. "See that hill?" Omo inquired as he pointed off to the right. "That was called Sentinel Peak back before the plague. Then Tucson fell on hard times, and George Nickels Sr. offered to buy the hill and the park around it for half a million eagles. In return, he promised to build a complex that would employ a thousand people. And he kept his word. A hotel, casino, and mall were constructed at the base of Nickels Peak."

"And the park?"

"It's gone. There's a playground, though," Omo replied. "Take the next exit. Once we enter the complex, there will be lots of cameras. I think some disguises are in order."

That made sense, so Lee took the next off-ramp and followed Omo's directions to a small shopping center. She remained in the car while he went to purchase the things they needed. Once Omo returned, he threw some packages into the backseat before sliding in next to her. "Let's find a spot where we can change without being seen. There are at least three cameras in this parking lot."

So Lee drove them into the ruins of an old housing development, where they could get out and don their disguises without being observed. Lee's outfit consisted of a full-length burqa similar to the one that Mrs. Fuentes had worn in LA. It was sky blue and hung all the way to the ground.

Omo was able to alter his appearance by turning his back to Lee and trading his cowboy hat and mask for a privacy hood. That, too, was an accepted piece of apparel inside the red zone and unlikely to attract attention. "What about our weapons?"

Lee wanted to know, as they reentered the car. "What if they scan us?"

The deputy laughed. "You must be joking. Everyone in the Republic of Texas has the right to carry a gun anywhere they want to. It's in our constitution."

Omo directed Lee onto West Congress Street. It led to Nickels Peak Road. They passed below a fancy-looking arch shortly thereafter and followed the signs into a large parking lot. It was early in the day, so there were lots of empty slots. Lee took one, got out, and locked the car. Shuttles were available, but they chose to walk. It didn't take long for Lee to realize that the burqa was too long. But, by holding on to the side seams, she could lift it up off the pavement.

Dozens of palm trees had been brought in and planted all around to give the impression of a desert oasis—and the mall was designed to resemble someone's fantasy of what a North African city might look like. The jumble of buildings included domed buildings, minaret-like spires, and boxy structures with arched windows. All of which bore Mediterranean colors. The goal was to transport customers out of their humdrum lives and into a state of mind where they would be willing to risk their hard-earned money.

But the police officers didn't see the *real* pièce de résistance until they passed through the so-called western gate and entered a large open area within. When they looked up, the pair could see the point where water shot out of the hillside, splashed into what appeared to be an ancient aqueduct, and was then delivered to the lake via a spectacular waterfall. That created a mist that drifted out to cool the mall's shoppers. Or so it seemed.

A more careful inspection revealed that most of the water vapor was being produced by misters concealed in the old-fashioned light poles that circled the lake and were used to support hanging plants. It was a clever way to not only add some ambience but combat the steadily rising temperature.

Logically enough, the mall had been built so that most of the stores enjoyed water views. That meant shoppers could walk an endless loop that would carry them past shop after shop until fatigue forced them into a restaurant, or they ran out of money.

It was important to appear normal, so the couple wandered in and out of stores, fingered merchandise, and conversed in low tones. "The whole place is lousy with cameras," Omo said, as they strolled down an aisle of women's clothing.

"And the merchandise sucks," Lee observed. "Most of these dresses are knockoffs of items manufactured in Pacifica. I have this top at home."

"Try to focus," Omo said. "We have a tail now . . . A woman wearing a flowered dress."

"Oh, *her*," Lee said dismissively. "My guess is that she works for the store rather than Nickels." And that theory proved to be correct because the woman stayed behind once they left the store.

More people were arriving all the time. That made Lee feel less exposed as they circled the lake and arrived in front of a second gate. This one promised to provide access to the "Medina," or oldest part of the imaginary city. And there, according to the signs, they would find the Palms Hotel and the Happy Nickels Casino. Both of which were bound to be of considerable importance to Mr. Nickels and his co-CFOs.

So they passed through the gate, followed a winding path past all sorts of small shops, and were delivered into the hotel's enormous lobby. Or were they in the casino? The two businesses were so intertwined, it was difficult to tell where one started and the other left off. Both were housed under a series of interlocking domes. And as Lee looked up, she could see the sort of intricate geometric designs that she associated with North Africa. Shafts of dusty sunlight entered through a cupola and streamed down to splash the tile floor. The temperature was almost *too* cool and kept that way at considerable cost.

The reception desk was a circular affair located directly below the cupola. Radiating out from that were pie-shaped sections of seats, various types of gambling setups, and restaurants with different themes. The whole thing was very impressive. But where to start? A feeling of hopelessness settled over Lee. Traveling to Tucson was a stupid idea. So what to do? *Keep looking*, she told herself, and followed Omo out into a well-furnished wilderness.

* * *

195

Amanda was terrified as she stood next to the door, metal tray in hand, and waited for the kitchen man to come. She'd been there for ten minutes by then—much longer than necessary. But it had taken days, no weeks, in which to build up sufficient courage. And should he come early, *before* she was ready, Amanda wasn't sure that she could summon the courage required to try it again. So she stood there, body trembling, waiting for the sound of his key in the lock.

Finally, after what seemed like an eternity, she heard movement outside. A knock followed. That was the signal to tighten her grip and raise the tray high. One blow, that's all she could be sure of, so it had to be good.

The door opened, and the kitchen worker stepped inside. Just as he did every day to retrieve the breakfast dishes. Except it was a woman this time . . . A fact that didn't register on Amanda's brain until the tray was already in motion. It came down hard, struck the back of the worker's head, and sent her sprawling.

Amanda kicked the door closed, just as she had imagined that she would, and rushed to administer a follow-up blow. It produced a dull clang. Amanda regretted having to hit the woman again but had convinced herself of the necessity days earlier. She was a prisoner, and prisoners have a right to escape. Or so it seemed to Amanda. That didn't stop her from checking the woman's pulse or being glad that there was one.

Then it was a race to remove the woman's clothes. That was a stroke of luck, actually, since she'd been expecting a man. A *small* man to be sure but a man nevertheless.

First, Amanda had to roll the woman onto her back in order to unbutton the shirt. That went pretty quickly but getting the kitchen worker's arms out of the sleeves proved to be more difficult than anticipated.

In the meantime, seconds and minutes continued to tick by. How long until somebody like Mac noticed the cart and wondered why the woman was taking so long? That's all it would take to bring Amanda's escape attempt to a disastrous halt. *Concentrate*, Amanda told herself as she pulled the shirt free. *Think about what you're doing.*

Amanda was wearing nothing more than a bra and panties

so as to complete the change of clothing speedily. All she had to do was pull the shirt on and remove the woman's shoes. Her pants were next and proved to be easier to cope with than the shirt had been.

Amanda tossed the trousers aside and went to work with the strips of cloth torn from one of her bedsheets. The plan was to bind the victim's wrists and ankles before gagging her. Hours had been spent on making that decision. What if the woman came to—and started to scream? Maybe the gag should be applied first. But if her hands were free, she would remove the gag. The "what if" process continued until Amanda had gamed every possibility she could think of.

Fortunately, the kitchen worker *didn't* come to. And Amanda was able to bind and gag her without interference. The pants were too big, but that was better than being too small. And by cinching the belt tight, Amanda could keep the trousers from falling down. Rather than wear shoes that were too large, Amanda chose to wear a pair of her own slip-ons.

With her heart beating like a trip-hammer, Amanda loaded the breakfast dishes onto the tray and carried it to the door. The trick was to hold it up with one hand while turning the knob and stepping out into the hall.

The stainless-steel cart was waiting. Amanda opened the cargo area, slipped the tray into an empty slot, and closed the door. Then she heard voices. Would the disguise work? There wasn't much to it. Another piece of the sheet had been used to fashion a harem-style veil similar to one she'd seen at a party. That would cover her nose and the lower part of her face. As for the rest, well, she knew that people see what they expect to see. And having grown up with a houseful of servants, Amanda knew how they could fade into the background unless one made a conscious effort to track them.

And sure enough, the men in the business suits didn't even glance at her as they walked past. Thus encouraged, Amanda pushed the cart toward the lobby. The rest of her plan was simple: She would take the freight elevator down to the tunnel, push the cart all the way to the hotel's kitchen, and leave as quickly as possible.

Would employees have an exit of their own? Amanda thought so . . . That would provide her with a quick way out. Then, she would have to wing it. There would be cameras, of course. But maybe, just maybe, she would manage to get off the grounds quickly enough to evade capture.

And after that? Well, there was whatever money might be in the wallet the woman had been carrying plus her own resourcefulness. Somehow she would find a way to make contact with her parents, and they would send help.

The thought made Amanda feel better as she pushed the down button and waited for the elevator to arrive. It took three long minutes. Finally, the doors parted, and rather than the full car that Amanda feared, the interior was empty.

The cart made a rattling sound as she pushed it onto the lift and touched the button below the word tunnel. The lift began to drop, and kept dropping, until it coasted to a stop. Then the doors slid open to reveal the twins known as Tom-Tom. Amanda felt a stab of fear as they stepped to one side. All she could do was put her head down and push the cart out into the lobby. The wheels rattled, and she was just starting to feel a sense of relief, when a hand grabbed the back of her collar. Another jerked her around. "Wait a minute," one of the twins said. "I recognize that smell."

"Yes," the other one agreed. "Remove the veil."

A hand tore the piece of sheet away, and Amanda saw the looks of recognition on both faces. "Amanda Screed!" the one called Ethan said. "What are you doing here?"

"She's trying to escape," Orson put in sourly.

"You're a very naughty girl," Ethan said as he sniffed the air. "Yes, it's you all right . . . My brother and I can smell things most people are entirely unaware of. Now get back on the elevator."

A shove accompanied the order, and Amanda fell. She didn't bother to get up. The escape attempt had failed, and the only thing she had to look forward to was some sort of punishment. The twins laughed.

* * *

After hours spent wandering around the mall and inspecting the hotel-casino complex, the police officers returned to their car. A short drive and a bit of searching turned up a midpriced hotel that catered to shoppers and gamblers on a budget.

Once they were checked in, the hard work began. Because even though the trip to the mall had left Lee feeling less than optimistic about their chances of success, she wasn't ready to give up. So she asked Omo to visit the city's Planning & Development Services Department in hopes that the deputy would be able to obtain a copy of the plans for the residence that sat atop Nickels Peak. As well schematics for the hotel, casino, and mall. It was a risky thing to do because even though such inquiries were legal, there was the chance that the inquiry would arouse suspicions.

Meanwhile, Lee spent the afternoon using the city's info net to search for information pertaining to where Nickels and/or the Ebben twins might be holding Amanda. Hours of effort turned up a single lead—and that was a brief article about a medical clinic to which Tom-Tom had given some money. By then Lee had concluded that free medical care was something of a passion for the twins. The reason for that was obvious given the extent of their physical problems.

But what if the clinic was a front for a surrogate farm? So Lee copied the clinic's address and continued her search. It was a fruitless endeavor, and she was happy to quit once Omo returned.

Fortunately, he had some good news to report—and that was the fact that he'd been able to get a copy of the building plans for the Nickels home, the hotel, and the casino. The information pertaining to security systems had been redacted, but everything else was there to see.

They spent the next half hour poring over the drawings, especially those related to the structures inside the hill and the home located on top of it. There was very little detail about the floors immediately below the house. Just two words spelled out in block letters: RESIDENTIAL QUARTERS.

That raised all sorts of questions. Quarters for whom? Guests? Staff? Or? There was a remote possibility that Amanda was being held there—but Lee didn't think it would make much sense. And Omo agreed. "We've got to be realistic, Cassandra . . .

Assuming Tom-Tom purchased Amanda, she's been sold to someone by now."

"True," Lee agreed. "The medical clinic I told you about is a better bet. I'm hungry . . . Let's go to dinner."

So they asked the clerk at the front desk for a recommendation, were directed to a Mexican restaurant called El Toro, and arrived to find that it was hopping. Two rounds of margaritas preceded meals consumed separately. A three-piece band was playing, and Omo asked Lee if she'd like to dance. *This is a mistake,* Lee told herself as she allowed Omo to guide her out onto the dance floor. *Never date your partner. That's rule number one. And this feels like a date.*

There were about six couples on the dance floor, and much to Lee's amazement, Omo could dance! Not just shuffle around the way most guys did but actually dance! The band was playing a Salsa tune, one of her favorites, and it was only a few moments before she fell into the familiar rhythm of one, two, three, back, five, six, seven. And then, in a surprisingly short period of time Omo added a turn, and Lee discovered that she was having fun. So they danced—and danced again. Before long, all of her worries dropped away.

Every now and then, they took a break, and when they did so, Lee sipped a rum and Coke. So that by the time the bar closed, she was feeling even happier. Something she didn't experience often and wanted to prolong.

There was a short drive back to the hotel, but without streetlights, it was a completely different experience. Most of the other guests were in bed by then although cracks of light could be seen around some of the curtains.

They got out of the truck, and Lee followed the blob of light produced by Omo's flashlight along a concrete path, past the deserted swimming pool, and up a flight of stairs. From there it was a short trip along the walkway fronting the rooms.

Lee fumbled for her keycard and felt a little tipsy as she slid it into the slot. The green light came on, and there was an audible click as the door opened. "That was fun," Omo said. "I'll see you in the morning."

Lee looked up at the mask. "It's a long way to your room,

Ras . . . At least twenty feet. Maybe you should stay here."

Omo looked down at her. The flashlight was still on, and the mask was half-lit. "Are you sure?"

"Yes," Lee said. "I'm sure."

"We can't kiss."

"No, but we'll make do."

Lee pushed the door open and towed Omo inside. It was pitch-black except for the glow produced by the clock and the indicator light on the TV. But that was enough.

Omo lowered Lee onto the bed and began to undress her. The process went smoothly at first. But then, as he attempted to tug her pants off, the Smith & Wesson got caught on the bedding. Lee giggled and tried to help. That led to an awkward moment in which both parties had to divest themselves of weapons and other police paraphernalia before they could proceed.

Eventually skin met skin, and the process of exploration could begin. Gently at first, then with increasing urgency, as they found the places they were looking for. "Be gentle, Ras," Lee said as she opened herself to him. "It's been quite awhile."

Their lovemaking was slow at first, deliciously so, but as both became more confident, the tempo started to increase. Before long, Lee dug her fingernails into Omo's back. "Please," she said. "I need you *now*." And he was there, helping her up and over, causing Lee to marvel at how intense it was. The result was an explosion of pleasure unlike anything she'd experienced before.

As Lee held Omo in her arms, and the afterglow began to fade, she felt a sense of guilt. And the first stirrings of fear. A rule had been broken. An *important* rule . . . And that opened up the possibility that one or both of them would be punished.

Lee pushed the thought away and listened as Omo whispered in her ear. "I love you, Cassandra . . . I know I shouldn't, but I do."

"And I love *you*," she said in return. Because she *wanted* to love him—and thought that she should.

Eventually, Lee got up and went into the bathroom before returning to bed. And that's where she was, propped up against some pillows, when Omo padded across the floor. Thanks to the light from the bathroom she could see that he had a long, well-muscled body, and a puckered patch of skin on his left shoulder.

A bullet wound? Probably. It was the sort of thing Omo would neglect to mention.

There were two mirrors in the room. One opposite the bed and another on the wall to Lee's left. That allowed Lee to watch Omo enter the bathroom. He stood in front of the sink, turned the water on, and lifted the mask. And that was when she saw his left temple and cheek.

There were a few patches of normal skin on which black stubble had begun to grow. But they were surrounded by currents of raw meat that flowed in and around archipelagos of black scabs. Lee winced and closed her eyes. Then she heard the water stop and the door close. The mattress gave as he sat down on it. Lee had been crying. But Omo didn't know that as he lay down beside her and threw an arm over her waist.

A door slammed somewhere, the clock continued to tick the seconds away, and Lee could feel his warm breath on her back. It was both a comfort and a threat. But she was wearing nostril filters *and* a mask. She would replace both in the morning. Sleep carried her away.

THIRTEEN

The Madison Medical Clinic was housed in a preplague business park which, judging from the for rent signs and half-empty parking lot had seen better days. The other tenants consisted of an accounting firm, an insurance company, and a florist.

Lee parked the rent-a-wreck out on the edge of the parking lot and handed the keys to Omo. "Here you go . . . Don't forget to pick me up."

Omo looked at her. His eyes were serious. "You're sure about this."

"No, but I'm going to do it anyway."

Omo made a face, but she couldn't see it. "Okay, let's get this over with. Give me a thirty-second head start."

He got out, and Lee waited for half a minute before opening the door. She could feel the full weight of the late-afternoon sun on her shoulders as she followed Omo across the parking lot. He staggered at one point, stumbled, and managed to regain his footing. Then he entered the clinic. Lee thought he was overacting, but figured it wouldn't matter as she entered the lobby just in time to see him collapse. The reaction was everything Lee had hoped for and more.

All eyes went to Omo, who was clutching his chest and gasping for breath. Someone called a "Code Blue" on the intercom, and medical personnel swarmed the lobby. Lee took that opportunity to slip through the door labeled authorized personnel only, and enter the corridor beyond it.

Lee hadn't gone far when it became necessary to step aside in order to let a woman pushing a crash cart hurry past. Would they use a defibrillator on Omo? That possibility hadn't occurred to either one of them. But Lee figured Omo would sit up and start talking if they tried to put the paddles on him.

Everything had gone perfectly up to that point. But Lee knew she had five minutes, ten at most, to find a hiding place and settle in. It wasn't easy. Which exam rooms and offices were in use that day? There was no way to know.

Lee paused to grab a pair of latex gloves from a dispenser as she hurried down the main corridor. Her head swiveled back and forth in hopes of spotting a refuge. Then she saw the door with the word storage on it and came to a stop. After a glance over her shoulder, Lee tried the knob. It turned, and the door opened when she pushed. She flipped the lights on and pulled the door closed behind her. There was a pile of cardboard boxes at the front of the room and a jumble of furniture in back.

Lee hurried to shed the burqa so it would be easier to move. Then, conscious of the fact that the room had *two* light fixtures, she pulled a chair over to the center of the room. The second bulb was starting to get hot, but she managed to unscrew it to the point where it went off. That cut the level of illumination by half.

With that out of the way, Lee hurried to collect the burqa before burrowing into the mass of junk at the rear of the room. There she found the desk and crawled under it. And that's where she was, busy congratulating herself, when Lee realized that the remaining bulb was still on!

That placed her in a quandary. Which was more dangerous? To leave the light on? Or go out and turn it off? Lee imagined the scene as a nurse opened the door to find a stranger in the room getting ready to turn the light off. *No*, Lee reasoned, *anyone who enters will assume that one of their coworkers left the light on. The safest thing to do is stay put.*

So she did. But what about Omo? What was happening to *him*? Surely it wouldn't take too long for the medical types to figure out that he was okay.

Wrong. More than two hours passed, and it was nearly closing time before Lee's phone started to vibrate. Omo's text message was short and to the point. "Still at the hospital undergoing tests . . . They can't figure out why my vital signs are so normal. One way or another, I will make it back there in time. O."

Lee smiled. Poor Omo . . . Her wait had been easier than his. She sent a brief reply letting him know that phase one of the plan had gone off without a hitch. Then, as she tucked the phone away, the door opened.

Lee couldn't see what was going on but she could hear. And it sounded as if someone was rifling through the cardboard boxes. Then came what might have been a grunt of satisfaction followed by a series of thumps. The light went out shortly thereafter, and Lee heard a click as the door closed.

Was that a normal click? Or was that the sound of a lock? If it was the latter, Lee was well and truly screwed. *Don't panic,* she told herself. *Everything is okay. The staff will leave, and once they do, you can come out of hiding.*

But even if that turned out to be true, Lee knew she would face a number of potential hurdles. Would one or more staff members decide to work past six? Would she be forced to deal with a security guard? And what about an alarm system? Or was the clinic relying on the barred windows to keep the bad guys out? All she could do was wait and see.

Finally, after giving the employees an extra fifteen minutes to get clear, Lee emerged from hiding. The first thing she did was to put the burqa back on so that cameras, if any, wouldn't be able to photograph her face. Then she tried the door. It opened smoothly, and she gave thanks as it clicked behind her.

Since Lee had no idea of who or what she might encounter, she had the Glock out and ready to go as she walked the halls. It wasn't long before she spotted a red eye up in a corner and knew the answer to one of her questions. The clinic was equipped with a security system, and it was on. But being a cop, she knew that the system was likely to have two settings. "Stay" would allow people to move around inside the clinic without triggering the alarm, while the "Away" setting relied on motion detectors that would trigger an external Klaxon if a mouse scampered across the floor. That would simultaneously summon the police and piss them off. So rather than run that risk, most businesses chose to use "Stay."

In this case, the alarm hadn't sounded, so Lee figured she'd be fine until it came time to leave. Then, lacking the proper code to enter into the system, she would be forced to open a door and let the system go bonkers. Would Omo be there with the car? She made a mental note to contact him prior to leaving the clinic.

But what about people? The alarm was on . . . That could indicate that everyone had gone home. It could also mean that one or more employees were working late and felt more secure with the system on. So Lee went from room to room, systematically checking to make sure that the clinic was clear. It also gave her an opportunity to identify which offices to return to.

But no one else was there. So five minutes later, Lee felt enough confidence to put the Glock away—and make a quick visit to the ladies' room. Then she returned to what looked like the main office. Would she be able to access one of the computers there? Lee figured she had a fifty-fifty chance. Creating, securing, and sharing passwords could be a pain in the ass. So a lot of businesses chose not to use them—especially if machines were shared. But some did, and the Madison Clinic could be one of those.

There were four workstations plus a lot of storage cabinets in the room. Lee chose the most organized desk and sat down. The swivel-style chair squeaked as she scooted closer. The screen was dark but came to life when she touched the screen. So far so good.

As rows of brightly colored icons wiped themselves onto the screen, Lee knew she was in. But what to choose? In addition to a variety of applications, there were lots of file folders on the desktop. The ones used most frequently? Sure, that made sense. But how to interpret the mysterious abbreviations? Take "PWAD" for example. What the hell did *that* mean? "People With A Disease?" "Patients With Accounts Due?" There was no way to know without wading into it.

So Lee went to work slogging through the folders, looking for any mention of surrogates, Amanda, or someone who might be Amanda. Hours passed. Omo sent messages every now and then.

According to the latest missive, he was outside, hunkered down in the car, eating a cheeseburger. Lee's tummy rumbled. There had been a candy bar in the lap drawer, but that was long gone.

More time passed. Lee's eyes were tired by then, she was exhausted, and gradually losing her ability to concentrate. Then she opened a folder named "SOPV," or Special Outpatient visits, and saw a list of names. All of them were female, all were in alpha order, and all of them had the same surname, which was Smith. That put someone named Amanda Smith at the top of the list. *Amanda?*

Lee struggled to focus. Could it be? Eleven girls all named Smith? All of whom were "outpatients"? And one of whom was named Amanda? That was interesting.

Suddenly, all of the tiredness seemed to drop away as Lee clicked the "Amanda Smith" file open and began to scan the woman's medical record. There were no mentions of fertility, pregnancy, or surrogacy. Nor did Amanda Smith have a diagnosis. But she had been subjected to physical exams every two weeks—the last of which had been carried out three days earlier!

And there was something else. All of the personal data fields pertaining to Amanda Smith were empty with the exception of her address. That read, "Nickels Peak, Tucson, AZ"!

And, after a quick check, Lee saw that the other ten were listed as residing on Nickels Peak, too. But, unlike Amanda Smith, eight of them were shown as "discharged." Did that mean they had been sold? Odds were that it did.

Lee felt a steadily rising sense of excitement as she looked at the Amanda Smith file again. The hill! Amanda was inside the hill! Or had been very recently. Keys clicked as she sent the file to a shared printer. That was when her phone began to vibrate. Lee turned it on, saw that Omo was calling, and thumbed the green bar. "Yes?"

"A rent-a-cop just pulled into the lot," Omo said grimly. "It looks like he plans to come inside. And that's not all . . . He has a couple of mutimals with him."

Lee felt a stab of fear. Humans weren't the only ones who were susceptible to *B. nosilla*. Animals were as well, which was how the term "mutimals" came into common usage.

A lot of the animal mutations were unpleasant to look at but harmless insofar as humans were concerned. But there were exceptions, like rattlesnakes that had become more venomous, bears that were measurably more intelligent than they had been previously, and dogs that behaved like wolves on steroids. Were two such animals about to enter the buildings? "Copy that," Lee said. "I'm coming out. Disable his car if you can . . . And don't come in. I'd hate to shoot you by mistake."

Lee thumbed the phone off and hurried to close both the file and the folder it was stored in. Maybe, just maybe, that would prevent the clinic's personnel from figuring out what she'd been after. Lee stood and made her way over to the printer. The file had printed by then, and she took it off the feeder. She had to fold the sheets twice before sticking them under her belt.

Then it was time to dump the burqa. Maybe there were hidden cameras in the clinic and maybe there weren't. But one thing was for sure . . . There was no way that she could fight while wearing a sheet.

Weapon in hand, Lee left the office and began to work her way toward one of the emergency exits identified earlier. She had only taken two steps when she heard a distant howl and a shouted command. "Get 'em, boys! Get 'em!"

Lee swore. How did the rent-a-cop know that someone was on the premises? Had a signal been sent when she opened the "SOPV" file? Or were the mutimals that good? It hardly mattered as a male voice came over the intercom. "I know you're in here, puke . . . And my dogs are coming for you! There's no point in trying to get away—so you might as well bend over and kiss your ass good-bye."

Lee was holding the Glock with both hands as she advanced down the hallway. Her heart raced as she heard a skittering sound off in the distance. That was followed by overlapping howls as two mutimals rounded the corner ahead.

They were *big*, at least the size of Great Danes, but looked like German shepherds. Their blue-black lips were pulled back to expose white fangs and pink gums. The mutimals growled in unison and charged straight at her, or tried to, since it was difficult for them to get sufficient traction.

Lee knew she would die if either one of the slavering beasts managed to reach her. So she fired at one, then the other in hopes of slowing them down. And she could see the blood fly as the bullets struck flesh. But the mutimals took the punishment and kept on coming.

So, having been unable to stop the brutes, Lee was forced to turn and run. She could hear the panting behind her, along with the frantic click of toenails, as the mutimals continued to gain on her. Then she saw an open door and ducked inside. Her pursuers banged into the door as she turned to pull it closed. They threw themselves at the barrier in a desperate attempt to get in.

"Okay, assholes," Lee said grimly. "You want some of *this*? Eat lead." Lee aimed dog high and emptied the pistol at a single spot on the door. The bullets made a respectable hole in the wood. That was when Lee shoved the Smith & Wesson into the aperture and pulled the trigger. The .357 magnum hollow points did what they were supposed to do, which was to cause an incredible amount of damage to whatever they hit.

BOOM! BOOM! BOOM! The noise was deafening in the small exam room, but that was a small price to pay as Lee triggered a fourth shot and waited to see what would happen. The answer was nothing.

Thus encouraged, Lee took a moment to reload the Glock before opening the door. The hallway was like a slaughterhouse, with two dead bodies and blood splatter all over the walls. A leg twitched. So Lee put a bullet into each skull just to make sure.

Then she crossed the hall to an ivory-colored PA box. She pushed the talk button. "Both of your doggies are dead, shithead. Come and get yours."

Rather than kill the security guard, Lee hoped to draw him away from the lobby. Having learned her way around the clinic, she hurried to a cross hall, where she slipped into a linen closet. By leaving it open a crack, she could peer out. It was only a matter of seconds before the dark bulk of the patrolman passed by. Once he was gone she slipped into the hall.

But he must have heard her because there was a shout followed by the crack of a pistol shot. The bullet missed her but hit the mirror at the other end of the corridor. It shattered into a hundred pieces. That was when Omo stepped out in front of her with a Colt in each hand. He shouted, "Get down!" and Lee had no choice but to obey. She dived forward, hit hard, and was skidding toward Omo when he fired both guns.

Lee rolled and scrambled to her feet. The Glock came up, but there was no need. The guard was down and clearly dead. She looked at Omo. "I told you to stay outside."

"You tell me all sorts of things," Omo replied. "Most of them are bullshit."

Lee smiled. "Come on . . . Let's get out of here."

They entered the lobby and left through the front door. And, much to Lee's surprise, the alarm didn't go off. That made sense, though, since it had been necessary for the rent-a-cop to turn the system off after he entered. So they closed the door and checked to ensure that it was locked. If they were lucky, it would be at least an hour before the patrolman was missed.

Thanks to Omo, the dead man's car had four flats. But the engine was running and the lights were on. That could attract attention so they turned everything off and locked all of the doors. They were in the rent-a-wreck and driving away when Omo asked the obvious question. "So? Any luck?"

"Hell, yes," Lee answered as she struggled to remove the printout from the waistband of her trousers. "Amanda was alive a few days ago—and I have a pretty good idea where she is."

Omo was at the wheel. He glanced her way. "I'm not going to like this, am I?"

Lee smiled tightly. "No, you aren't."

George Nickels's day began the way it always did, with a one-hour workout regimen, followed by a shower. Then, rather than eat at home, he preferred to make his way over to the hotel-casino complex and have breakfast in one of the many restaurants there. But not in a predictable manner.

That kept the staff on their toes, helped to ensure good service, and gave him a chance to table-hop. There was nothing customers enjoyed more than a two-minute conversation with the big boss. "Treat people with respect, and they'll come back." That's what George Senior had taught him, and it was true.

On that particular morning, he had chosen to eat in the Keno Room, which was adjacent to the so-called lounge where the game was played. Keno enthusiasts weren't high rollers for the most part—but they were very fond of the all-you-can-eat buffet in the restaurant.

Nickels was very careful about his diet, however—and always had the same breakfast. It consisted of coffee . . . At least two cups, a bowl of oatmeal, and a slice of organically grown cantaloupe.

Sometimes Nickels ate alone, and sometimes he invited a restaurant worker to join him. Some employees looked forward to such opportunities, and some dreaded them. But both groups had to agree that the boss was willing to listen.

After breakfast, Nickels went out to the lobby, where he could be seen running a finger over ledges prior to boarding the elevator that took him up to the executive suite. He had a large office with a view of the peak, the home that sat on top of it, and the column of water that shot out of the hillside.

Nickels liked his coffee hot, *very* hot, and a metal thermos was waiting for him as he circled around to the other side of his desk. It was a beautiful slab of Arizona marble resting on a custom-made frame. Nickels sat with his back to the view as he poured himself a cup of coffee, anointed the brew with cream and sugar, and took an experimental sip. It was perfect.

Then it was time to turn the computer terminal on, enter a six-digit code, and start the working day. The first task was to review the run sheets related to all of his legitimate business concerns. That included the hotel, the casino, and his percentage of what the mall shops brought in. And thanks to years of practice, he could identify problem areas and sweet spots with ease. Each item, good or bad, was written down so he could discuss them with the Ebben twins.

Once that process was complete, it was time to scan the reports related to the other profit centers. Those included drug smuggling, loan-sharking, and a high-end surrogate business. The kind reserved for only the wealthiest and most discriminating of clients. And, for the most part, those enterprises were doing well . . . Although there was a shortage of product.

After finishing one cup of coffee, Nickels poured another. Then he signaled his readiness to start what promised to be a long day by touching a black button. In keeping with a long-established tradition, the Ebben twins entered his office first.

They were dressed in a blue blazer, a white shirt with no tie, and khaki trousers. Based on their expressions, Nickels could tell that Orson was worried and Ethan was feeling good. "Good morning," Nickels said. "Please have a seat. What's going on?"

"You've seen the run sheets by now," Ethan said. "So you know that the bottom line looks good."

"That's true," Orson agreed, "but we have a problem."

"We *might* have a problem," Ethan said. "It's too early to be sure."

Nickels was used to that sort of bickering and nodded. "Okay, tell me about the problem that we might have."

"Someone broke into the Madison Medical Clinic last night," Orson said darkly.

"They didn't break in," Ethan corrected him. "A woman entered the facility and hid."

"That isn't important," Orson said impatiently. "The point is that they weren't after drugs. They went straight to the computer system and logged on."

Nickels frowned. "And I care because?"

"You care because we use the clinic's personnel to provide health care for our norms. They come by once a week to deal with minor health problems and perform physicals. Our customers are very finicky in that regard and insist on lots of documentation."

"Yes," Nickels said mildly, "I know. So the intruder had access to our records?"

"They did," Orson confirmed. "But they looked at a lot of other stuff, too."

"And that's why there's no reason to get excited," Ethan put in. "There's a strong possibility that the information they were after had nothing to do with the surrogacy product."

"Maybe," Orson allowed. "But when a security guard happened by, and went inside to perform a random check, they shot him. And his mutimals, too."

Nickels thought about that. "Have we got pictures of them? Or fingerprints?"

"No prints," Orson replied. "But we have a lot of pictures. Check your e-mail. I sent some samples."

Nickels opened the message and scrolled through the photos. "Why am I looking at a man who is lying on the floor?"

"He faked a heart attack to distract the staff," Orson replied. "That allowed the woman in the blue burqa to enter the clinic and hide until the employees left. She's the one who trolled the computer system for information."

Nickels kept going and stopped. "She took the burqa off . . . And she could be a norm."

"We think she *is* a norm," Orson said. "And there are very few norms in the Republic of Texas. That makes the situation all the more unusual."

"So what are we doing to identify her?"

"Chief Dokey is on it," Ethan said helpfully. "He's going to check with the Crime Information Center to see if we can match faces. As for the guy with two guns—he was wearing a mask. That will make the task more difficult."

"Okay, good work," Nickels said. "Better safe than sorry. Send the photos to security and tell them to keep an eye out for these people. What's next on the agenda?"

"Senora Avilar is waiting to see you," Ethan replied.

Nickels looked from one face to the other. "So what do you think? Should we sign up for her program or not?"

"I think we should," Orson answered. "Assuming the price is right."

Nickels nodded. "Okay, but how much can we afford?"

"No more than 250,000 a month," Ethan put in.

"I'll aim for two," Nickels replied.

"That sounds good," Orson said, as the twins got up to leave. "I wish we could tell her to screw off . . . But, given the consequences of that, anything under 250 is a viable proposition."

The twins left, and Senora Avilar was shown in a few moments later. Avilar's carefully coiffed black hair had been highlighted with a single streak of white, her red lipstick matched the pantsuit she wore, and there was a much-practiced smile on her face. "Senor Nickels . . . This is a pleasure."

Nickels's arm whirred as he went out to greet her. That was when he realized that there were only two digits on each of his visitor's well-manicured hand. "The pleasure is mine, Senora . . . Please. Have a seat. Would you care for some coffee or tea?"

"Gracias, no," Avilar said as she sat down. "I had breakfast a short time ago. You have an impressive complex here . . . Very impressive indeed. But what are we? Seventy miles from the border? That is well within striking distance. Does that concern you?"

Avilar's eyes were like chips of obsidian. Now Nickels realized that there would be no financial foreplay—no attempt to make the occasion seem like anything other than what it was: a form of extortion. He could pay her, and through her the generals who ran the Aztec military machine, or he could sit in his office and wait for the first missile to fall. So it wasn't a question of *whether* he would pay . . . But how much. "I *do* worry about that," Nickels said. "Not just for myself, but for my employees, and the citizens of Tucson."

"Because they are your customers," Avilar said coldly.

"Yes," Nickels admitted. "But for other reasons as well. I was born and raised here."

"On Aztec land," Avilar said sternly. "But that will change one day. In the meantime, there will be people who support the corrupt officials in Austin and will be hung with them, and those who support restoration. Realizing that those who support our cause are likely to prosper once the war is over."

Her meaning was clear. Senora Avilar was offering more than interim protection . . . She was selling a long-term insurance policy. And that sounded good . . . Or would if the service was affordable. "You make some excellent points," Nickels conceded. "What sort of contribution would you and your associates be looking for?"

"Three hundred thousand per month," Avilar said without hesitation. "Paid in nubucks or in gold."

That was interesting. It seemed that the Aztecs had faith in both Pacifica, and its currency but were so confident of victory they wouldn't accept eagles. Thus began a process of offer and counteroffer that eventually wound up at 225 nu per month. A sum that was twenty-five more than Nickels had been hoping for—but twenty-five less than the maximum the twins had suggested. "Okay," Nickels said finally. "It's a deal . . . But if a bomb or missile falls on Tucson, the whole thing is off."

"You will have to accept some hits," Avilar responded airily. "It would look suspicious if you didn't. But I think it's safe to say that your property and the surrounding area will suffer very little damage."

"Good," Nickels replied. "I will ask my co-CFOs to work out the details with you and your staff. My compliments to General Contreras. We've done business in the past."

"Yes," Avilar said as she stood. "He speaks well of you—and told me to tell you that he looks forward to staying in your hotel during the occupation."

Nickels saw Avilar to the door. Then it was time to have another cup of coffee and do some serious thinking. Maybe the Aztecs would seize control of Arizona, and maybe they wouldn't. Things could go either way . . . But it was important to formulate a backup plan. Something he could fall back on if things went wrong. And that would require money . . . Lots of it. His phone buzzed, but the call went unanswered.

A thirty-second story about the Madison Clinic shooting aired on the 11:00 p.m. news, but other than that, the incident received very little coverage. Was that because the break-in was small potatoes compared to the terrorist attack in Dallas? Or had Nickels and his cronies been able to figure out which file Lee had been interested in—and were using their influence to minimize coverage? Both possibilities were credible.

But while there hadn't been a lot of coverage, photos of Lee had been aired, along with a request that viewers contact the police if they saw her. Fortunately, Lee had been wearing a mask. Still, there was reason to be concerned. That's why she was wearing a cheap wig, face veil, and faking a limp as she entered the hotel. The plan was for Omo to arrive separately so that they wouldn't appear as a couple.

As Lee crossed the lobby, she felt the familiar emptiness at the pit of her stomach. Would some sharp-eyed security person see the similarities between the woman in the wig and the person in the clinic? If so, they would swarm her.

Lee approached the check-in counter and identified herself as Marsha Crowley. The clerk had so much loose skin on her face that Lee was reminded of a Shar Pei. She welcomed Lee to the hotel and entered her name into a computer. "Yes, here we go . . . You're staying just the one night?"

"Yes, that's correct."

"Good. I have you down for a king-sized bed and a no-smoking room."

"Perfect."

"Okay then, the deposit will be the 230 eagles, a hundred of which will be refunded if you don't incur any additional charges."

Lee was ready for that. Credit cards were a thing of the past, and cash or cash equivalents were king. She slid the appropriate number of notes across the desk. The clerk gave her a receipt, a keycard, and a twenty-eagle chip in return. "Please accept this gift—and enjoy your stay. The elevators are over there."

Lee thanked the woman, towed the suitcase over to the lifts, and felt a sense of relief. Things had gone well so far. The elevator carried her up to the third floor. From there, it was a short walk to room 306. She entered, left the suitcase by the dresser, and went over to the window. Her room faced the artificial lake and the mall beyond. Her cell phone rang, and she answered. "Hi there."

"Which room?"

"I'm in 306."

"I'll be there shortly."

Lee waited for the knock on the door and went to open it. Omo towed his suitcase into the room. "Okay, we're in. Now what?"

"Now we wait for evening," Lee replied. "I think it's safe to assume security is tight around the clock. But, if we find her, we'll have a better chance to escape when it's dark."

Omo shrugged. "So we'll wait. Who knows? Maybe we can find an enjoyable way to pass the time."

Lee laughed. "Really? You want to have sex with someone who looks like I do?"

"The wig is hot."

"You're a sick man."

"Yup. Close the curtains."

Lee obeyed, felt his arms encircle her waist, and let herself go.

Jimmy was pissed. And for good reason. His supervisor, a troll-like man named Huggins, had assigned him to night duty. Never mind the fact that it wasn't his turn. And, if that wasn't bad enough, he'd been sent to 409 to clear a really gross backup in the toilet. Now it was off to 306 to fix the AC. The tool cart made a rattling noise as he pushed it off the elevator and down the hall. Three-zero-six was on the left. He knocked on the door and was careful to announce himself. "Hotel maintenance!"

The door opened, and a woman wearing a veil gestured for him to enter. He did, and that was when he saw a man dressed in a uniform very similar to his own. The man said, "Howdy," and pointed a Taser at him.

Jimmy went rigid as fifty-five thousand volts hit him, he lost motor control, and began to fall. The man stepped forward to catch and lower him to the floor. As the current went off, the woman slapped a pair of cuffs on his wrists. Jimmy opened his mouth to swear, but that was a mistake, because the man took the opportunity to shove a washcloth into his mouth. Jimmy was trying to spit it out when the woman taped it down.

So Jimmy kicked with his feet, or tried to, but couldn't. Not with the man pressing down on his legs. He felt something tighten around his ankles and knew he'd been hog-tied. He couldn't move but he could hear. "Got the keys?"

"Yup."

"Got the radio?"

"Yup."

"Okay . . . Let's do this thing."

Jimmy heard the door close and tried to roll over. He couldn't. The bed . . . He was tied to the bed. Would Huggins come looking? Or would he be forced to lie there until the maid came in the morning? The answer was important because Jimmy needed to pee.

The empty suitcases had been left behind—and the cart rattled loudly as Omo pushed it down the hall. He was dressed in an outfit that was nearly identical to the one that the maintenance man had on. Lee had chosen business attire which, when combined with a name tag and clipboard, made her look like a manager.

The elevator was on another floor, according to the number displayed on the indicator above the doors. So they had to wait. Lee made use of the time to monitor the radio. She couldn't eavesdrop on security because the handset was locked to the channel used by the hotel's maintenance personnel. There wasn't any chatter about a missing worker, though . . . And she chose to interpret that as a good sign.

The doors opened to reveal the very person Lee feared the most: another maintenance person. She was a heavyset woman who was wearing glasses so thick they looked like goggles. She leaned forward to peer at Omo's name tag as he pushed his cart in next to hers. "Ruiz? I don't think we've met."

"That's because he's new," Lee said, as the doors closed. "My name's Debbie . . . I'm with HR."

"Okay," the woman said, as the lift stopped on the second floor. "Welcome aboard, Ruiz. My name is Collins. Give me a holler if you need any help. There's a lot to learn."

"Thanks," Omo said. "I will."

Lee felt a tremendous sense of relief as Collins left, and the doors closed behind her. Thankfully, the elevator passed the first floor and went directly to the tunnel level.

A food cart was waiting there, but the worker in charge of it was busy filing her claws, and barely glanced at them as they got off. There was only one way to go—and that was down the well-lit tunnel.

Omo pushed the cart as Lee examined her surroundings and sought to memorize any details that might be helpful later on. A well-lit exit sign drew her interest. If they were forced to run, the stairs might provide a quick way out. "Uh-oh," Omo said, as they approached the east end of the tunnel. "I see a problem."

Lee saw that a security guard, no, a uniformed *policeman*, was stationed in front of the elevator. And he was armed with an assault weapon. Was that something new? Or was that the norm? "Get ready to take him out," Lee said from the corner of her mouth.

Omo nodded. The Taser was in front of him, in among some tools.

"Good evening, Officer," Lee said. "How's it going?"

"Just fine," the cop said noncommittally. "I'll need to see your ID cards."

The officer produced a grunt as Omo shot him in the chest, and neither one of them bothered to break the man's fall. Lee was calling for an elevator, *any* elevator, and Omo wasn't close enough.

An elevator arrived seconds later. Once the doors hissed open, Omo towed the cop aboard. Lee followed with the cart. Then it was a simple matter to close the doors and push the stop button.

By the time the policeman had regained control of his body, he was wearing his own cuffs, and plastic ties from the cart had been used to secure his ankles. He was about to say something when Lee slapped a piece of duct tape over his mouth. So far so good . . . But their luck was running out. Had the attack been captured by a camera? Of course it had . . . That meant a whole shitload of trouble could be on the way.

Lee said, "Shit, shit, shit," as she ran a finger down the list of potential destinations. The choices included, residence, guests, and storage. So Lee stabbed the button next to the word guests and hoped for the best. She turned to Omo as the elevator went into motion. "Give me half the keys . . . We can open doors faster that way."

Omo slid a fistful of keys off the five-inch ring and gave them to her. Then he removed the Colts from a toolbox and stuck them into his waistband. That left his hands free to use the rest of the keys and the assault weapon that was slung over one shoulder.

The doors parted as the elevator came to a halt. Lee pushed the stop button and led Omo out into a hall lined with steel doors. Omo scored the first victory and called Lee over. But when they opened the door, it was onto an empty suite.

Undeterred, they went back to work. A second unit was empty, too . . . But Lee had a premonition as she opened the next lock. This was the one! And sure enough, as the door swung open, there was Amanda Screed. Her hair was different, and she had a black eye, but the face matched the photos Lee had seen. But there was no joy in the young woman's face. And the reason for that became obvious as the man with two heads stepped out of the bedroom. He was armed with a machine pistol, and Omo was about to draw the Colts, when a gun barrel prodded his back. The assault rifle was confiscated moments later.

"You're going to be sorry," one of the heads said.

"But not for long," the other added. "Not for long."

FOURTEEN

"**P**lace your hands on your head! Spread your feet!" The orders came in quick succession as the prisoners were disarmed. Lee's veil was ripped off so that a police officer could check her ID. Fortunately, a pair of nostril filters were still in place, but it was important to avoid breathing through her mouth. "Well, look what we have here, a norm from LA!" he said. "What's the matter, honey? Did you take a wrong turn or something?" The cop had pink eyes and blubbery lips. Lee could smell the garlic on his breath.

"That ain't nothing," another officer said. "It looks like Arpo sent one of his boys down to poke around."

"Chief Dokey won't like that," a third man predicted. "Take that hood off . . . Let's see what ugly looks like."

The hood came off, which prompted the first officer to say, "Eew, that's gross! Put it back on."

"Cut the crap," one of the twins said irritably. "Take them upstairs. The girl, too."

Both prisoners were cuffed prior to being pushed and shoved out into the hall. Lee was scared and for good reason. Except for the man she assumed to be Tom-Tom, the rest of them were uniformed police officers. That meant there was no hope of a rescue.

The elevator ride took less than a minute. And once the doors opened, the prisoners were herded along a curving window, past a bar, and out into a well-furnished great room. Nickels was seated in a leather chair and talking on a phone. A servo whirred as he lifted a hand to signal for silence. Lee took note of the way Nickels had chosen to emphasize his physical deformities rather than try to conceal them. It was an act of defiance and one she could relate to.

Nickels looked from Lee, to Omo, then to Amanda as he tucked the phone away. "It was a mistake to do business with your father. If I had the whole thing to do over again, I'd tell him to fuck off."

Amanda was clearly surprised. "You spoke to my father?"

Nickels laughed. "That's right . . . You don't know! Your father asked me to loan him half a ton of cocaine, and I agreed, but only if he gave me some collateral. And *you* are that collateral."

"That doesn't make any sense," Lee put in. "Why would Bishop Screed want to borrow half a ton of coke?"

"So he could sell it," Nickels replied, "and use the money to recruit more members. Believers who would require more churches, donate more money, and vote the way he wants them to."

"But he *hates* mutants," Lee objected. "That's fundamental to his religion."

Nickels laughed. "No, that's fundamental to his *business*."

"So you never intended to use Amanda as a surrogate," Omo said.

"No, I didn't," Nickels said. "I took a risk, and that was a mistake. Bishop Screed was supposed to make his first payment a week ago. He didn't. So I plan to send him one of Amanda's fingers. That should jog his memory."

"Maybe it will," Lee allowed. "But what if Screed wrote her off? What if he *never* planned to pay?"

Tom-Tom had placed both sets of ID on the table next to Nickels. He opened a case and peered at Lee. "I wouldn't like that. You're from LA?"

"Yes." The nearest mutant was ten feet away. Was that enough distance? Lee hoped so.

"Why did you come here?"

"Amanda was kidnapped. That's a crime."

"That's it? Nothing more?"

"Bishop Screed put pressure on the mayor—who put pressure on the chief of police."

"*See?*" Nickels said triumphantly. "The Bishop cares."

"Or he wants it to look as if he cares," Lee put in cynically.

Nickels sighed. "You may be right . . . If so, I will send people to kill the bastard."

He turned to Omo. "How about *you*? Why are you here? Sheriff Arpo is making a big mistake if he thinks he can extend his reach to Tucson."

"I'm on vacation," Omo said matter-of-factly. "And I had nothing better to do."

Nickels laughed. The sound had a harsh quality. "She's pretty . . . I get that. But this isn't going to end the way you hoped. That's what happens when you think with your dick."

Then, turning to the police officers, Nickels spoke again. "Take the trash out, boys . . . You know what to do. And stop by the payout window in the casino when you get back. You'll like what's waiting for you."

Amanda was sobbing by then. She'd been used, by her father no less, and left to die. And the police officers sent to find her were about to be killed. "I'm sorry!" she shouted, as the other prisoners were taken away. "I didn't know!" There was no answer.

Lee's mind was racing as she tried to come up with a plan by which she could turn the tables on her captors. None was forthcoming. The police officers were professionals and not about to provide the prisoners with an opening.

So that left Lee with nothing to do but think during the subsequent elevator ride and the long march through the tunnel. Why had she been so stupid? The whole notion of invading the complex was insane. Somewhere along the line, her sense of determination had been allowed to overwhelm common sense, and now she was going to pay the price.

Worse yet, *Omo* was going to pay the price, too. Like Conti, he was in love with her—and like Conti, that was going to get him killed. Of course, *she* was going to die this time, and that was fair. Was there an afterlife of some sort? A place where she would see her father? And did she want to? Because if Frank Lee wasn't a murderer, he was something damned close.

Lee's thoughts were interrupted as one of the officers shoved her into an elevator. It took them up to the level located directly below the hotel-casino complex. Then they were escorted through a maze of pumps, boilers, and other equipment to an exit sign and a flight of stairs. "Hurry up," one of the men said. "We ain't got all night."

The stairs led up to a door that opened onto a moonlight-glazed parking lot. Lee felt the cool air touch her skin, saw three squad cars parked side by side, and heard the distant tinkle of music. Lights flashed as one of the cars responded to a remote. Once the doors were open, the prisoners were ordered to get inside. A wire-mesh screen separated the front seats from those in back. The car lurched slightly as two of the officers got in the front, and the third offered a wave.

That cut the odds by a third . . . But so what? Lee couldn't see any way to take advantage of the situation as the engine started and the officer in the passenger seat called in. "This is Two-Ida-Four. We'll be 10-10 (out of service) for half an hour or so."

The response was matter-of-fact. "Copy that . . . Over."

So that's what they were. A chore to be taken care of before a return to duty. "How's it going back there?" the cop on the right inquired. "I hope you don't shit your pants . . . This car stinks bad enough already."

Both officers laughed as the car sped up an on-ramp and onto I-10 south. There wasn't much traffic because of the blackout, and most of the vehicles around them were doing sixty or so. Lee considered an attempt to signal the people in the other cars but quickly realized how futile that would be. So what if the prisoners in the back of a police car pounded on the window? That's what prisoners do.

It was too dark to make out the street signs, and Lee didn't know the area all that well, so it meant nothing to her when the squad car left the freeway. That was followed by a series of turns as the car continued generally south before taking a final left. As it did, the wash from the lights slid across a sign that said, landfill. Of course . . . The perfect place to dump a couple of bodies.

The cruiser continued for a bit and came to a stop in front of a double gate. The driver remained behind the wheel as his partner got out. The stench of rotting garbage flooded the car and caught at the back of Lee's throat.

After unlocking the gate, the second officer got back in, and the squad car pulled ahead. Thanks to the moonlight, Lee could see some low-lying buildings, a row of recycling bins, and the dark bulk of a bulldozer. Then the surface of the road began to deteriorate as the car lurched through some major potholes. "Okay, that's far enough," the driver said.

"Works for me," the second man said cheerfully. "Let's get this over with."

The cops had their weapons drawn as they opened the back doors and ordered the prisoners to get out. The officers were divided at that point, and Lee thought about trying to charge the cop on her side of the car. Maybe she could head-butt him. No, the bastard was too far away for that.

Maybe she should run then . . . The cop would fire, but there was the possibility that he would miss. Yes, Lee decided, some chance was better than none. But wait . . . What about Omo? She couldn't leave without him. Then it was too late to execute her plan as she was ordered to circle around and stand beside her partner. His hands were cuffed in front of him, but he could still use them to pull the hood off. His face looked like raw meat, and there was defiance in his eyes. "I'm sorry," Lee said.

"Me too," Omo replied.

Both police officers stood with their backs to the car and weapons raised. Lee closed her eyes. The shots came in rapid succession. But the hammerlike blows that Lee expected never struck her body. She heard a grunt, assumed it was from Omo, and opened her eyes.

Both of the cops were down, and a man was standing over them. She couldn't make out his face, only a long, lean body, which was silhouetted in front of the car. At least one of the policemen was still alive. "Please! No!"

But it appeared that the man was enjoying himself. "What's wrong, pig . . . Does that hurt? I hope so." The man fired, and the cop jerked in response.

Omo took a step forward and stopped as the long-barreled pistol swung around to point at him. "Don't try it asshole. I want Detective Lee to live a little longer. You're expendable."

Lee tried to think—tried to focus. "You're the Bonebreaker . . . You followed me. *How?*"

The man with the pistol laughed. "Trackers the size of BBs. They're in your clothes, in your luggage, you name it."

"But *why?*"

"You know why . . . For those who died. I'm the one God sent to kill the monsters and their progeny. That's why you're going to die the way your father died. But not yet! I, and I alone, will decide the how and the when. So leave this place, return to Los Angeles, and wait for me to summon you."

The gunman had already begun to back away and soon faded into the night. Then Lee heard an engine start and knew that a serial killer was getting away. There was nothing she could do about it though . . . Nothing at all.

"That is one crazy motherfucker," Omo said calmly.

"Yes," Lee said, "he sure as hell is." Her body had begun to shake by then, and Omo put an arm around her shoulders.

"We're alive."

"Yes, I guess we are."

"Maybe we should take a look at those guys . . . Check for a pulse."

Lee nodded and followed Omo over to the bodies. Thanks to the light from the moon, and the patrol car's parking lights, they could see fairly well. A quick check confirmed that both men were dead. "Now what?" Omo said.

"Collect their weapons," Lee suggested. "I'll check the trunk."

Lee went over to the car, opened the driver's side door, and pulled the trunk release. She heard it open and went back to take a look. The trunk light was on. There was a lot of gear inside, including a large first-aid kit, a toolbox, and more. But none of that held any interest for Lee. What she wanted was front and center. She said, "Bingo," and removed a tac vest from the pile. It was heavy with ammo and gear and the acronym "SWAT" was emblazoned across the front of it.

Most patrol officers didn't carry weapons in the back of their squad cars, but members of the SWAT team did, and Lee was pleased to see a second vest, plus some additional firepower. She was still taking inventory when Omo arrived. "Here," he said as he gave her a Glock 19. "There's one in the chamber. I checked."

Lee slipped the weapon into her empty shoulder holster and accepted a couple of spare magazines to go with it. "Thanks, Ras . . . How 'bout you?"

Omo was wearing the hood again. A gun belt was buckled around his waist. "I have a Glock."

"There's a 12-gauge up front," Lee said, "and look at this stuff . . . We're ready to rumble."

"Meaning what?" Omo wanted to know.

"I have two choices," Lee replied. "I can make a run for the border right now. Or I can go back, get Amanda, and make a run for the border."

Omo looked at her. "Where do I come in?"

"You don't."

"I know what you're trying to do," Omo replied. "But here's the deal . . . If you're going after Amanda, so am I. Not because I'm in love with you, but because I'm a cop, and you need some backup."

Lee felt torn. On the one hand, she didn't want Omo to risk his life for her. And she was concerned about the true nature of his motivations. But he was a cop—and a good one.

Ultimately, it came down to his final argument. It might be possible to rescue Amanda, but she wouldn't be able to do it alone. Two people would be the absolute minimum for such a raid. She looked at him. "You're sure."

"I am."

"All right, let's gear up. The patrol car will allow us to get in close. After that? Well, things are likely to get interesting."

The next half hour was spent revising the way the vests were loaded, checking their newly acquired weapons, and testing their com gear. Then it was time to get in the car and head back to the hotel-casino complex. Both of which were open twenty-four/seven. Omo was driving, and that left Lee free to think. "Remember the trip through the tunnel? And the exit we passed? Let's find the point where the stairs reach the surface. Maybe we can use the exit as an entrance."

"Sounds good," Omo said, as they left I-10. "We're about ten minutes out."

Lee nodded. "Okay, put out the call."

Since both of the dead cops were male, Omo was the logical choice to call in. "This is Two-Ida-Four. We have a terrorist attack, repeat terrorist attack, taking place at four-one-one North Central Avenue. It looks like they're parachuting in. Code 6A. Oh shit, they blew up a building!"

Then, as the dispatcher started to respond, Lee killed the radio. "They blew up a building? Where did that come from?"

"I was ad-libbing."

Lee laughed. "Well, that should keep 'em busy for a while."

Once they entered the vast parking lot that served the mall-hotel-casino complex, Omo wound his way over to the open area that separated the hotel from Nickels Peak. And sure enough, there was a small, shedlike structure, right where they thought it would be. And when Omo turned the headlights on for a brief moment, Lee saw the emergency exit sign. "Okay," she said, "let's do this." The hope was that they'd be able to leave the same way they went in. So Omo parked with the car headed out—and was careful to lock the doors.

Omo had replaced his hood with a knit mask issued by the Tucson Police Department. He was wearing a SWAT helmet and a face shield over that. He made his way over to the door, tried to turn the knob, and found that the barrier was locked. "Stand back," he said. "It's time to use the master key."

The so-called master key consisted of the patrol car's 12-gauge shotgun loaded with eight "breaching" rounds specifically designed for opening doors. The trick was to destroy the hinges rather than the lock because that might jam. There was some risk, however, since the shells were designed for wood doors.

Omo stood at an angle, fired, and saw the top hinge part company with the door frame. Tiny bits of metal peppered his face shield, the Kevlar vest, and his forearms. They stung but did no real damage.

So Omo pumped another door buster into the chamber and blew the second hinge away. The door sagged and gave when Lee stuck a tire iron into the gap and pushed. She said, "Nice job, Cowboy," and Omo felt a silly sense of pride.

He thumbed two additional rounds into the shotgun as Lee led the way down a flight of steep stairs to the tunnel level below. Then it was time to pause as she cracked the door and peeked into the hallway. "It's clear. Let's go for it."

Omo had slung the shotgun across his back by then and was holding a six-shot 40mm grenade launcher instead. It was loaded with canisters of pepper spray in the hope that they would be able to incapacitate people rather than kill them.

But Lee was carrying an ugly-looking submachine gun (SMG) and was ready to use it if necessary. Omo followed her down the tunnel, turning occasionally to check their six. He figured that an alarm had gone off the moment they forced the door. Maybe, if they were lucky, a rent-a-cop would be sent to investigate. If so, he or she would see the cop car and assume that Dokey's goons were responding to some sort of problem. And if a *real* police officer showed up? Then the poop would hit the fan in a hurry.

Lee was happy with the way things had gone so far—but knew that couldn't last. And her premonition came true as a pair of stainless-steel doors opened to reveal a load of well-dressed passengers. Guests perhaps? Leaving some sort of function? Lee raised her weapon so that the barrel was pointed at the ceiling. "Sorry, folks . . . We're running a routine security sweep. Nothing to worry about. Have a nice evening."

One of the men raised a hand by way of an acknowledgment, and the group left for the casino, chatting merrily as they went. Lee felt a sense of relief and followed Omo onto the elevator. Having been there only hours earlier, she knew that the level labeled guests was the one she wanted. She pushed the button.

As the car rose, Lee prepared herself for trouble. It seemed likely that security had been strengthened since their last attempt to free Amanda. Lee was ready to fire as the lift came to a stop, and the doors opened. But there was nothing to fire at. The elevator lobby was empty. Omo stood ready to provide cover fire as Lee took a peek around the corner. There was no one in sight.

That meant absolutely nothing, of course. The corridor had been empty last time as well. The trap had been waiting *inside* unit G-3. Lee waved Omo forward. He switched to the shotgun and pointed it at the door. There was a loud BOOM, quickly followed by a second blast. The door shattered. Lee kicked it open and went in ready to kill. The apartment appeared to be empty. Omo stood guard while Lee raced from room to room. Amanda was gone! She swore. "Maybe she's in one of the other apartments."

So Omo went down the hall firing on door after door. Lee was right behind him, ready to dash in and check each apartment out. All of them were vacant.

By that time, Lee was both frightened and frustrated. Had they walked into an even larger trap? Was Amanda being held at some other location? If so, the chances of finding her were nearly nonexistent. "I think we should go upstairs and pay Mr. Nickels a visit," Omo suggested. "Maybe Amanda is there. But even if she isn't, we can arrest Nickels and take him with us. We don't have jurisdiction, but who knows? Maybe Sheriff Arpo can trade him for Amanda."

Lee looked at him. "You're a freaking genius! Let's go."

"Well, I'm a freak anyway," Omo said. But Lee didn't hear him.

Somewhere between the guest level and the floor above, Lee felt all of her doubts drop away. She was going to do what she had to do, whatever that turned out to be, and God help anyone stupid enough to get in the way.

The elevator doors opened, and there was a cop! He looked at them, frowned, and went for his gun. Lee shot him in the head. The second and third bullets were superfluous, but the submachine gun was set for three-round bursts, so he got more than his share.

Omo was already on his way to the bar and great room by

then. The shotgun was slung across his back, and the grenade launcher was ready to go. A party was under way, about two dozen nicely dressed people were standing around holding drinks, and most of them were looking his way. Which was to say in the direction of the shots heard moments earlier.

As Omo aimed the launcher at the crowd they backed away. "Hold it right there!" he ordered. "Drop the drinks and place your hands on your heads! Do it *now!*"

Lee had arrived by then and fired a burst over their heads. The bullets passed through the blackout curtain and shattered a window on the far side of the room. That was when she saw motion out of the corner of her eye and turned just in time to see a man and the chair he was seated on disappear! Nickels? Yes . . . But wait . . . A bikini-clad girl was chained to the platform! "There she is!" Lee shouted. "It's Amanda! Free her . . . I'll cover the crowd."

Amanda could hardly believe her eyes! Here, out of nowhere, were the police officers who had been sent to their deaths! And not only were they alive, they were heavily armed and in charge. She was fumbling with the leather collar when the man came to help her. "Don't worry," he said. "We'll get you out of here this time."

Amanda felt the collar drop away and immediately went over to where Mac was standing with her hands locked behind her neck. Amanda could see the fear in the other woman's eyes as she reached in to tug the stun gun out of its holster.

Amanda heard the male police officer yell at her but ignored his command in order to aim the stun gun at Mac and pull the trigger. Nothing happened. Amanda looked, saw the brightly colored safety, and thumbed it off. Then she tried again. Mac knew what was coming and tried to fend it off with her hands. The shock put her down hard, and Amanda was kicking the woman in the head when Omo grabbed her arm. "We don't have time for that," he said. "My name is Omo. Come with me."

* * *

Lee was still holding the crowd at bay by aiming the submachine gun at them. "Stay here. If you try to follow us, we will kill you." And with that, she backed away.

Omo had pushed the stop button prior to getting off the elevator, so it was still buzzing when they arrived. Lee paused to grab the Glock that lay a few feet away from the dead policeman. She gave it to Amanda. "Hold it straight out in front of you, aim, and pull the trigger. Can you do that?"

Amanda looked up from the pistol and nodded. "But stop pointing it at Lee," Omo said. "Come on, let's move."

They piled onto the lift and rode it down to the tunnel without incident. Nickels was on the loose. That meant members of his private security force *and* the police would be on the way. So Lee figured that an armed reception committee would be waiting for them when the elevator came to a stop. But the only person there was a surprised kitchen worker with a hot cart. He stood with his mouth hanging open as two heavily armed cops and a girl in a bikini left the lift and began to run.

Amanda took two steps, realized there was no way she could run in high heels, and paused to kick them off. Then she had to sprint in order to catch up with the others. And that was when she heard Omo yell, "There they are!" and saw a hastily constructed barricade in the distance. It consisted of two golf carts parked crosswise across the tunnel. At least a dozen people were hiding behind the flimsy barrier, and they opened fire.

Amanda saw the police officers hit the floor, so she took a dive as well, and hit hard. The Glock skittered away, and she had to crawl after it. Meanwhile, bullets were glancing off the ceiling, walls, and floor and zinging all about. That meant it was only a matter of time before somebody took a hit. Then she heard a chugging sound as Omo fired a short, stubby weapon. That sent an object hurtling down the corridor. There was a flash of light and a loud boom as one of the golf carts took a direct hit.

But in spite of the damage, more than half of the security people remained unharmed and came charging out of the swirling smoke. That was brave, and it was smart, since they knew that the grenade launcher was a long-range weapon. And if they could close in on Omo, he wouldn't be able to use it effectively.

Tom-Tom was in the lead. The twins couldn't run very well, but they came shuffling forward, firing from the hip. Lee responded with a burst from the SMG. Two bullets went wide but the third hit Ethan and killed him instantly.

The dead head flapped wildly as Orson continued to advance shouting incoherent swear words and sobbing at the same time. Suddenly a grenade struck his chest and blew his body apart. By that time, all the security people were down, and the tunnel looked like a slaughterhouse.

Amanda had to run barefoot across blood-slicked concrete in order to follow the others through a maze of bodies to the exit beyond. Omo opened the door and held it for her. She ran up a steep flight of stairs, came to another door, and pushed it open. Cold air hit her mostly naked body and caused Amanda to shiver, but she didn't care. She was free!

Lights blipped as Omo aimed the remote at the cop car and all of them hurried to get in. "Buckle up," Omo advised. "This could get interesting."

Omo took off, with the roof lights lit and the siren on. Meanwhile, Lee was on the radio providing a mostly accurate report about the fight in the tunnel. Except, according to her, ". . . The perps are heading into the hotel. We need backup, and we need it bad."

Maybe the goons were onto the fact that Two-Ida-Four had been hijacked. Or maybe, in the midst of all the confusion, they would buy the latest false report and send every available squad car to the hotel-casino complex. Especially since they had corroborating reports by then. And, judging from the number of police cars that passed going the other way, the trick was working.

Omo could see better with the headlights on. There wasn't

much traffic, but what there was hurried to get out of his way. A series of deftly executed turns took the car onto I-10 northbound. There was no plan. Maybe that was an oversight. Or maybe it was because neither of the police officers had thought they would get that far.

Having been left to his own devices, Omo was going to make a run for Phoenix. Sheriff Arpo would be pissed, there would be all sorts of hell to pay, but they'd be safe. And Lee had no objection to that so long as it worked.

But as Lee eyed the highway ahead, she could see lots of red brake lights and stuttering blue lights up ahead. It was a checkpoint! The Tucson police knew the people they were after would head for Phoenix and were determined to stop them.

They were in the fast lane. Omo saw the problem, too, said "Hang on!" and whipped the wheel to the left. That took them through a "turnaround" in the concrete barrier that separated northbound traffic from southbound traffic. Such passes were normally used by the police as a way to access accidents more quickly.

But rather than turn south, the way he might be expected to, Omo went *north* and into oncoming traffic. Lee swore and held on to a grab bar as a horn blared and a semi missed them by inches. Then they were speeding up the inside shoulder with lights flashing and siren bleating. Cars swerved, ran into each other, and piled up.

Shortly thereafter, Omo saw an opening and drove diagonally across the road in order to reach the opposite shoulder. Once there, he continued northbound, which forced southbound traffic to move left. That triggered a series of fender benders as he waited for an opportunity to exit the freeway. That chance came as Omo pulled up alongside an off-ramp.

But in order to take advantage of the escape route, Omo had to slow down and make a hard left. Unfortunately, the car's turning radius wasn't up to the challenge and he had to brake or hit a concrete retaining wall. Tires screeched as he was forced to back up and turn some more. Rubber burned as Omo stomped on the gas. Moments later, they found themselves on North Freeway Road. It paralleled the freeway and was lined with shabby homes, small businesses, and empty lots. "What we need is a major road that will take us west!" Omo said. "Keep your eyes peeled."

Lee understood, but there wasn't much she could do to help. She caught a glimpse of the brightly lit roadblock as they passed it for the *second* time. When she glanced back over her shoulder she saw Amanda's frightened face beyond the wire-mesh screen. Flashing lights were visible through the back window. "We have a cop car on our six," she warned.

"Yeah, I know," Omo said grimly. "I'll shake him."

Even though the blackout was in effect, traffic signals were still working, and Lee saw one up ahead. It was red. Omo slowed but blew through it as he took a right-hand turn onto West Grant Road. He continued on for three blocks before taking a sudden right. That was when he killed the light bar, pulled in under an apartment house, and turned the engine off.

All three of them were looking back through the rear window when the squad car roared past with lights flashing. That was Omo's signal to turn the engine on, back out, and return to West Grant Road. Then, with everything except the parking lights extinguished, he drove along at the legal limit. And with no streetlights to give it away, the squad car would look like any other vehicle unless someone got up close.

Lee stared out the back, expecting to see the cop car appear at any moment, and was glad when it didn't. "Nice work, Cowboy . . . Let's continue for a few miles, look for a good ride, and pull it over."

Omo glanced at her. "You would do that to mom and pop?"

"I'll be sorry," Lee said. "But we need some new wheels. When the sun comes up, this thing will be very easy to spot."

"Excuse me," came a voice from the back. "But could we stop somewhere and buy some clothes? I'm freezing."

Lee looked back, remembered the bikini, and chuckled. "I'll bet you are. Crank up the heat, Ras . . . Maybe that will help."

There was a moment of silence. Then Amanda spoke again. "Thank you. I will never forget what you did."

"You're welcome," Lee told her. "And, based on what I've seen, you're well worth saving."

"You heard what Mr. Nickels said," Amanda replied. "About the deal with my father."

"Yes, we heard," Lee said.

"That means Mr. Nickels will try to get me back, hoping that my father cares."

Omo glanced toward the back. "Does he?"

Amanda was silent for a moment. Her voice wavered. "No, I don't think he does."

It was a harsh assessment but one that neither one of the people in the front seat could argue with. "Hold on," Lee said. "We'll find you something to wear soon."

The Roadhouse was spacious inside, with plenty of tables, and a stage surrounded by chicken wire. The girl with the blue hair didn't need any protection, however. She had a rich, sultry voice, and knew how to use it. So as she sang a song called "Laura's Eyes," even the pool players paused to listen. And Lenny was no exception. He had tentacles rather than arms and used one to grab his beer. It was the fourteenth of the twelve he allowed himself to have each night. The ice-cold liquid felt good going down, and Lenny felt the tears begin to well up as the song came to a sad conclusion.

But tears weren't permissible in the Roadhouse. So Lenny fought them back and swore as his phone began to vibrate. He pulled the device out of his hip pocket and made used of a tentacle tip to turn it on. There was no message. Just a photo of his three-year-old son looking into the camera and laughing. That was Sally's way of telling him to come home. No lectures, no threats, just a picture of Jimmy.

Lenny felt a surge of guilt, put the cue stick down, and said good-bye to his friends. Except they *weren't* his friends, not to Sally's way of thinking, and he had a dim awareness that she was right.

Lenny knew the way to the front door by heart—and that was a good thing since he was a bit wobbly by then. An elongated version of his shadow shot out onto the ground when he opened the door and disappeared as springs pulled it closed.

Gravel crunched under Lenny's cowboy boots as he crossed the parking lot to where Big Hoss was parked. The especiale was a thing of beauty, and next to his family, the thing he loved most in the world.

Lenny paused at that point and was taking a pee, when the cop car came to life. It was parked next to his truck and Lenny raised a hand to shield his eyes from the light as the headlights came on. And that's where he was, dick in hand, when the girl in the bikini appeared. She shook her head and waggled a finger at him. "Peeing in public is illegal," she said. "And you're drunk. Give me your car keys."

Lenny had experienced hallucinations before and learned to ignore them. So he was busy stuffing his penis back into his pants when Omo Tasered him. Lenny felt his muscles lock up as he toppled face forward onto the patch of wet gravel. Hands patted him down. "Here we go," a female voice said. "I have his keys."

"Good," a man said. "Let's get out of here."

There were crunching sounds, followed by the roar of a very familiar engine, and the rattle of gravel. That was when the phone started to vibrate, and Lenny knew he was in trouble.

FIFTEEN

After stealing the SUV, Lee, Omo, and Amanda drove south until they came to Highway 86. They sure as hell couldn't go east, not with the entire Tucson police force searching for them, so they went west.

After an hour of uneventful driving, they entered the town of Sells. It was obvious that the locals weren't following the blackout regulations. Lights could be seen in some of the houses, and most of the vehicles had their headlights on.

As they drove around town, it quickly became clear that only one business was open at that hour, and that was the brightly lit Crazy Coyote gas station and convenience store. So Omo pulled in, left the engine running so that Amanda could stay warm, and followed Lee inside.

Like many stores of its type, the Coyote stocked a little bit of everything. So Omo shopped for food while Lee went back to examine a small collection of clothing. Most of it was the sort of stuff that truck drivers and construction workers might buy.

When they arrived at the cash register, a man with a pointy head was there to serve them. Omo was no physician, but it looked as though pressure from the cranial deformity was pushing the man's eyes forward and to the sides.

The sight of that made Omo feel grateful regarding his own mutation. That was one of the realities in the red zone. No matter how bad your condition, was someone else was worse off. The clerk was curious and began to ask questions as he tallied their purchases. "So," he said casually, "where are you folks headed?"

"To Tucson," Omo answered. "To visit my family."

"Yeah, I'm looking forward to seeing your mother," Lee said sarcastically.

The clerk laughed. "Fifty worth of gas plus the merchandise comes to 127 eagles. Or eighty-five nubucks if you prefer." It seemed that both customers were low on cash because they had to rummage through their pockets and combine what they had to come up with enough money. That didn't surprise the clerk since half the people who came through Sells were short of cash. So he rang up the purchases, dispensed a small amount of change, and said good-bye.

As the couple left, the clerk watched them go via a security camera, made use of a joystick to zoom in on the truck's license plate, and wrote it down. The police were looking for a very similar couple . . . It was all over the news. Cop killers, that's what the folks on Channel 7 said, and a large reward had been offered. Enough money to pay for the operation he needed. The clerk thumbed his phone and began to dial.

The sun was rising in the east as the Aztec army crossed the border at a point roughly halfway between San Luis and Nogales. Hundreds of vehicles were involved, and each of them sent a rooster tail of dust up into the cold air as they lurched through gullies and raced across the flat spots. But it was General Santiago Jocobo Contreras and the crew of his command car who entered the Republic of Texas first.

That accomplishment would look good in his next report. But it was largely meaningless because the only thing that barred the way was a border post manned by eight Republicans and a mangy dog. The latter was the only member of the detachment who wasn't taken by surprise.

And that was the plan . . . To take the enemy by surprise, drive a wedge between the Republic of Texas and Pacifica, and put points on the board quickly. Besides, Contreras couldn't attack cities like Tucson and Phoenix without cutting off the flow of protection money that was pouring in from more than a dozen wealthy "clients." That stream of income would have to be sacrificed before too long, but why hurry?

So rather than burden himself with prisoners Contreras told his men to kill the Republicans and spare the dog. He liked dogs and detested people who were cruel to them. One of the soldiers yelled "Remember the Alamo!" just before a quick rattle of gunfire took his life.

Then, as airplanes arrived to support them, the vehicles took off again. Within minutes, they were inside of the Barry M. Goldwater Air Force Range. The huge reservation had once been an important military base. And soon, thanks to his leadership, the range would serve the Second Empire. The thought pleased Contreras as he waved his tanks forward. What was the saying the nortenos liked to use? "Payback is a bitch?" Yes . . . And the time had come.

After departing the town of Sells, Omo, Lee, and Amanda continued west until they found a likely-looking side road. Then they turned off. The deserted ranch was a quarter mile to the north and to the left of the dirt track. After parking the truck behind a decaying outbuilding, it was time to go through their purchases and divvy them up.

Amanda hurried to put on some clothes and was grateful to be warm, even if she looked somewhat comical in a Minnie Mouse mask, voluminous gray hoodie, and men's running shorts. They were baggy and cinched in at the waist. A pair of clunky work boots completed the outfit. Omo laughed when Lee pointed a flashlight at the girl.

"Don't forget this," he said as he gave Amanda one of the pistol belts acquired from the cops at the garbage dump. It was too big, so she wore it bandito style across one shoulder and over her chest. Her Glock went into a black holster.

"Now that's scary," Lee commented. "Let's eat."

The women sat down twenty feet away from Omo to eat their

meal. The food consisted of desiccated corn dogs, cookies, and bottles of water. There were chips and candy bars for later on. "Okay," Lee said, as they gathered around the truck's tailgate, "we need a plan. I don't know about you—but I'm fall-down tired. So let's grab a nap. Then we'll get up and head west. I wish we could call for help, but I forgot to search the guy at the bar for a phone, and the Tucson Police Department took ours."

"Not to mention our badges," Omo said gloomily.

Lee nodded. "Right, which means we're going to run into trouble once we reach the border. But that's then, and this is now. Amanda? What do you think?"

"That sounds good," the young woman said. "I'm in."

Lee knew they should post a lookout. But all of them were exhausted, and if they stood watch, that would leave them that much more tired. So she discussed it with Omo, who agreed.

Lee thought she could sleep in the front passenger seat by lowering the back a bit. Amanda made a place behind her by getting rid of a kid seat, and Omo crawled into the cargo compartment, which he shared with a mishmash of guns and equipment.

Though less than perfectly comfortable, Lee fell asleep right away and awoke what seemed like seconds later to find that the sun was up and her watch was buzzing. She got out of the truck, planning to find some privacy. Then she saw the contrails that crisscrossed the sky and knew that something was up. Planes, military planes, *why*? An exercise of some sort or . . . ?

Omo was up by the time she returned to the truck. He pointed upward. "You saw the contrails?"

"Yeah . . . They're hard to miss."

"We've been listening to the radio," Omo said. "It sounds like the Aztecs crossed the border west of here and are headed north. They're making good time, and our troops, which is to say Republican troops, were concentrated around Nogales."

"Damn it," Lee replied. "They could cut us off from Pacifica or force us to travel north. We need to haul ass."

"Roger that," Omo agreed. "Let's roll."

A few minutes later, they were on the highway and headed west toward Ajo, Arizona. From there, they planned to go north to Gila Bend—then west to the border crossing at Yuma. A route that should allow them to cross north of the advancing army.

Lee was at the wheel. She was careful to obey the speed limit rather than get pulled over by a cop. And the plan seemed to be working until they neared Ajo. That was when Amanda glanced up through the moonroof. "Look! There's a helicopter directly above us!"

Lee swore as the low-flying aircraft passed over, sped away, and began to turn. By that time it was no more than ten feet off the ground and blocking the road. The Tucson PD markings were plain to see, as was the cop who stood in the open doorway. He aimed an assault weapon at the SUV and Lee saw it wink repeatedly as a series of pings were heard. She said, "Shit, shit, shit," as she gritted her teeth and pushed the accelerator to the floor.

The especiale leaped ahead as if to reach the helicopter and kill it. The seemingly suicidal move forced the pilot to pull up or die in a fiery collision. But something was wrong with the truck. Steam was pouring out from under the hood, which meant that a hose had been severed or there was damage to the radiator. They would have to bail out, but *where*? It had to be a place that offered some cover. Otherwise, they would be shot before they could mount any sort of defense.

"They're on our tail," Omo warned. "Open the moon-roof!"

"No way," Lee answered. "Your pistol won't bring it down—and I want you to stay strapped in."

Lee saw the bridge in the distance as the copter kept pace with the truck and bullets punched holes through the roof. One of them nipped her shoulder before burying itself in the seat. Then, as they approached the bridge, Lee swung the wheel to the right. The SUV left the pavement and slid through loose gravel. Lee stomped on the brakes as they nosed over an embankment and skidded down toward the dry riverbed below.

A hard left caused the truck to lurch around and almost flip. But the wheels came down, and their luck held. They were under the bridge and protected from above. "Bail out!" Lee shouted. "Grab the food and weapons! We're going to need them."

Omo ran around to open the tailgate and load stuff into Amanda's arms. Lee leaned in to grab the grenade launcher

Omo had used earlier. The chopper would land, then the cops would get off, and a firefight would ensue. That's what Lee assumed—but she was wrong.

There was a loud roar and the helicopter appeared off to her right and slid *under* the overarching bridge! Two cops stood framed in an open side door and were firing assault weapons.

Lee had fired grenade launchers on previous occasions but only on the range. So she was no expert. But the target was extremely close so she pulled the trigger. The grenade entered the chopper head high, struck something, and exploded. The results were spectacular. The pilots lost control of their ship, a rotor blade sheared off as it hit a bridge support, and that caused the helicopter to corkscrew into the ground. There was a loud crash and a cloud of dust as the aircraft hit the dry riverbed. That was followed by a loud whump as the fuselage exploded into flames. Thick black smoke poured out of the wreckage, to be carried away by a light breeze. "Nice shot," Omo observed. "But we're in the extra deep doo-doo now."

Lee knew what he meant. The truck was inoperable, the Tucson Police Department would redouble its efforts to find them, and they were facing a wasteland. All they could do was take whatever they could carry and start walking.

The outlaw and two members of her gang lay sprawled on top of a rise where they could look south. Planes were dueling overhead as flyboys and girls from the Republic of Texas tried to stop the Tec air force. Then, if they managed to do so, they'd go after the vehicles on the ground.

For her part, Jantha Sysco didn't want to fight the Aztec army. No fucking way. That would be stupid. But she didn't have a lot of choice. Not if she wanted to keep what she'd worked so hard to steal—which was a stash of gold, silver, and platinum worth well over 2 million nubucks. The totality of which was stored in an old bunker deep inside the Barry M. Goldwater Firing Range.

Did the Tecs know about the treasure? No, that seemed unlikely, since Sysco had gone to great lengths to keep the exact location to herself. A life-insurance policy of sorts intended to keep members of her own gang from murdering her.

But could the invading army stumble across the bunker? Yes, they could. And if the big cloud of dust was any indication, the Tecs were making good time. There was a bright flash as a distant plane exploded, and the one-winged fuselage cart wheeled out of the sky. "So, who's winning?" a woman named Nevada wondered out loud. She'd been a stripper prior to joining the Grim Skull Gang and functioned as Sysco's second-in-command.

"Beats the hell out of me," Sysco replied. "But right now, I'd put my money on the Tecs. Or, I'd put the Tecs on our money, since they're so damned close to it."

The Monkey, or Monk for short, had a face that bore a striking resemblance to that of a chimp. He turned to look at Sysco. "Are you saying that they are going to overrun our stash?" he demanded.

"Yes, I am," Sysco replied although she thought of the loot as *hers*. Because in spite of previous promises to split the stash with the gang, it had always been her intention to keep it for herself. But now, with everything at risk, it looked as though she might have to keep her word. "So we need to go down there and get it."

"We'll need a couple of trucks," Monk suggested.

"Indeed we will," Sysco agreed. "And a plan. A *good* plan. Let's head back to camp and talk to the gang. Then we'll head south, get in position, and pull our stuff out. If we can avoid the Tecs, we will. But if we can't, then they're gonna get hurt."

It was midafternoon, and the sun was like a malevolent presence as Lee climbed up out of a gully and paused to catch her breath. She was hot, sweaty, and dehydrated. Not to mention exhausted. Two hours' sleep wasn't enough, but what choice did they have? "March or die." She'd heard that saying somewhere—now she understood what it meant.

Artificial thunder rolled across the land as a plane broke the sound barrier. Lee looked up to see a contrail etch itself onto the sky. An Aztec plane? She thought so. But the occasional mutter of what might be artillery fire suggested that the Republicans had been able to rush some reinforcements to the area.

That wasn't Lee's concern, however. According to the map taken from the truck, the Barry M. Goldwater Firing Range was about twenty miles wide. A car could cover that distance in less than thirty minutes on a highway. But they were traveling cross-country on foot. So assuming things went well, they might be able to cross the firing range in two days. *If* they could make the water last . . . And that was a mighty big if. Lee heard the crunch of gravel as Omo arrived next to her. "See anything?"

"Nope. Just a whole lot of desert. How's Amanda holding up?"

"Very well all things considered . . . The girl has grit."

"That's for sure. Okay, let's get going . . . I think we should take a break and wait for nightfall if we can find some decent shade. Holler if you see anything."

But Omo *didn't* see anything. Nor did the others. So all they could do was trudge across stretches of hardpan, skid down into dry riverbeds, and climb out of them. It was thirsty work. They had what remained of the water that Omo had purchased at the convenience store. Fourteen eight-ounce bottles of it. Would that be enough? It seemed doubtful, but they had to try.

So they kept walking. And Lee made an effort to think about things other than the next sip of water. Every now and then, they passed old bomb craters, tanks that had been used for target practice, and signs warning them that live munitions might be lying around.

And there were cars, too . . . Most were postplague especiales that had been driven out into the desert for one reason or another and broken down. And judging from the campfires adjacent to the metal carcasses, and the graffiti that covered them, the cars were used as landmarks by the gangs that frequented the area.

They were passing a van adorned with a well-executed skull and riddled with bullet holes when Lee noticed the fresh tire tracks. *Lots* of them. She knelt in order to take a closer look. The others arrived moments later. "Motorcycles," Omo observed. "And a couple of four-wheeled vehicles as well. All headed south."

Which was strange since the outlaws stood a good chance of running into the Tecs if they went south, and Lee was about to say as much, when Amanda spoke. "I wonder where they came from?"

That was an excellent question. Did the bandits have a camp close by? A place where Lee and her companions might be able to obtain more water? Or did the tracks run all the way up to the highway that ran along the firing range's northern boundary? Because if they did, and the threesome chose to follow them, they'd be even worse off. Omo looked at Lee. "What are you thinking?"

So Lee put her thoughts into words. Should they continue west? Or turn north in hopes of finding water? The decision was unanimous. They would go north for two or three miles and turn west if they failed to find a camp. "Okay," Lee said, "the sun's low enough to create some shade. Let's find a spot to rest before heading north."

A ten-minute walk took them to the bottom of a rock-strewn gully and a long strip of shade. They had just settled in when the sound of an engine was heard. The prop plane appeared a few moments later. It was flying low, no more than three hundred feet off the ground, and headed due west. "Don't move," Omo advised. "Any sort of motion could attract their attention. It will be difficult for them to see us in the shade."

"Who are they?" Lee wondered out loud. "The Aztecs? Or the Republicans?"

"I think the plane belongs to the Tucson Police Department," Omo replied. "And that ain't good."

Lee wanted to find a place to hide but knew Omo was right. Movement could give them away. So she was careful to remain still until the plane disappeared, and the sound of its engine had faded away.

They had to wait or run the risk of being spotted from above. But once the sun went down, the fugitives followed the tire tracks north. Even though there was some risk associated with using occasional blips of light from the torch, it was necessary in order to follow the tracks.

It was difficult to judge distance under such circumstances. And since Lee didn't have a pedometer, she was forced to use her watch. They would walk for three hours. Then, if they came up empty, they would turn west. That was the plan. But roughly an hour and a half into the trek, they heard an engine start, sputter, and die. Sound could carry a long way out in the desert. But Lee could tell that this was close, *very* close, and sensed that the camp was directly ahead of them.

From that point on, it was necessary to advance with considerable caution. There were bound to be sentries, and it wasn't long before Omo spotted one off to the left. Amanda followed as he slipped from shadow to shadow.

Now that night had fallen, it was cold in the desert. Monk put his coffee mug down in order to hold his hands out over the fire pit. It consisted of a metal tub half-filled with sand. Because the container was buried six inches below the desert's surface, the glow couldn't be seen beyond fifteen or twenty feet.

Such precautions were necessary because the Grim Skulls weren't the only human predators in the area. The Thunder Hands and Diamondbacks roamed the desert as well . . . Both of which would be happy to loot the encampment.

That's why Monk and two Skulls had been left behind, while Sysco and the rest of the gang rode south. The task was to remain sober and protect the encampment that Sysco called Home Plate. Though not located on high ground, Home Plate was surrounded by an oval-shaped enclosure of fanglike rocks that stuck up out of the ground and would provide cover if the Skulls were attacked. Desert-style camo nets were strung overhead, and had been good enough to hide the camp from planes up until then although Monk feared that the gang's tracks were visible from the air and could lead people to the camp. So would they have to move now that planes were crisscrossing the area? Maybe, but that kind of decision was above Monk's pay grade.

He took a final sip of coffee, put the mug aside, and stood. It was time to make the rounds. His path took him past a line of tents, a two-thousand-gallon water truck that had been stolen from the town of Sentinel, and over to a rank of second-string motorcycles.

That's where Monk paused to throw a leg over the trail bike he'd been working on. He flipped a switch, stood on the kick starter, and was rewarded with a stuttering roar. He was smiling when the engine died. Monk swore, got off, and continued on his way. He would work on the trail bike later.

The machine-gun emplacement on the west side of the camp was unmanned and would remain so until the rest of the gang returned. Monk paused at the latrine for a minute before resuming the walkabout. It was dangerous to sneak up on Twitch—so Monk produced a whistle and heard one in return. But as he approached the clutch of boulders where Twitch was stationed, Monk could tell that something was wrong. There was quite a bit of starlight, and Twitch had boobs! Monk was reaching for his pistol when something hard was rammed into his back. "Maricopa County Sheriff's Department. Place your hands on your head and . . ."

The outlaw wasn't having any of that. He had his hand on a gun when Omo fired the Taser. The results were delightfully predictable, and it was only a matter of minutes before Omo and Amanda had the bandit trussed up, and laid out next to an equally incapacitated sentry. "Come on," Omo said, "let's find Lee."

Lee had circled right, and she was easing around a rock, when someone jumped her from above. The weight drove her to the ground. And had the assailant been able to pin Lee there, the fight would have been over. But the outlaw was off-balance and rolled away.

That gave Lee enough time to turn over and raise the Glock. She couldn't see her target at first, but then a section of stars disappeared as the bandit stood. Lee fired twice and heard a meaty thump when the bandit fell. Then she whirled, weapon at the ready, but there were no additional attackers. Gravel crunched as she went over to check the man's pulse. There was none.

Omo called Lee's name before showing himself. "Are you okay?"

"Yeah . . . I think so. Were there others?"

"Two. I stunned them, and Amanda tied them up."

"Granny knots," Amanda said as she appeared out of darkness. "Lots and lots of granny knots. That's the key."

Lee smiled. "Well done. Now it's time to look for some water."

"A water tanker is parked inside the camp," Omo said. "And there are some dirt bikes, too . . . At least a dozen of them. Backups, probably—but who cares? How would you like to ride the rest of the way?"

Lee remembered the burst of engine noise and felt a sudden surge of hope. "Show me," she said eagerly. "This could be the break we need."

The next twenty minutes were spent test-starting bikes—and that was easy to do since very few of them were equipped with ignition locks. Then it was time to choose what they thought were the best candidates, roll them over to a trailer that had the words fuel hog painted on its flanks, and fill them up.

Once the process was complete, it was time to scrounge some knapsacks, load them with necessities, and mount up. Lee had been careful to choose a bike with a long seat so Amanda would have room to sit behind her—plus a sissy bar that would prevent the girl from sliding off the back. "Hang on to me," Lee instructed as she threw a leg over the machine. "And don't let go." Lee dealt with the kickstand, thumbed a button, and felt a sense of satisfaction as the engine roared. Gravel spewed out from under the back tire as she followed Omo out of the encampment.

Confident that the outlaws would manage to free themselves, the threesome left them behind and turned north. It was good to be on a bike, *any* bike, and Lee felt a surge of joy as she followed Omo's taillight out into the desert. They would go straight north for a while before turning onto I-8. At that point, they would be no more than thirty miles from Yuma. From there, they would be able to enter Pacifica, and the long journey would be over. Lee opened the throttle and felt the wind press against her face.

The plane banked as it circled Yuma, Arizona. The blackout was supposed to be in effect, but the streetlights were on, and the Tecs had left the city alone. *Why?* Especially since Yuma was only twenty-five miles from old Mexico. Maybe the locals were paying protection money to the Aztecs.

But Nickels figured that the answer might be a bit more

complicated than that. The city was *very* close to Pacifica. So close that if the Aztecs attacked Yuma, the citizens of Pacifica might view that as a threat and form an alliance with the Republic of Texas. So even as they sent forces deep into Arizona, the city of Yuma had been spared.

Nickels felt the plane level out and start to lose altitude as the pilot prepared to land. The trip to Yuma was a pain in the ass, and dangerous, too, since Tec fighters were flying missions nearby. But, as his father liked to say, "If you think the snake's going to bite, kill it yourself. Don't wait for someone else to take care of it."

And the old man was right. This snake *could* kill him if he wasn't careful. Especially given the threat to his holdings in Tucson. Yes, he was paying for protection, but how long would it be before the bastards wanted *more*? When that occurred, he would need the cash Screed owed him to start over somewhere else. And Amanda Screed was critical to getting the money back. Unless the bishop didn't care about her, that is . . . But the fact that an LA police detective had been sent to rescue the girl argued that he did.

The thought made Nickels feel better as the landing gear touched down, the engines roared, and the plane started to slow. It took about five minutes to exit the runway and taxi to a hangar. The copilot hurried to open the door. Cold air flooded the cabin, and Nickels noticed that the sky was lighter as he made his way down the stairs to the tarmac.

A black SUV and a small group of people were waiting for him. Chief Dokey came forward to shake hands. The officer was well outside his jurisdiction, so he had chosen to wear plain clothes. The suit was tailored to minimize Dokey's hump, and Nickels could see the shit-eating grin on the man's moonlike face. "Good morning, sir . . . How was your flight?"

Machinery whirred as Nickels took the other man's hand. "It was a pain in the ass," Nickels said truthfully. "So, how are we doing?"

"Pretty well," Dokey answered carefully. "The local police chief isn't giving us a whole lot of support—but he isn't getting in the way, either. He knows we're after some cop killers."

"I guess that's the best we can hope for," Nickels said. "Rumor has it that he won't take a shit without getting permission from Pacifica first. And if he knew that we're gunning for an LA police detective, he'd have a cow. Are we ready?"

"Yes, sir. A drone located them shortly after sunset last night. And we had a team on the way to stop the fugitives, when they stole some dirt bikes and got away. Right now, they're on Interstate 8 and coming this way. The plan is to intercept them before they enter Yuma."

"Excellent," Nickels said. "But don't hurt the girl."

"Yes, sir. My men understand that."

"I'm glad to hear it. Let's go."

A plainclothes police officer opened a door, Nickels got in, and pink sunlight spilled over the horizon as the SUV sped away.

As Lee came up behind a slow-moving semi, she checked her rearview mirror before pulling out to pass. Then, with the throttle wide open, she pulled ahead. A quick check confirmed that Omo was right behind her. The dirt bikes weren't intended for that sort of riding, however. Their engines were too small, Lee's motorcycle was burdened with a passenger, and the knobby tires weren't ideal for highway use. Of course, none of that mattered so long as they managed to reach the border. And as lights appeared in the distance, their chances of success looked good. Or so it seemed until Amanda yelled in her ear. "Motorcycles! Coming up fast!"

Lee glanced back over her shoulder and saw that Amanda was correct. She eased off the throttle and fell back next to Omo. Her plan was to warn him but there was no need to do so as one of the pursuing bikes pulled up beside him.

Lee saw the gun, accelerated in order to take Amanda out of the line of fire, and heard a series of pops. She glanced back and was happy to see that Omo was still in the saddle. The initial shots had missed, giving him an opportunity to brake and pull in behind the gunman.

A scabbard and sawed-off shotgun had been attached to the bike when Omo stole it. He pulled the weapon free, allowed the barrel to rest on his handlebars, and fired. The rider was thrown forward, his bike went down, and Omo swerved to avoid it. A horn blared, and the semi braked, but it was too late. There was a horrible screeching sound as the bike was sucked under the big rig and dragged along the highway.

Meanwhile, Lee had problems of her own. Bikers had pulled up on both sides of the motorcycle and were trying to force her off the road. They couldn't shoot . . . Not without hitting Amanda or each other. Their purpose was clear: to recapture the girl.

They were motioning for Lee to pull off the highway when Amanda took charge. She had the Glock, and her arms were free. So as the riders continued to close in, she fired. Not at them, but at their tires, and at close range it was impossible to miss.

A bike swerved, turned sideways, and flipped. It was still turning end for end when Amanda switched to the other side and fired again. A black-clad rider fell off his motorcycle, and Omo's front tire hit the body. The deputy caught some air, landed on his rear tire, and found himself in a wheelie. He forced the front wheel down and raced to catch up. The border was only a few miles away.

Thanks to the drone that was following the fugitives, Nickels had been able to watch the entire debacle via the laptop perched on his knees. He was furious. So much so that he would have cheerfully killed Chief Dokey had such a thing been possible. But it wasn't since the entire operation was being carried out by members of the Tucson Police Department. "Shoot the detective," he ordered. "Maybe Amanda will survive the crash and maybe she won't. If she dies, we'll send one of her hands to the bishop and freeze the rest of her."

Dokey gave an order, and the SUV accelerated up an on-ramp and onto I-8 westbound. They were ahead of the motorcycles at that point and in a position to cut them off. Nickels was forced to move aside as the sunroof slid open, and a police officer stood. "Slow down!" Dokey ordered. "Get next to them!"

Nickels understood the necessity of that. If the officer fired straight back and hit the detective, the bullet might pass through her and hit Amanda.

But as the cop pointed his pistol at the lead motorcycle, Amanda stood on her foot pegs, and took hold of Lee's collar. That left her right hand free. Thanks to the low-flying drone, Nickels could see the whole thing via his laptop. He ducked but the police officer standing next to him couldn't. Two of the bullets that shattered the rear window hit him waist high, and a third nicked the driver's throat. The SUV swerved alarmingly as he brought both hands up to stop the sudden gush of blood.

Fortunately, Dokey managed to lean in and grab the steering wheel. Then, with no pressure on the accelerator, the truck started to slow. The SUV was slow rolling as the bikers raced by. Nickels looked out the window just in time to see Deputy Omo flip him the bird. Then they were gone.

Lee saw the line of cars and trucks up ahead and knew they were waiting to enter Pacifica. By all rights, she and Omo should get in line and wait, but to do so could be fatal, so she steered the bike between two lanes of vehicles. Omo followed. That caused people to honk, shout threats, and open their doors to block her.

Lee didn't care. Her goal was to reach Pacifica, and nothing else mattered. She saw three kiosks, all manned by heavily armed soldiers and drove straight at them. They tried to wave her off, and one raised a weapon, but he was forced to jump out of the way or be hit.

Then they were across the border but far from safe. Lee knew it would only be a matter of seconds before the soldiers opened fire, so she braked, and killed the engine.

Amanda was smart enough to see the danger and hurried to get off the bike. "Raise your hands," Lee told her, "and keep them there. I'll do the talking."

Omo had arrived by then and was quick to do the same thing. But none of them were given an opportunity to talk. Orders were shouted, searches were carried out, and the presence of so many weapons led the soldiers to all of the wrong conclusions.

Finally, after being taken into the adjacent administration

building, they were separated and placed in holding cells. There were other prisoners as well—most of whom were mutants.

Hours passed as different interrogators came and went. All of them asked the same questions over and over again: "Who are you? Where is your ID? Why did you force your way into Pacifica?" And so forth.

Lee was careful to keep her answers consistent and hoped that her companions would do the same. Eventually, she was given a meal, some disposable toiletries, and allowed to lie down. The overhead light was eternally on, the mattress was thin, and there was a lot of noise. Sleep came quickly though, and when someone called her name, she was reluctant to wake up. "Detective Lee? You have a visitor."

Lee swung her feet over onto the floor and stood. Two people were waiting on the other side of the bars. An army sergeant and Deputy Chief of Detectives Ross McGinty! "Well I'll be damned," McGinty said. "It *is* you! We thought you were dead."

Lee felt an unexpected desire to cry but held the tears back. "Deputy Omo is here, too . . . *And* Amanda Screed."

McGinty nodded. "Her father will be thrilled. Perhaps you would like to make the call."

"No," Lee said harshly. "I think a surprise would be best."

McGinty's eyebrows rose incrementally. "I get the feeling there's a lot to catch up on." He turned to the sergeant. "Open the cell. She's one of ours."

SIXTEEN

Two days had passed since Lee and her companions had crossed the border. During that time, they had been flown to LA, where they were debriefed by the chief of detectives, the chief of police, and the mayor. All of whom were eager to call a press conference and pat themselves on the back.

But they couldn't. Not so long as Amanda maintained that her father was responsible for the kidnapping—and not so long as two police officers were there to back her up. So the best the authorities could do was to get on the right side of the situation by bringing charges against Screed and allowing the poop to hit the fan. Members of the Church of Human Purity would be furious. But could the church survive in the wake of Screed's arrest? Only time would tell.

So finally, after what seemed like an endless sequence of meetings, Lee was allowed to go home for the third night in a row. She took a shower, put on a robe, and made some tea. Then she went into the living room to sit on the couch. Everything was fine, or should have been, but she felt guilty. She could have invited Omo to stay with her. Come to think of it, why hadn't she? And if not him, then *who*? He was funny, brave, and in love with her. *And you sure as hell aren't getting any younger,* Lee thought to herself.

But deep down Lee knew what the answer was and didn't like it. Omo was a mutant, and that meant both of them would have to wear masks all of the time. And if either one of them made a mistake, she would be at risk of contracting *B. nosilla*. It was a daunting prospect. So fear was part of it.

But the truth lay even deeper. Try as she might, she couldn't forget the horror that was Omo's face. She should ignore it, *wanted* to ignore it, but couldn't. Lee felt a sudden and overwhelming sense of grief. Sorrow for him and for herself. Because in the final analysis, Lee wasn't the person she'd hoped to be. She was something less, and the realization hurt.

Or did the truth lie elsewhere? What if she loved Omo, *truly* loved him, would that make the necessary difference? The problem was that she didn't know. Which was why she curled up on the couch and cried. Pictures of her father looked on, but as always, they were silent.

The police sealed off the block on which the Screed mansion was located at 0500 hours. Shortly thereafter, uniformed officers went door to door and told neighbors to remain in their homes. Once that process was complete, two squad cars pulled up in front of the house. Uniformed officers got out, ordered the guards to stand aside, and opened the gate. That allowed three unmarked vehicles to enter the grounds and pull up in front of the house.

While other officers hurried off to secure various exits, and a helicopter hovered overhead, McGinty, Lee, Omo, and Amanda approached the front door. They were in plain clothes, and Amanda's face was hidden by a veil. As Lee rang the bell, she could hear a muted beeping sound. Was that an alarm? Triggered by one of the gate guards? Yes, that seemed likely. And there was a porch camera. That meant the Screeds could see the people standing outside.

The beeping noise stopped, and a male voice came through the speaker mounted over their heads. Lee thought she recognized it as belonging to Bishop Screed. "Chief McGinty? Is that *you*?"

"Yes, it is," McGinty replied. "Please open the door."

At least a full minute passed before the door opened to reveal Bishop Screed. He was dressed in burgundy robe, gray pajamas, and expensive-looking slippers. But his ginger-colored hair was tousled, and he was clearly angry. The shotgun was held over the crook of his left arm—like a hunter in the field. His eyes flicked from Omo to Amanda and back. "*Mutants?* You have the nerve to bring mutants to my house? Damn you, McGinty . . . The mayor will hear about this!"

"We have a search warrant," McGinty said. "Please surrender the shotgun. You can give it to Deputy Omo."

Like a father confiscating something dangerous from a child, Omo stepped forward to take the shotgun. "That's better," McGinty said. "Why don't we step into the parlor? Then I can explain."

Screed frowned, started to say something, and apparently thought better of it. He did an abrupt about-face prior to leading them into a room filled with overly ornate furniture. "Now," Screed said, "what's this silliness about a search warrant? Surely you can't be serious."

"Oh, but they *are* serious," Amanda said as she removed the veil. "Hi, Daddy," she said. "Did you miss me?"

Screed stared, and his face went pale. "Amanda? You're alive? Thank God! Our prayers have been answered."

"Have they?" Amanda inquired sweetly. "I don't think so. You gave me over to a man named George Nickels as collateral for a loan that you didn't intend to repay. And you knew what that would mean. Eventually, Nickels would send you some of my fingers in an attempt to get his money back. And when that failed, he would kill me. But you didn't care—and now you *are* going to pay."

"That's a lie!" Screed roared. "I don't know where you heard such nonsense—but none of it is true."

"Yes, it *is* true," Lee said as she spoke for the first time. "Both Deputy Omo and I were present when George Nickels described the agreement with you. And his admission was consistent with the evidence gathered during the days that led up to the statement. That's why you will be charged with kidnapping and a variety of other crimes, including drug trafficking. Place your hands on top of your head . . . You are under arrest."

That was when Cathy Screed spoke. Lee hadn't noticed the woman's arrival and turned to look at her. Mrs. Screed's blond hair was in disarray, and she looked older without any makeup.

Of more importance, however, was the anger in her eyes and the chrome-plated semiautomatic pistol clutched in both hands. It was pointed at her husband, and the barrel wavered slightly. "You rotten, lying bastard!"

Bishop Screed held both hands palms out as if to stop any bullets that might come his way. "Don't believe them, Cathy . . . None of it is true. I *forced* the mayor to put Detective Lee on the case. You know that."

"He was trying to cover up," Amanda said coldly. "And he assumed that Cassandra would fail."

There was a series of loud reports as Cathy Screed pulled the trigger. She managed to fire three shots before Omo grabbed her arm. The fourth bullet went into the ceiling. Bishop Screed jerked as a bullet hit an arm, another smacked into his chest, and the third struck his left shoulder. Then his eyes rolled back in his head, and he fell over backwards. There was a loud thump as the body hit the floor. McGinty went to check on him.

"Good shooting, Mom," Amanda said coldly. "The bastard deserved to die."

Lee went over to where Cathy Screed stood and gently removed the gun from her palsied hand. "I'm sorry, Mrs. Screed, but it's my duty to arrest you for the murder of your husband."

Uniformed cops surged into the room with weapons drawn. Cathy looked at them and back to Lee. Her eyes were empty. "I didn't know."

Lee turned to a female officer. "Search her, read her rights, and take her downtown."

"Can I go with her?" Amanda inquired.

"No," McGinty said. "But you can get her some lawyers. Maybe, if they handle this correctly, your mother can get off with a light sentence."

McGinty turned to Lee. "Go downtown and file a full report. Then you'll be on leave. I'd give the same set of orders to Deputy Omo if I could."

Lee and Omo left the house, drove a sedan back to the headquarters building, and flashed their new badges to get in. "I've got to check in with Arpo," Omo said, as they took an elevator up to the sixth floor.

"That'll be fun," Lee replied.

"Yeah," Omo said. "It will." Then, after a pause, "I'd like to take you to dinner."

Lee looked at him. "That would be nice, Ras. Kind of like the old days."

"There's a place in Freak Town," he said. "A restaurant with special booths. We can eat there."

"Okay," Lee replied. "What time?"

"I'll pick you up at six."

Lee spent the next couple of hours filling out reports; and then she went home. There was plenty of housework to do, and she left the TV on while she did it. Word of the murder at the Screed mansion was out by then, and the press was having a field day. The mayor was giving serial interviews flanked by the chief of police and the chief of detectives, and everybody was waiting for Amanda to release a statement.

Lee's phone began to ring around 3:00 p.m. And it continued to ring until she turned the ringer off. That was a sure sign that her role in bringing Amanda home had been mentioned, which, when combined with the still-recent bank shootout, would be enough to set the media on fire. A quick glance outside confirmed her suspicions. Three remote trucks were lined up in front of the apartment house.

So she closed the blinds and went back to work. Then, having completed her chores, she put in a call to Omo. It was only fair to warn him. She was ready by the time Omo pulled up in an unmarked car with lights flashing.

Lee left the apartment, locked the door, and made her way out through a storm of flashing lights to the car at the curb. "What was it like in the red zone?" a reporter shouted. "Is it true that you killed a bunch of cops in Tucson?" another demanded. Followed by, "I love the skirt! Where did you get it?"

Then she was in the car, and they were pulling away. "I ran into the same thing," Omo told her. "They're calling me 'the masked mutant,' and styling me as your sidekick. As for you, you're the killer cop who eats nails and shits fire."

Lee laughed in spite of the empty feeling at the pit of her stomach. She *had* to tell him, *had* to hurt him, and wanted to cry.

Omo took an indirect route in an attempt to shake any members of the press who tried to follow them, but eventually pulled into the area called Freak Town and drove down the main street. There was lots of neon, and as Lee looked out through the passenger-side window, the area and the people who lived there no longer seemed strange. Not after weeks spent in the red zone.

Omo pulled in behind a restaurant called the Back Booth and parked the car. Then he escorted her in through the rear door. The main room was divided up into boxlike enclosures, all equipped with interior blinds. Some were up, and some were open, allowing Lee to see glimpses of people sitting across from each other.

A hostess in a burqa-style "baggie" appeared and showed them to a booth. Once inside, Lee saw that a partition of antibacterial mesh separated one side of the enclosure from the other. Omo's blind was down. But once he raised it, she saw that he was wearing a different mask. A formfitting affair that hid his disease-ravaged skin but revealed his mouth. But could *B. nosilla* have entered the enclosure with her? Lee was wearing nose filters but still had to breathe. All she could do was hope for the best.

The mesh did very little to block sound, so they were able to communicate freely and discuss what they planned to have. Orders were taken via an intercom system. When their drinks arrived, Omo hoisted a bottle of Arriba beer. "To us! We made it back alive."

Lee raised her gin and tonic. "Yes, to us." The words sounded flat and empty. And she regretted the need to utter them.

"So," Omo began. "I spoke with Arpo."

"And?"

"And he reamed my ass. It seems Chief Dokey wants to charge me with murder, among other things."

"Uh-oh," Lee said sympathetically. "That's bad."

"It would be," Omo agreed, "except that somebody shot Dokey in the head. My guess is that Nickels hired someone to do it. It's an object lesson for the rest of his employees."

"That makes sense," Lee agreed. "And Nickels?"

Omo shrugged. "The bastard is in good health as far as I know. Anyway, McGinty asked the mayor to call Maria Soto.

You may remember that she's president of the Maricopa Board of Supervisors. And she wants me back . . . More than that, she promised that Arpo will give me a promotion."

Lee grinned. "Arpo will be thrilled."

Omo laughed. "No, but he'll go along to get along."

"Congratulations, Ras . . . You deserve it."

"Thanks. But there's another possibility as well. Chief Corso offered me a job here . . . Leading a unit that will be focused on mutant-related crimes."

Lee could feel the walls closing in on her. "That's terrific, Ras! You're in demand. What's it going to be?"

Lee couldn't see all of Omo's face, but she could look into his eyes and saw the pain there. She could beg him to stay but hadn't, and he understood what that meant. "I'm going home," he said. "There's my family to think of—and a new job to do."

"Yeah," Lee said, as a lump formed in her throat. "Who knows? Maybe there will be an opportunity to shoot Arpo's son again."

Both of them laughed, then the food arrived, and talk turned to their past adventures. The media trucks were gone by the time Omo dropped Lee off, and she knew it was good-bye. "Take care, Cowboy . . . I'll be thinking of you."

"You too," Omo answered. "Watch your six." And with that, he was gone.

Lee watched the taillights dwindle to dots and disappear. Then she made her way up to the apartment, unlocked the door, and went inside. It felt cold and lonely. So she turned on some music, made some tea, and sat on the couch. It was time to cry. But the tears never came.

Rather than remain in LA and spend all of her time hiding from the press, Lee decided to leave town. The first step was to test-ride her bike and check to make sure that it was tracker free. Then she packed clothes and other necessities into the Harley's twin panniers, turned her phone off, and hit the road.

There was no plan. Just a desire to get away. And Highway 101 seemed like the perfect choice. It led her north through Santa Monica, Santa Barbara, and Santa Maria. And there were smaller towns, too . . . Places like Pismo Beach, Los Osos, and Cambria. All of which were located next to the ocean, where she could take beach walks and get her feet wet.

The days were easy. But no matter how good the view from a particular restaurant might be, dinners were lonely affairs, often shared with a book, while lovers chatted at neighboring tables. Then it was off to whatever hotel she was staying at, where she was careful to avoid watching TV lest the real world find her.

But, eventually, the long string of sun-drenched days came to an end, and it was time to return. Rather than go back the way she had come, Lee chose to point the Road King east. Then, when the road intersected I-5, she turned south.

Traffic was every bit as bad as she expected it to be. But thanks to the bike, she could weave in and out of traffic. A tactic she disapproved of when other people did it.

It was getting late by the time Lee got home and found the note that had been shoved under the door. She felt a sense of foreboding as she opened it. "Cassandra, I tried your phone, but it went to voice mail, and your mailbox is full. Please contact me right away. Sean."

Jenkins never called her Cassandra, never slipped notes under her door, and never said "please." So Lee dug her phone out of a pocket, turned it on, and made the call. Even though it was past quitting time—Jenkins answered right away. "This is Jenkins."

"This is Lee. I just got home. You wanted to speak with me?"

"Yeah," Jenkins replied. "I do. I was about to leave. Can I buy you a drink?"

"Sure . . . Where?"

"I'll meet you at the 911 in twenty minutes or so."

The 911 was owned and operated by an ex-cop and a popular spot for law-enforcement officers to hang out after work. "I'll see you there," Lee said.

"Good," Jenkins replied. Then the line went dead.

Lee hurried to shower and put on some fresh clothes. It seemed natural to slip the pistol harness on and clip the new Smith & Wesson to her belt.

Then she left, mounted the Harley, and rode it to the 911. The parking lot was full, but the attendant knew her and was willing to squeeze the bike in.

Lee thanked him and went in through a side door. The bar was more than half-full, very noisy, and decorated with all manner of police memorabilia. That included an old squad car that sat at the very center of the huge room with lights flashing. And Lee knew that back on the west wall, in among hundreds of photos, was a picture of her father.

The proprietor's name was Ed Murphy. He had a bulbous nose, two chins, and a hearty manner. "Well, look who's here! Good to see you, Cassandra . . . Chief Jenkins is in cell nine."

Lee thanked him and exchanged greetings with people she knew as she made her way back to the booth with the number 9 spray painted onto it. Like all the other "cells," it was surrounded by wire mesh on three sides.

Jenkins saw her coming and smiled. "How was the vacation? Good I hope." There was something forced about the way he said it, and Lee felt a sudden emptiness in the pit of her stomach. "Don't bullshit me, boss," Lee said as she slid onto the bench across from him. "You could give a shit about my vacation."

Jenkins made a face. "Sorry . . . It's hard, that's all."

Lee frowned. "*What's* hard? Did something happen to Omo?"

"No, not so far as I know."

"What then?"

"It's McGinty . . . He was murdered."

"*Murdered?* When?"

"A few days ago."

"Shit! Do we have a suspect?"

"Yes," Jenkins answered soberly. "We do. The chief's head and torso were found next to the Hollywood Freeway. There was a note in his shirt pocket. Plus a photo. Here's a copy of both."

Jenkins pushed a piece of paper across the table. When Lee looked at it, she recognized the block printing right away. "TO DETECTIVE LEE: WELCOME HOME. THE BONEBREAKER." And below that was a copy of the Alma Kimble photo. X's had been drawn through both of the police officers. Lee felt something akin to ice water trickle into her veins. The Bonebreaker had returned—and he was ready to dance.

ACKNOWLEDGEMENTS

Many thanks to my daughter Allison for her technical advice. The college education paid off!

ABOUT THE AUTHOR

William C. Dietz is an American writer best known for military science fiction. He spent time in the US Navy and the US Marine Corps, and has worked as a surgical technician, news writer, television producer, and director of public relations. He has written more than 40 novels, as well as tie-in novels for *Halo, Mass Effect, Resistance, Starcraft, Star Wars,* and *Hitman*.

williamcdietz.com

For more fantastic fiction, author events, exclusive excerpts,
competitions, limited editions and more

Visit our website

titanbooks.com

Like us on Facebook

facebook.com/titanbooks

Follow us on Twitter

@TitanBooks

Email us

readerfeedback@titanemail.com